Say Yes to the Princess

At the sound of her name, Her Serene Highness glanced up.

Looking into her face was like coming to the end of a deep cave and seeing the sun. Killian inhaled slowly. Their gazes locked, and held, and she closed her book. A tingling in Killian's chest followed the gentle arc of the book cover.

I'm sorry, he wanted to say.

I've been given no choice.

Do your worst.

I'm sorry.

Please.

She stood and dipped into a reverent curtsy. Killian had never seen a curtsy quite so smooth or deliberate, a thing of beauty.

She, he thought, *is a thing of beauty.*

Her hair was unadorned save a thick velvet ribbon. She wore only a small cross on a silver chain around her slim neck and oval pearls at her ears. She held her book in both hands, clutching it to her chest.

All around her, bored royalty glittered and drank and surveyed the ballroom with haughty judgment. She was somber and graceful and appeared to be patiently biding her time. Her head was slightly bowed; he couldn't see her eyes.

I want, Killian thought, the desire as powerful as it was simple.

I want her to look at me again. I want to see her face.

I want her.

Also by Charis Michaels

Awakened by a Kiss
A DUCHESS A DAY
WHEN YOU WISH UPON A DUKE
A DUCHESS BY MIDNIGHT

The Brides of Belgravia
ANY GROOM WILL DO
ALL DRESSED IN WHITE
YOU MAY KISS THE DUKE

The Bachelor Lords of London
THE EARL NEXT DOOR
THE VIRGIN AND THE VISCOUNT
ONE FOR THE ROGUE

Say Yes
TO THE
PRINCESS

A HIDDEN ROYALS NOVEL

CHARIS MICHAELS

AVONBOOKS

An Imprint of HarperCollinsPublishers

SAY YES TO THE PRINCESS. Copyright © 2023 by Charis Michaels. All rights reserved. Printed in the United States of America. No part of this book may be used or reproduced in any manner whatsoever without written permission except in the case of brief quotations embodied in critical articles and reviews. For information, address HarperCollins Publishers, 195 Broadway, New York, NY 10007.

First Avon Books mass market printing: July 2023

Print Edition ISBN: 978-0-06-328006-9
Digital Edition ISBN: 978-0-06-328007-6

Cover design by Nadine Badalaty
Cover illustration by Juliana Kolesova
Cover images © Shutterstock

Avon, Avon & logo, and Avon Books & logo are registered trademarks of HarperCollins Publishers in the United States of America and other countries.

HarperCollins is a registered trademark of HarperCollins Publishers in the United States of America and other countries.

FIRST EDITION

23 24 25 26 27 BVGM 10 9 8 7 6 5 4 3 2 1

For my father-in-law, with love and gratitude.
Thank you for reading all of my books within the first
twelve hours of their release; thank you for hand-selling
them to everyone you encounter; and thank you for that
early critique, years ago, in which you said, "I like to put
just one thought in a sentence and end it with a period
before going on to the next."
Although I failed in this dedication, the first line of
the book is for you.

Say Yes
TO THE
PRINCESS

CHAPTER ONE

London
September 1803

*K*ILLIAN CREWES WAS known as the Royal Fixer.

He "fixed" things: lapses in judgment; gambling debts; amusing friends who were, in fact, petty thieves. He recovered runaway lovers, bribed judges to release careless relatives from jail, and redacted press reports about late-night escapades in public fountains. More than once, he'd disposed of a dead body.

Sometimes, he performed these duties under the title of "Equerry to the King"; other times, he was nameless hired muscle. He was nimble and resourceful, occasionally threatening, and spoke only when necessary. Little-known fact, he was also the second son of an earl.

His late father's title had gained him access to life at court, while his late mother's *profession* positioned him as the man on whom the palace relied to take out the rubbish.

In short, he was a very creative, very private *solver of problems*, and on the first day of September 1803, Killian Crewes was asked to creatively solve the private problem created by a certain French princess.

Distract her . . . occupy her . . . enchant or even *seduce* her—these had been the palace's suggested fixes to solve the problem of the princess. Methods didn't seem to matter, so long as Killian redirected her from the current spate of trouble she'd been making in the royal court.

First, however, he had to determine *who* the French princess was.

Oh, Killian knew the girl's name, and he knew she was one of many courtiers and hangers-on in St. James's Palace. She was called Her Serene Highness, Princess Regine Elise Adelaide d'Orleans. She was a glorified houseguest living under the protection of the British royal family.

To seduce her, Killian would require more than her name, but the problem was Her Serene Highness traveled in a pack. She was never without a small entourage of ladies-in-waiting, and they dressed in identical black bombazine. Ebony hats. Onyx-colored gloves. Black woolen drapey things that could be a cape or could be the bunting from a funeral pyre. Worst of all, they wore veils that obscured their faces like a dense vapor.

They marched around Mayfair, four blackbirds in formation, and it was impossible to tell who was the lead bird.

"Why not ask the royal dukes which one she is?" wondered Hodges, Killian's manservant, speaking of the sons of King George. They stood at the edge of Portman Square, watching the as-yet-unidentified princess and her entourage bear down George Street.

"Because the royal dukes *do not know*," Killian said, leaning his shoulder against a tree. "I've asked. They don't keep track of their sisters' friends. And we dare not suggest to the king or queen that none of us has the slightest idea, do we?"

Hodges could best be described as Killian's "manservant," but a more accurate title was "man of all work." Royal fixing was rarely a one-person job. But the older man sometimes forgot that the work was not guaranteed; they were employees, just like the footmen and the grooms. As such, they could be sacked if their services did not meet expectations.

"We're meant to consistently prove our value, Hodges—remember?" Killian went on. "How valuable do I appear if I cannot identify the girl I've agreed to seduce? No. Wait. Let me tell you: *I appear to have no value.*"

The more invaluable Killian was to the king, the more work they sent his way—princesses to entertain, for example. The more work, the more money, and the king and his sons paid handsomely. Money, however, wasn't the only thing he earned. His role as royal fixer also allowed him inside knowledge and *access.*

The crown owned half of England and most of London. It was a profitable but cumbersome portfolio, and from time to time, the royal family would *sell* less desirable properties. Killian used his position inside the palace to *buy* these cast-off properties on the cheap. He was the first to know and the last to place the winning bid.

In essence, he came to the palace for a salary, but *stayed* for access to condemned boarding houses, vacant shops, and old taverns.

One day, perhaps very soon, he hoped to have acquired enough derelict property to sustain himself as a proper landlord instead of a lackey. He hoped to have earned enough money to restore the properties to safe, livable structures. And also to provide for his young nephew. And to set up Hodges with a pension. And to work for himself and himself alone.

But not today. Today he would carry on as fixer, making money by entertaining Her Serene Bloody Highness and keeping her occupied.

If he could determine which of these women she was. And why she was rambling about London. And the most effective way to distract her.

Princess Elise was obscure French royalty living in exile in Britain. Killian's research hadn't yet turned up exactly how close she was to the French throne. She'd been harbored by the royal family, safe these last ten years from the voracious guillotine of the French Revolution. Her first five years in England had been spent with an aunt and uncle in Kent, and the last five in St. James's Palace, as a companion to King George's daughters.

Apparently, the black dresses and veils were a new addition to the princess's wardrobe. According to the king's sons, her presence in court could formerly be described as "unremarkable"; now she trudged about in a death quartet, needled the royal family with probing questions, and was generally in everyone's way.

"That's some mourning attire," observed Hodges now, watching the princess's black-clad entourage navigate the maze of walkways in Portman Square.

"Is it me," asked Killian, crossing his arms over his chest, "or does she look less like a mourner and more like a woman-shaped hole cut into the wall?"

Hodges snorted. "If her father lost his head to the guillotine, maybe she has no choice but to dress in black."

"I don't care if she wears black, or pink, or floral sofa upholstery; if I'm meant to distract her, I need to know who she is."

Given so little information about the identities within the princess's entourage, Killian had made up little names for each of them. In his own mind, he tracked them as the Tall One, the Little One, the Nervous One, and the One Who Walked like a Duck.

"So you reckon that's what happened?" Hodges speculated. "The princess's parents got . . . ?" He made a gesture like the drop of a blade.

"I believe that's the commonly held view," Killian remarked. "She arrived in England alone, save the nun who delivered her. The timing is right. Except for King

Louis's daughter, the only way French royals escaped the guillotine was to flee the country."

At the moment, Princess Elise and Co. appeared to be bound for St. James's Catholic Church. Or at least, the church would likely be her performative destination. Yesterday she and her ladies had called to the church but not remained—not for Mass, not even long enough to dip their black-gloved fingers in holy water. They'd gone in one door, waited three minutes, and slipped out another. A quarter hour later, they'd turned up in a bookshop in Camden.

"In they go," remarked Hodges, watching the women file into the church.

"So they do," said Killian, shoving off the tree. "I'll bet you ten shillings they're out the alley door and on their way in five minutes . . ."

CHAPTER TWO

$\mathcal{H}$ER SERENE HIGHNESS, Princess Regine Elise Adelaide d'Orleans, had begun to wonder *when*, if ever, she'd last felt *serene*.

Also in question, the elevated designation of "highness."

At the moment, marching down George Street, her ladies surrounding her in their usual formation, she felt neither serene nor elevated. She felt a strange combination of exhilaration and fatigue, like a person sneaking out of prison after waiting up all night.

She hadn't waited up all night, and she wasn't a prisoner (well, not really); she'd slipped away from St. James's Palace when one of the king's daughters saw a mouse and swooned. The ensuing panic disrupted the routine of an otherwise boring afternoon. While everyone else leaped onto chairs, Elise had rallied her ladies. Now they were halfway to what she hoped was a golden nugget of new information. Another piece of the puzzle that was her missing brother.

"Juliette," Princess Elise called, whispering to her cousin. "Faster, if you please. He's come. Again."

"Mr. Crewes?" Juliette asked in a breathless trill. The younger woman halted in the middle of the walkway and craned around. The stop was so sudden, it caused Kirby to collide with her; her stillness had a ripple effect on

Marie. The group splintered in different directions like pins in a lawn game.

Elise swallowed a noise of frustration and swept up both Kirby and her cousin Juliette by the elbow, ushering them along.

"Yes, it's Mr. Crewes." Elise looked over her shoulder. "We may be forced to linger for Mass today—at least until the homily. Hope he loses interest."

"I should like to proffer the suggestion," began Juliette, "that Mr. Crewes is not someone to *evade* during these forays outside the palace, but rather someone we might use to our *advantage*."

Elise ground her teeth. Of course Juliette would see him as an advantage. Juliette's life was not at stake, nor her sanity. Also, Juliette viewed every man as an advantage, while Elise saw anyone who stalked her as a threat.

"Hasn't Mr. Crewes been a trusted courtier for years?" Juliette continued. "Doesn't his alliance with the king and queen make him honor bound to protect us? Like an escort?"

"He is bound by *greed*," Elise corrected her, "to *mind us*. Like a nursemaid. *If* we're very lucky. Greed could also motivate him to knock us in the head and toss us into the river. Turn here."

The lurking presence of Mr. Crewes had enchanted Elise's cousin Juliette since the first time they'd noticed him. Now every new sighting inspired the younger woman to comply less and preen more—a remarkable digression, considering her tendency to petulance and vanity.

But Cousin Juliette had always been the most challenging member of Elise's entourage. Elise would have dismissed her years ago, except—

Well, for one, there were few other candidates for the job of attendant to a twenty-five-year-old exiled princess.

Second, Juliette was Elise's cousin and therefore the only noblewoman among Elise's ladies-in-waiting. Cousin Juliette was meant to remind everyone that Elise was an *actual* princess (albeit exiled) with *actual* claim (albeit distant) to an *actual* European throne (albeit dismantled).

Now Elise wondered why she or her ladies bothered. The Prince of Wales and Queen Charlotte might have offered Elise a safe haven once upon a time, but that had been years ago, and Elise's welcome had long since worn thin. She grew more conscious of her outsized place with the royal family every day.

And what of the imposition to herself? She was so very purposeless and idle, so displaced. She missed her real family like a part of her body had been cut out.

While hiding in England may have saved Elise, her life in exile had been a truncated, sort of *half existence*. She had no freedom and no recourse to regain it.

For years, she'd simply gone along, mimicking the motions of daily life in a fog of grief and fear. Then, one month ago, she'd been traveling back to London from the seaside estate of Gloucester Lodge in Weymouth with King George's daughters. As she rode along, bored and uncomfortable, she made a chance sighting of a man. An achingly *familiar* man.

Her brother.

His Serene Highness, Prince Gabriel Phillipe d'Orleans.

She'd never been more certain of anything in her life.

The man was young—well, younger than Elise—but no longer a child. His hair was sandy brown like hers, although that wasn't the bit that caught her eye. The striking thing about the man was that he looked *exactly* like a younger version of their late father.

Everything about him—his posture, his build, and especially his face—was so familiar to Elise, she sat up and stared out the window, nose and two hands pressed to the glass. She gasped so sharply, King George's daughters shot up and craned to the window to see what had caught her eye. How disappointed they'd been by the sight of a wholly undistinguished man, standing in a patch of sunlight in a market square amid a milling herd of horseflesh.

But not Elise.

Elise had been forever changed.

By the time he was a tiny speck on the horizon, she'd convinced herself that the young man was her long-lost brother, Gabriel. She'd found him—or, at the very least, she'd caught sight of him. She was alone and directionless no more.

It had been ten years since she'd last seen Gabriel, the night before they'd fled France. He'd been only eight years of age, confused and terrified but trying so hard to be brave. Elise had been fifteen, and their sister, Danielle, only a toddler. The night after their father's execution, the three of them had been separated, spirited out of France, and hidden in exile for their protection.

Since that night, Elise had not heard even a glimmer of news from her brother or sister, and she assumed they'd not survived.

Until last month, when she'd seen a man who might be—who *must be*—her brother somewhere along the Road to Land's End, which had been the route taken by the royal caravan from Weymouth to London.

The sighting had set off something inside of her; it was . . . a motivating event. Seeing her brother had been the hard shove to an immovable rock that finally sent it rolling downhill. She'd rolled slowly at first, then faster, then faster; now she felt unstoppable.

She would find that man who was surely her brother. She would extricate herself from her tedious, periphery position in the British court. She would claim some semblance of a normal life. Together, she and her brother would find their baby sister. In the process of this, she might relocate her own self.

The sight of her brother had conjured a forgotten boldness; it had prodded her to step outside the shadowy, borrowed life she'd been living and turn her face to the sun.

Except she hadn't turned her face to the sun. She'd covered it in a veil, because although this new boldness was motivating, it was also frightening. Boldness was not necessarily braveness.

It didn't help that St. James's Palace wouldn't endorse or assist in her plan.

They'd objected almost immediately to her search for the man who might be her brother. Firmly. With no appeal. The king and queen hadn't personally objected, but their ministers, the fussy men who darted about the palace with dossiers clutched to their chests, had done it on their behalf. They sought her out and said *no* in every way imaginable except for the words *It's forbidden*. She might be an exiled princess, forgotten and ignored, but she was royalty. It would be unseemly to give her an order outright—not if they could *dissuade* her instead.

They began by curtailing her access to the queen. After that, they instructed other courtiers to ignore her questions. They closed doors and locked libraries and interrupted her mail. Elise was no longer included in events where she might speak to senior members of court. Finally, her old friend and newest lady-in-waiting, Marie, was summoned from a convent in Ireland to appease her.

And then, most chillingly of all, the palace had dispatched this . . . "minder" to stalk her.

Killian Crewes.

He kept his distance inside the palace but dogged

her every step on the outside. She'd known who he was, of course; these many years in the palace had afforded her ample time to study the key players. In the broadest sense, Killian Crewes was a schoolmate of the royal dukes. More to the point, he was the shady man in fine clothes with fine manners whom the royal family summoned when something inside St. James's Palace had gone awry.

When the king's fifth son, Ernest, had made too many shady investments, Killian Crewes had been called in to make the problem disappear. When King George's seventh son, Adolphus, had taken up bear baiting, which resulted in several maulings, Mr. Crewes had been appointed to conceal the details, pay off the injured, and ship the animals to Bavaria.

He made unsavory people vanish, caused missing diamonds to appear, and reimagined bastard infants as wholly legitimate, long-lost nieces.

And now here he was, trailing Elise everywhere she went.

For better or worse, this was not her first experience with a stalker. She'd been followed before, and she'd been captured before. She'd seen her own father killed in the most gruesome manner; a shrewdly planned public execution, drawn out over one terrible afternoon, forever seared into her memory. She understood very well the danger that lurked within royal courts. Fear had been her companion since the age of fifteen; it took the shape of bumps in the night, and mob-ruled crowds, and men who followed her.

It was miserable to be afraid, but not miserable enough to stop trying to break free.

CHAPTER THREE

𝒯WO DAYS LATER, Killian followed the princess and her ladies to a hostler's yard in Tottenham Court Road. For women who'd been (for all practical purposes) *sequestered* these last five years, they were surprisingly difficult to track. Then again, who better to spring a metaphorical lock than someone trapped in a palace-shaped cage? Their use of Holy Mass as a cover to ramble farther afield had been their first sign of stealth, and Killian had upped his game. Now he was intrigued in spite of himself.

"Reckon they don't see us?" Hodges asked. The two of them stood at the edge of a hostler's pen, observing the princess and her entourage from a distance as they fed apples to the horses.

"They see us," Killian said. "They're more aware of their surroundings than the night watchman. They view me as protection surely, like a sort of guard. They've seen me in the palace. They know I am a friend of the royal dukes and therefore a friend to them."

"Hardly rushing up to say hello, are they? Not even a smile in your direction."

"I've not met the girl, Hodges. They cannot acknowledge me without a proper introduction. If I'd *met* Her Serene Highness, I'd know which one she is."

Hodges considered this for a moment. Then he asked, "Why do you think they want you to keep her busy?"

Killian shrugged. "I've been told only that she's 'up to something from which no good can come.' Cryptic, as usual. Edward said that her habits have changed, and wildly so, and it doesn't sit well with the king. There are foreign visitors due to visit the palace, apparently, and they don't want her to approach them." Killian thought about this a moment, then added, "I assume."

It wasn't uncommon for Killian to be summoned by the palace to manage an undefined problem, pay an unnamed debt, or control a shadowy person. There was value to the royal family in not having to explicitly state what they paid him to do.

According to His Grace Edward, the Royal Duke of Kent, King George's fourth son, Princess Elise had undergone a marked sort of . . . transformation of late. She'd evolved from disengaged and forgettable to unpredictable and nosy. Not to mention, Her Serene Highness had begun to vanish from court life. She and her ladies-in-waiting were frequently absent from tea, absent from dinner, allegedly napping when King George's daughters took their afternoon stroll 'round the palace grounds. The king wanted to know why. What was their business when they left the palace? With whom did they meet?

So far, Killian's only answer had something to do with horses. Today they'd come to Tottenham Court Road and crowded around a wholly indistinguishable hostler's yard. Three days ago, it had been a bookseller's shop that specialized in books on animal husbandry; specifically, the wall of books devoted to horseflesh. Beyond that, there was little rhyme or reason to it.

At this point, Killian had far more questions about the princess than he had answers, but he couldn't approach her inside the palace. Queen Charlotte was restrictive of her daughters and their friends, especially when it came to men. His orders had been clear: distract Princess

Elise, but not at the expense of King George's daughters. Killian was not to be a fox in the henhouse.

"In the end, I suppose they're afraid she'll bolt," Hodges guessed.

"Honestly?" Killian said. "I don't get the impression that they'd care if she ran away. But she doesn't run, does she? She always returns to St. James's, only to do it again. If she intends to remain under the protection of the palace, she mustn't . . ." Killian trailed off, unwilling to say the words.

"Roam free?" Hodges mused.

"*Ask questions,*" Killian said grimly. Question-asking seemed to be the behavior that most troubled the palace.

"According to certain members of palace staff, the princess has begun a letter-writing campaign to every exiled relation she can locate. She pilfers newspapers from breakfast. She makes direct appeals to the royal family and their ministers," said Killian.

"Direct appeals about what?"

"About her exile. About other exiled French royals. About the location of her missing family members."

"They mean to keep her in the dark," Hodges theorized, "and quiet."

"Probably," Killian said on a sigh. The truth of this unsettled him somehow.

"What's the matter, Kill?"

He was shaking his head. "I don't like this job. I don't like the target, and I don't like the means. I would politely decline it except for the warehouses."

"Limehouse?" asked Hodges.

"Aye. I've already paid the architect for plans to restore them. I cannot walk away from the opportunity to buy them."

Of all the derelict properties Killian had ever bought from the Crown, he'd coveted a certain run-down block of riverfront warehouses in Limehouse most of all. The area was infested with crime, and the buildings were crumbling with age, widely considered too run-down to ever be of value. But Killian thought differently—there was always potential near the river—and he *wanted* those warehouses. If he did this job, if he pleased the king and was paid for his work, he felt sure he could finally move on the bloody warehouses.

"Well, it's not like they're asking you to harm the chit," reflected Hodges.

"No," said Killian. "They simply want me to make her *invisible*. England is at war with France. It's not a good time for King George to be harboring a nosy French Princess."

Hodges made a whistling noise.

Indeed, thought Killian.

"She cannot ask troubling questions. She cannot march about London with no stated purpose. She cannot be a bother. I've been brought in to make certain she is none of those things. Whether I like it or not."

"By taking her to bed," said Hodges.

"Something of that nature." Killian sighed, staring at the quartet of women beyond the horses. "Apparently she's too high-ranking to lock up and too much trouble to hide. Instead, they want her distracted. So, I'll court her. I'll *dazzle* her into . . . *being a very good girl*. Or similar."

"No wonder they put you on her."

"Yes," Killian said. "No wonder."

CHAPTER FOUR

"I BELIEVE MR. CREWES to be a very great friend of the royal dukes," Cousin Juliette remarked, eyeing Killian Crewes across the paddock. "Surely we needn't *evade* someone who is friendly with the sons of the king."

He's moved in closer today, thought Elise. Marie and Kirby stood by dutifully, indulging Juliette's complaints, waiting for some cue from Elise. She glanced at Marie. *He grows ever bolder.*

If the palace meant to restrict her, to really restrict her, Elise almost wished they'd simply lock her up. She abhorred being tracked and watched and stood over. When she'd fled France all those years ago, she'd been pursued relentlessly by men on horses, men with dogs, men tearing through the forest on foot like phantoms. For five terrifying days, she and Marie had huddled in carriages and stowed in boats, scurrying like mice.

The fear born of that summer was lodged inside of Elise like a jar on a shelf. Whenever she felt followed or watched or, God forbid, chased, the jar was opened, and something like panic escaped. It was one of the reasons she languished in the British court for so long. She was largely ignored inside St. James's Palace. The lid had remained on the jar. She'd been left alone. Until now. Until the palace had stopped ignoring her and appointed this man to . . . to . . .

Well, she couldn't guess at his precise assignment, but it could hardly be good.

"Here you are, Juliette," Elise said, handing her cousin an apple. "Can you tempt the mare to eat while we wait?"

"I think Mr. Crewes is ever so handsome," Juliette remarked, slipping the apple beneath her veil to take a bite. "Don't you think he's handsome?"

"I've not considered his appearance, Juliette," said Elise. This was a lie, and the reality of it annoyed her. Elise's many years of observing courtiers had allowed her ample time to study the appearance of Killian Crewes. Why him? Elise couldn't say; her eyes had simply always . . . located him. After she'd found him, her attention had . . . lingered. She'd *watched* him. Oh, the irony that now, he watched her. If the odd little tingle in the pit of her stomach had returned—the one she'd barely noticed before but now felt as familiar as his face—there was no accounting for it. She could not control her stomach.

While the handsomeness of Killian Crewes did not interest her, he had another quality that never went unnoticed. The man was *cagey*. And strategic. And, in a manner . . . enterprising? He never seemed to be enjoying himself in the palace, not like the other members of the royal court. It was more like he came to the palace to survive.

If Elise also viewed the palace as a means for survival, well . . . perhaps like recognized like.

And maybe she wouldn't have noticed these traits if he'd not been so very distinct from the other men in court. While the other friends of the royal dukes were jovial or irreverent—courtiers were meant to be diverting, after all—Mr. Crewes spoke very little and smiled less. He slipped through parties with an air of almost . . .

grimness, a weariness, not a fatigue so much as a worldly sort of *knowing*. Unless Elise was mistaken, he looked like a man who wished he didn't know quite so much.

Here again, Elise felt some kinship. She, too, had been forced to know so many tragic things—things she hated to know. Her life had been turned inside out to escape all those terrible *known* things.

In general, the sons of King George and their raucous friends enjoyed an inherent sense of *entitlement*, but Killian Crewes seemed to lack their privilege. He kept out of the light. He was never far from a door, or a concealment, or a shadow.

And of course, lately, he was never far from *her*. Not so close as to approach—not yet—but close enough to appear at various points about London, lurking just steps away.

"Even if you don't find him handsome," Juliette was saying now, swinging her apple core back and forth by the stem, "you cannot disagree that he is well-connected. To the sons of the king."

"The royal dukes have a wide array of friends, Juliette," Elise said, holding out another apple for the mare. "And *some* of them are welcome to dinner, and afternoon tea, and church on Sunday. While *others*—Mr. Crewes among them—are rarely seen in the light of day. Instead, they come in the dark of night, by way of back doors, and they do God knows what after all decent company have gone to bed. The queen would never welcome an introduction of Mr. Crewes to her daughters. He is never announced at balls. He does not travel with the family. He is not welcome to approach me inside the palace, and yet he stalks me outside? I could go on and on—but do you take my meaning? He skates the periphery of respectability. It's the prerogative of the royal dukes to fraternize with whomever they like, and it's my prerogative to *avoid Killian Crewes*."

"Don't *we* skate the periphery of respectability when we scuttle away from the palace at every opportunity?"

"We do not scuttle, Juliette. Every step need not be a *promenade* for the benefit of gentlemen in court. We have business outside the palace and only short snippets of time to manage it. Gabriel is not just my brother—he's your *cousin*. Can you not see the value of these sojourns?"

"I didn't *say* he wasn't my cousin. What I'm *saying* is, I hardly think we'll stumble upon him while we dart about the town, interrogating stable boys."

Elise took a deep, calming breath. "We do not endeavor to *stumble* upon him. We're trying to learn more about horse traders between here and Weymouth. And who better to tell us about horse traders than men whose job it is to mind horses? I've said this. Repeatedly. If you cannot get into the spirit of searching for my brother, can you not simply enjoy the liberty of walking about freely beyond the palace?"

"Perhaps. If ever we called to a shop or a tearoom. Somewhere diverting or with interesting people. But *no*. Until finally, Mr. Crewes comes along, and he is interesting, even if you don't find him respectable. Yet also, *no*."

"It's not Mr. Crewes's lack of respectability that unnerves me," said Elise on a sigh. "It's the fact that he's been somehow attached to *surveil* me. I don't relish being managed, Juliette. The thing that happens after surveillance is management. And what happens after management could be anything from confinement to death. Please, I implore you, ignore Killian Crewes."

CHAPTER FIVE

*I*T WAS THE princess's visit to Tattersall's that propelled Killian, finally, to approach her.

Tattersall's was an urban horse market comprised of stables and subscription rooms, a counting house, and covered alleyways on the edge of Hyde Park. It bustled with gleaming stallions, uniformed grooms, and hunting dogs. And gentlemen. So many gentlemen. Well-heeled buyers perused thoroughbreds and breeding stock, while race enthusiasts traded stories of fortunes won by a nose. The combination of money and sport was so enticing, gentlemen congregated on the premises even when the market was not open for business. Certainly in the month of September, when the weather was still fair and owners planned the crossbreeding for future seasons, the market was a crush of finely dressed men and pedigreed horseflesh.

There were, however, very few women, and certainly no women marching about in a foursome wearing deep mourning attire. In all of their rambles, Killian had never once felt the women were in danger. He'd taken their safety for granted; he could see that now.

"And you'll stride right up to them, will you?" Hodges asked, trailing him through a covered alleyway near Tattersall's stables. They followed the princess's entourage from several yards away. A plodding ox cart lumbered through the intersection and obscured his view. Killian swore, stepping around the cart.

"That's the idea," he mumbled, scanning the market for a clutch of black. They were vulnerable here. He shouldn't let them out of his sight. "We cannot tail them forever. I'm meant to be seducing her, not being led on a merry chase by *four* women, one of whom *might* be her. It's a little pathetic, really, that she's evaded me so long."

"What did the servants say about her?" Hodges mused. "Hazel eyes? How will you make out the color of her eyes through the veil?"

"I've heard too many conflicting descriptions to rely on servants' gossip. I intend to identify her by her regal"—he let out a tired breath—"bearing."

"Her what?"

Killian ignored the question. The truth was, he had no idea how he would identify her. Ordinarily he would simply ask, but successful seductions began by making a woman feel known and chosen, not . . . guessed.

He frowned and took off his hat, using it to shade his eyes. "Do you see them? I've lost sight. How could we misplace four women in mourning dress amid a milling crowd of gentlemen and horses?"

"There," said Hodges, making a terrible face. "She's there."

Killian followed his gaze to a line of empty wagons and carts parked on the periphery of the market. The vehicles stretched for six acres at least; they were the conveyances of every trader who'd traveled to London from the country. The princess's entourage was clustered near a gap between two wagons, and beside them stood a tall, thin man in a shabby coat and dirty boots. His head was bare, revealing a tangled mop, and he held a crooked stovetop hat in his hand. He used the hat to gesture between the row of parked vehicles.

Killian stopped walking. He'd lost them for two minutes, and they'd managed to engage the dodgiest degenerate in the market. The man was unknown to Killian, but he'd spent enough time with lowlifes and malcontents to identify threat when he saw it. Criminals, unlike princesses, were easy to identify.

"*Don't do it . . .*" Killian muttered tiredly, watching in frustration as one member of the entourage—the Little One—separated from the foursome and took a step between the two wagons.

"But what could they want with the likes of him?" huffed Hodges, catching up.

"God only knows."

Killian started walking again, faster now. Meanwhile, Little had stepped between the wagons, looked back, and said something to the Tall One. A tense exchange ensued between the two women. A line of men walking arm in arm stepped in front of Killian, and again he couldn't see. He swore, stepping around them, and now the Tall One moved to join the Little One between the wagons. Little wasn't having it, and Tall returned to the pack.

Killian's sightline was cut again by a boy pulling a horse on a lead. When he stepped clear, Stovepipe was beside Little, flicking his hat in the manner of a parent ushering a child down the road.

The Tall One called out, but Little stayed her with a hand, pivoted to the muddy path between the wagons, and walked deeper into the field.

"*No, no, no . . .*" whispered Killian, trotting now.

Meanwhile, Stovepipe was in no rush. He took his time, savoring the sight of her picking her way through the mud, skirts held high. His face was lit with avarice; the held-breath expression of a hunter watching a rabbit hop into his trap.

When Little disappeared from view, Stovepipe looked right and left, tightened his gloves, and hurried after her.

Killian swore again, sidestepping an old man carrying a bucket of sloshing water, and ran.

"Hello," Killian called when he reached the three remaining members of the entourage. Perhaps they answered or perhaps they didn't, but Killian didn't stop.

He called over his shoulder, "Forgive me my haste. Killian Crewes. I'll just have a look . . ."

He didn't finish. He'd no idea *which* member of the entourage had disappeared between the wagons and really—did it matter? Little could be the princess, or a lady-in-waiting, or Mary, Mary Quite Contrary; in any event, nothing good would come of following this tosser into a field of empty vehicles.

She was gone, of course, by the time Killian reached the tail of the first wagon. He cocked his head and listened. The day was breezy, and snatches of conversation wafted from every direction.

Swearing, he dropped to the ground, holding himself horizontal above the mud. He scanned beneath the vehicles for a black skirt and cheap boots.

He found them quickly, two rows over. They were in earshot, but he dared not call out yet. He didn't want to send them running deeper into the field. He didn't want a chase. He didn't want a fight.

I don't want this job, he thought, vaulting up.

Moving silently and quickly, whipping carefully around corners, he approached Stovepipe from behind. This took another ten seconds, and Killian edged around the last cart to see Little being ushered up the steps of a wagon.

"A word, if you please," Killian called, keeping his voice calm, almost bored.

Little had already stumbled into the wagon, but Stovepipe teetered on the top step.

"Bugger off!" Stovepipe spat before disappearing inside.

"You must be joking," muttered Killian.

He was up the steps a moment later, breaking his way in with a boot to the door.

Two faces whipped in his direction. Little's veil remained enigmatically in place; Stovepipe's features were red and distorted.

"Now that I have everyone's attention," Killian continued, "I would ask you to step *away* from the lady. Hands in plain view."

Stovepipe looked between the woman and Killian, weighing his options. Whatever the transaction here, he was very loath to let it go. He looked at the side of the wagon, considering escape. The vehicle had no covering, but the walls were high.

He looked back to Killian. Stovepipe had several inches on Killian, but the wagon was confining, and there was a woman in the mix. Despite his fine clothes, Killian knew how to handle himself in a fight; any idiot would discern this.

Stovepipe took two steps back. He looked again to the side of the wagon. "Keep back, gov," he snarled, assessing the woman like a piece of furniture he intended to pitch over the side.

"You will regret it," Killian remarked, "if you touch her. Depend on it."

"Arrêtez. Stop." This came from the woman. She said it twice, once in French and once in English.

Killian blinked. He'd not expected her to speak. His only expectation had been to recover her. He was just about to ask her if she was hurt when Stovepipe darted right.

Killian lunged, swiping for the man's wrist, intending to wrench his arm behind his back.

Stovepipe was faster, ducking behind the woman to shield himself. Killian wouldn't advance on the woman, and any coward would know it. Killian was forced to fall back.

Stovepipe used the space to lift his rangy arms up the side of the wagon, jump, and catch hold of the top plank. Kicking and pumping filthy boots, he shimmied himself up and over, disappearing to the other side like a squirrel.

The woman let out a noise of frustration, brushed past Killian, and leaned from the entrance to the wagon. She looked right and left, but Killian already knew. Stovepipe was gone.

"Are you hurt?" he asked, coming up behind her.

"No," she said dismissively. "He's vanished. You've frightened him away."

"*I've* frightened *him*?"

"Yes, of course. He's run to God knows where. And before he sold me the information."

"Forgive me—he was meant to sell you *what*?"

"Never mind," she said in French. "Do not trouble yourself; it's no business of yours." She took up her skirts and clipped down the steps.

"Wait," Killian called, but she ignored him, trudging through the vehicles.

"I should like to help you," Killian tried again.

"Oh, this was 'help,' was it?" she called, turning left beside a rickety cart.

"Yes, of course. I—"

She wasn't listening. She didn't even look at him. She wound her way down one row, then the next. When she cleared the last vehicle, the waiting entourage came into view. She sped up, plunging herself among them. They closed ranks around her like the slamming of a gate.

"*Wait*," Killian tried again, half laughing now. How had *he* managed to become the threat? Him? She felt threatened by *him*?

If *this* woman happened to be Princess Elise, he was so very buggered. Seduction canceled. Payout *not* earned. Warehouses lost.

He came to a stop beside the four women and held up his hands in a gesture of supplication. "Please," he said. "I beg of you. Might we . . . begin again? I should like to introduce myself."

In a silent swivel, four black-netted heads turned in his direction.

"And ascertain that everyone is unharmed."

Nothing.

He continued, "That man was . . . not a safe man."

No response.

"Will you tell me his business with you? How did he compel you to follow him?"

No reply.

"It's me, Highness," Killian pressed, speaking to all of them, "Mr. Killian Crewes, Equerry to the King. Queen Charlotte would not forgive me if she knew we'd crossed paths and I'd not offered myself to your service. Pathetic introduction, I know, but I should like to be useful."

"Like to be useful?" repeated one of the women in French.

Killian searched the veiled faces for the source of the question. The Little One. Of course. *God save me*, he thought, *from the Little One*.

"Yes," he said cautiously. "Useful. *And* to make your acquaintance—to be introduced, if we can manage it."

"You've done enough, I should think," she said. "Honestly, I'm shocked you would approach us in this way."

"Shocked because . . . ?" He trailed off. He was so confused.

She let out a tart, French-sounding noise of irritation, raised a gloved hand, and swiped the veil back. She blinked up at him with her face open and bare.

The unexpected sight of her features rendered him momentarily speechless. The shadowy lines and shades he'd seen only in outline had become . . . human. She was an expressive, living, boldly beautiful thing. She was also furious.

Her eyes were hazel, large and intelligent, her face heart-shaped. Her mouth was slightly open, sucking in angry little breaths.

Killian felt an odd spark inside his chest, the strike of a match, a tiny flame lighting up the corner of an abandoned room. A burn.

He took a step back.

"*Why,*" the woman asked in French "*in God's name* would we want an introduction to *you*?"

"Me?" he repeated stupidly.

"*Yes.*" A scoff. "*You.*"

And then Killian knew.

She was the princess. Easily identified by one feature alone: her *disdain*.

Killian encountered disdain so frequently, it had become as expected as a cloudy day. His father may have been an earl, but his mother had been a dancer. They'd been married in the end, but that almost made it worse. The only thing less respected than a dancer was a dancer who'd managed to become a countess.

Were there *some* scenarios where the son of an earl and a dancer overcame the social obstacles of his birth? Yes, possibly, but this had not been Killian's experience. His half brother had made certain of that. He'd been a living vessel for the disdain of polite society for as long as he could remember, their contempt whispered at a velocity meant to shatter. A quietly known, pointedly painful thing.

Oh, he had the favor of the royal family, but they regarded him as a reliable henchman with a very high price, or an enterprising friend who unburdened them of their shite properties. It was a different kind of disdain, but disdain all the same. Regardless, an exiled princess would not welcome his introduction. Of course she wouldn't. She would see him, she would discern the disparity, and she would feel only disdain.

This has been a fool's errand, he thought.

The palace is mad if they believe I can make friendly, chummy progress with a princess.

And seduction? They could forget seduction altogether. Perish the thought. He was a fixer, not a bloody . . .

Well, he was no one to whom she cared to be introduced.

CHAPTER SIX

*E*LISE FORGOT THE degree to which the veil obscured her vision. When she lifted it, even the most mundane scene looked . . . well, it looked a little resplendent.

Surely this was the only reason Mr. Killian Crewes appeared anything like "resplendent"—which he did, undeniably, staring down at her with warm brown eyes and long, black eyelashes and a pretense of overblown gallantry. Elise clung to the pretense because she wasn't sure what to do with the brown eyes or the long lashes. As men went, she knew him to be markedly *un*gallant. He was known in court by his grimness and spareness. He wasn't cordial or affable—he was playacting. It was chilling, really, how well he feigned his concern.

"Let us not pretend, Mr. Crewes," she told him. "It feels rather jarring to fumble through an introduction now, after we've endured your stalking for nearly a month."

"Stalking," he repeated hollowly.

"Yes. And hounding. We've been terrorized, honestly, by your constant lurking presence."

Elise's anger spiked, just saying the words. The *gall* of the man. Forgetting the fact that he'd run off a possible informant. Granted, Mr. Latchfoot had been a shiftless, likely *unreliable* informant, but still. Now they'd never know. He was gone, and in his place: Killian Crewes.

Faux chivalry, feigned concern, and the pretense of knowing which one of them was the real princess.

Ha.

Elise had only removed her veil because it was clear he had no idea who she was (or wasn't). In this, the mourning dresses had worked. It gave her a small measure of freedom.

Next, Cousin Juliette peeled back her veil. After that, Marie's veil came off. Finally, with shaky reluctance, Kirby. The plan had always been for the four of them to act in unison. When they behaved the same, it curtailed assumptions about who was who.

"But you'll not deny it, surely," Elise went on. "Have you not trailed us for weeks, silently *watching* us?"

"By 'not denying it,'" he asked flatly, "do you mean admitting to this?"

"And what of Mr. Latchfoot?" she went on.

"Who?"

"The man in the wagon whom you frightened away, likely never to be heard from again? And before we'd managed to procure one morsel of the information he'd promised."

"What information?"

"None of your concern, that's what. But let me be clear, *no business* of the princess is of any concern to you, Mr. Crewes."

"Forgive me. I endeavored to *watch over* Princess Elise. For the sake of safety."

Elise shrugged deeper into her cape. "The princess has not felt safe. The princess has felt *hunted*."

He opened his mouth. He closed it. He adjusted his stance and crossed his arms over his chest. He bowed his head ever so slightly. "My apologies."

And now it was Elise's turn to be speechless. As apologies went, it sounded almost genuine. His voice was quiet. The faux aplomb was gone. His intonation was spare.

And then he repeated the two words. *"My. Apologies."* He did not smile. He looked . . . bored.

Elise narrowed her eyes, considering this change in tone. And now he was *bored*? He'd stalked her across London and they finally met so he could portray . . . *boredom*?

He also looked somehow *detached*. Before, he'd watched her as if he was curious about what she might do. Now he watched her as if he didn't care, as if he was being paid to watch her.

"I'm afraid I cannot accept your apologies, sir," Elise said. The words came out before she'd considered them. It was pride talking. He would convey boredom? Detachment? Fine. Apology rejected.

How old is this person? The question popped into her mind. He'd stopped paying attention and, as a result, her attention was piqued.

Not so very old, she thought. There were lines at the corners of his eyes, but they appeared to be born of the sun, not of fatigue or ill health. His health, in fact, appeared to be very robust indeed. He stood tall and broadshouldered. He'd bounded into the wagon with athletic grace. He'd followed her through the wagons with no effort. He stared down at her with neither distorted eyesight nor impaired hearing. She felt fully, vividly *seen* by Mr. Crewes. Not watched, *seen*.

He was *not* old, she thought. Elise herself was twentyfive, too old to be a debutante, slightly younger than an old maid. Despite this, she often felt about fifteen, her age at her father's execution. Grief and fear had stunted her maturity. Other times, she felt as old as a crone: tired, purposeless, weary. The only one left.

It didn't matter how old or young she felt. The truth was, she was a grown woman, and he was a grown man. For the first time ever, she longed for the seclusion of the veil. She should have some barrier between his eyes and his eyelashes and herself.

"I'm afraid you'll have to excuse us, Mr. Crewes," Elise heard herself say. She wasn't prepared to contemplate him as a grown man; she wasn't prepared to contemplate him at all. Her plans to find her brother were larger than the tempting puzzle of Mr. Killian Crewes.

She added, "We must see the princess home before tea."

"Permit me to hail a hackney cab," he said. "Or send my man for a carriage."

"That won't be necessary."

"I insist." He sounded like it didn't matter.

This had the distorted effect of making her want him to do it. Elise pushed the desire away and reached for her veil, smoothing the mesh over her face. The other women promptly followed suit.

"It is the strong preference of the princess to walk," she said.

"I will accompany you," he said.

"No, I don't think so."

Her heart pounded. She had the errant thought that she could do this all day. He could say one thing and she would say the opposite. His tone could suggest that he didn't care and she could, inexplicably, care quite a lot.

"The princess is not safe without some escort," he said. "This Mr. Latchfoot, whomever he is, does not mean you well."

"Do not trouble yourself with the intentions of Mr. Latchfoot. Do not trouble yourself with anything to do with . . . Her Serene Highness." She detested invoking her own title.

He stared at her, but did not challenge this.

Elise began to back away. She watched him watching her retreat, daring him to make the next offer. His face and form were clearer now, despite the veil. All those annoyingly resplendent details like eyelashes and the scar beside his mouth were locked in her memory. She didn't want to see the stubble on his jaw or the wisps of hair that curled from beneath his hat.

She turned and strode across the market. Her ladies fell into formation behind her. For the first time since he'd begun to follow her, she had the powerful urge to look back, to see if he would trail behind them. She dared not. She wanted to, but she didn't.

"As you wish," he called after her, his voice clipped. After a beat, he added, "*Highness.*"

Elise missed a step. Marie, so very nimble, rushed to steady her.

Highness? She looked to her friend. Had he referred to Elise as Highness?

She couldn't see Marie's expression behind her veil, but she knew her friend was raising an eyebrow.

The desire to look back was a physical force, an invisible hand taking hold of her chin and turning it. Had he known all along that she was the princess? Had she given herself away? Did he guess?

In the end, Elise didn't look back. She squeezed her eyes shut and opened them again. She breathed out. Gaze forward, head tall, she strode through horses and men and hounds. She could feel his eyes on her back like he'd pinned a target to her cape. It burned and tingled. The loose hairs on the back of her neck stood up.

She was unsettled—she could admit that. It had been

an unsettling day. Everything about their exchange had
been disorienting and unexpected and alarming.

What it *wasn't*, she also admitted, was frightening.

Elise had not been afraid.

For the first time since he'd begun to follow her. Inexplicably, almost imperceptibly, there *was no fear*.

CHAPTER SEVEN

$\mathcal{K}$ILLIAN WAITED THREE days to be sacked.

He thrashed about his house, scowling at documents he didn't read, unfurling maps he didn't study, and regretting . . . all of it.

He'd been hired to do a job—hired by the bloody *King of England,* no less—and he'd failed. In fact, he'd done the opposite of the job; he'd "terrorized" his charge rather than seduced her. The princess would complain; hell, the princess *should* complain. She wasn't enchanted. She was angry.

But honestly? It wasn't even the impending dismissal that bothered him. It was the regret. He regretted his own ineptitude, and it couldn't be undone.

Five times a day, Killian shoved up from his desk, stalked to the window, and glared into the garden. The Lamb Street town house in Bishopsgate was one of the first condemned properties he'd bought from the Crown, and he'd devoted four costly years to restoring it. He'd intended to sell it, but found it to be so comfortable and well-appointed, he'd made it his home instead. The walled garden behind the house was his refuge. While architects and builders had made the structural renovations, he'd installed the garden himself. There were two soft plots of green sod bisected by a thin gravel walk, a smattering of trees, and a stone reflecting pool.

Looking out the window now, he saw none of this; he saw only the blight beyond the gate. Eventually, he'd bought the surrounding properties, but he'd not yet earned the money to renovate them. They leaned at odd angles up and down Lamb Street, gutted by fire or rotting with neglect. With no future payouts as the Royal Fixer, there would be no money to repair them.

So be it. Fine. These were unexpected challenges, certainly, but Killian would solve them by selling other properties and rethinking the scale of his future. He was nothing if not adaptive and resourceful. This, also, wasn't the regret. The source of his regret was *her*.

The encounter at Tattersall's would not leave him. Over and over, his brain retraced the memory of their exchange. It was like reading the same page of a terrible book again and again. Despite his best interests, he thumbed to it ten times a day. He'd underestimated her, an amateur mistake. He'd made assumptions about her cleverness, which was considerable, and her gullibility, which, in fact, she did not possess.

He'd been so very wrong about all of it. And it made no difference what the palace wanted. Her Serene Highness would never consider Killian Crewes—not as a paramour, or even an amusing friend. Her Serene Highness had not even allowed him to *fetch her a cab*.

It had been arrogant and foolish of him to offer any service to her, and oh, how Killian *hated* playing the fool. He was not a distinguished man, not respected; he wasn't even necessarily well-liked, but *he was no fool*.

Except at Tattersall's. Except with her.

It hadn't been a shaming, per se. She was not cruel. He could pretend this, but it was untrue. There'd been no dressing him down or turning away as if he wasn't there. She'd simply told him no. Her rejection had been an uncomfortable reminder, a little note tucked into his pocket: he could fix many things—low things, criminal things, things that were sloppy drunk or blinded by conceit—but he could not, should not, endeavor to engage people who were above him.

And Princess Elise was so very far above him.

At least I'll never have to see her again. His chief consolation.

Regret was one thing, but the threat of making repeated overtures to a bloody princess and enduring her dismissal was more than he wished to contemplate.

"I'll never see her again," Killian mumbled on the fourth day, still waiting for some rebuke from the palace.

He tossed a pile of architectural schematics on his desk and shoved up. The plans were rubbish now, of course. He'd been just about to file them away when he heard Hodges coming into the front hall.

"Kill?" the manservant called from the entryway.

"In the office," Killian shouted back.

"Delivery," Hodges said, leaning into the door and holding out an envelope. "It's just come. I intercepted a boy on the steps."

"What is it?" Killian asked, staring at the smooth, stiff envelope like poison in a dram.

"The boy didn't say."

"What boy was it?"

"Messenger. I've not seen him before."

"From the palace?"

Hodges was confused. "Not liveried, if that's what you mean."

Without looking down, Killian slid a finger inside the flap and ripped.

"What's it say?" asked Hodges.

"It is an invitation," Killian said flatly. "To a ball. At St. James's Palace. Tomorrow night."

"Well, look at you," Hodges crooned with a whistle. "A proper guest to a royal ball."

"Indeed."

Killian stared at the invitation like he'd accidentally picked up someone else's gloves.

Social gatherings with the royal family were not unknown to Killian; during the Season, he was in and out of St. James's Palace several nights a week. But rarely, if ever, did he receive an *invitation* to the home of the king. He was not seated at dinners. He didn't dance or exchange pleasantries with gentle guests.

He joined events already in progress, played cards, listened for gossip, and stood guard over drunken relations. He removed imposters and chased randy dignitaries from the hedge maze.

"I'd not yet mentioned this to you, Hodges," Killian finally said, "but there is a good chance they're about to cut us loose—cut *me* loose."

"Cut? What'ya mean?"

"The sack. No more work from the palace."

"Bollocks," said Hodges.

"I . . . I failed miserably with the princess, didn't I? She will have complained about our encounter at Tattersall's. Not to mention, the job was to entertain her. It's been a fortnight since I was assigned to her, and I've done nothing of the sort. Actually, I've somehow managed the opposite. Perhaps they mean to tell me at this ball."

Hodges was shaking his head. "I'm doubtful they devote time at royal balls discussing the likes of you and your job, Kill. It's more for dancing and drinking and the like."

"*No*, I mean they'll use the crowds and revelry as an excuse not to explain. They'll dismiss me, and I'll go. A public fete provides so many convenient distractions, doesn't it? The awkwardness of parting ways will be smoothed over."

Hodges shrugged and turned to go. "If that happens, it'll be the first time a royal duke has thought about something so common as awkwardness."

"There has to be a reason for the invitation," Killian called after him. "Perhaps—perhaps they mean to pass along the princess to some other hired fixer? Perhaps I'm meant to . . . to *brief this person* at the ball?"

Killian stared down at the invitation, conjuring up the image of Princess Elise. Heart-shaped face. Green-brown eyes. Olive skin that seemed so very supple against black silk. He heard her voice in lyrical French and crisp English. And then he thought of some other man taking over the truly questionable work of "occupying" her.

"I'll need the onyx suit," Killian heard himself say.

"Right," Hodges yelled from the stairs. "Might also consider a haircut."

"Aye," Killian said, looking again to the invitation.

It was miserable to fail at a job that any idiot could do, a job he didn't even like.

It doesn't matter, he told himself.

And she doesn't matter.

And no one cares.

I do not care.

FIVE DAYS LATER, standing in the glittering ballroom of St. James's Palace, glass empty, hair freshly cut, Killian repeated this mantra—*I do not care*—like a song stuck in his head.

"Ah, there you are, Kill," said His Grace Edward, the Royal Duke of Kent, fourth son of the king. He carried a boiled lobster on a dinner plate that slid back and forth between wedges of shiny lemon.

"Highness," Killian said carefully, bowing. Edward was a few years older than Killian and had been several years ahead of him at Eton. In the line of royal dukes, Killian's closer association was the king's *fifth* son, Ernest. They'd been classmates in school. When it came to business, however, the king generally dispatched Edward to direct Killian. The two men were cordial, but they weren't old friends. If they meant to sack him, naturally they would send Edward.

"You've come right on time. Excellent. My mother is not likely to let the girls out to play for long."

"Pardon?" asked Killian.

"The French girl. Princess Elise. I can hardly introduce you properly if the queen has squirreled her away to her nunnery."

The daughters of King George lived in a section of the palace known formally as the Queen's Chapel and informally as "the nunnery" because the queen kept the girls and their companions under restrictive schedules and tight surveillance. The queen was jealous of their time, determined to have her daughters remain at home to attend her in old age rather than marrying and having families of their own. There was little access to outside callers, especially men. King George's daughters were allowed to preview the first hour of any nighttime fete— but only the first hour. And the girls were positioned away from the general revelry. No man was permitted to approach them without an advisor or member of the family.

"You've been working your magic with her outside the palace, I know, but the king is impatient to have her taken in hand sooner rather than later," Edward told Killian. "We cannot tarry another week—another day, in fact. The king wants her dazzled into submission *now*. Tomorrow, if you can manage it."

"Dazzled into sub—"

"She's a cold, remote little chit, isn't she?" conceded Edward. "I had no idea until I endeavored to locate her myself. Wanted to *herd her* in your direction. Standoffish and difficult, that one. I can see now why my father wants her numbed and docile. But never you fear, we'll work together to *pin her down*, won't we?"

Killian stared at him.

"Come on, then," Edward said, making a summoning motion with his lobster. "The queen will lock up the girls soon enough, and our chance will be lost. I waited until Mama was otherwise engaged, but if we move quickly, we won't have to stand on ceremony."

Edward trudged across the ballroom, and Killian followed, trying to disguise his confusion. He stacked and restacked the royal duke's words in a different way, hoping they'd make sense. Killian was not being sacked. He was being thrust more deeply into the ploy. The objective remained, only now it was more specific. Render the princess "numb." Make her "docile." Tomorrow, if possible.

"Highness?" Killian began, searching for the least damning way to reveal, *She does not like me.* He searched also for a way to suggest that "numbing" an otherwise harmless princess was, surely, an overstep.

The words were not found. Instead, he did something that he rarely, if ever, did in his work as fixer: he asked for more details.

"Highness?" Killian began. "But can you say what His Majesty has in mind for this . . . 'distraction' I'm meant to enact?"

"Well, it's become less an issue of 'what' and more, 'when.'"

"Right," allowed Killian, annoyed. "There's a schedule now."

"Indeed. And the schedule is: as soon as possible. A proper flirtation should begin tonight. Honestly, the flirtation should have already commenced. Why do you think I summoned you to this ball?"

Killian wouldn't answer that. Instead, he said, "Noted. 'As soon as possible.' But how distracting am I meant to be?"

Edward giggled. "Oh, you know"—the royal duke made a wide, circular gesture with his plate—"flatter her, scribble out a few lines of soppy poetry, whisk her away on little jaunts through the countryside, close the carriage curtains and make her see stars."

Killian's head began to pound.

"When we thought of you for this job, we envisioned you . . . in a way . . . *charming her*?" mused Edward. "The goal is to make her lose interest in nosing about Crown business and foreign affairs. Diplomatically we're not really meant to *tell* the girl what to do, you see. And we cannot trap her in the palace—she's not a prisoner— but the troublesome meddling and attention-seeking must stop. Likewise, these *rambles* of hers. She believes herself to be invisible in that ghastly black attire, but of course the opposite is true. If she leaves the palace in your company, we hope she'll dress to please *you* rather than shock anyone who has the misfortune of turning a corner and catching sight of her. We thought the two of you might do the typical, courtship-y things . . . the opera, Hyde Park promenade . . . an exhibition. Picnicking? Why not? A few days at the seaside would not be remiss." He wiggled his eyebrows at Killian.

"Just to be perfectly clear—because I've heard you say 'seduction' from the beginning—the king means for me to engage in behavior that is less than . . . respectable? With the princess?"

Edward made to walk away. "Do whatever is necessary to shut the girl up. Delight her so thoroughly, she doesn't *realize* she's being shut up. *That* is what we mean. If you can manage this without getting her in a family way—all's the better. But then again, if she's breeding, we'll have the perfect excuse to remove her from the palace altogether, won't we? We can stick her in a convent and be done with it."

Killian stopped walking.

The duke felt him fall away and turned. He lowered his lobster. Frowning, he stalked to Killian's side.

"If you're asking what lines should or should not be crossed," whispered Edward, "I'd say, *don't*."

"Don't?"

"Don't ask." Edward gave Killian a knowing look. Killian blinked at him, and the royal duke added, "We trust you to get the job done."

With this, Edward pivoted and resumed his march across the ballroom.

Killian stood motionless, staring at the thick, rounded shoulders and emerging bald spot on the back of Edward's head. He'd been asked to do many unsavory things in service to the crown—ugly things, illegal things—but this?

This?

He was just about to say something—he wasn't certain what, but something—when Edward turned around and studied him with an expression Killian had never seen before.

"Killian, I've been meaning to tell you," the duke said coolly. "The four old warehouses in Limehouse? You know the ones? You had some interest in them, did you not?"

Killian narrowed his eyes. *Surely not.*

"Would you believe," continued Edward, "that our agents in Bond Street have sent word—just this week, in fact—that we're to offer the warehouses up for sale very soon?"

"In fact, I cannot believe it," Killian said slowly.

It was no *accident* that Edward should mention the warehouses here, now. The royal dukes were largely ignorant of the property owned by the Crown. And yet, they'd clearly gone to the trouble tonight. They were educated enough to offer Killian an effective bribe.

Why is this girl so important to the royal family? Killian wondered.

But Edward was underway again.

"Ah, there she is," the royal duke said. "My sister promised she'd get her here, and without that ridiculous veil, thank God. Oh, and she's worn gray—how *festive*." Edward rolled his eyes. "No matter. You'll make her feel like a diamond—I've seen your ministrations before. After I've made the introductions, you may get right to it. No more beating 'round the bush. This introduction should have been done properly from the start. Oh well— water under the bridge. We'll see to it now. I'll make it so very clear that I give you my blessing, et cetera, et cetera. Your handsome face and dashing form will do the rest. You can make some plan for a diversion—then off you'll go. Honestly, tomorrow would not be too soon. It cannot be said enough. We want to please the king, don't we?"

And now he turned back to shoot Killian a wink, one of a hundred such winks Edward had shared with him over the years. It was Killian's custom to answer that wink with a subtle salute, but tonight Killian could only stare—stare and follow the son of the king through the ballroom, trying to breathe around the icy block of dread in his throat.

"Bonjour!" called Edward, approaching the section of the ballroom set apart for his sisters and their friends. It was a wall lined by tall urns of flowers and burly footmen. Plush sofas and divans were scattered in a shallow half circle; the daughters of King George—easily the least happy women in the ballroom—and their friends draped themselves on the plush seating in various poses of boredom and wistfulness. Three of the women held little dogs in silk bows, panting in the warm ballroom. There was a parrot on a perch. Servants hurried in and out with trays of refreshments. The women made little reaction to the royal duke, but Killian felt their collective attention lock on him like cats watching a mouse.

"How miserable they all look," tsked Edward. "Pity, my mother allows my sisters to *attend* court balls, but she does not permit them to dance."

Killian smiled at the women—a reflex. In general, female courtiers enjoyed Killian's smile; in general, they enjoyed Killian. He knew better than to *grin* at the daughters of the king, but their friends were a different story, and he'd engaged in dalliances with a myriad of female courtiers over the years. Before Princess Elise, any "fix" involving a female courtier had been quick and easy work.

That was before.

Now the royal family expected Killian to play the Pied Piper to a woman who would sooner give him the cut direct.

"Princess Elise," called Edward, shouting to a seated figure on the periphery, her head bowed over a book.

At the sound of her name, Her Serene Highness glanced up.

Looking into her face was like coming to the end of a deep cave and seeing the sun. Killian inhaled slowly. Her eyes went to Edward first and then Killian. Their gazes locked, and held, and she closed her book. A tingling in Killian's chest followed the gentle arc of the book cover.

I'm sorry, he wanted to say.

I've been given no choice.
Do your worst.
I'm sorry.
Please.

"But will you allow me to introduce an old friend, Princess?" Edward boomed to her. "He's wanted to make your acquaintance for some time. I've been remiss in not doing the honors."

Edward came to a stop before her, and she stood, glancing between the royal duke and Killian. The royal duke beamed down, and she dipped into a reverent curtsy. Killian had never seen a curtsy quite so smooth or deliberate, a thing of beauty.

She, he thought, *is a thing of beauty.*

Her hair was unadorned save a thick velvet ribbon. She wore only a small cross on a silver chain around her slim neck and oval pearls at her ears. She held her book in both hands, clutching it to her chest.

All around her, bored royalty glittered and drank and surveyed the ballroom with haughty judgment. She was somber and graceful and appeared to be patiently biding her time. Her head was slightly bowed; he couldn't see her eyes.

I want, Killian thought, the desire as powerful as it was simple.

I want her to look at me again. I want to see her face. I want her.

And then it occurred to him: he hadn't been simmering to embers because she'd *rejected* him; he'd been rapidly catching fire . . . *because he wanted her.*

The truth was as obvious and brilliant as a full moon on a clear night. This wasn't darkness, this was illumination.

He was attracted to the princess. He could deny it,

except when had self-delusion ever served him? It was best not to pretend; his half brother had shown him that.

Fine. So he wouldn't pretend, but he also couldn't act on it. A French princess and the Royal Fixer? It was like a trowel being attracted to a rose. Perhaps they existed in the same garden, but to very different ends.

Wasn't it always like this? Killian and his regrettable habit of wanting things he could not have.

And now the king had charged him with *courting her*—when Killian really should stay as far away as possible. *Remoteness*, that should be the order of the day. The only way to survive.

Why keep company with someone he wanted—and a member of royalty, no less—so that he could see her, and hear her, but never have her?

Because you're being paid to entice her.

And if you don't do it, they would put some other blaggard on the job.

"But have you *made* the acquaintance of the Honorable Mr. Killian Crewes, Your Serene Highness?" Edward was asking.

"Yes, I have met him," Princess Elise said simply. Her gaze slid again to Killian's and, because he was not a coward (but rather a fool?) he met that gaze. He felt a jolt—a sort of . . . *resonance* in the air. It felt like a very long note from a very large tower bell. The vibrations of the look blocked out everything else. Killian heard no music and saw no revelers; there were only the waves of energy ricocheting between them.

And now it was his turn to say something.

"It is a pleasure to make your acquaintance again, Serene Highness," he said. *There*, he thought. *Something.*

Princess Elise did not return the salutation—she didn't even acknowledge it. This amused him because naturally she would not deign to respond to him. She simply stared up at him with a placid, waiting expression.

He was just about to ask her about her journey home from Tattersall's when Edward spoke again, gesturing with the plated lobster.

"At the risk of embarrassing you with ruthless flattery, Princess Elise," said the royal duke, "I'd like to tell you a little secret. Mr. Crewes here—whose father was an earl, by the way . . . Earl of Loondoch, isn't it, Killian?"

"Earl *Dunlock*," Killian corrected him.

"That's right, whose father was Earl *Dunlock*. The secret is that Mr. Crewes has *noticed you* among the women of the court. How do you like that, Princess?"

"I neither like it nor dislike it," she said, "but I do find it very hard to believe."

"Oh, believe it," Edward assured her, making a circling motion with his lobster.

Killian felt his expression tighten into something like mortification. He blinked, striving for blankness. He might perish from the horror of the moment, but God help him, his face would betray nothing more than bloody, bleeding blankness.

"*And*," Edward was saying, "because I am such an obliging fellow, and also because I know Killian to be the very best sort—and you a mature woman of whom my sisters are so very fond—I saw fit to do the honors."

"The honors?" Elise asked in the same moment Killian said, "Highness—"

"Oh, no," scolded Edward, "there's no place for shyness now. We've done the deed. Your cleverness and fine manners will win the day, never you fear, Killian. Perhaps you will ask her to dance? Dare I suggest it?" The royal duke looked hopefully back and forth between them.

Even if the woman did not despise Killian—which

she did—this would be an excruciatingly awkward exchange.

Even if Killian had descended on the ballroom with an air of the forbidden and a hint of danger—the two qualities that seemed to make court women fall at his feet—Killian would be at a loss for words.

If her head were filled with loose buttons instead of a brain, she could not be more confused by the graceless "introduction" from the royal duke. Surely. It was beyond comprehending. Even Killian was confused.

He looked to her and felt loose buttons in his own head. He searched for something, anything, to make the moment less painful.

"Come now, let us not be timid," Edward soothed, determined to prolong the awkwardness. "If you're troubled by the queen's restrictions, might I suggest you make some arrangement to meet outside of this ball? Even on the best night, these parties are overwrought and overwarm and deafeningly loud, are they not? You have my blessing to make your own diversion. Enjoy some pastime beyond the gates of the palace if you like."

Killian struggled to keep his mouth from falling open. Never in all his years of service to this family had he been so strong-armed or marched about. Rarely, if ever, were there specifics about time and place. What in God's name was so threatening to the king about this small, quiet woman?

"Highness—" Killian began, speaking with no idea of what he might say next. His only goal was to stop the flow of words from the royal duke's mouth.

"Mr. Crewes is," revealed Edward, "the owner of various properties in and around London, Princess Elise. Did you know that?"

The princess looked at Killian.

He could only stare at her.

"And," Edward went on, "he rides out frequently to inspect them—"

"In fact, I do not—" cut in Killian.

"*In fact*," Edward spoke over him, "he has his eye on a new property in Limehouse. This is just outside of London, on the river—do you know it? Limehouse?"

"No," said Princess Elise, but she'd perked up. She looked as if the royal duke had just held up a map of buried treasure and asked her if she knew the meaning of the large black *X*.

"Indeed," said Edward, "we were just speaking of it, weren't we, Killian? Imagine how lovely it might be to have a companion to join you when you next visit it. The sale could happen any day."

"I would never imagine—" Killian started.

"I'll do it," said Princess Elise, cutting them both off. The royal duke beamed at her.

Killian blinked. He could not have been more surprised if she'd dissolved into a cloud of smoke.

"I beg your pardon?" Killian began slowly.

In the same moment, Edward said, "Oh, lovely! You see, Killian, I told you she'd take a shine to you."

"Is Mr. Crewes's property near the Road to Land's End?" the princess asked, speaking of the main thoroughfare from London to the southern coast of England. Her voice had taken on a pointed, almost urgent note. She sounded less like she'd taken a shine to Killian and more like she'd missed the last mail coach to Dorset.

"Not far," mused Edward, even while Killian said, "No. It's not. Limehouse is in the opposite direction."

"Now, Princess Elise," coaxed Edward, "there'll be no need for veils or even ladies-in-waiting when you're in the company of Mr. Crewes. Killian has served my family for years. He's a gentleman. You will be safe with him, and—"

He paused, winked at the princess, and continued with a grin. "Well. Never you fear. Wear something pretty and leave off the suffocating veils. How much better to take in the scenery? This is my advice to you."

"Just to be clear," Killian said, "the property of which Edward speaks is an area wholly unsuitable for a lady—"

"But could you *reach* the Road to Land's End from the unsuitable area?" pressed Princess Elise.

"Not really," said Killian on an exhale. "And furthermore, I should never conceive of bringing a woman to inspect a warehou—"

"Who is to say what is close and what is far as we enjoy these last rays of summer and the roads are dry?" cut in Edward with a chortle.

I am, Killian thought. *I am to say it. Me. The man being bullied into dragging this woman to crime-ridden dockyards for reasons that are largely unclear to me— other than to remind me that I want these warehouses, and you have them, and you'll sell them to me if I'm a very good little solider.*

Killian eyed the lobster on Edward's plate, wanting to swipe it up and stab himself in the eye with a claw.

"It would be my pleasure to accept," Princess Elise said, dipping into a shallow curtsy.

"Lovely," Edward crooned. "I'll leave the two of you to sort it out. Take a small amount of care not to disrupt the queen—this is my one word of caution. Her priority is my sisters, so never you fear. If you're careful not to trouble her with your comings and goings, she shouldn't—"

"I know how to evade the queen," said Princess Elise.

A flash of irritation tightened Edward's face, and Killian thought, *You reckon? It grates to be told what's what, doesn't it?*

"So you do," Edward conceded. "Well then—off you

go. I've done my good deed for the day. You may thank me later, Killian. Princess Elise? I've no doubt he'll prove to be a very diverting companion, indeed."

"Goodbye," Princess Elise said flatly, almost dismissively.

Edward's face flashed again with irritation. He nodded stiffly, shot Killian a look meant to convey something that Killian couldn't possibly identify, and left them.

After a glance at his sisters, the royal duke wound his way through the crowd with his lobster.

Killian watched him go, marveling that someone with his leadership role in the country—fourth in line to be sovereign, in fact—could be so tactless and coarse.

He glanced back at Princess Elise. She, too, was marveling at the royal duke. Or perhaps she was cursing the man to the devil. What she *wasn't* doing was looking at Killian. With very great purpose, she *refused* to look at Killian.

Killian, now fully exhausted by this night, studied her openly. At Tattersall's, he'd seen her uncovered face for what? Five minutes? Meanwhile, he'd been reckoning with her rejection . . . with her ladies, milling about, just steps away . . . with what might've happened in the empty wagon if he'd not reached her in time. He'd identified her as beautiful in that moment, but he hadn't had the opportunity to understand why.

Her nose, he now saw, was decidedly French, prominent and interesting and balanced by her large eyes. Her lips were full, light pink, textured—they put him immediately in the mind of a kiss. Her cheekbones were high, her skin radiant. Her face was as unique as it was symmetrical.

As Killian stared, he felt something like a brisk wind rattle the scaffolding of his heart. He shifted, not sure if the brackets would hold. Instead, the sight of her lifted years of cynicism and callousness and bore it away.

He wanted to reach out and tuck his fingers beneath her chin, tip her face upward, and see more.

He wanted her to look at him.

He wanted to feel the wind again.

Of course he would not touch her chin or any other part of her. It was unclear *what* he would do with her— inside this ball or out of it—but he knew for certain that he would *never* touch her.

He was just about to say, *I apologize*, when she turned to him and said in French, "Should we dance, Mr. Crewes?"

CHAPTER EIGHT

"WHAT, EXACTLY, DID the royal duke mean by that conversation?"

This was Elise's first question. Mr. Crewes was leading her, wordlessly, to the dance floor. Meanwhile, Elise was not without words. Elise had *so many words*.

The question was bold, but boldness seemed to be the order of the night. Edward's comments had been more than bold: they'd been forward and presumptive and mildly transactional. Elise had never before spoken to the King's fourth son, and she hoped to never speak to him again.

For whatever reason, she didn't mind speaking to Killian Crewes.

"Pardon?" Mr. Crewes said, not looking at her.

"Am I to believe," Elise said, "that *you* wish to . . . in a manner . . . *court* me?"

He didn't answer. He slowly closed his eyes in a pained sort of *I-will-not-survive-the-night* expression. He didn't look like he wanted to dance with her, let alone court her. He looked like he'd been handed the carcass of a dead animal and asked to pretend it was his living pet.

The band began a waltz and, without another word, Mr. Crewes took her up and swept them into the sea of dancers. Despite the wide chasm he maintained between their bodies, he led them capably through the steps. It had been many years since Elise had danced—a lifetime ago—but her feet remembered the count. She also remembered that there were two ways to go about it: sailing about the dance floor in a thrilling whirl of skirts and elbows, or bobbing along, proficient and pleasant.

At the moment, they bobbed.

"The reason I ask," Elise went on, looking at his clenched-jaw profile, "is that the royal duke's introduction made very little sense, and I'm confused."

Still he said nothing, so she continued. "For example, I've already been outside the palace in your company—if not *with you*, then certainly *adjacent to you*. You've revealed no interest in 'courting me'—not then or now."

Again, he made no comment.

Elise went on. "Another thing you've done that was decidedly un-courtship-like was to interfere with my important transaction with Mr. Latchfoot—"

"You're welcome," he said, spinning them in a half turn.

A joke. Alright. Elise had not expected this. She bit her lip to hide her smile.

"Then," she continued, "you introduced yourself in the most artificial way. After that, you *shouted my identity* into the crowded market despite my obvious desire to remain anonymous.

"And yet *now*," she finished, "Edward would have you play suitor to me? *Me*. An exiled, on-the-shelf Frenchwoman who's been all but invisible in court for five years?" She made an exasperated sound. "Perhaps *confused* is a poor word for what I am. Perhaps I simply want to know how to proceed. With you. You seem to be ever-present in my life, Mr. Crewes. As constant as my footprint. But in what vein? Stalker? Interference? Suitor? Should I fear you, evade you, or flirt with you?"

They came to the corner of the dance floor, and he spun her, dropping his hand from her shoulder to her waist to effect the slightest little hop, whirling them through the bend.

Oh, Elise thought, feeling herself smile. The simple dance had evolved into something more athletic and breathless. They'd left the realm of counting steps and begun to sail. Her face felt flushed, and her heartbeat kicked up. It was . . . exhilarating. It had been so long since Elise had felt anything exhilarating, or joyful, or diverting; it was like the first truly warm day of spring after months of winter. It was like sunlight.

Meanwhile, he said nothing. He made no expression. He wouldn't look at her.

But he was an excellent dancer—she would give him that.

At least he's not lying, she thought. If he didn't speak, he didn't lie to her.

So . . . he wasn't a liar (so far as she knew), but he *was* a puzzle, and Elise had always rather enjoyed puzzles. Curiosity felt good—it felt alert and alive—and she'd once been very good at figuring things out.

In the days since Tattersall's, Elise had repeatedly unfolded the puzzle of Killian Crewes to make guesses about him. She'd hardly solved the puzzle, but now here were all these new pieces.

He was an excellent dancer but endeavored to hide it.

He was working on behalf of the royal family to . . . to . . . *attach himself* to her (this clue was still very unclear), but he wouldn't talk about it.

He was the son of an earl and the owner of properties but also somehow running errands for the king.

Later tonight, Elise would take up these pieces and turn them over in her mind, trying to make them fit. For now, she struggled simply to keep up with his dancing.

The music from the bandstand swelled, and he spun them again. Elise missed a step.

"Sorry," she said. "I have not danced since—" She looked at their feet. "Since I left Paris."

"That long." A remark, not a question.

"Ten years at least."

"How old are you?"

"Twenty-five. How old are you?"

He ignored her question. "Waltzing at age fifteen, were you?"

"I was, in fact. I debuted at fifteen. I'd just finished my first season when we were—when I left France."

Mr. Crewes gave a nod and made a wide loop to the right, zigging and zagging to circumvent two other couples, and spinning again. When the music swelled to its robust conclusion, he whirled her to a stop on the edge of the dance floor. Elise was breathing hard, her smile impossible to hide.

Mr. Crewes released her and took a step back.

Elise put one hand to her chest and gave a winded laugh. "I'm not conditioned for spinning. Dancing with you feels a little like waltzing and a little like swinging in my childhood garden at the Palais-Royal."

"My apologies," he said.

Elise rolled her eyes.

"What?" he asked.

"Oh, the very great burden of it all. Dancing. At a ball. And with someone whom you've . . . how did the royal duke put it? 'Noticed'? You sound so very miserable— it's funny."

"I'm happy to amuse you."

"I'd not go so far as *amusement,* but you should see your face. Honestly, it makes my point. Would a suitor scowl down at the object of his affection? Edward has been misled about your regard for me."

He narrowed his eyes, crossing his arms over his chest. He looked like a boxer who'd been challenged to a fight by a child.

Elise considered this. He felt challenged, did he?

"Why is the palace attaching the two of us?" she asked. "To one another?"

"I don't know."

"I don't believe you."

He frowned. "Fine: the king and queen are worried that you're . . . bored."

"And they put you on it because . . . ?"

"I am the opposite." He sighed. "Of boring."

He looked back at her. There was something about that look—impatient and annoyed and yet also . . . sympathetic. It was arresting. Elise felt a flipping sensation in her stomach. He was correct about one thing. She wasn't bored.

"How odd," she ventured. "They've never before cared whether I'm entertained or not. Why now?"

"Perhaps they've seen the error of their ways."

Elise raised her eyebrows, pretending to consider this. "To what lengths are you permitted to go, Mr. Crewes, to vanquish my boredom?"

"You ask a lot of questions, Highness."

"And yet I've learned almost nothing. My days are marked by asking and asking and asking and being told, 'You don't need to know.'"

He stared at her.

"I *do* need to know, Mr. Crewes," she told him. "And I'll not carry on, accepting ignorance, just because my alleged boredom troubles King George."

"Noted," he said. He took a deep breath. "Look, Highness, I'm not in the position to *answer questions* about the palace—largely because I know very little. They actually don't tell me, and I don't ask. What I can say is this: I do what I want, when I want, how I want. I serve the king, but in my own way. You are"—he took a deep breath—"you are safe with me."

And now Elise felt the flipping again, more pronounced this time. She held an armful of puzzle pieces, far too many to consider on the edge of the dim dance floor, and she didn't want to drop a single one.

One piece in particular was solid, and weighty, and she wanted to squeeze it in her hand. How had he said it? *You are safe with me.* It sounded like the truth. His face, handsome and a little anguished in the candlelight, looked like the face of someone who would *tell her the truth*.

She would take it, she thought. She had few other options. And if nothing else, he was a means to travel outside the city.

"Where will we go?" she asked.

"What?"

"When we leave the palace. If you'll not take me to Limehouse, where shall we go instead?"

He stared at her a long moment. Finally he said, "Where would you like to go?"

"Well . . ." she began. She was suddenly cautious. It was one thing for him to vouch for her safety, but quite another for him to agree to squire her about, wherever she wanted to go.

"Let me guess," he cut in. "Dorset. Via the Road to Land's End."

Elise blinked at him. Perhaps he *would* agree to squire her around. Perhaps he would agree to whatever she wanted.

"Would that be possible?" she asked.

"Anything is possible, apparently," he said. "We've been given carte blanche by a royal duke, haven't we?"

She was just about to ask him how far they could

travel in a day, when the music behind them changed from a waltz to a rousing composition of ascending notes and the herald of a trumpet. The dancers cleared the floor, and a procession of costumed performers filed into the ballroom, pulling a small gold wagon studded with jewels. The performers concealed the contents of the wagon from view, but Elise looked closer and discerned glimpses of a shadowy figure crouched inside.

"Not this, God save me," grumbled Mr. Crewes, turning away.

"What is it?"

"Nothing worth watching, I assure you. The Prince of Wales favors this lot. I find them appalling."

"Why?"

Mr. Crewes ran a tired hand over his forehead. "They'll have some wild animal chained inside the wagon. They'll—"

"A wild animal?" exclaimed Elise. "Like a bear?"

"God only knows. I haven't the stomach for it."

"But perhaps I'll take just a peek? The queen never allows us to stay at these balls long enough to enjoy the entertainment."

Mr. Crewes held up his hands. "Off you go then. I think you'll find the word *entertainment* applies very loosely."

Elise shot him an impatient look and stepped to the side, trying to see. The edge of the dance floor was suddenly crowded, and it was difficult to get a clear view. She moved forward but was jostled back by other guests. The enthusiasm of the revelers surprised her—cynical boredom was a hallmark of most courtiers—and she paused a moment, weighing her desire for a look against the effort of fighting a crowd. But then she heard gasps of delight and intermittent applause; she heard the performers making a show of greeting the Prince of Wales.

Elise was intrigued in spite of herself. She squared her shoulders and tried again to nudge her way to the front.

"Highness?" Mr. Crewes called tiredly from somewhere behind her, but she waved him back. Squinting, she tried to see through gaps in the crowd. The troop of performers—all men, dressed in exotically colorful costumes—were wheeling the little wagon to a stop in the center of the dance floor. Once in position, they spread their arms with a flourish and opened ranks to reveal the form behind the bars.

Elise craned, straining to see. She dodged the elbow of one man and the fluttering fan of a woman. Finally, she made out the crouching figure of . . . a giant cat. Mr. Crewes had been accurate. It was a tiger, based on illustrations she had seen, his sinewy body huddled in a defensive hulk behind the bars of the wagon.

Elise recoiled. The sight of the proud creature paraded through a raucous ballroom horrified her. She took a step back. This wasn't worth fighting the crowd; this wasn't worth even the turn of her head. How correct Mr. Crewes had been.

She changed course, trying to escape, but a large man rushed up behind her, and she collided with his chest. She let out a yelp and hopped sideways. The hop slammed her into a crowd of women pushing forward to see. Elise swam through the wall of silks, pawing for a way out. The revelers seemed to have multiplied, there was no end to them, they stacked against her, pushing arms and clawing fingers, eyes wild.

From the direction of the dance floor, a performer began to describe the strength and speed of the captive tiger. His voice boomed facts about razor-like teeth and knifelike claws. Someone must have prodded the beast, because she heard a feral roar. All around her, the crowd burst into applause. Unprepared for the sudden clapping,

Elise ducked her head like someone had hurled a handful of gravel.

Head down, breath coming in shallow pants, she tried again, winding her way through an ever-tighter scrum of revelers.

Out, she thought, her heart thudding like a hammer in her chest. *I need out.*

For every step forward, she was knocked back two. Elise tried to drag in a deep breath, but her lungs had begun to do the tight, hard, clamping thing, to be stingy with air. She tried again and the effort burned her throat. She made a strangled, rasping sound. Not this again. Not here.

I need breath, she thought, trying to keep hysteria at bay. *This is fine. I'm fine. These are courtiers, rushing to see a show. I am not the target. I'm not behind the bars of the wagon. I'm safe. This is survivable.*

She looked left. A couple walking arm in arm closed in, threatening to sweep her into the heart of the crowd. She looked right. A scrum of men barreled to her, jumping and pressing on each other's shoulders to get a better view. Straight ahead, a servant lost his battle with a toppling tray, upending its contents. Crystal goblets slid in every direction, and champagne launched into the air. A plume of cold liquor splashed across Elise's face, stealing her breath. She tried to raise her hand to wipe it away, but her arms were pinned to her sides by the crowd. Her vision swam with the avaricious, drink-lit faces of courtiers.

Elise had just opened her mouth to scream, when the men to her right popped apart like billiard balls. And then there he was, Mr. Crewes, stepping among them, tall and solid, a scowl on his face. He took up her wrist with one hand and settled the other on the small of her back. He ushered her forward, breaking through the crowd with his shoulder. Elise fell against him, pinning herself to the hard column of his body. A moment later, they were at the edge of the crowd.

"What happened?" he asked. "Did someone harm you? Why is your face wet?"

Elise couldn't answer. She breathed in and out, in and out, sucking air in rapid shallow breaths.

"What do you need, Highness? How can I help?"

She shook her head, working to catch her breath. "Forgive me," she breathed. "I—I'm not comfortable in crowds. I shouldn't have—"

Two young men darted forward then, knocking into her, shoving her against Mr. Crewes's chest. He caught her up with one hand and shoved back at the men with the other. "Mind yourselves," he snarled at them. Pivoting, he put himself between Elise and the crowd.

"I should've escorted you to the front so you could have a look," he said. "This is my fault."

He'd not released her, and she shook her head against his heartbeat. "It's mine," she rasped. "I didn't comprehend what it was. If I'd known, I wouldn't have gone. I had no business venturing into it. I'm unnerved by crowds. In France . . . when they came for us . . . the prison . . . when my father was—" She couldn't finish.

Mr. Crewes swore under his breath and lowered his head to her ear. "Let me return you to the king's daughters."

She was only half listening. The sounds of the terrified tiger mixed with the palpable enthusiasm of the crowd. In a booming voice, the handler announced he would coax the animal from the wagon.

Elise felt her lungs constrict again. She raised a shaking hand to cover her eyes. She tried to draw another deep breath, but the air wouldn't come. Her chest was a tight, wet knot. Inside her gloves, her hands were slick with sweat. She struggled with them, trying to peel back the kidskin.

"We're going," Mr. Crewes said. He moved her from his chest and tucked her to his side. Elise pivoted but continued to struggle with her gloves. Her breath sawed in and out.

"Highness," he said, "walk."

"What?" she rasped.

"*Walk.*"

Elise latched on to the sound of his voice: calm, measured, a little irritated. She walked.

"Never you fear, gentlemen, ladies," boomed the performer from the dance floor. "The beast is ferocious but we keep him securely bound on a chain of solid gold . . ."

The crowd surged and shouted words of encouragement. Two women rushed past them, shoving hard against Mr. Crewes's shoulder. One of the women toppled forward and let out a drunken hoot. Elise was lashed with a tangle of course, perfumed hair. The woman giggled and clutched at Elise's arms, steadying herself. Elise tried to pull free, but the woman's weight and lack of balance pulled them downward. Before Mr. Crewes could extricate her, another wave of spectators spilled around them, threatening to take Elise and the woman with them. Elise felt like she was being ripped in two. Cold fear poured through her, filling her like floodwater in a cellar. She was drowning and freezing at the same time.

"Bloody hell, they must be joking with this," Killian Crewes grumbled, and he unceremoniously extricated the other woman from Elise and attached her to her friend. Then he lifted Elise's stiff body and carried her— not unlike a coatrack—away from the women, away from the roiling crowd, away from the screaming tiger. He strode to the rear of the ballroom, one arm looped beneath her bottom, the other braced across her back, a palm between her shoulders. Elise closed her eyes and held on, clenching his cravat in sweaty handfuls.

He went through a door, through another door, around a corner, down two flights of steps, and deposited her in the quiet dimness of a deserted passageway.

Elise's mind was a riot of terrible sights and sounds and the memories of an angry mob and barred wagon. The experience was still so very vivid, it could've happened yesterday. She gasped for breath, trying to force her lungs to function.

She dragged up her head and looked wildly around. They were alone. No crowd. No shouting. The terrorized tiger in the golden cart was gone.

Thank you, she thought, eyeing him in the dark. *Thank you.* She closed her eyes again.

"You're alright," Mr. Crewes said. "Breathe, Highness. Breathe. You're alright. Careful. That's it."

Gently, he nudged her against the cool stones at her back and then stepped away. Elise shook her head and reached for him, clutching the lapels of his jacket to pull him back.

"Right," Mr. Crewes grunted, letting her pull him. He fell on top of her, the weight of his lean body pressing her against the wall. She reveled in the solid, immovable heft of him, and buried her face into his chest. She was a bucket tossed into the river, and he was the large, dangling hook that kept her from being swept away. She hung herself on him while the current of fear and grief slowly drained. He moored her, holding her up. He was a tight, safe place; the safest she'd ever felt in the fortress of St. James's Palace.

She should have felt trapped, but she didn't.
She should have felt obliged to him, but she didn't.
She felt . . .

Well, she felt entitled, and she had no idea why. He owed her nothing. He'd told her not to look at the tiger. By all accounts, he didn't even like her.

But he'd done exactly what she'd needed, at precisely the right moment. And he'd done it with a precision and urgency that felt almost . . . dutiful. She couldn't remember the last time someone had looked after her in this way. Protected her. It was silly and fanciful and useless, but she felt a little like a princess in his presence.

"Can you speak?" he asked softly.

"What?"

"Talk to me, Princess."

"Yes, alright," she rasped, saying the words into his chest. She cleared her throat and repeated, "I can speak."

"Good. If you can talk, you can breathe."

"When I'm . . ." she tried, wheezing between words ". . . *when I feel* panicked . . . my heart races and I can't catch my breath . . . This accelerates everything else."

"My mother was prone to episodes like this. It is miserable, I know."

And just like that, Elise was thinking about Mr. Crewes's heretofore unmentioned *mother*. What an odd notion. He seemed so very independent and grown; she couldn't picture him as a vulnerable child. He didn't seem to require a mother.

"Your mother is . . . deceased?" she clarified.

"Let us never allow panic to get in the way of probing questions," he grumbled. "Yes. She is deceased."

"May God rest her."

Mr. Crewes cleared his throat. "Thank you."

She took a deep, unobstructed breath. She became aware of the smell of him. With every breath, she detected soap and whiskey and *him*.

For his part, Mr. Crewes did little more than *stay*. He wedged himself against her, motionless, and simply . . .

remained. He hadn't touched her, hadn't held her; he'd braced his forearms on either side, palms by her ears, boots wide at the hem of her skirt. He waited. But when the full-body trembles stopped and her legs again would support her weight, he slid his hands from the wall and gathered. It could have been one minute or an hour. She made a small sound, half whimper, half moan, and buried her face deeper into his chest. She held to his lapels with both hands.

"You're alright, Highness," he whispered, and dropped his face on the top of her head, resting his lips on her hair.

Elise's eyes had been closed, but now she blinked them open. There was almost no light. She raised her head, just a little. She felt . . . better. Her breathing was almost normal. Her heartbeat had slowed.

"I'm sorry," she whispered into his coat. "Mr. Crewes."

"Don't apologize."

"That performance—" She stopped. It would be stupid to relive it in her memory.

"I, for one, was grateful for the excuse to leave it," he said. "I've suggested to the royal dukes that they reconsider their patronage of that particular troupe. Not only are they devoid of talent, someday their captive beasts will eat one of them alive. Now, that is a performance I would be willing to watch."

"You saved me." The thinnest whisper.

He tensed around her. He cleared his throat. "How do you usually cope? When you feel panicked?"

"Usually I flee to my bed and curl up beneath the covers. I . . . I constrict myself tight and hard like a nut. I imagine a brittle shell around me, and I weep. Until I can no longer stay awake."

"Do you want your bed now?"

"No," she said. She did not want her bed.

"Has the panic faded?"

"Yes. It has." The truth. "Thank you."

"Can you breathe?"

Elise nodded.

He was too tall for her to see over his shoulder. She tipped her head up, seeking light, and scraped her tear-streaked face through the folds of his cravat. This motion felt cleansing, and she tipped her head higher still, moving her face over the stiffness of his collar to the warm skin of his neck.

Her cheek nuzzled his throat, soft skin against the scruff of his whiskers, and his body went rigid.

How curious, Elise thought, because the feeling of his warm, rough skin actually made her more relaxed. She felt soft and light. She breathed in the smell of his skin. She made another whimpering noise—she didn't know why—and her lips grazed the skin of his neck. The feeling, she discovered, was not unpleasant.

In fact, it was very pleasant indeed.

She shifted, swiping her lips against his throat a second time. His body went rigid again. He felt like a rope about to snap.

Elise's breathing hitched, puffed out, hitched again. It wasn't hysterical breathing; it was . . . anticipation. She wasn't suffocating, she was energized.

Without thinking, Elise licked her lips. This afforded the tiniest little swipe of her tongue against Mr. Crewes's neck. His skin was tangy from sweat.

On a hiss, he let out a curse, low and miserable.

Elise paused, trying to decipher this hiss. Did he sound miserable because she'd licked him? Or because she might not lick him again?

It felt like an invitation. She swiped her tongue again. The royal duke had just introduced Mr. Crewes in a way that suggested he would be open to—well, that he would be open.

"*Highness*," he rasped. A warning. His voice was raw, and the sound of it felt somehow like a lick to her own skin. Gooseflesh rose on her arms.

She licked his neck a third time, and he made a growling sound. She scraped her mouth over the spot she'd licked, reveling in the warm, stubbly prickle of it.

"*Highness*," he repeated, another whispered hiss. "*Your Serene Highness*," he breathed into the whorl of her ear.

Something about his voice, and his breath, and his lips grazing her skin, caused her legs to wobble. He caught her up, of course. His arm slid around her waist, locked, and held her hard against the wall. Her breathing increased, her eyes dropped closed, and she burrowed her face deeper into his neck. Warm, molten pleasure dripped down her body like honey. She was coated with sensation, inside and out. She felt as if she glowed.

"*Princess*?" Mr. Crewes said, breathing into her ear.

She made a muffled sound of acknowledgment.

"*Elise*," he whispered, long and slow, and she breathed in the sound of her given name. Shimmers of warm . . . *aliveness* (for there was no other word) burned at every place he touched: his mouth on her ear, his arm on her waist, his chest against her throat. A new place also, awake for perhaps the very first time, tingling ever so intriguingly. The tingling wanted a shift, wanted *her* to shift, just a little, to *lean* into his thigh.

"What do you"—he huffed into her ear—"want with"—another huff—"the Road to Land's End?"

What? she thought.

Her brain had been a swirl of delicious tingles and his hard thigh and *leaning*. She could barely remember the Road to Land's End. She didn't answer. She shifted to the right, hooking an ankle over his calf.

Mr. Crewes grunted and hiked her a bit higher on the

wall, widening his stance. Elise grimaced; now his thigh was just out of reach. She made a noise of frustration and skimmed his neck with her teeth—an almost-bite.

He swore and pressed his lips closer to her ear. "What's in the Road to Land's End, Highness?"

"Villages," she said into the skin of his neck. "Markets."

"A man?" he wanted to know.

"What?"

"On the Road to Land's End? Do you seek a man?"

"Oh," she said. "Yes. A man."

Mr. Crewes pulled his head from her ear so suddenly, she cried out. She hadn't yet finished with that . . . position.

Killian slid her down the wall until her feet hit the ground. He released her and took a step back.

The loss of his body felt like a tumble from a window. Her hands went out.

Mr. Crewes scowled, looked away, and yanked at his ruined cravat. With a jerk, he pulled it off. He wiped the skin of his throat.

"Is it?" he confirmed bitterly.

"I beg your pardon?"

"Is it *a man*? This search of yours in Dorset. Or, *on the road* to Dorset?"

Slowly, Elise nodded. "Yes, it is a man. My brother. Gabriel."

Mr. Crewes stopped wiping. "What?"

"Prince Gabriel d'Orleans, my younger brother," she told him. "That is the man I seek on the Road to Land's End."

He'd not moved from his frozen position. "Why?"

"Oh, well," she began, wrapping her arms around herself, willing her brain to keep up with his questions. "Because I caught sight of him—or I caught sight of a man I'm certain *could be* him—out a carriage window on the roadside."

"When?"

"Last month. We were on the return journey from Weymouth, and—"

"*Who* was returning from Weymouth?"

"The queen and her daughters. Wherever the queen and her daughters go, so do I."

Mr. Crewes unfurled his cravat with one sharp crack. He flicked it two times, shaking it out. "Continue," he said.

Elise held up her hands. "What more would you have me say? You asked who I seek, and it's Gabriel."

"Your brother?" he confirmed.

"Yes."

"Your brother, *the prince*?"

"*Yes.*" Now she was irritated. This request had devolved into an interrogation.

"And you wish to see him because you're . . . what? Estranged?"

She shook her head. "I wish to see him because we've been separated these last ten years, and I thought he was dead. He was hidden in another part of England when we entered exile."

"Why?"

"Why was he hidden," she asked, "or why was he in a different part of the country? You're staring at me like I'm the tiger in that cage."

He closed his eyes and took a deep breath. "Why," he amended, "were you separated in exile?"

She shrugged. "For our safety? Because there was no time for another plan? I'm not certain. We were told only a handful of things about survival and haste. Honestly, your guess is as good as mine. I've been permitted to know almost nothing about the circumstances of my exile."

"I find that difficult to believe."

"I assure you, sir, it is even more difficult to endure. I am safe. I am provided for. I live in a palace with one of the most influential families in Europe. The suggestion is—what more need I know?"

"And so you know nothing of your brother?" he said, marveling a little.

Elise looked at the floor and then up again. "No, nothing. And we've a sister, too. Danielle. She was a baby when we entered exile. I know nothing of either of them." Elise's eyes began to sting.

"And you've been disallowed to communicate with these siblings? No letters? No reunion can be arranged? The revolution in France has been over for ten years."

"I told you, Gabriel was believed *dead*."

"Believed by whom?"

"Well . . . the aunt and uncle who first harbored me in England—this is what they believed. Also, King George and Queen Charlotte. Other exiled French aristocrats with whom I'm allowed to correspond, my mother included. It is . . . the commonly held view."

"You've a mother exiled elsewhere?"

She waved a dismissive hand. "She is Spanish and has returned to Spain with a lover."

"For what reason would your brother be concealed from you—dead or alive?"

Elise shrugged. "I suppose because of the line of succession? Should France ever restore the throne, he would be a contender. Life is less complicated for many people, I believe, if he is dead."

"This makes no sense," he said.

"This is what I'm trying to tell you. It's senseless. And no one else cares if Gabriel is alive. If they do, they care only to ignore him or conceal his location. If he is alive, he could, in theory, upset the aspirations of French royalists. But I don't care who is king of France. I care only that the brother who was so very dear to me is *alive*. The sister, too. When I saw Gabriel, it was like a . . . a resurrection. I am not alone. He is alive, living a different life. So be it. A different life is more than no life at all. If we found each other, perhaps we could search for our sister, too."

"Highness," he began, sounding skeptical. "A *sighting* gives you very little to go—"

"*It's him*," she said, standing up very straight, raising her chin. "I've not seen Gabriel for ten years, he's a man now, but I know the man I saw was my brother. He was selling horses in a market. No one will hear me, but I know it to be true. And I am determined to find him."

"So these rambles about London and questions about exile have been to discover a long-lost brother?"

She nodded again. He stared down at her as if she'd told him they would *walk* to Dorset.

Elise wondered why the palace wouldn't have explained all this to him. She'd assumed the function of Mr. Crewes's stalking (originally) and proposed affection (tonight) had been to keep her *away* from her brother. But there was no mistaking his tone. He did not know.

On the heels of this realization came the glimmer of a possibility.

"But will you help me find him?" she asked. Her voice was a whisper.

He turned away.

"Mr. Crewes?"

"I'm thinking."

"You've no interest in pressing your suit," she tossed out. "That much is clear. The royal duke is a terrible liar. So, fine, so you're meant to guard me, or watch me, or contain me. I don't care. I am accustomed to being guarded and watched and contained. Life in England keeps me safe from the guillotine, but I am hardly free. However, if you don't have explicit orders that *prevent me* from searching for Gabriel, perhaps you could *help* me."

"My orders are . . ." he began, but he didn't finish. Slowly, he folded the linen of his cravat into quarters.

He said, "I don't know anything about a lost brother."

"Perhaps the less you know, the better? You've said as much yourself. But what about tomorrow? Could you help me tomorrow?"

He laughed bitterly.

Elise frowned. It was imprudent to ask this of him—*him*, of all people. Imprudent and reckless and unexpected.

And yet—

He was nothing like she expected. He *seemed* trustworthy—only time would tell on that score—but he was wholly capable, of this she had no doubt. He'd extracted her from the ballroom as if he were leading her around a puddle. Also, he was available to the highest bidder. This, too, had been said. He was hired by the king, but he worked on his own terms.

Elise had very little money, of course, far less than King George, but she would worry about the debt later. If only he would . . . help her.

"You don't like me at all," she said—an observation and also a test.

"Yes," he said, making a scoffing sound. "*I don't like you at all*. That's it."

He ran a hand through his hair and tugged at his collar, now open and free of the cravat. Elise stared at the triangle of skin below his clavicle. Her mouth had been there. She'd *tasted* that spot.

He turned away. "You must go."

"Go . . . ?" She was lost in the maze of this conversation.

"*To bed.* To your quarters in the Queen's Chapel. The other girls have been gone for nearly an hour. What was it Edward said about your comings and goings and Queen Charlotte?"

"Fine, yes, alright. This is true. But *will you help me*? The royal duke said we were to enjoy an outing together. We've been given leave. This is my chance. If you will help me, *this is my chance.*"

"I'll walk you to your quarters," he said, ignoring her question. "I cannot be seen near the door, but I'll go as far as is prudent."

"*Will you help me?*"

"*I cannot be seen near the door,*" he repeated, enunciating the words slowly, "*but I'll go as far as is prudent.*" He looked her dead in the eye, a pointed, knowing look.

"I'll take that as a yes," Elise said. She inhaled a deep breath. For the first time in weeks, she felt like she'd made progress. She'd been trying to shove open a very thick, very heavy door, and finally, it had budged. Just an inch, but movement had occurred. She could see a tiny sliver of light.

"Thank you," she added. "And now you may walk me to my quarters. Or, as close as is prudent." She moved closer and extended her hand to take his arm.

He stepped out of reach, frowning at her hand. "I don't think so." Bowing slightly, he made a sweeping gesture and motioned for her to precede him. "*After you. Highness.*"

Elise narrowed her eyes. And now he would follow her. More pieces of the puzzle. Fine. She had been a princess, once upon a time.

She placed her hand on the cool, rough wall of the passage and led the way.

CHAPTER NINE

$\mathcal{T}$HE NEXT MORNING, a beautiful new carriage with two chestnut bays and a driver clattered into the mews beside Killian's house in Lamb Street, along with a note from St. James's Place.

> *Killian,*
> *Please enjoy exclusive use of this carriage with the princess. To facilitate your seduction. For as long as it takes. Let the enchantment commence.*
>
> *Edward, Duke of Kent*

The conveyance, for which he had not asked and in which he would orchestrate *no* seduction, angered Killian. He'd crumpled Edward's note and pitched it into the fire.

"I'll arrange for my own bloody carriage, thank you very much," Killian told Hodges. "Why not deliver a bed with the princess strapped to it? It would be no less subtle."

I should walk away. The thought flashed through Killian's mind for the hundredth time since last night.

He thought of sending his own note to the palace, thanking the lot of them for the many fortuitous years, and declining this job with respect.

He thought of simply disappearing, making do with the property and money he'd earned—never to be seen from again.

He thought of America, or Australia, or—

There was no option to refuse. He had a nephew for whom he was responsible, the boy's mother, two maiden aunts—

And the princess.

Another thought that had plagued him all night.

Killian was not, he knew, *responsible* for Princess Elise—not for her future or her present, not for her fits of panic or her missing brother. He owed her nothing; in fact, he'd only just met the woman, and he'd been tasked with something that felt very much like *sabotaging* her.

How could one man be responsible for her well-being and also with sabotaging her? He could not.

Or, he couldn't without some nonnegotiable adjustments to everyone's view of what would happen next.

The *new* plan—*Killian's* plan, which he'd conceived at roughly two o'clock in the morning—was to skate the fine line between serving as a *Glorified Nanny* to the princess and her *Special Friend.*

Special as in alive and nearby, not distinctive, valued, or even well acquainted. *Friend* as in a platonic, benign acquaintance.

Being *responsible* for her played no part.

Dancing with her played no part.

Touching her played no part.

Breathing her in like she was a buttery croissant after living on gruel his entire life? *Not a part.*

Whispering into the small shell of her ear? Pressing her into stone passageways? *Absolutely not a part.*

Caring whether she searched for *some man* on the Road to Land's End . . . or fifty men . . . or her long-lost brother?

None of this was part of the nanny/special-friend plan.

The new plan was meant to represent how *little* he cared.

The new plan circumvented any future interludes in dark passages or the repeat of what was surely a *one-time* lapse in self-control.

Do not remember it.

The thick fog of desire in the passage last night had been so very dense and intoxicating, and it had been selfish and irresponsible for Killian to breathe it in. He could only cope by shutting out the memory. He bolted it behind a door in his brain like the sealed hatch to a deadly mine.

The alternative, which was to descend into the cool, dark memory of it, allowed two very dangerous illusions to float in his mind: hopefulness and want.

Of course he wanted to touch her. When had he not wanted rich, exclusive, beautiful things that were entirely unavailable to him? He'd wanted her since the moment she'd revealed her face.

And of course, he wanted to be the hero who restored her missing brother and a potential King of France.

But that had not been the assignment, had it?

Actually, the first bit—seducing her—had been *precisely* the assignment, but he refused to touch her casually now only to inspire her resentment in the future. He was a fixer, not a lothario. And he knew the pain of tempting himself with something he couldn't have in the end.

But the second bit—the fuss about a missing brother—was the *opposite* of the assignment. He could see that clearly now. If the missing brother was in line for the French throne, naturally King George wanted to put her off the scent. The last thing St. James's Palace needed was to incubate a plot to reorder the French monarchy. The assignment was to distract her, to "numb her," so that the brother remained as dead as everyone wanted him to be.

If Killian wanted to receive the payout from this fix (which he needed)—and the offer of the warehouses (which he also needed)—if he had to survive spending days . . . weeks . . . with a woman *so very off-limits to him*—he must stay on task. He must forget about their encounter in the passageway except to make certain there was no repeat of it.

If last night's interlude had been step one in a working seduction . . . if she'd felt the burning lick of desire . . . well, he had, too. So be it. He was doing the job he'd been hired to do—but he would take it no further.

He would "occupy" the princess, but on his own bloody terms, which meant leaving Princess Elise no more miserable than when he found her.

She would not be "ruined."

She would not fancy herself somehow "in lust with him."

And she would never be, God help them, "breeding," as Edward had so callously put it.

He would escort her up and down the Road to Land's End. He would watch from a safe distance as she turned over every haystack, looking for the man who could be her brother or could be any of thousands of horse traders between London and Dorset.

He would do only what he could tolerate (first and foremost), while indulging her search (second), and fulfilling the assignment of the palace. In that order.

Hopefully. Possibly. If a miracle occurred and he could achieve it.

After a clean shave and hot breakfast, Killian devoted the next twenty minutes to donning and discarding five different jackets and waistcoats. In the end, he told Hodges to make the choice. The result was a combination of deep aubergine and dark vermilion, with gray trousers and black boots. He might dread the task at hand, but he refused to turn up looking like Captain of the Bourgeoisie.

Next he went to the mews for his horse. Edward's loaned carriage and driver had not left the alley, and Killian took one look at the glistening new carriage and realized that *of course* she and her ladies should have it as their conveyance. She should glide along on its sleek wheels and view the world from its springy height. Nothing less would do. They would be far more comfortable, and people on the road would give way to its understated elegance. She deserved the very best.

And yet she'll settle for you, Killian thought.

Pretending.

To be her Special Friend.

Killian climbed into the saddle and signaled Tom Coachman to walk on. Killian would follow on his stallion, Mayor.

Their schedule had been designed by the princess last night. He'd wound through the passages of St. James's Palace behind her, and she'd rattled off her plan for their great escape. For someone who'd been traumatized (first) by Satan's Rolling Menagerie of Jungle Cats, and (second) by Killian's heavy breathing and hungry . . . pressing, Her Serene Highness had been remarkably clearheaded. Killian would be lying if he said it did not thrill him, just a little, to hear her accurately inform him of the best times and ways to slip away from the palace.

And just like that, they were collaborating. She'd gone from not allowing him to hail her a cab to instructing him to collect her on the side of the road.

Glorified Nanny, he reminded himself. *Special Friend.*

The princess had suggested they convene outside

the palace wall in a sprawling meadow known as The Green Park. Staff and deliveries came and went from the south and north palace gates, while The Green Park bordered to the west. Comings and goings were limited to groundskeepers and palace hunts, and the parkland was so dense, pedestrians were easily swallowed up and concealed among the hedges and stands of trees.

Killian had agreed because—why argue? It was as good a plan as any, and he'd been given permission by Edward to do far more than simply take her on a ride.

Glorified Nanny, Killian said again when he reached the appointed wall at the appointed time the next morning. *And Special Friend.*

And that is all.

"Wait here," he told the coachman when they came to The Green Park wall. There was a gate for pedestrians, and Killian guided his horse through. Shading his eyes with his hand, he scanned the lush emerald meadow for a quartet of black.

"Oh," said a familiar voice, "you've come on horseback."

Killian nudged Mayor around.

Princess Elise stood in the shade of a tree, a stack of notebooks hanging by a belt in one gloved hand. She was alone, no ladies, no maid, no chaperone. She wore a dress of smoky lavender, the color of the sky at dusk before a stormy night. She appeared perkily awake, eyes bright, chin high, a woman who'd been up and dressed for hours. Her skin glowed. She was neither smiling nor frowning. She regarded him with calm, keen interest.

She was, Killian thought, the freshest, most naturally beautiful thing he'd ever encountered in a lush meadow. Or under a tree. Or anywhere. He wanted to slide from his horse and walk to the tree for no other purpose than to get a closer look at her.

"Shall we go?" she prompted.

"Where are your ladies?" he asked.

"It's only me today, I'm afraid. I'll be nimbler if I travel alone."

Killian thought of her nimbleness. He thought of her alone with him. This was not the plan.

"Who will attend you?" he asked.

"Oh, I've no need of attendants. The ladies only traveled about London with me to conceal my identity."

"And how will it be concealed without them?"

She shrugged. "It won't. I'm not quite so vulnerable in your company, surely."

Killian shifted in the saddle, taking a metaphorical bite out of this declaration. How good it tasted, he thought, that she felt safe with him.

"Where is your manservant?" she asked pointedly.

Killian blinked at her. He couldn't really explain why he'd asked Hodges to stay behind. Not even to himself. The servant accompanied Killian almost everywhere he went, serving in every capacity from lookout, to drinking mate, to valet. For whatever reason, it had simply felt . . . superfluous to include Hodges on this particular job. In hindsight, the exclusion had been an imprudent choice. Also reckless.

"Hodges had other business," Killian finally said. "But what of a chaperone? For Your Serene Highness."

"You are my chaperone."

Killian frowned. Was it possible she did not understand the English word for chaperone? Unless he was mistaken, *chaperone* was a French bloody word.

"No," he tried.

"Yes," she countered.

Killian opened his mouth and then closed it. Inside his chest, his heart gave a double beat because—fool that he was—he relished exchanges like this. Last night, before she'd panicked, it had been no different. If she wanted something, she told him how to give it to her. It was provoking. It was . . . arousing. He was a little aroused by her ordering him about, and this was the opposite of the plan.

"Wasn't this your excuse," she asked, "for the stalking and the hounding? You were protecting me? Watching over me? Chasing away Mr. Latchfoot? *You* are my chaperone, Mr. Crewes."

Who will protect you from me?

He wanted to say it, but he reminded himself that Her Serene Highness would view the Royal Fixer as her security detail and nothing more.

"What of your mourning attire?" he said. "Your veil?"

"Will there be a test of skill, Mr. Crewes, to accompany this interrogation? I've slipped away from the palace undetected, but I cannot loiter here. Timing is everything with these evasions."

"Forgive me."

"You are forgiven. Shall we go?"

No, he thought, *we should not go*. The two of them couldn't embark on a journey outside London. *Alone*. Together. He didn't care what the royal duke said.

"I saw myself more of a *shepherd* on this journey," he said, "not a . . ."

". . . a guide?" she provided.

"*Private escort*," he said.

"If I might answer your many questions in one breath," she sighed, "the black dresses unnerve people, and they are bulky and overwarm. My ladies complain and squabble and are insubordinate, particularly Juliette. I've one true friend among them—"

"Which?" he cut in.

"I beg your pardon?"

"Sorry. If it wasn't plainly obvious, I didn't know

which member of your entourage was, er, *you* and which were your ladies. I distinguished the four of you by . . ." And here he drifted off, clearing his throat. Why was he telling her this?

"By what?"

"By the most discernable features I could identify despite the mourning costumes."

"Really? What was my discernable feature?"

"I don't remember."

"Come now, I would hear it," she said.

He exhaled. "Fine. Smallness."

She considered this for a moment and then nodded. "Perhaps I am the smallest one. And my friend is Marie. The nun."

"The tallest of the lot?"

"That's right."

He inclined his head. "This had been my guess."

"How astute you are. You'll not be surprised that the four of us are widely different women—both in appearance and personality—when the mourning clothes are off. I'm gratified, at least, that the costumes were effective. You are not an easy man to confuse, surely."

Killian had no response for this. He nodded, regretting the topic of his piss-poor surveillance.

Elise eyed him for a moment more and then continued. "As I was saying, Marie knows that you and I are setting out alone. What else . . . ? Oh, the veils. The veils are terrible, and I hope never to wear them again. Those are my excuses, but really we must go. The palace guards canvass this path every ten minutes. But what of a mount for me?"

Killian made a sound that was half cough, half choke. "A mount?"

"I'm not an accomplished rider, but I am motivated. I can—"

"I've a carriage for you, Highness," he cut in. And now he did slide from the saddle. He took up Mayor's bridle and began to pull him in the direction of the carriage.

"I implore you to reconsider," Princess Elise said, following behind him. "I don't require a vehicle all to myself. My view of the villages will be better from horseback."

"There are windows," he said.

"I should like to be with you," she said.

Something like a cool breeze fluttered the drapes on the windows of Killian's heart. It should have felt too cold or been too bright, but it wasn't. The statement invigorated him. *I should like to be with you.*

He stepped through the little gate. He put one hand to the stones and leaned for half a beat, collecting himself. *Glorified Nanny. Special Friend.*

The princess rounded the corner, saw the carriage, and shook her head.

Killian wanted to laugh—naturally she would be displeased with a private luxury vehicle—but he said, "I will ride with*out*, and you will ride within. You may design this outing, Highness, but only to a point." He crossed to the carriage and held open the door.

"Edward said—"

"Edward is not here, is he? In you go."

Princess Elise paused a moment, contemplating the open door.

"To be honest, I'm glad Edward is not with us," she said finally, speaking on a sigh.

"Very good." He didn't want to know.

"They've all but forbidden me from speaking Gabriel's name—the lot of them. Searching for him would be out of the question. How agreeable you are, Mr. Crewes, now that you're no longer stalking me."

She gathered her skirts and clipped up the steps, settling on the ivory velvet seat.

Killian stared in after her, his brain hanging on the suggestion that she'd been "forbidden" to speak the name of her own brother.

"You're certain you'll not ride in the carriage?" she asked, peering out.

The carriage was small and sleek, but she was not a large woman, and the ivory velvet seemed to swallow her. She looked like a beautiful moth captured in an expensive box.

"Mr. Crewes?" she prompted.

"I will ride," he said.

She stared at him a moment more, her hazel eyes narrowing. Then she sat back against the seat. "The Road to Land's End?" she confirmed.

"I believe you mentioned it ten or twelve times."

"How far along the road can we travel in, say . . . three hours and still make our return? It would be risky to be absent from the palace for longer than six hours."

Killian was familiar with the Road to Land's End because it was the route from London to his childhood home, Paxton Dale. Also, he'd pored over the map in the middle of the night.

"We can make Lyne, perhaps, before we turn 'round? What have you told them about your absence today?"

"Staff and residents of the Queen's Chapel have grown accustomed to me slipping out for hours at a stretch. There is some vague suggestion of church, or visiting French prisoners of war in hospital, or calling to bookshops. My friend Marie is aware of my actual destination, but everyone else?" She made a shrug, the gesture of someone aware of her own insignificance. "But can you tell me: How many towns and villages will we encounter between London and Lyne?"

"Six or seven? Depends on traffic leaving London and what you consider to be a village. Are we meant to stop at every hitching post?"

She shook her head. "Only villages large enough to host a market day. When I spotted Gabriel, the village was in the midst of their weekly market. He was surrounded by horses, making a trade. I cannot say why, but I believed him to be the *trader* in the transaction, *not* the buyer."

"So you're in search of a horse trader . . . somewhere between London and Dorset . . . who you saw at market . . . in an unnamed town?"

"Yes," she said. "That's right."

"And you've no idea if the town was nearer to Dorset or London?"

"No."

"You are aware that the Road to Land's End is more than one hundred thirty miles long?"

She grimaced. "I hate my vagueness on this, but I can make no reliable guess. I'm sorry."

He gestured to the driver. "We should away. It'll take some time to reach the outskirts of London; after that, the road will open up to countryside. If you see an area you'd like to investigate, rap on the carriage wall to alert the driver."

"Very good. Thank you, Mr. Crewes." She fixed her gaze ahead, steadfast and hopeful. Killian's heart tumbled forward and knocked against the wall of his chest.

"Walk on," he told the driver.

For a quarter hour, they lurched through London traffic. If the princess was uncomfortable, she gave no sign. He could, he realized, align his horse with her window and see her elegant profile. Her gaze did not waver from the road ahead. Killian, in contrast, barely saw the city. He was grappling with the notion of this missing brother.

Again and again, his mind returned to her statement,

They've all but forbidden me from speaking Gabriel's name.

It was one thing for the palace to oppose a manhunt for a missing French royal, but to forbid her from speaking his name? She was hardly a high-placed courtier, but she was a guest of the palace, invited by the Prince of Wales and the queen herself.

He should, Killian knew, put it out of his head. One of the things that made Killian an excellent fixer was that he moved quickly, and he never stewed. He was in and out with no time to—

With no time to *care*.

He was ruthless and efficient and saw problems cleanly solved. This would be no different. It didn't matter if she was forbidden from discussing her brother or her parents or her pet fish.

He was the Glorified Nanny and Special Friend.

They cleared the congestion of the city, moving into wide swaths of green meadow flanked by freestanding houses in clusters of two or three. When they reached the River Crane, a queue formed on either side of a small bridge. Traffic slowed and ultimately stopped as travelers waited their turn to cross.

Killian nudged his horse beside the carriage and tapped on the glass. "Highness?"

The glass windowpane was attached on hinges at the side, and she swung it outward with a squeak.

"Yes?" She peered up.

"Were you free to discuss your brother with the royal family when you . . . as you describe . . . *spotted him* out the window of the carriage? Could you raise the topic in that moment?"

This, he told himself, was not "caring." This was research.

"Oh," she said, peering at him through the open window. "Well, the sight of him was . . . How can I describe it? It was like a small sort of eruption—that is, an eruption in my consciousness. I was gazing out the window, seeing nothing, thinking of nothing—and then there he was, as familiar as my own hand. And so I stared, and I think I even cried out. But also, I devoted valuable minutes to sort of . . . *reckoning with* seeing him."

"Reckoning with it?" he repeated.

"Yes. In other words, I said nothing."

"So you told no one in that moment?"

"No. After I reckoned with it, I felt overwhelmed by the *reality* of seeing him. And after *that*, more time was given to talking myself *out* of the possibility that it was, in fact, him. The whole experience was an odd mix of monumental and solitary."

"And you told no one in the moments following?"

"Correct. But later that night, I told my two ladies-in-waiting."

"I see," said Killian.

The princess gave a small nod and pulled the window shut.

Killian, however, did not see. He rapped the glass with his knuckle. The princess pushed it open again.

"Can you remember any distinguishing features from the town where you saw this person you believe to be your brother?"

"No, I'm afraid I cannot."

"Right."

She swung the window shut.

After a moment, she opened it again. "I know this lack of attention discredits me, but I can only say that it was one of countless unremarkable villages and unremarkable markets one might see traveling on an unremarkable road."

Killian rolled his shoulders. For all the mud and traf-

fic, he'd always considered the Road to Land's End to be
rather scenic.

"Please understand," she went on, "before I experienced this . . . sighting of my brother, my life in court
was a fuzzy, sleepy sort of blur. It was part boredom,
part purposelessness, and part lack of control. Everything I did was entirely at the mercy of the queen and
her daughters.

"Visits to the seaside only increased this . . . stupor.
And Queen Charlotte and the girls love nothing more
than a holiday to Weymouth. We travel there repeatedly
in spring and summer. It's an agonizing journey for me,
a test of endurance every time we go."

A gust of wind blew, fluttering the ribbons of her hat.
Above them, the cloudy sky had begun to stratify into
ever-darkening layers of gray. She blinked against the
gust.

"Why do you so dislike traveling to Weymouth?"

"Oh, well, because before, when I was—well, before
my exile, my family had a villa in the South of France, in
Villefranche-sur-Mer, on the Mediterranean Sea. It was
one of my very favorite places in all of France.

"Weymouth, in contrast, is located in Dorset, which
is on the English Channel. The town is dismal and misty,
even in the summer, and the water is beige, with angry,
spine-cracking waves. Not that I was ever given the
opportunity to bathe in it, despite how much I delight in
sea bathing. The royal family prefer to *gaze* at the sea,
not swim in it. So journeys to Weymouth made me . . .
homesick, I suppose you might say? Or more acutely
homesick?

"I was presented with the sea, yes, but the *wrong* sea,
with a family that is not my own, and long, chilly days
spent *observing* the water in which I wished to swim."

The wind blew again, and she turned her face into it,

squinting. After a beat she said, "At least at St. James's, there is a secluded bench in the gardens and an out-of-the-way window seat where I may be alone with a book or my embroidery. Weymouth is far smaller, and there is no escape. Traveling to Weymouth is a pointed reminder of all I've lost."

Killian nodded. "I'm sorry."

She gave a sad, small smile, retracted into the carriage, and pulled the pane shut.

Ten seconds later, the window squeaked open yet again. "It's not my intent to complain, mind you. Truly. I would have met a terrible end if not for the British royal family. However . . ."

"You may say anything to me," he said, "including complaints." Killian glanced at her and realized this was the least Glorified-Nanny/Special-Friend thing he could've said. She was staring at him with bright eyes, softened by gratitude, wet with tears. Inviting a woman to tell him anything—nay, to complain—was, perhaps, the most seductive thing he could've said.

She looked as if she was being sold something shiny and indulgent by a peddler, and she wasn't sure if it was real or paste.

"Thank you," she said, and shut the window for what would, surely, be the last time.

They crossed the bridge and the road opened up, carriages and carts spreading out. The driver let the horses have their legs, and they made admirable time from the river to Hampton, the first town beyond London.

The sky was darker now, the clouds sinking ever lower, but Killian knew it would be pointless to mention the weather. She would not be deterred by something so inconsequential as rain. Her gaze was locked on the horizon; her anticipation was so charged, he felt it outside the carriage.

When they reached Hampton, she pushed open the window and asked to be let out in the center of town. Killian did as she bade—at last, something that aligned perfectly with his plan. He would trail her about the sleepy village, he would watch over her, he would answer questions about the miles to Dorset—all the while making *no investment* in what she was doing.

He would not think of dreary Weymouth, or the respite of a lone bench in the gardens of St. James's Palace, or seeing her brother but having no one to share her joy.

He would be her Glorified Nanny and Special Friend.

CHAPTER TEN

"NOT TO BELABOR the point," Mr. Crewes said, ushering her into the carriage, "but when you claim to be forbidden from speaking about your brother—are you not permitted to speculate on Gabriel's whereabouts, or can you literally not utter the man's name?"

They'd just completed a half-hour circuit of Hampton and she'd forgotten his questions about her brother. The village had been . . . if not a wellspring of information, a very good start. She'd spoken to the blacksmith, the groom who tended the horses in the inn's stable, and two barmaids inside the tavern. It hadn't been easy to walk and make notes, but she was determined to take down every detail.

She settled on the carriage seat, tapping her notebooks into a neat stack, and Mr. Crewes shut the door behind her. She was staring at the closed door when he pulled the tiny window open and studied her through it.

"What about my brother?" she repeated.

"You've said someone in the palace has forbidden you from asking about your brother. But *how* forbidden?"

"Oh no. We'll not start this again." She scooted across the seat and pushed open the door.

"I should be happy to answer your questions, Mr. Crewes, but I'll not continue braying through the window like a donkey, thank you very much. If you have questions, you must travel *inside* the vehicle and converse with me like a civilized person." She looked at the sky. "Also, it's about to rain. In case you hadn't noticed." She pulled the door shut.

That would be the end of that, she thought. He would not join her in the carriage. He would not ask more about her brother. He preferred the rain to her company. She knew this because he'd not accompanied her through the streets of Hampton. He'd stood in the town center, one foot on the ledge of a gurgling fountain, silently watching her call from shop to shop. He did not care. He was present but not collaborating. He wasn't rude, but he was hardly good-natured. She was shocked, in fact, that he'd asked so many questions.

"He doesn't care," she mumbled to herself, buckling her notebooks with the belt. "And he's not sympathetic. And if he helps at all, it will be out of pity. Or to spy."

"I will smell of the road," said Mr. Crewes, climbing into the carriage. "I would apologize, but you commanded it, didn't you?"

Elise stared wordlessly as he folded his long, lean body into the ivory cocoon of the vehicle. He was big and dark against the pale interior, and he'd been correct about the scent. The small space was immediately filled with the smell of leather, and wind, and the musky notes from last night that were distinctly him. There were also the sounds: his spurs *chinking* against the seat, the muffled rustle of his overcoat, the creak of leather gloves.

Elise couldn't have been more surprised if he'd transplanted her to the coachman's box and told her to drive the vehicle herself.

To his credit, he kept himself very contained, no sprawling or spreading. He adjusted his hat to accommodate the seat and crossed his arms over his chest.

He looked at her.

Elise blinked back.

"Unless you've changed your mind," he said.

"Where is your horse?"

A look of discomfort chased across his face. She didn't mean to discourage him by asking, but he'd been so adamant about his mount when they set out.

"I dispatched a boy to stable him in Hampton," he said. "I'll collect him when we come back through. I'll not impose upon you for long. You may answer my question and then I'll pass the journey outside seated next to the driver."

"I am happy for the company," she said. But was happiness the reason her heartbeat had kicked up? Or why the air in the carriage felt charged? He was so very close. Bright memories of last night—the dim, cool passageway . . . the safety of his arms . . . the taste of his neck—flickered through her mind.

For a long moment, he stared out the window. Then he took a deep breath and turned back to her. "Are you satisfied with your discoveries in Hampton?"

Elise said nothing at first, staring at his face. She'd known so few men while in exile. Queen Charlotte's household was kept almost entirely separate from the royal court, and men like Killian Crewes were exactly the sort who would never be welcome. Dark eyes, sharp jaw, rough with stubble, even so early in the day. A coiled sort of energy rolled from his body like the piercing note of a taut guitar string.

"Highness?" he prompted.

"Yes," she said. "Hampton. The villagers were very forthcoming. No one knows of a horse trader who fit Gabriel's description, but no one knows *any* of the traders who turn up on market days. The trade of this village is more in"—she referenced her notes—"lavender candles and soaps. Even so, they set up market on the first Monday of every month. I've taken it all down. I'll come again when the market is on."

"You intend *return trips* to each of these villages?" he asked.

"Of course."

"Of course," he repeated.

Their eyes locked, and Elise felt a current pass between them. The carriage, already so small, shrank to exactly the size of their two bodies.

"I've but one purpose in my life now. To find my brother. After that, our sister. However I can manage it." She chuckled to herself. "I find it hard to believe you didn't know I've been forbidden from discussing Gabriel."

He raised his eyebrows, the expression of, *Well I* don't *know.*

Insolent, Elise thought, and then she let out a little laugh.

"What?" he asked.

"Forgive me. I am not accustomed to speaking to men." The notion of *insolence* had not crossed her mind in ten years.

"I admire the way you speak."

"The way I speak? Oh, my accent."

"No, your accent is barely discernable. It's simply—"

"What?"

"It's nothing."

"Come now—you've raised it. You must tell me. It's simply . . . ?"

He sighed again. "Your voice is very earnest. And level. I'm not accustomed to it."

"To what are you accustomed?"

Again, he raised an eyebrow. Something about that

arched brow, and his long lashes, and his brown eyes made her chest hot. Who knew she was so fond of insolence?

"You mean the other women in court," she guessed. "You're accustomed to breathless and . . . *chirpy*?"

His mouth hitched up.

She guessed again. "Bored and cynical?"

He cocked his head. His eyes were so direct. It should have caused her to look away. She stared back instead, feeling energy bounce back and forth between them.

"You are straightforward," he finally said. "It feels very genuine. Royal court is typically navigated with artifice and betrayal."

"Spoken like a man who's experienced both, I dare say."

"Spoken like a man who has been the source of both. It's often my job to rewrite the truth, and I get paid based on how effectively I do it. You, however, say what you mean. You ask what you want to know. Nothing more, nothing less. I find it very . . . refreshing."

Elise considered this. *Refreshing.* She wondered when, if ever, she'd been considered "refreshing." Bracing dips in cold rivers were refreshing; lemon ices were refreshing. Exile had turned Elise into someone who was tepid and silenced and inconsequential. And yet he saw her as "refreshing."

"Thank you," she said.

He gave a nod.

"In the spirit of saying what I mean," she said, "here's the truth of it. I've been disallowed from raising the topic of my brother inside the palace. I'm not meant to say his name. I'm not meant to speculate whether he's alive or dead. I cannot discuss the line of succession to the French throne or his place in it. *Especially* I may not speak of where in the world he might be or the possibility that I've seen him alive."

"Not meant to discuss this *with whom*?"

"Well, with the queen, first and foremost. The day after our return from Weymouth, I approached her with my account of seeing Gabriel. She listened but made no comment. The next time I requested an audience, I was told the queen would not receive me. The pattern has been the same with her aids and advisors, her ladies-in-waiting, even her daughters. They ignore me and then they become . . . unavailable. In the end, an aid to the Prince of Wales sought me out and informed me, in no uncertain terms, that if I wish to remain a welcome guest to the royal family, I must *stop asking* about Gabriel."

"Or what?"

"Well," she said thoughtfully, "he offered no 'or what.' To his credit, he did ask me if there was anything he could provide that would calm or comfort me. Some . . . consolation."

"And you could not be consoled?"

"Well, I asked to take leave of the palace and visit my uncle, who is exiled somewhere in Austria—and he said no, it was unsafe, and also not in the budget. I asked to meet with French scholars at the Society for French Literature—and he said no, it was inappropriate and the opposite of 'calming.' And so finally I asked to have a guest call on me in London—this is my friend Marie, the nun. She delivered me from France when I entered exile. This, thank God, he permitted. She had been cloistered in Ireland, but they sent for her. She joined me as a lady-in-waiting and has been a great friend and ally to me. I cannot say what I would have done without her.

"Even so," she finished, "every other restriction has endured. The locked rooms, the closed doors, the silence from the royal family. They quite literally ignore me in plain sight. And then, of course, you turned up, following me wherever I go."

"But you're not deterred?"

"On the contrary, I am emboldened. With every dismissal, I've become more determined to leave the palace—to leave London altogether—and find him. It's been as if I've . . . *awakened*. These last ten years have been so very lonely—lost years, truly. My grief over the execution of my father, the horror of fleeing Paris? These evolved into a sort of . . . numbness. I did not speak for the first two years after leaving France. I lived with my aunt and uncle then. When their daughter, my cousin Juliette, came of age, we were installed in St. James's Palace to secure Juliette's place in court. Juliette's advancement had been the plan all along— it's why my aunt and uncle took me in. They knew that eventually I would be a royal courtier, and I would take my cousin with me. And so I went along, keeping quiet, going through the motions in a haze. Imagine the haze lifting only to discover . . . no one cares. And no one will help."

"And your plan has never been to simply . . . run away?"

She turned and stared out the window. "Marie and I have discussed this. But the truth is, I'm emboldened, but not reckless. I feel too vulnerable to leave the protection of the palace. The political climate in France is . . . unclear to me. It felt very risky, indeed, to simply travel the streets of Mayfair, asking grooms and stable boys about horse traders along the Road to Land's End. That is the reason for the veils and my ladies. When my family fled the country, nearly every citizen of France wanted us dead.

"I will find a way, however." She sighed. "I cannot live out my days as a forgotten, silenced houseguest. I simply . . . cannot. The opportunity to leave London in your company was a straw grasped. Honestly—you, Mr. Crewes, have shown more interest in me and my plight than anyone beyond my three ladies-in-waiting."

"I'm not interested," Mr. Crewes assured her. The words came so quickly, she let out a little laugh.

"*Not interested*," she repeated. "I will take that into account."

"I am . . ." he began ". . . trying to understand. Nothing more."

"Well, if you can make sense of it, you're cleverer than I."

She was just about to ask him to estimate the time to the next village when a loud *crack* cut through their conversation, splintering the hushed intimacy of the carriage.

Elise clapped her hands over her ears, and Mr. Crewes lunged to the window, craning to see out.

The sound was accompanied by a repetitive jolting—a, *rap-rap-rap-rap*—of the carriage wheels. The smooth sway of the vehicle was replaced by violent, rhythmic lurching. It felt like the carriage was being bounced down the road like a ball.

"We've cracked a carriage wheel!" Mr. Crewes said, yelling over the din. "Brace, Highness. Hold on to the seat and lodge your feet against my seat. The driver will have to—"

He never finished.

He was cut off by the angry sound of splintering wood, the scrape of metal against metal, the coachman's shouts, and the sounds of panicked horses.

Elise felt a sudden, jolting *whoosh*, the carriage lurched, and the vehicle careened over, falling sideways. Elise was pitched from her seat, arms flailing, legs akimbo. She felt Mr. Crewes's arm band around her waist two seconds before she hit the side of the carriage, her ear to the wall, with a hard, painful *thwack*.

The last thing she saw before closing her eyes was Mr. Crewes's body, coat flapping, hat falling, coming down on top of her.

CHAPTER ELEVEN

$\mathcal{I}$T WAS DIFFICULT, Killian realized, to fold his body *over* her while also holding himself *off* her.

The carriage was immobile, lying on its side in what Killian could only assume was the middle of the road. Princess Elise huddled beneath him in a tumble of lavender silk and white petticoats. She was on her back, twisted slightly, with her legs tucked up and to the side. She sucked in deep, quivery breaths—a wretched sound, but better than no sound at all. Breathing meant a beating heart.

"Careful, Highness," he said, speaking to her shoulder. "Careful. Are you—Can you understand my words?"

Her breathing paused, he heard only heartbeats, and then she nodded.

He said a silent prayer of thanks and widened his legs, working to hold himself off her. She shouldn't survive a carriage accident only to be crushed by a large panting man.

The jarring impact of the accident had come and gone very quickly, but the terrifying sounds had gone on and on. First a loud knock, then splintering wood, and finally the chaotic jangle of tack and panicked horses. The loudest sound of all had been lacquer carriage colliding with hard road. The most harrowing sound had been the desperation of the driver. They'd heard him scramble, panicked and grunting, to cut the horses loose. After that, it was only their own heavy breath and the disappearing drum of hooves as the animals ran.

And now, silence.

"Highness?" he asked again.

"Yes?"

"Are you—"

With no warning, another sound rent the air: the clank of metal and shattering of glass. The lantern that hung from the top of the carriage, he guessed, gave up its fight with gravity and dropped to the road. Princess Elise cried out.

"*Shhh*," whispered Killian.

She answered with a frightened murmur, and he could feel her trembling beneath him. Something inside Killian also gave up the fight, and he lowered himself gently on top of her like a sheet of chain mail.

"I have you," he said. "It's over. That was the last of it."

She made a small noise of compliance and burrowed against him.

You feel nothing, Killian told himself, feeling every inch of her body beneath his chest, his thighs, his groin.

This doesn't matter, he thought, knowing nothing else mattered.

"Highness," he forced himself to ask, "do you think you've been injured?"

"I don't know."

"Right. Well, keep breathing and—"

"Are you well, sir?" A third voice broke into the toppled carriage—the driver, peering down from the door above. In their sideways world, the door functioned like a hatch on the now-ceiling.

Killian lifted his head only enough to see him. "We're alive, Tom. That's all I can say at the moment. I've yet to assess the princess. The left rear wheel, was it?"

"Aye," said the coachman. "There was a low spot in the road, washed out by rain and traffic. We hit the spine of a sharp rock at a bad angle. This carriage wasn't meant for highway driving, honestly. I said as much to the royal duke, but His Grace was adamant. Still, I take full responsibility, Mr. Cre—"

"The roads are dangerous, Tom," cut in Killian. "Everyone knows this. It's not your fault. Are the horses injured?"

The driver shook his head. "Don't seem to be. I've cut them loose to run. The gelding went down, but only for a second. I'm giving them their legs. When he settles, I'll have a look."

"See to them," Killian said, "but stay close. And keep any Good Samaritans at bay if you can. The princess took the brunt of the fall, and I must assess her. For the moment, we are catching our breath. Oh, and look to your own head, Tom. You've a gash, and it's bleeding."

"'Tis only a scrape, Mr. Crewes. Nothing to worry about. If you're in no rush, I'll leave you. The horses will be impossible to recover if I let them run too far afield."

Killian nodded, and the driver slid from the side of the vehicle.

"Do you think he's badly hurt?" The princess spoke into the space between the wall of the carriage and his shoulder.

"Do not move."

"I'm not moving. Is he hurt?"

"I don't think so. All of us appear to be very lucky indeed. But you must be careful not to move, Princess. If you've broken a bone, it could be dangerous to shift it. Also, the window beneath you could have shattered."

"The window is intact," she provided. "But are we . . . upside down?"

"We are, in fact, *sideways*. We've been dumped

onto the wall of the carriage. The *opposite* wall of the carriage—the one with the door—is above us. It's where we've just seen Tom. When the carriage went over, I grabbed for you. God only knows if it helped or hindered. I'm trying not to crush you."

"I am not crushed," she said. "And I would know if I'd broken a bone, surely."

"If you are in shock, the pain may not register. Can you take inventory of your body? How do you feel when you move about?"

"I feel . . . uncomfortable," she reported. "And my notebooks are pressing into my leg. And then there's you. On top."

"Too heavy."

"No, it's not that," she said quickly. She cleared her throat. "I want to make sure my notes on Hampton are secure."

He was relieved. He didn't want to crush her, but he also did not want to move, not really. Meanwhile, she shifted and wiggled and burrowed more tightly against him. With every move, Killian's body, previously so tense and flexed, began to loosen. He'd fashioned himself into a protective shell, but he was rapidly becoming less shell-like and more . . . *draped*.

"Before paperwork," he said, "we find broken bones."

She shifted again.

"Please stop moving."

"Are you hurt?"

"No, Princess. I'm not hurt."

"Why shouldn't I move?"

Because we're lying together in a tangled heap, and you're a beautiful woman and I'm an ogre (obviously) and it's arousing, he thought.

He said, "The only way to get you out of this carriage is to pull you through the door above us and then lower you to the ground. It will be strenuous and physical. If you're injured, I must know before we try." It was an answer, even if not to the question she asked.

Carefully, he began to peel himself up. Their current position was impossible to justify.

"And now?" he asked. "Did you feel pain when I moved?"

She turned her head to watch him.

He crouched on a knee beside her. "Princess?"

"I want to sit up. I want my notes."

Killian stared at the small, soft curl of her body. Her head was pressed beneath a seat, her legs tucked up. Her hat was gone, and her dress was bunched up to her knees.

"Right," he said.

"Right," she repeated.

Grunting a little, she squared her hips, knees now pointing upward. She flattened her shoulders against the carriage wall beneath her.

"Pain?" he asked.

She shook her head. The new position—legs bent, knees up—caused her bunched skirts to fall and expose her legs to mid-thigh.

She reached out to adjust the layers of silk, but Killian whispered, "Let me."

She dropped her hand.

This is entirely necessary, Killian thought, smoothing her skirts from thigh to knee. *Any gentleman would do this. Assessing her is the sensible thing to do.*

It can't be helped.

"I want to help you," he breathed.

"Alright."

"Good."

"Good." She raised an eyebrow.

"Thank you."

"You're welcome."

He let out a sigh. She was taking the piss. "So, Highness," he began, "what I mean to do is touch—" He stopped and cleared his throat. "I will touch all of you. That is, I will touch *most* of you."

"Is that . . . a request?"

"It was a statement."

She raised the eyebrow again.

Killian frowned. He endeavored to take this seriously, but he was alone in the seriousness. Apparently. Fine, he thought. If she felt well enough to tease, she would likely survive. And this examination was about her survival. Only. And nothing else.

He raised his hands, hovering them above her body.

He looked at her again. This time, she *laughed*.

"What?" he asked.

"You look like a pianist about to play a particularly challenging sonata on my ankle."

Killian narrowed his eyes—*challenge accepted*— and dropped his hands to her feet. She wore small ivory boots. He covered the laces with his palms and gave them a gentle squeeze.

"Oh . . ." she said.

He yanked his hands away. "Pain?"

"No. It was simply . . . I didn't expect it."

"Hold still," he grumbled, moving his hands to her ankle. The round bone of her ankle was small and delicate. He could feel the warmth of her skin through the silk of her stockings.

"What about this?" he rasped, probing his fingers higher.

She shook her head. Her laughter had faded away.

"Tell me the moment you feel anything amiss," he lectured, trying to sound clinical—trying to *be* clinical.

Any man would do this, Killian repeated in his head. *It can't be helped. It is the proper thing to do.*

He worked his way higher by inches, sliding gentle fingertips over the contours of her leg, testing, exploring, learning the shape of her. She was small, but also firm. He could feel strong muscles and soft silk and the warm temperature of her skin.

With each glancing touch, he paused, waited for some reaction, and increased the pressure. He was thorough and careful and observational. Only his hands moved, but their bodies were somehow drawn closer. Her legs, previously only imagined, were in his grasp. Her stockings, previously beyond his wildest dreams, slid against his fingertips. She spoke no words, but she cooperated. He touched her and she reacted. A murmur. A sigh. Soft sounds that gratified and aroused him. Killian felt his own body respond, hardening urgently.

"Your legs are strong," Killian rasped.

"I walk every day," she said. "An hour at least. In any weather."

"This has served you well," he said, looking to her.

She'd bent her head to the side, watching him grip and loosen, grip and loosen. Her lips were ever so slightly parted. Her eyes had dilated, black pupils in a ring of hazel. She had a look of focused anticipation—as if the most crucial spot would be the very next place he touched.

Killian's breathing hitched. He swallowed. His erection had hardened to a heavy pike, but he ignored it and kept moving. Only when he reached her knees did he pause. The hem of her dress was balanced there. Could he slide his hands under her skirt? No—no, he could not. He would continue the examination on top of her dress.

But first, he thought, *her knees. Quickly. Just to make absolutely certain.*

Without stopping to think—in fact, banishing all

thought—Killian slipped his right hand beneath the frill of her skirt. Ever so gently, he nuzzled the ball of her knee with his open palm.

The princess sucked in a slow breath. He looked up.

She made no further sound, staring at him with half-lidded eyes.

Killian returned his attention to her knee. Moving slowly, he traced it with one finger, sliding it into the shallow indentation beneath.

"And how is this?" he rasped.

With one knuckle, he probed the soft hollow under her knee.

The princess whimpered. It didn't sound like pain.

He tried again, repeating the move, nuzzling beneath her knee.

"Princess?" he breathed. He wondered if he could hear her response over the thud of his heart.

He didn't wait for an answer; he traced a small, quick circle with his knuckle beneath her knee.

Princess Elise sucked in another breath and *clamped down*, folding her leg around his hand. Killian jumped, unprepared for the sudden move, and tried to swipe his hand back. She squeezed harder, not letting him go, and tipped her knee and leg—*tipped all of herself*—to the side. His hand was still trapped beneath her knee, and when she fell sideways, he went, too. He was given no choice but to follow his hand and be pulled down over her.

"Highness?" he rasped, speaking into her shoulder.

She answered with giggles.

"Princess?" he demanded.

She turned her face up. Her eyes were squeezed shut, and her lower lip was caught in her teeth. She was shaking with laughter. "Sorry, sorry, sorry," she gasped, blinking her eyes open. "I'm . . . I'm ticklish. There. *Right* there . . . that bit. Forgive me." She turned her head to the side as if trying to ride out a wave of sensation.

Killian wiggled the fingers trapped tightly between the underside of her knee. She gasped again and clamped a hand over her mouth. Her body shook.

"Right," he drawled, watching her face contort. He made an effort to slide his hand free, but even the slightest movement caused her to clamp down harder.

"Highness," he repeated, a note of warning in his tone.

"I'm sorry." She chuckled.

He tried again to free his hand. "Princess Elise."

She shrieked, a shrill little chirp of a sound that Killian knew he would hear on his deathbed. Again she squeezed his hand beneath her knee.

And now Killian fought his own smile.

It was impossible *not* to smile at a beautiful woman laughing beneath him—at *this* beautiful, laughing woman.

Well, now he could make a ruling on potential injury: she'd suffered no breaks. Her body appeared to be in perfect working order. And this examination was superfluous. And he was a randy blaggard.

And yet . . .

And yet he found himself fighting the urge to keep going—to take the next, natural step. Beautiful woman, beset with giggles . . . a tangle of arms and legs . . . his erection lodged against her hip . . . his heartbeat pressed to her ribs. He was five inches from her mouth. He was one *tickle* away from . . . everything else.

He could barely, barely keep himself from closing in. Years of manners and civility strained against voracious, panting, *want*.

This woman was a Princess of the Blood and he was the Royal Fixer. There was no choice but to pull away. He *would* pull away. *I will, I will, I will*, he thought. *In ten seconds, I will.* It would be bitter, resented work, but he would do it. He would sleepwalk through it, but he would do it.

In ten more seconds.

Meanwhile, in his mind, he squared her beneath him. He hiked the ticklish knee to his shoulder. He dipped his head and captured her mouth—

Killian blinked, and the princess swung into focus: hazel eyes wide, lips parted.

Reality, as cold and prickly as February sleet, moved over him. He thought of the assignment from Edward.

Distract her.

Mesmerize her.

Seduce her.

He was, in effect, doing all of these, and the realization was enough to make him stop. If he didn't, he would be acting out the very seduction they'd ordered. And Killian Crewes was many things, but Seducer of Young Women wasn't one of them.

Drawing a shaky breath, Killian rolled up. His hand was still under her knee, and he gave it a tug. She seemed to understand, and released it. He sat on his heels against the far seat and ran a hand through his hair.

"I'm sorry," she offered in a whisper. She scooted into a sitting position.

"Careful," he said gently.

"I'm—That is, I'd forgotten that I am ticklish. Under my knees. I haven't been—"

She cast around for her notebooks.

"You've done nothing wrong," he said.

"I am not frequently in such close . . . proximity. To others. It's been a very long—"

She stopped again. Finally, she said, "I am not accustomed to being touched."

A cold wind whipped across Killian's heart, peeling back loose shingles. It was painful to watch her struggle.

"Don't apologize," he said, watching as she tightened the belt around her notebooks.

This was the second or third time she'd mentioned living in . . . well, in something like lonely seclusion.

And what were the ramifications of *that*? For one, no other man had tickled her beneath her knees. Perhaps he shouldn't be gratified by this, but he was.

Mostly it meant she would be highly susceptible to *staged seduction*.

He'd thought she would not want him, but really it would be no contest. Killian knew that women found him exciting and challenging and scintillating. He could take easy advantage—something that the royal dukes had obviously known. He'd been an easy tool, compliance and effectiveness practically guaranteed.

Except he would not be used, and she would not be deceived. He could get the job done without orchestrating some illicit diversion that lasted ten minutes, or ten days, or even ten months.

"Mr. Crewes?" she asked. Her eyes searched his face. "Should we be worried about your wellness? Have you broken bones?"

"I'm fine," he said, rising. "No worse for wear. The important thing for climbing out is that you can move easily and support your own weight. Tell me if you feel otherwise?"

"Yes, alright."

She was confused. He could see it in her face. He'd explored her body and draped himself over her, and now he would barely look her in the eye.

It can't be helped, Killian thought, casting around for his gloves and hat.

When he glanced at her again, she was studying his profile.

"Let's see what's become of the driver, shall we?" he said, reaching for the door above them. "That's thunder, if I'm not mistaken. Naturally we would have rain on top of everything else. We need to get you out of this vehicle."

CHAPTER TWELVE

*E*LISE WAS HOISTED outside in one swift tug.

She'd stood in the center of the carriage, arms above her head, while Mr. Crewes knelt on the top of the over-turned vehicle and lifted her by her wrists. She cleared the doorway like a vole popping out of a hill. When she was up, he caught her around the waist and clutched her to his hip.

Elise breathed in the fresh air of outside, cool but damp from the threat of rain. After the dim, cramped carriage, the world beyond was vast and bright. Middle-sex unfurled before her in a patchwork of green. The wreckage of the carriage was less picturesque—it wob-bled drunkenly beneath them in a sideways heap. The three remaining wheels jutted to the side like the legs of a dead bug.

The driver of the carriage, muddy and stripped to his shirtsleeves, stood on the ground and shouted up stam-mered apologies and excuses for the accident.

"She'll need a moment, Tom," Mr. Crewes said. Elise gave a wave and smile, hoping to absolve the man.

"It's best to sit," grunted Mr. Crewes, "but the lacquer is slick. Hold on." He lowered first her, then himself, un-til they sat on the edge of the carriage side, feet dangling.

"How do you feel?" he asked.

"Lucky, I suppose?"

"There's a brave princess."

Elise felt a small burst of warmth every time he referred to her as a princess. Not because she cared about the title, but because it felt like an endearment. She felt . . . noticed, and upheld, and a little . . . honored? She felt special.

Thunder cracked, and they looked to the sky. Graphite-colored clouds slid together in uneven layers, obscuring the sun.

"We cannot tarry," he said. "If I collect you 'round the waist, can you be handed to the road?"

"I can slide."

"If you can slide, then you can also be handed down."

Before she could protest, he dropped to the dirt and reached for her. He fastened large hands around her waist. "Ready, set, down you go."

On reflex, Elise covered his hands with hers, securing them to her waist.

When she was down, he asked, "Can you stand?"

Elise nodded, but she held fast to his hands at her waist.

"You're alright," he said, eyeing her.

Don't let go, she thought.

"Princess?" he asked slowly.

Elise nodded again, but she couldn't seem to release him.

Mr. Crewes took a step back, his hands trapped beneath hers. "*Princess*," he repeated. He moved to retract his hands, but she held them fast.

She gave the slightest little shake of her head. *No, please. Not yet.*

He swore under his breath and looked away, but he squeezed her waist tighter. Then, he tugged her closer, just a little. The tightened grip felt so very good, Elise closed her eyes. She wanted to lean against him. She wanted—

I've hit my head, she thought. *Cleary. I am addled.* She sucked in a breath, forced a smile, and dropped her hands from his.

"Forgive me," she said briskly. "Of course I'm well."

He eyed her, searching her features. Finally, slowly, he slid his hands from her waist. The move was so very gradual and pronounced, it sent a frisson of fuzzy warmth from her belly to . . . to lower, to the very center of her.

Elise blinked up at him, saying nothing, trying to hold on to the last tendrils of the fuzz and heat and the lingering imprint of his hands.

He cleared his throat. "There's a drystone wall just there . . . do you see it? It's too jagged for you to sit, but you could lean against it."

"I'm perfectly fine to stand," Elise said.

"So you are. Right. Well, stand you shall. Tom and I will hoist the carriage upright. We cannot leave it in the road."

How odd it felt, Elise thought, to speak in such formalities after his examination inside the carriage. He had touched her so intimately, so deliciously. He'd hovered above her. He'd *almost* kissed her—she was sure of it.

But no more. There was work to be done. There was a storm coming. Say what you would about the English, but they could anesthetize any situation with stiff cordiality and the threat of inclement weather.

"I'm not an invalid," she said. "Include me in whatever you need."

"Use the time to catch your breath and make certain you are . . . sound. The less you're seen on the roadside, the better we'll be."

"What do you mean?"

"People are drawn to things they don't see every day. And this story has managed to get better and better as the minutes tick by. First a carriage accident, and now a beautiful woman has been extracted from the wreckage."

Elise eyed the small crowd that was gathering beside the carriage. People pointed and gawked, and children ran 'round the wreckage looking at it from every side.

Was it so very necessary, she wondered, to be secretive here on the side of the road? She'd spent weeks zipping about London, face covered, flanked by an entourage dressed in identical black. Now she was miles from the city, in the distant company of a few rustics who were more curious about the accident than her. And anyway, *he* was here. Could she not pause her constant worry about safety and identity for ten minutes? Could she not rely on Mr. Crewes to interfere with any harm that might come to her?

Perhaps she could not. Perhaps she was being careless. Perhaps she was a poor judge of what was safe and what was not. It was impossible to say, really, because her prevailing thought at the moment was, *Did he just say I was beautiful?*

"I've suggested everyone keep back," he said, "for the well-being of the lady."

"Very considerate," she said, "but the lady is quite well."

"'The lady' is, in fact, a princess," said Mr. Crewes, "and I'm not yet convinced of her wellness. If you tuck yourself here, between the wheels, you are mostly blocked from view. When we begin to hoist the thing up, you can move to the wall."

"Off you go then," said Elise, brushing the wrinkles from her skirts. She'd grown weary of reassuring him of her wellness. Although—whose fault was this? She'd clung to his hands and stared imploringly into his face. No wonder he thought she was damaged.

Elise frowned. She was not, by nature, a clinger. She didn't pine, except possibly for her brother and sister, and she did not fixate.

The act of clinging to someone's broad back—which was exactly the thing upon which she'd been fixated—was not only odd, it didn't make any sense. Was it possible she'd been somehow *starved* for human touch these years in exile and didn't realize it? She'd been barely noticed in St. James's Palace, let alone *touched*.

When she thought of the many things for which she longed in exile—and there had been quite a few—*touching some man* would have never made the list. In fact, it had been her extreme preference to push most people away. She'd become almost an island unto herself.

Until now.

Now, the desire to touch, to be near, to *smell* this man, felt akin to something like . . . *falling*. It wasn't intentional, or graceful, or managed; it was wild and careening and propelled by ruthless gravity. The desire was unstoppable and inevitable, and it made Elise feel a little like the toppling carriage, hell-bent for the hard, flat road.

And whatever in the world would she do with *that*?

As if missing her brother and sister and *freedom* were not enough?

Meanwhile, he seemed perfectly keen to breathlessly explore her legs in one moment and revert to brusque formality the next.

Elise took a deep, cleansing breath.

In the distance, the carriage driver and Mr. Crewes spoke to a circle of men. Elise peered around the damaged vehicle, examining the three intact wheels and the shattered fourth, now a splintered mangle of wooden spokes and metal. Around the other side, she could hear female voices of assembled passers-by, making speculation about the accident. They spoke in hushed, worried tones, marveling that no passengers or horses had been injured. Elise was touched by their obvious compassion, especially for the animals, and she poked her head around the side.

A woman saw her face and smiled gently, giving a little wave. Elise smiled in return, but withdrew to the safety of the spot between the wheels. She looked to Mr. Crewes. Every minute or so, he pivoted to check her position and raised his brows, the universal expression of, *Are you alright?*

Elise nodded, and he turned back to the men.

The nod wasn't a lie—she *was* alright. She was grateful she hadn't been relegated to the wall, or worse, packed into some stranger's carriage and returned alone to St. James's Palace. Soreness was setting in, but she could move freely, walk from here to there, and idly spin the jutting wheels of the carriage. She could also acknowledge—realist that she was—that her stomach spun like a carriage wheel every time he looked at her.

So, fine, she thought, *I enjoy his company. Fine.*

And his touch. Also fi—

Actually, she thought, *these sentiments are out of order.*

She enjoyed his touch—and her regard for his company came and went. Since she was stranded with him, surely it was better to *abide* him rather than to be, for example, repulsed by him. Or bored. Or afraid. There were worse things, surely, than feeling attraction—and yes, she was honest enough to call a spade a spade—for a man who had helped calm her during a fit of panic and cared for her after a carriage accident.

If feeling "attraction" was foolish, or pointless, or immature, well—perhaps she was owed a bit of foolishness. She had witnessed her own father's execution, and fled her home, and was currently locked in the bottom drawer of exile. Foolishness was long overdue.

"Madam?" called a gentle voice from the other side of the carriage.

Elise poked her head around, grateful for any topic that was *not* her attraction to Killian Crewes.

"But were you injured in the accident, madam?" the woman continued. She was middle-aged, short, and round, with a kind face and a tame ferret peering out from the circle of her arms.

"Would you not take a seat here beneath this tree?" continued the woman. "The ground may be a bit damp, but I've a blanket and can offer some refreshment. I've ale and bread here, and I should be happy to share."

"How kind," Elise said, "but remarkably, I was unharmed, thank you so much. I hope the wreckage has not impeded the progress of your journey." She picked her way around the toppled carriage.

"Oh no, our wagon can go around, but my husband is a right *bear* of a man and can help the driver move the thing, if he'll allow it. He's just there, speaking to the gentlemen." She pointed to Mr. Crewes and the other men.

"Oh, so he is," said Elise. "Your willingness to help is a credit to you, madam. Thank you."

"'Tis nothing. We're gratified no one was hurt. It's a miracle, really. And there is no rush on our account." The woman and her ferret looked down the road. "We're on our way home to Sunbury. It's not every day you see a carriage flipped on its side, is it?"

"No, I don't suppose it is. But, forgive me, did you say you are from Sunbury? The next town to the west?"

"That's right, madam. Born and bred."

Now Elise closed the distance between them. "But

would you mind if I might ask you a few questions about your village? Specifically about the day the town holds market? Also, I've a portrait here of a man. I've actually come into this area for the purpose of learning more about him—he's a lost . . . relation. Here it is—the portrait. The man for whom I search may look very similar to *this* man, his late father. Can I impose upon you to have a look?"

"But of course, madam. Oy! But look at him in his fine clothes and feathered hat. He must be a man of some means . . ."

"Yes, yes—he was a . . . successful man, you might say—but his face? Can you look closely and try to remember some resemblance to someone who might frequent Sunbury? A horseman, perhaps . . . ?"

Ten minutes later, Elise was surrounded by women and children, discussing the market day in Sunbury. The small portrait of her late father was passed from hand to hand, and speculations came very quickly and colorfully. Elise longed for her notebook inside the carriage.

One of the women had just relayed the story of a donkey bought at market last winter, when the voices began to peter out, growing first hushed and then stopping altogether. Elise palmed the portrait and frowned, looking around. The women were staring, their eyes cautious, at something behind her. Elise turned to see Mr. Crewes, tapping his hat against his hand.

"If you'll excuse me," Elise said.

"What's happened?" asked Mr. Crewes, rounding the side of the carriage.

"Nothing has happened," she said. "I was speaking to the bystanders. They are . . . concerned."

"They may be concerned, but they are also curious and chatty and lead country lives that can best be described as unremarkable. The more we say to them, the more they will discuss it up and down the countryside. Please have a care, Highness; I am trying to protect you and your reputation."

"But I've not said my name," she told him.

"No name is required, I assure you, to relay the story of an unmarried lady and gentleman who climbed from the wreckage of a carriage and passed about the likeness of a missing prince."

"I've said no names," she repeated. "And anyway, I fail to see the problem. If my brother hears that someone is searching for him, perhaps he will make the effort to seek me out. This was always my plan, Mr. Crewes—whether I go today or tomorrow or next week. This is what I did in Hampton."

He closed his eyes and exhaled—an expression of forced patience—and then examined his hat, jammed it on his head, and walked away.

Elise glared after him. He would dismiss her? She might be a lesser royal, forgotten and forsaken, but she was worthy of a finished thought.

She hurried after him. "I am worthy of a finished thought."

He kept walking. "Your worth, Highness, is not in question here. You are worthy of a family, and a home, and a rich, full life—but I cannot give you these, can I? The only thing I can give you—or, that I've *endeavored* to give you—is a pleasant afternoon, seeking some answers in a village or two. I have failed in that, clearly, and you've been nearly killed in this heap of a carriage and compelled to become a spectacle on the side of the road."

He came to the drystone wall and stopped. Elise trudged behind him, waiting for the moment when she was told some version of *no/stop/quiet/disappear*.

"I am not a spectacle," she said.

"You," he said, spinning to her, "are the most intriguing thing anyone has seen for a year."

The most intriguing thing that you've *seen*? she wondered, but she said, "I . . . I'll consider what you've said. Perhaps I am being reckless."

"Don't be cooperative, Highness," he said. "It actually makes this more difficult."

"What does that mean?"

"Nothing. Forgive me. We are racing the weather and I've—I am wrong to unburden my frustration on you."

She paused, realizing that he had *not*, in fact, told her *no/stop/quiet/disappear*. She thought about what he'd said instead. She took a deep breath.

"Apology accepted," she said. "But can you tell me your plan?"

"Right. Well, Tom and I will work with these men to put your carriage to rights and drag it from the road.

"Next, I'll have Tom return you to Hampton and hire some conveyance. After the storm passes, he can see you safely back to London. Could you ride bareback, do you think, the three miles to Hampton?"

Elise frowned. "No, I could not ride bareback even a quarter mile. I've never ridden astride, even with a saddle, let alone bareback."

"Fine, you can ride with Tom."

"Meaning . . . ?"

"Meaning, you'll sit in front of him on the horse and the two of you will share the mount for the short distance to Hampton."

"Are you suggesting that I sit in Tom Coachman's *lap* for three miles?"

"Yes. That is what I'm suggesting."

"And where will *you* be?"

"I'll wait with the wreckage until Tom can send men with a rig to haul it away."

"Why cannot *Tom* wait with the carriage and *you* convey me to Hampton?"

"Because of propriety."

"*Propriety*?" she repeated. "What is proper about me riding in the lap of a coachman?"

"Tom is a career servant who has been in the employ of the royal family for thirty years. He'll inspire no . . . *misgivings*. The limitations of a carriage accident and a storm are understood. *If* you are waylaid in Hampton because of weather, or *if* there are no suitable vehicles for hire—and there is a high likelihood of both—he will install you at the local inn until morning, when an alternative can be sorted."

"But you could—"

"*I* cannot escort you to an inn, Highness. Not with half the county watching our progress with rapt attention. Do you know where coachmen lodge at inns, Princess? In the stables. I, however, would take a room inside, a fact everyone knows. Everyone also knows—whether it's true or not—that *my* room and *your* room would most likely be the same. Do you see?"

Elise was shaking her head. "If I must gallop down the road in the lap of a servant, I should like Tom to take me the opposite direction, to Sunbury. I've already seen Hampton."

"No," he said.

"*Yes.*"

"The reasonable thing to do is to return to Hampton," he said. "I wish I'd included my manservant, Hodges, on this outing. What had I been thinking?"

"Hodges counts as yet another strange man in whose lap I would not ride. Look, Mr. Crewes, if the day has been ruined, if we're rewriting the plan, why not allow me to move even the slightest bit forward, rather than retrace my steps?"

He was shaking his head. And now her desire to touch him was replaced by her desire to shake him.

"If you mean only to hire a vehicle to convey me to London," she asked, "why is Hampton better than Sunbury?"

"Because," he ground out, "Hampton is larger and more prosperous and home to Hampton Court Palace. Perhaps you've heard of it? A rather consequential dwelling inhabited by King Henry VIII? Sunbury, in contrast, is smaller and less established and directly on the banks of the river. There is no palace and therefore few visitors—oh, except for the scrum of common dockworkers who travel there for their jobs and then loiter in the alehouses to drink. It is no place for a princess."

"Ha! These will be the words etched into my tombstone, *No place for a princess*. And what care have I for alehouses? I mean to interview locals who can tell me about the horse trade on market day. The women I've just met have given me names, Mr. Crewes. Specific townspeople I should ask about my brother. Please—I cannot allow this opportunity to pass. If I must bounce down the road in the lap of poor Tom, then at least let there be some usefulness in the end."

"How did I know this would happen?" he asked himself. He swiped off his hat and ran a hand through his hair. "I cannot ask Tom to take you to Sunbury. It's an unfair request."

"Good. I prefer not to involve him. I will walk."

"It's too far to walk."

"You will convey me."

"So you'll ride in *my* lap, will you, but not Tom's?"

Elise felt her face redden, but she did not look away. Slowly she raised her eyebrows. *Yes*, she thought, *I will ride in your lap*.

Mr. Crewes swore under his breath.

Elise waited.

"Fine," he said. "Here is another offer—the *only* other offer, so prepare yourself to pick one or the other. There is an estate not far from here. It's called Paxton Dale. We could take refuge there for the night."

"Who could take refuge there?"

"You and I," he ground out.

"One of your properties?"

"No. It is the home of my nephew, Earl Dunlock. Also in residence is his mother, the Countess Dunlock, and two elderly aunts. It's no St. James's Palace, but we'll be out of the rain. And we won't be . . . alone. We can pass the night there, borrow the earl's carriage, and visit Sunbury first thing in the morning. I can have you back to St. James's Palace by early afternoon."

"But will it be a great imposition for your family to receive us unannounced?"

He grimaced again and stared at the sky. "First, I do not regard them as my family. Second, I don't see that we have a choice."

"Well, if you're certain . . . I should like that very much. It's presumptive of me to accept, but that is how desperate I am for more time away from London. How far is your estate?"

"Paxton Dale belongs to my nephew—it is not mine. And first I must work with these men to set the carriage to rights. After that, a half-hour ride, perhaps? Can you manage?"

Riding in your lap? she thought.

"Yes," she said, "I can manage."

CHAPTER THIRTEEN

KILLIAN COULDN'T REMEMBER the last time he'd ridden a horse with no saddle. Sometime in boyhood, surely. *Never* before had he ridden with a woman in his lap. And wasn't that a method of delicious torture beyond his wildest dreams?

It wasn't the nearness to her—her face tucked against his neck, her bottom lodged against his groin—nor the arm she'd snaked around his waist, nor the hand she'd slid beneath his waistcoat to clutch his shirt. It wasn't even the relentless *bounce, bounce, bounce* of her against him as the horse cantered down the road.

It was *all of these*. They hadn't gone five yards before Killian wondered if this was some sort of existential test.

He'd never been so aroused while also so very worried. There was weather to consider; also the certain disaster bringing a *princess* to Paxton Dale.

If nothing else, he'd stopped trying to convince himself that any of this was necessary—that she would meet a terrible end if he didn't haul her to Paxton on his lap. Why self-delude? He *wanted* to pass the day with her, to know her, to touch her.

Still, he could explain it away if necessary. The note he'd scrawled to the royal duke hit all the high points: carriage accident, impending storm, a night spent under the watchful eyes of two maiden aunts at Paxton Dale.

But if ever he intended to survive his attraction to this woman, he should be honest with himself about how much he wanted her.

"Mr. Crewes?" she asked suddenly.

It would be too much to ask, naturally, that she bounce quietly on the most urgently desirous part of him and not also talk to him.

"Yes?" he answered.

"Is there some unsettled quarrel or ill-will between yourself and your nephew, the earl?" She was leaning into him, her shoulder to his rib cage, her ear to his throat.

"No," he said, "no quarrel."

"You are fond of him?"

"I am, in fact, fond of him," Killian said. "He is only eight years old."

And now she tipped her chin to stare up at him, her face a breath away. "The earl is a child?"

"Yes. He can be a bit exhausting at times, but he is sweet-natured and curious. I have found him . . . impossible to dislike, despite my best efforts."

"What does that mean?"

"I hated his late father—the previous earl. My half brother. Peter, he was called. The dislike was mutual; in fact, the discord *originated* with Peter. I had so very much wanted to adore my older brother."

"How odd, to think of you . . . adoring someone. You seem so . . ."

I adore you, he thought, but he said, "It's true, I dislike most people. But I especially disliked my older brother. However, when you meet Bartholomew—"

"Bartholomew?" She laughed. "That's a very big name for an eight-year-old boy."

"Yes, well, his mother's view of the world can best be described as 'outsized' and 'with emphasis.'"

"What did she intend to emphasize with the name Bartholomew?"

"Whatever she can get—for the boy, that is."

"So it is this *woman* you do not like? Your sister-in-law?"

Killian sighed. "No. But I've tried very hard to dislike her, too. She is ambitious, but her motives are pure. She wants the best for her son. And she is completely without guile. And grateful."

"Grateful to whom?" Every time she looked up, the tip of her nose barely, barely missed his chin.

"I cannot believe you wish to hear this story."

"Believe it." She sighed, snuggling closer.

Killian gripped the gelding with his thighs, readjusting the princess in his lap. If anything would diffuse his arousal, it was discussion of Bartholomew, his mother, and Paxton Dale.

"Fine," he said. "Pearl is grateful because—"

"I beg your pardon. *Pearl?*"

"Pearl is my sister-in-law, Bartholomew's mother. She was married to my brother, Peter. She is the current countess."

"You are *familiar* with this person," the princess realized. "You refer to her by her given name."

"We are not familiar so much as . . ." He paused, considering. "Let us just say that I tend to forget she is a countess. When you meet her, you'll understand."

"I . . . I wish you would refer to me as Elise," she said softly.

"Not a good idea, Highness."

"Why?"

"Because *we* are *not* familiar." A lie, as she was sitting in his lap, clinging to his shirt, and asking personal questions about his family. In this, they must pretend.

"In the passage last night, you called me Elise."

"I was trying to break through the tempest of your panic. It's a tactic I used with my mother—referring to her by her given name. It generally helped."

"Oh," she said, sounding disappointed. After a moment, she said, "May I call you Killian?"

He closed his eyes. The way her slight French accent looped through the double *L*'s in "Killian" made him sound more interesting than he was, like a version of his name that was for her use only. An endearment. He loved it.

"I am at your service, Highness," he said. "You may call me whatever you like."

"Very good," she said. *"Killian."*

He wondered why the sky hadn't yet opened up and dumped bracing rainfall on their heads. He wondered why she was not rigid and uncomfortable in his lap. He wondered why they'd wrecked their carriage close enough to make Paxton Dale an option.

He no longer wondered if this was an existential test, because now he knew.

The wind had increased, and she molded herself against him. Lightning on the horizon added to the atmosphere. They needed only to be chased by a bear.

"But go on," she urged, "you were explaining that your sister-in-law is so very grateful to you . . ."

He frowned. A bear attack, he thought, would be preferrable to this.

On a sigh, he said, "She's grateful because . . . before she and the boy turned up . . . *I* was the earl."

"You?"

"Yes. For about ten minutes. My father has been dead for many, many years, but my half brother, Peter, was the firstborn son and the rightful earl. But then *Peter* died. As my father's second son, I became Earl Dunlock."

"But was your brother old or unwell?"

"No. He was relatively young, hale, and hearty. He died from a blow to the head when he fell from his horse. We were not familiar; in fact, we were estranged—the hatred I mentioned. Even so, he was a known sportsman and an active member of London society. He was perfectly healthy, but his horse missed a jump."

"Why were you estranged?"

"We had a history of . . . oh, let's call it *conflict*. And our father was dead. And there was no reason to socialize; there was no reason even to speak. I had virtually nothing to do with the earldom. Paxton Dale had been my boyhood home, but after my mother died, I never again visited."

"How difficult it is to imagine," she murmured, "considering I want nothing more than to locate my brother."

Killian rolled his shoulder. "Ours was an animosity set in motion by Peter at the earliest age. I was scarcely out of the nursery. His distaste and resentment for me were . . . insurmountable."

"And then he died with that resentment?"

"Yes, I suppose he did. He was dead, resentment and all—and I was Earl Dunlock."

"*Oh*," the princess whispered, rapt.

"Yes," said Killian. "I had much the same reaction. Shocked did not begin to describe it. However, I rallied quickly and set about assuming the title. I removed myself from life inside St. James's Palace and ceased the work I do for the king. I moved to Paxton Dale. I threw myself into the running of the estate."

"And so the title was a windfall? You wanted it?"

This question gave Killian pause. The desire he felt for the earldom was one of the cruelest ironies of his incredibly ironic life.

Yes—he wanted the earldom. He wanted it so much,

he saw scenes from what might have been in his dreams at night. He dreamed of it even now: brightly vivid, incredibly specific vignettes of himself as earl, going through the mundane motions of daily life at Paxton Dale. He saw himself sheering sheep with tenants. He saw himself hosting meetings with neighboring gentry about improvements to county roads. He dreamed of the bloody *roses* he would plant in the manor house garden . . .

"I would have been honored," he told her, "to do my duty toward the earldom, if it had come to me. But it didn't, did it? Or it did—but only for a month. And now it is in the hands of my brother's son. That is the way the system works."

"But your brother had a wife and child and you didn't know it?"

"Ah, but here the plot thickens. My brother was not the bachelor that I and all of society thought him to be. This is what I meant about Pearl—"

He stopped and began again. "This is why the *countess* is so grateful to me. Peter had—unbeknownst to anyone—*married* a young dancer he met while on a hunt in Essex. But instead of introducing this girl to society, instead of acknowledging her publicly as his countess, he smuggled her to Middlesex and installed her in a gamekeeper's cottage in a far-flung corner of the estate. The entire arrangement was made in secret— hidden from all but the most trusted servants.

"Pearl accepted this arrangement—for what reason, I have no idea; when you meet her, you'll understand my confusion—and lived in the forest, eventually bearing them a son. And then Peter died unexpectedly, and Pearl bided her time for a month. I was scarcely installed in Paxton Dale when she marched on the manor house, Bartholomew in tow, and informed me who she was and the identity of the boy. She claimed Bartholomew was the rightful earl. At the time, he was barely three years old."

"Why did she wait a month?"

"Her strategies remain a mystery to me, honestly. But the War Office would do well to study them, because hers is a tenacity and cunning that would benefit England in any conflict. She's deuced effective at getting what she wants."

"And she wanted . . . ?" speculated the princess.

"*She wanted it all*," said Killian.

"*No*," said the princess.

Killian sighed wearily, remembering that bright autumn morning. "Yes."

"And . . . and it was true? She *was* the rightful wife to your brother, and her son was the new earl? Despite the fact that no one knew of her? But if this is true, why hadn't he made some provision for her?"

"I believe the provision he made was this cottage in the woods on estate grounds. She does not discuss their relationship with me, but I think perhaps he was a little ashamed of her? She's a very pretty girl if you like that sort of thing, but she's also very raw. And, as I mentioned, a dancer by trade.

"Also," Killian continued, "Peter was bollocks at planning ahead. She, however, is perfectly adept at it—some might say she is a genius at planning. She had a detailed account of their fortuitous meeting in Essex, the special license that saw them properly married, the name and direction of the vicar who performed the ceremony. She had records of Bartholomew's birth. She'd been so very meticulous about all of it—and why wouldn't she be? Honestly, I've no idea how Peter managed to keep her hidden for as long as he did. I suspect she had some larger plan and was merely biding her time in the forest. Regardless, she made quick work of me. I required no larger plan. She wanted the title for her son, and the house for the two of them—she wanted it all—and she would accept nothing less."

"But was she . . . hateful about it? It's no small thing to unseat the accepted heir and stake a claim to an earldom. And to make said claim with a *child*?"

Killian chuckled. "And there lies the rub, doesn't it? She was not hateful about it. She was . . . terrified, honestly, to approach me. But her love for her son and her desire for a better life gave her the courage—that is, I assume this is what drives her. God only knows. She is incredibly determined and ambitious—but she presumes nothing that is not rightfully hers. And she is . . . well she's perfectly cordial about it. Cordial but insistent.

"By all accounts, one would expect her to be an unlearned woman, entirely devoid of manners. You would assume her dreams are small and her ambition amounts to little more than a payoff. But you would be wrong. Her manners are self-taught but in working order. She seeks constantly to improve herself. Apparently she hounded a local shopkeep in her village until he taught her to read as a child. Certainly she'd read and comprehended every page of the documents that prove the legitimacy of herself and the boy."

"I cannot believe it," said Princess Elise. "But what a remarkable history. I wonder why your brother didn't simply take her as a mistress? If he intended to hide her from the world? Why marry her? In France, no effort is made by men to seclude their mistresses. In fact, both of my parents engaged in open affairs. My mother has exiled to Spain with her lover."

"Oh, yes, you mentioned this," he mused. "It did take me by surprise, if I'm being honest. And it takes quite a bit to surprise me. I assumed you'd been orphaned."

"It is custom in French court to be raised primarily by nannies and governesses, and it was no different in the Palais-Royal. I've received four letters . . . possibly five . . . from my mother during the ten years of my exile? She was a member of the Spanish royal family before she married my father, and after he was killed, she fled to Madrid with this man who is her lover. She's living—that is, she's *probably* living—in a villa on the Mediterranean Sea."

"I don't know what to say, Highness. I'm sorry."

"Yes, I am sorry, too."

Killian thought of his own mother, doting and generous.

"I've had the opportunity to observe a different version of motherhood in England," she said. "My aunt is silly and showers affection on my cousin Juliette, but she wants the best for her daughter and is very attentive. Juliette lives in London now obviously, but my aunt calls on her constantly. Even Queen Charlotte, with her suffocating restrictions, shows open love for her daughters. It has made me wonder how I might have benefitted, even in exile, from the figure of a mother who *wanted* me, who was searching for me.

"In this," she finished, "open affairs among husbands and wives are not ideal. We were never first in the heart or mind of our mother."

Killian shook his head, brushing the top of her head with his chin. He told her again that he was sorry. The number of extramarital affairs that he'd been asked to "fix" in St. James's Palace was incalculable. Dalliances were exciting and provocative, but at least one party was always left with an emotional wound. It was one of the many reasons Killian would not "seduce" this princess. She had enough heartache in her life.

"But what I don't understand," the princess was asking, "is your brother's intent. If he relocated her to his estate only to regard her like some sort of kept woman—separate and hidden—why go to the trouble of marrying her?"

"That's the question of the decade, isn't it? All I can say is, he takes after our father?"

"Meaning?"

Killian sighed, loath to tell this bit, even after all these years. "My late mother—the one who suffered the fits of panic—was *also* a dancer."

"Oh," the princess said.

"Yes," Killian said. "*Oh*."

"A ballerina, was she?"

"No," Killian said.

"Oh," she said again. Simply. No judgment.

He took a deep breath and finished it. "*My* mother was a dancer, but my father's *first* wife—Peter's mother—was a gentlewoman. Her father had been a viscount. She died in childbirth along with the infant that would have been Peter's brother. Peter never recovered from the loss. My father was, by all accounts, also mired in grief, but eventually he met my mother at a club in London. She was very beautiful and vivacious, and they fell in love. Their love was so very deep and abiding, he married her."

"Oh, so you're suggesting a pattern. The men in your family prefer dancers."

Not me, he thought. *I prefer princesses.*

He said, "Well, my brother married a dancer and kept her a great secret, but my father spit in the eye of society and flaunted his dancer wife. My mother was his countess in every way—the love of his life—a sentiment no one ever forgave."

"He was ostracized?" guessed the princess.

"He was ribald and verbose and rather effective in

the House of Lords. No one challenged him, really. And that's the great cruelty, isn't it? *He* was forgiven, largely, for marrying a dancer. My mother, however, was never forgiven for becoming a countess. Especially by her stepson. And when I was born, Peter had a *new* vessel for his scorn."

"He resented you?"

Killian nodded. "A sentiment he made certain was shared throughout society."

And here Killian paused again. This story was as familiar to him as the road to his home. It had been repeated by neighbors, classmates, and courtiers at St. James's Palace. He'd learned very young that it was impossible to hide it, or go around it, or to reconstruct it. Instead, he'd built it into his reputation and wore it like a breastplate over his heart.

And honestly, he no longer felt the emotional pain of it—truly, he did not. Yes, his beautiful, sweet-natured mother had been rejected and ridiculed by the women of society. Yes, his older brother had been resentful and mocking to him; his humiliations when they were in school were diabolic. He'd accepted all of it. Also, he'd used it to his advantage. His mother's reputation made it possible for the king to close his eyes and hold his nose and dump his royal dirty work into Killian's lap. His brother's cruelty made Killian shrewd and cynical, skills that made him very good at his job. He was able to charge the palace a small fortune for the effort.

And yet . . .

And yet now he waited for the princess to react. To be appalled by his lineage, or be put off by his baseness, or feel pity for the sliver of time he was an earl.

"But this is the most remarkable family story I've heard since my own," she said. Her voice was deeply thoughtful. She sounded . . . captivated. "And so this alleged sister-in-law turns up, claiming to be the mother of the child earl. But did you . . . endeavor to send her away?"

Killian said nothing, readjusting the two of them on the horse.

Each time she said the unexpected thing, the *compassionate* thing he wanted to bury his face in her hair. He wanted his hands on her hips, on her ankles, on the arch of her foot. He wanted to spin her to sit astride him and take . . . any part of her she would give, her throat, her lips, *all of her.*

He wanted to cease talking about his strange, cobbled-together family and consume her.

But of course he could not. In all honestly, he couldn't be—well, he shouldn't be—ferrying her to Paxton Dale. He should be fifty *miles* from her. It was unwise to be so close to someone he wanted so very much.

"Killian?" she prompted. "What did you say to her?"

Killian took a deep breath. He would not consume her. He would . . . discuss his sister-in-law and his nephew. He would continue to want her through it all, but he would not permit himself to experience intimacy with her.

"Well," he began, "at first I said nothing. I've a procedure in the . . . 'favors' I do for the palace. It begins with observation. You watch, you wait, you learn patterns and habits and weaknesses. This was no different."

"Is this why you stalked me for days and then allowed the royal duke to introduce us?" she asked.

"I 'stalked' you for days because I had no idea who you were in the entourage."

She made a snickering noise. "The mourning attire and the veils. The one piece of useful advice given to me by my mother. Her infrequent letters tell me virtually nothing except the weather in Spain, her own ro-

bust health, and the recommendation of black veils and
dresses for a safe and uniform entourage."

"Nothing about the situation of your brother and sister? Nothing about an end to your exile?"

"No, nothing. Never mentioned. In fact, actively omitted. You would"—the princess sighed tiredly—"have to
make her acquaintance. To comprehend."

"Right. Well, one might say this of Lady Dunlock, my
brother's widow. She defies explanation. Not for the same
reasons, obviously, but . . . You'll see, soon enough."

"So she is . . . terrible?" asked the princess.

"Terrible? No. Not to me. I cannot say that she's . . . fit
company for a princess, however."

"She's sheltering me from a storm and protecting the
reputation no one cares about but you. That is, unless she
refuses us. Is that a possibility?"

"No. She will not refuse us."

"Because you did not refuse her?" she guessed.

"Because it will thrill her to host a princess."

"Rumpled and streaked with mud from the road and
sharing a horse with no saddle?" she asked.

"Absolutely."

"And you? When she came to you—why did you not
refuse her?"

Killian sighed. "I'll tell you what I noticed first: she's
a devoted mother. Overlooking other failings, this is obvious. She has never demanded more than is rightfully owed
to her son. She is . . . decent, I suppose you could say."

"Oh," she said, "I'd not expected this. But of course
you must see all manner of indecency at court. The contrast to the larger world must be striking."

*I'll never encounter anyone in the larger world like
you*, Killian thought. He said, "Yes, the contrast is
striking."

"And so she turned up," surmised the princess, "and

she was a proficient mother, and you did not challenge their claim to the earldom because . . . ?"

"Well, I'd planned to offer her money to go away instead. I kept her close, going so far as to install her and the boy in guest rooms. I didn't want her spreading rumors in Hampton or, God forbid, London, until I learned the amount required make her disappear. I summoned the family solicitor and sent a note to my banker, preparing an account that would support her and the boy in America or Scotland or wherever she wished. Then I began to study her documentation."

Killian paused in the story, remembering the fortnight he spent, researching Pearl's claim to the earldom for her young son. After everything. His poor, tortured mother. His own battle to be accepted in society. It seemed like a lifetime ago—not the effort to disprove Pearl, but the waning hope. The last vestiges of what might have been before he comprehended the very great futility of it all, the naivete. The desperate maneuverings of a man who yearned for some claim to respect and legitimacy.

In the end . . . *of course* he would not be earl. Of course.

"And you knew?" the princess asked softly. "When you looked into it, you knew?"

"Yes," said Killian. "I knew."

"But you'd already inherited, and she was an anonymous dancer, and her son was a child. You could've sent them away. You had a plan to pay them to go away. It could have worked."

"Yes," he repeated. "I could have."

"But you did not." She looked up at him, one of a dozen times she'd tipped up her face. This time, she dragged her lips along the contour of his throat and jaw. It wasn't so much a look as a prolonged nuzzle. Killian closed his eyes, breathing in the smell of her. He forgot about the title and the house and his nephew. There was only the movement of the horse, and this dark afternoon, and her. His loins, now rock-hard, throbbed with the most delicious burn.

She swiped her mouth along the corner of his lips; a nip, a nibble—an invitation, a request.

Killian closed his eyes, fighting the urge to take what she offered, fighting the urge to swallow her whole.

"Princess," he hissed, a warning, but he did not retreat. He held his head perfectly still, hoping she'd do it again.

He was just about to tip his face down, to lose himself to her, survival be damned, when the sound of galloping horses trampled his thoughts.

Killian paused, hovering a hairbreadth from her lips.

"Hallo!" came a shout from behind them.

"Oh, God," whispered Killian. He dropped his forehead to her hair.

"Hallo lonely traveler!" the voice said again, closer now, pitched over the advancing sound of the horses' hooves. "I say, hallo!"

"What is it?" the princess asked, turning in his lap. Every move she made was delicious torment.

"It is . . ." Killian began, clearing his throat ". . . the embodiment of everything I've just explained."

"What?"

And now they were overtaken by three horses: a uniformed groom on the left; on the right, a thin, upright woman; and between them a small, chubby boy with an expression of delighted curiosity on his round pink face.

"Lonely traveler!" bellowed Bartholomew Crewes, Earl Dunlock, the boy cantering beside them.

"My lord," called the woman. It was Bartholomew's nanny, Mrs. Pile. Her voice was firm but patient. She pushed her horse to keep up. "Do not crowd the man. Do not startle his horse. If you please."

Princess Elise spun in his lap, gaping at the boy and the woman.

"Uncle?" said the boy, gasping in recognition.

His nephew always greeted him like he was his favorite person, believed lost at sea, restored to life. Killian would be lying if he said he grew weary of it.

"Uncle Killian, but you said you'd not come for a fortnight!" Bartholomew half sang, half shouted. He kicked his horse into a gallop and darted ahead, then broke right and circled back, riding a wide loop around the three other horses.

Princess Elise giggled, and whipped around, watching him.

"You've come you've come you've come!" the boy shouted, his chubby face thrown back, eyes closed, hat in his hand, waving in the air.

After he'd circled them two times, he sidled up to Killian, cramming his hat on his head. "But is that a girl in your lap Uncle why are you riding with a *girl*? Where is Hodges? And what of a proper saddle? *Where is your stallion Uncle this is a gelding where is Mayor?*"

"Have a care, my lord," sang Mrs. Pile, "and *do not* crowd them, *please*."

"But Mrs. Pile, it is Uncle Killian and he has come to see me and brought a girl!"

"So he has," said Mrs. Pile. "Pleasure to see you, Mr. Crewes. The earl's enthusiasm defies explanation, as usual. But are you quite alright? We did not expect you until mid-month."

"Thank you, Mrs. Pile. Hello, Bart," said Killian, readjusting the princess. She sat a little taller and put a hand to her hair. All the while, she watched Bartholomew with delight.

To Mrs. Pile, he said quietly, "It's business as usual with the earl, I see."

"It is, in fact," said the nanny, flashing him a pained smile.

"Shall we give them *room*, my lord?" Mrs. Pile said to the boy. "Remember what we've said about allowing others to draw breath and regard you from a safe distance lest we overwhelm? Remember we must allow them time to have a thought in between your great many questions?"

"But it is only Uncle Killian," explained the boy, gesturing to Killian with an open palm.

"Is it?" asked Mrs. Pile. "Is it *only* your uncle? Or have we, perhaps, stumbled into mixed company? Might we now demonstrate our finest manners, regardless? Might we wait for an introduction?"

"We might," allowed Bartholomew, his voice one decibel quieter. He studied Killian with the attention he might give a magician who was about to reveal how he pulled a rabbit from his hat.

"Never you fear about my horse, Bartholomew," said Killian. "Mayor is quite well. I've stabled him in Hampton. But can you listen very carefully and be on your best behavior as I tell you why I've come, and why I have no saddle, and about my . . . companion?"

"Oh yes Uncle I am listening I actually have two guesses—no I actually have three guesses—but you may say the real answer first and I will tell you if I guessed correctly. Wait! Should I tell you my guesses first so that you know that I am telling the truth?"

"My lord," began Mrs. Pile wearily, but Killian waved her off.

"Under normal circumstances," said Killian, "I would hear your guesses first; however, considering the storm and our rather uncomfortable means of travel, I should like to cut to the chase."

"I've seen the lightning," reported the boy gravely.

"Indeed. Can you promise to listen carefully, all the way to the end, before you interrupt? Can you furthermore be a proper gentleman, not to mention a good host, and lend a hand as we make these last few miles to Paxton?"

"Oh yes Uncle I can do—as you know I am a gentleman although I do not know what may be required of a good host I shall look it up in the library when I get home and Mr. and Mrs. Pile well help me."

"Of course they will. I knew I could rely on you, but are you listening?"

"I am listening ever so carefully Uncle oh but if only I had some parchment and a pen—"

"It might be noted that you are currently riding a horse, my lord," cut in Mrs. Pile gently. "Dictation is not expected. I believe your uncle means that you might be silent and allow him to tell us?"

Before the boy could interrupt again, Killian said, "Today, the carriage in which I was riding hit a rock in the road, splintered a wheel, and was wrecked."

This invoked a gasp of delighted horror, as Killian knew it would. The boy exclaimed, "Uncle but did it—"

Killian held up a hand and the boy fell silent.

"The carriage was new—part of King George's private collection—and rather nimble and quick, but the coachman hit a sunken spot in the road, and it ended up on its side."

"Oh Uncle how many times have I read of this—"

Killian silenced him with another hand.

"By some miracle, everyone was unharmed, including the horses. We were very lucky. However, we were also stranded on the roadside with a storm coming on. That is why I am riding a chestnut bay with no saddle. He was one of two horses pulling the carriage.

"Now, about the lady. I am doing a favor on behalf of King George and his sons. You remember the favors I do on behalf of the king?"

"Like the time you snuck up on an assassin outside the king's hunting lodge and attacked him from behind and wrestled him to the ground and held your blade to his throat but then had mercy and knocked him unconscious instead?" The boy pantomimed this exaggerated version of events.

"Yes," said Killian, "favors like that. However, today my favor was to escort one of the king's very important guests into the countryside. And that guest is here, on the horse with me. She was in the accident, and we find ourselves stranded. And her name—are you ready?—is Princess Regine Elise Adelaide d'Orleans. She's known in her country as Her Serene Highness. Her uncle was King Louis XVI of France and grandfather was King Louis XV."

A second, more astounded gasp escaped the boy, as Killian knew it would.

"The Well-Beloved!" the boy shouted and the young earl set off in another gallop, ringing them again with his horse.

"What the devil does he mean by that?" Killian mumbled, watching him.

"My grandfather was known in France as the Well-Beloved," said the princess quietly, watching him.

"Ah," said Killian. The boy's knowledge of history—in fact his knowledge of most things academic—astounded him.

"Hallo your majesty and welcome to the second road outside the first road to my home of Paxton Dale in Middlesex in the country of England! But should we bow, Mrs. Pile?" asked Bartholomew, sidling up.

"I cannot say, my lord," said Mrs. Pile. "However, I

believe your uncle bade you *listen* as he explained what he might require of you."

"We do not bow, as she is a French princess and we are English. She does, however, outrank you, so—"

"But I am an earl I am the seventeenth Earl Dunlock—"

"So you are, and she is what's known as a Princess of the Blood, and—considering she is stranded and in my care—she will be a guest in your house, if you will have her."

"Oh of course Uncle of course we shall have her it would be an honor wouldn't it Mrs. Pile to have her in our home in fact she may sleep in my bedchamber and I shall sleep on the floor so that she may be—"

"No one need sleep on the floor," said Killian. "As you know, Paxton has twenty bedrooms, and she is only one woman. Perhaps we'll allow the housekeeper and your mother to select a guest room for her. But you may sit beside her at dinner, if you like. Perhaps you can even . . . practice your French?"

"Oh but does the princess speak French?" asked the boy.

"French is, in fact, her native tongue."

He spurred his horse forward again to trot another circle around them. The princess laughed, and it was such a delighted, pretty sound. Killian readjusted her on his lap; he wanted to absorb it.

"Bartholomew," he called, "come to me and listen carefully. I should like to reach Paxton Dale before the storm—it's a miracle it's held off for this long. Can I rely on you to ride ahead and tell your mother and Mrs. Short-well that I've come and brought an esteemed guest? Also, tell the aunts, if you can get them to comprehend."

"The aunts?" the boy exclaimed in distaste, making a face.

"Yes, the aunts. They'll know the protocol for hosting

a royal guest better than any of us. This may come as a shock to you, but riding around and around in circles is not the thing. Can you do this?"

"Oh yes Uncle but are you really coming to Paxton with the princess?"

"Yes, Bartholomew, we are really coming. If you can go before us and prepare the house and staff."

"I can do it Uncle!" exclaimed the boy, digging his heels into the sides of his horse and bolting ahead.

"And you're off, Mrs. Pile," said Killian, watching him go. "My apologies."

"Very good, Mr. Crewes," the woman said with a chuckle, spurring her own mount forward. "If you'll excuse me, Mr. Crewes, Highness."

"You're a good woman, Mrs. Pile," Killian called after her.

"We do work, daily, with the boy," vowed the nanny, looking over her shoulder as she galloped away.

Killian snickered. To the groom beside him, he said, "Donnie, I was going to ask that we trade mounts so I might have the saddle, but we're so close now, why don't you stay with the earl and Mrs. Pile? We'll be along shortly. When we arrive, can you personally see to this gelding? He's from His Majesty's stable and has had the very devil of a day."

"Very good, Mr. Crewes," said the groom, and he clicked at his mount and hurried after the boy.

When the last of the hoofbeats had faded away, Killian said, "Princess Elise? I give you the Earl Dunlock."

The princess had studied the boy as he'd circled them, flanked them, and shouted at them. Her expressions had been curious and disbelieving, but also delighted. Intuition suggested that she would not be *unkind* to the boy—he wouldn't have brought her here if he'd believed she would be unkind—but there was always the risk that she would judge, affect some haughtiness, or make fun. This would be the reaction of almost every other woman he'd ever met in St. James's Palace.

Killian held his breath. He was biased—this he knew—but he had grown to love Bartholomew. He loved the boy enough to want the earldom for him. Perhaps she—

"I want to kiss you," the princess stated.

The words hit him like the unexpected strike of a gong, reverberating through his body, settling in the very spot where her round bottom bounced against his lap.

Well, this answered the question of whether she was put off or haughty.

His mind raced with all the replies he wanted to make—*God yes*, and *Come here*, and *Please*—but he couldn't, of course. He was her Glorified Nanny and Special Friend. He could only keep silent and hold his breath.

"Why could that be?" she wondered out loud, turning to him. "Why do I want to kiss you?"

He wouldn't look at her. They were so very close to Paxton Dale.

"Do you know . . ." she began, facing the road again ". . . it's been ten years since I've thought of something as frivolous as kissing?"

Killian did not answer.

"In fact, that's how long it's been since I've wanted anything for myself—anything at all. It's only the last month that I've wanted to find my brother and sister."

She waited, but Killian didn't trust himself to speak. He could not encourage this—he couldn't.

"I've shocked and alarmed you," she guessed. "I've shocked and alarmed myself—and why? For what?"

"It was the carriage—" His voice broke and he started again. "It was the carriage accident, Highness. You hit your head."

"I think perhaps it *was* the carriage accident," she observed. "But not my head. I think perhaps it was your careful inspection of my unbroken bones. It's also this horseback ride. And last night in the passage. And the story of your family."

"They are not my family."

She spun back to him. "They are entirely your family. Do not deny the adoration that boy feels for you. I've so little family—I've *no* family—and I see a rich, abiding *love* between you and the earl. And it takes my breath away. And that, I suppose, is why I want to kiss you."

Killian kept his eyes on the road.

"Killian?" she prompted.

"Princess."

"*Killian.*"

He could feel her staring at his face. As seductions went, it was unintentional, and one-sided, and unstudied. But his mouth watered, and he squeezed the horse's mane. He wanted to give her what she wanted. He wanted to vanquish that calm, chatty speculation from her voice. He wanted to show her why she really wanted to kiss him.

Finally he said, "You are not . . . available to me."

"And who regulates my availability?" she demanded. "To you or to anyone else?"

"It is the order of things. You know this."

"The 'order of things' was severed ten years ago, along with my father's head. I know of no such order."

Killian sighed. "If you were not beaten and battered by the day's events . . . if you'd not been treated with such neglect by King George and his lot . . . you would not want me anywhere near you. Certainly you would not want me—"

He stopped and then started again: "You would not want *that.*"

"Please don't tell me what I want," she said softly, straightening. "My motivations—what I want and don't want—are the only things over which I have absolute command. I can choose what I want. I don't care what you say about the order of things."

She's angry, he realized. *Good. Anger and affection cannot coexist. Let her be angry. Let her be terse and cold and clipped. Let her stew.*

The one thing she couldn't do was batter his self-control. He was not made of stone. Well, one area of his body was, in fact, very stonelike.

But if he couldn't resist her, he would not be able to *help* her. He would play into the hands of the palace, design the seduction they wanted—"numb" her with no regard for her future, let alone his.

He was the fixer, and she was a princess, and they *would not kiss*.

"I won't tell you what you want," he said, "but I will tell you what I want. I want to do my job. And *my job* is to manage situations. I'm meant to *improve* things, not complicate them. Kissing is complicated."

She stared at him a moment longer, studying his face. Killian looked away. They'd come to the parallel walls of hedgerows that flanked the drive to Paxton Dale. He required all concentration to guide the unsaddled horse into the turn.

"Can you imagine," the princess said quietly, "how weary I've grown of being told no by every quarter of St. James's Palace?"

"You are weary, Highness. I understand."

"And what's worse? Being *managed*. Telling me not to complicate things with a kiss is another form of management, Killian."

"You're killing me, Princess."

"Killing you, am I? Meanwhile, *I* fight to live," she shot back. "Inside my own mind and body, I am fighting to actually live a real life."

"I believe you. But will you believe this? I am on your side."

"No," she said, turning her face to the wind. "I don't believe you."

Killian exhaled. The moment had passed. He was relieved by this. Relieved, and also so very dejected. It didn't matter. She was no longer snuggled against him. She didn't cling to him so much as clamp down for balance. Her body was tense on his lap.

"I wish I'd not revealed my desire for a kiss," she announced.

"No regrets," he told her, and then he clutched her against him, kicked the gelding to run, and galloped the last half mile.

CHAPTER FOURTEEN

*I*F IT HAD been Killian's goal to shake every coherent thought from her head, he had succeeded. The questions she wanted to ask—indeed, the righteous indignation in which she'd wanted to stew—became secondary to simply *holding on.*

The horse thundered down the road, rattling her teeth, and she was given little choice but to cling to him for her very life. When the manor house finally swung into view, she saw only a jostled red-and-gray blur.

"But is it a walled estate?" she called as they clattered to a wide, low arch between two gatehouses. The arch led through a high wall; inside the wall was a verdant garden. A house rose just twenty yards away, but Elise was distracted by the beauty of the garden.

The centerpiece was a three-tiered fountain gurgling; beyond the fountain was a broad oval of grass ringed by a crushed-rock drive. Irregular beds of mixed flowers bracketed the drive at uneven angles like points on a loosely drawn star. It wasn't grand or sprawling, but it perfectly suited the Tudor mansion with the arched front door.

The house was built of knobby red brick but trimmed at corners, doors, and windows with gray carvings that rose to high arches. The facade was flat, extended slightly for three fat gables. Parapets dotted the roof at even intervals.

"Killian," Elise breathed, whipping around when the horse spun in the opposite direction, "how beautiful."

"I've always thought so," he said, sadness in his voice. He busied himself with quieting the horse.

Elise twisted on his lap, trying to keep the house in view. What a sacrifice it must have been to relinquish this home and grounds to a child.

"Uncle!" came a cry, accompanied by the banging open of the front door. "We are ready to receive the princess!" said the boy earl, erupting from the inside, three dogs on his heels. "Everyone is to be on our very best behavior!"

The dogs lunged for the horse, barking and jumping. The animal reared up, and Elise felt Killian's arm clamp her to him again. He pressed down on her back, leaning the two of them over the mane as he struggled to keep them astride.

"Call off your dogs, Bartholomew," Killian grunted.

"Sorry Uncle! Socks, Bun-Bun, Patrice—heel heel heel!"

This command, issued along with running and arm waving, was met with total insubordination. Elise squeezed her eyes shut until the horse stopped dancing and Killian loosened his arm. Three grooms rushed to help, settling the gelding and taking him by the bridle. The dogs, still barking, were shepherded along the side of the house by the earl and a stableboy.

"Will you be handed down, miss?" asked a groom beside her leg.

"Address her as, Highness, James," Killian said to the groom, gripping her around the waist. "I'll assist with the dismount, but have a care. She may be unsteady on her feet."

Elise's legs *were*, to her great annoyance, largely unreliable. Soreness from the accident was setting in, and her body had conformed to a strange, numb position in Killian's lap. She faltered slightly when her feet hit the shifting gravel.

Killian was off the horse in an instant, one hand on her waist, the other on an elbow.

"Can you stand?" he asked softly.

She winced, forcing her stiff muscles to work. "Yes, yes, I can stand. I need to walk a bit, that's all. Was it necessary to sprint the last half mile?"

"It did feel necessary to sprint," he said. "In the moment."

Elise shot him a glance, but he wouldn't look at her. *Fine*, Elise thought, shaking out her legs and pulling away. *Evade and dismiss*.

She looked around, taking in the serene beauty of the house. One of the dogs darted around the corner with the earl huffing in pursuit.

"Bun-Bun, no!" the earl bellowed.

"Where is your mother, my lord?" shouted Killian.

"She is coming she was taking her pianoforte lesson when I reached Paxton and then I told her you were coming and bringing a princess she said she would change her dress from the pink to the yellow or perhaps the green but probably the yellow!" The boy lunged in one direction then the other, trying to catch the small yipping dog.

"Should we send for a book on dog training, Bart?" Killian asked.

"But is there such a book Uncle?" asked Lord Bartholomew. "I should love to train my dogs and perhaps get one or two more which I would also train—"

"Let us pause with *three* unruly dogs, if we might. Seize command of this lot before we toss in another? I'll have Mr. Pile put in for a book."

A stable boy rushed to help contain the earl's escaped

dog, and the trio disappeared around the side of the house.

"This garden rivals the grounds at St. James's Palace, Killian," Elise said. "Wild and contained at the same time."

"Thank you," he said. "I began work on it as soon as Paxton fell to me. It had been neglected for many decades, but the land is fertile, and there was some vague outline from a century ago. Paxton was my boyhood home. I grew up fantasizing how I would restore it if it were mine."

Elise nodded, acknowledging the sad note of longing in his voice. Oh, how the pieces of the puzzle had multiplied today. Killian designed gardens. This particular garden was wild and contained because he understood the beauty of those two qualities. The storybook mansion behind it had been his home as a boy.

She glanced again at the property. Her travels with the royal family had acquainted her with more than a few country manor houses, but Paxton Dale was unique. It was rustic in a sort of well-worn, Gothic way, but no less grand. It looked distinctively English with a dash of continental fairy tale thrown in.

"But how old is the house?" she asked.

"It was original to King James, actually," he recited. "A hunting lodge built in the 1200's. It was remodeled in 1650 or so. Thankfully the earl at the time preserved bits of the king's original lodge. This is why you see ancient masonry exposed here and there. The renovations I've done aimed to preserve both eras. It's a hodgepodge, really, but hopefully a harmonious one."

"Indeed," Elise said, nodding. "I love it."

"I . . . will not argue with that sentiment," he said.

Elise wanted to ask him why he did not live here with

his nephew—the boy clearly adored him—but movement caught her eye from the direction of the house. She looked up. The doorway, previously vacant, was now occupied by a cluster of liveried servants. Standing to the side of the staff, her body mostly hidden from view, was a young blonde woman in an orange gown. The woman peered out with curiosity and something like . . . *trepidation* plain on her face.

Elise smiled and gave a little wave. *Hello?*

The women's eyes grew larger; she looked to one of the servants, whispered something, and looked back.

She appeared to be Elise's age—no more than thirty, certainly, and very pretty. She was curvy and soft, with large eyes, creamy skin, and a splatter of freckles across a pert nose—all the hallmarks of a classic English beauty.

Elise took another step closer, and the woman vanished behind the crowd of servants.

Elise glanced at Killian. A groom had approached him, and he gave some direction about the horse.

Elise looked back to the door. Now there was movement among the collected servants, and the woman Killian had referred to as Mrs. Pile pushed her way to the front. The nanny raised her eyebrows at Elise, gave a respectful nod, and then whispered behind her. A lengthy exchange ensued, but the woman in orange remained out of sight. A cat slunk to the threshold of the door, rubbing against Mrs. Pile's leg, and an orange-clad arm appeared from behind the door to scoop it up. Finally, after more discussion, the young woman in the orange dress peered around the edge of the door again, stealing a look.

Elise smiled.

The woman's eyes grew larger still, and she looked to Mrs. Pile. The older woman nodded her head.

"What's happening?" asked Killian tiredly, sending the groom away.

"I cannot say for certain," Elise said slowly, waving again to the woman who now clutched a cat.

"Oh," he sighed, "there she is. Well, there's no going back now. Remember, you chose this. You could be in Hampton's finest inn right now."

"But what do you—"

Now the woman in orange was in motion, gliding out the door. When she broached the threshold, she pitched the cat into the shrubbery. She descended the steps with hands slightly outstretched and posture uncomfortably straight, a pose of forced grace. Her expression was what Elise might call *terrified resolve*.

"*Greetings*," intoned the blonde woman. "And welcome to Paxton Dale, Your Highness." Her Essex accent was very thick and distinctive, even to Elise's French ears.

When she reached the bottom step, she dropped into the deepest and most pronounced curtsy Elise had seen since she left her uncle's court in France. The fabric of her dress was clearly fine, trimmed with velvet and overlaid with lace, but the style and color were eye-wateringly pronounced—bright, and low-cut, embellished like a fancy orange curtain tassel.

"Princess Elise," said Killian blandly, "may I introduce you to Lady Pearl Crewes, Countess Dunlock."

And now Mrs. Pile made her way down the steps, her progress natural and efficient. The liveried servants spilled out behind her, taking up position in two rows on either side of the steps. Mrs. Pile stopped behind the young countess and whispered something to her.

Lady Dunlock's head popped up. She looked as if she was bracing for a loud boom.

"Lady Dunlock," Killian continued, "this is Princess Regine Elise Adelaide d'Orleans."

"It is an honor, your majesty," said Lady Dunlock, bowing her head again.

"Apologies," said Killian to the top of the countess's head, "for turning up unannounced, and with a guest to boot. I've been tasked by the palace with giving the princess a tour of Middlesex, and we've run into a spot of trouble with our carriage. Busted wheel—a near miss, actually. Considering the weather, I was compelled to bring the princess here rather than sort out whatever unfit conveyance we might find in Hampton. Can you and Bart spare a room for the princess for the night?"

Lady Dunlock was nodding, slowly at first, now wildly, rising from her curtsy. "Yes, Killian, yes—of course. How delighted we would be to host her." She skittered forward and sank into another curtsy, orange ribbons fluttering.

"I might suggest that Princess Elise is a *French* princess," drawled Killian, "and being as we are *English* and *not* French, we need not affect a posture of quite so much reverenc—"

"Your generosity is a credit to you, my lady," cut in Elise. She would not embarrass her. Elise reached for the countess, clutching both hands in her own. "I'm so grateful to you and your son. We've endured quite an ordeal with the carriage, and your home is an oasis, truly. Thank you."

"Oh, but you're so very welcome, Highness. Of course we are at your service. I've bade the maids to prepare the finest guest room. I've ordered a hearty supper. I've—"

In that moment, one of the earl's dogs emerged again, darting between them, sending the hem of Lady Dunlock's gown flying.

"Bartholomew!" shouted Lady Dunlock. "Keep the dogs away from the princess or they'll not step another foot inside the house! Do you hear?"

"We are trying, Mama!" called the earl, trudging after the dog. "She likes the princess and some princesses are

fond of dogs so you should ask her before you threaten to turn the dogs out everyone has a different view on dogs!"

The boy trotted past and Elise laughed. Lady Dunlock gaped at her, clearly terrified she would see some offense.

"I do, in fact, like dogs," said Elise, staring after the chase.

"Sorry?" called a crackly voice from the doorway, redirecting everyone's attention. "But did someone say *chintz*?"

Elise looked up to see two very old women, one thin and wiry, the other plump and round, standing on the top step. They squinted into the garden.

"Aunts," said Killian, "may I present a guest of King George, Princess Regine Elise Adelaide d'Orleans of *France*. She has endured a carriage accident on the road from London and will pass the night as your guest.

"Princess Elise, may I introduce you to Ladies Millicent and Margaret, sisters of my late father. They are the longest-standing residents of Paxton Dale."

"How do you do," said Elise, bobbing into a shallow curtsy. "Thank you ever so much for offering this safe haven from my calamitous day."

"I knew they weren't saying *chintz*," said the second aunt. "Why would we be summoned to the garden to view chintz? Killian's brought a *girl* who is *French*, God preserve her. Which part of France, my dear? Not Paris, I hope."

"Well," began Elise, "when I lived in France, in fact I did pass much of the year in Paris. At the Palais-Royal. In the premièr arrondissement. Do you know it?"

"So you say," remarked the wiry aunt. "But are you acquainted with Lady Racine Huxtable-Ducet?"

Elise bit back a smile. "I don't believe I have had the

pleasure. But it has been many years since I was in Paris. I've lived in England these last ten years."

"She would not know Lady Racine, of course," scolded the round aunt, "as Lady Racine is *Bavarian*, not French."

"Lady Racine is as French as a bouillabaisse," the wiry aunt informed her.

"But how long will you be with us, my dear?" asked the round aunt. "I shall write Lady Racine and ask when she was last in Paris. Perhaps she might make the journey from . . . But where has she settled? She took up with that count she met on the brigantine to Naples, and they moved to . . ."

"Malta," the other aunt declared.

"Bedfordshire," the plump aunt remembered at the same time.

"Bedfordshire?" exclaimed her sister. "Why, Lady Racine—"

"Forgive me, Aunts," cut in Killian, "but I should like to have the princess shown to a guest room before the clouds open up. Perhaps we could revisit the topic of Lady Racine, the count, and their new home over dinner."

"Oh, but she will stay for dinner?" asked the round aunt.

"Indeed," he said.

To Lady Dunlock, Killian said, "Perhaps you and Mrs. Shortwell might help Princess Elise get settled? She may require a few things, considering hers was only meant to be a brief morning sojourn from St. James's, and now she's stranded here overnight."

Lady Dunlock was nodding assuredly. "Absolutely, Killian. We are at her service, aren't we, Mrs. Shortwell?"

Behind them, a woman in an apron agreed indulgently. "Yes, my lady, we shall see to anything the princess may require."

"Thank you," Elise said, allowing Lady Dunlock to sweep her up the steps. The countess chattered nervously about how very glad she was to host such an esteemed guest, about the great many comforts Elise would encounter at Paxton Dale, about her lifelong dream of meeting a real princess.

Elise allowed herself to be swept away, but she cast a look over her shoulder at Killian. The aunts had descended upon him, inundating him with requests and observations. He bore it all, nodding along, but not before he looked up to catch Elise's eye.

His expression said, *You asked for this.*

What I'd ask for, Elise thought, *was a kiss.*

The single-mindedness of her desire for him no longer surprised her. Everything about him . . . and this house . . . and the care he obviously bestowed on these people . . . invited her to want him.

Actually, what it invited was . . . something more than want.

Elise could sense movement in the area of her heart, the first stirrings after ten years of hibernation. Stretching, feeling the way, seeking.

She paused for a moment, reveling in the feeling. Was it a surprise, Elise wondered, that she felt something like *love* for Killian Crewes?

Yes. Yes, she supposed it did surprise her. She'd only just met him.

"Oh, but you look like you might faint, Highness," observed Lady Dunlock, stepping back. "Do you feel light-headed?"

Yes, thought Elise, *I do feel a bit light-headed.*

She said, "Forgive me, my lady. I find myself succumbing to the comforts of your lovely home. Please lead the way."

CHAPTER FIFTEEN

𝒟INNER AT PAXTON Dale was generally an elaborate, overblown affair, and tonight would be no different. Pearl ordered the moon in soufflés and sauces and set the ballroom ablaze with every available candle. Oh, the irony. Killian's brother would sooner have him eat from a pail of scraps on the kitchen stoop than entertain him in high style. His widow, in contrast, treated him like the prodigal son.

Killian didn't mind so much. If Bartholomew was meant to eventually enter society, he should become accustomed to a certain standard of living. And Killian did not begrudge his sister-in-law basic comforts.

However, Killian was careful not to portray too much fondness for any visit to Paxton. The more he appeared to enjoy his time here, the more they would expect him to remain. And remain. *And remain.* The lot of them never failed to mention how happy they would be if he abandoned London, relocated to Middlesex, and moved in.

But Killian was determined to function as provider, steward, and advisor and nothing more. It was his strong preference to lend support but not invoke his heart. And, he had some measure of autonomy in London. In London, he wasn't forced to stand witness to someone else embodying the earldom that would have been his.

Most importantly, someone had to actually *work* for

their living to provide for all of them. It was no small thing to refurbish an estate, support two elderly aunts and one windowed countess, and educate a boy in the manner befitting a future earl. Killian had put a plan in place that should eventually see Paxton Dale prosperous and self-supporting, but it would need another five years at least. Herds had to mature, crops had to grow, tenants had to be trained, and investments made. As it now stood, the first cut of any money Killian earned went to Paxton.

When, eventually, the estate could sustain itself, Killian hoped to build his own small holding with whatever money was left. This was an entirely different plan, much longer in scope, and he'd not yet decided where. The enemy of the plan—nay, the death of it— would be to simply give up and move into a guest room at Paxton Dale like a desperate relation.

Tonight, however, he embodied every inch of the Desperate Relation. He had no change of clothes for dinner, and his coat was wrinkled and layered with dust from the road. He had axle grease on his gloves, and his boots had been ruined.

The princess, he was shocked to see, had been furnished with an evening gown, slippers, gloves, and jewelry. He might not have recognized her if he'd not *collided* with her rounding the corner to the great hall, his hands filled with ledgers.

"Bollocks," he swore, not seeing who it was. He hopped back as his paperwork slid to the floor.

"Sorry," she laughed, stooping to gather the loose parchment.

Killian stood above her, his mind caught between surprise and something like . . . dazzlement. The gown was a soft apricot—that nameless color where light orange met ripe pink. The silk was light as a feather, fanning out in a pool around her. Her head was bowed over his paperwork, revealing her slender neck and a half moon of creamy shoulders.

"Is it too much to hope," she said, scraping the papers into a heap, "that these were in no particular order?" She looked up, flashing a smile of half chagrin, half question.

Killian felt his breath catch. Her face shone in the candlelight, all traces of fatigue and travel gone. Her hair had been smoothed from her face and secured on the sides with pearl-studded pins. Matching pearls hung from a single strand around her neck. The gown had tiny puffed sleeves that dropped to a square neck—the décolletage lower than anything Killian had seen her wear.

She looked, he thought, like royalty: regal, and beautiful, and ordained.

"Highness," he clipped, the only available word. He sank beside her, reaching for his ledgers. "Forgive me."

"You are forgiven." She chuckled and pulled back, watching him gather his papers in a clumsy schoolboy fashion. He felt his face redden—he was actually blushing—and he cleared his throat. It had been a great many years since he'd been unsettled by the sight of a beautiful woman.

"Where did you acquire the gown?" he asked gruffly, shoving up.

"The countess," she said. She struggled to stand. Almost too late, he remembered to extend his arm to her.

"Pearl?" he asked. That made no sense. She favored tight silk and a profusion of rattling, flapping embellishments. Also, she outweighed the princess by a stone. Her dinner attire always put him in the mind of sausage casing that fell into the fripperies bin. This dress was vivid but simple. It flowed loosely down the princess's slight frame in a whisper of silk.

"I believe," said Princess Elise, "that she may have borrowed it from one of your aunts. Which one, I cannot say."

"Margaret," guessed Killian. He saw now that the style was several decades out of date. He'd never considered his maiden aunt to be fashionable, but perhaps Princess Elise could make anything look beautiful.

"It was too long," said the princess, "but a maid was able to quickly tack up the hem. I hope it's not inappropriate for me to accept the countess's invitation to dinner—and to dress up as if I'm a proper guest. I considered declining, but then I thought, why not? The accident was inconvenient, to be sure, but the result is a brief holiday from my real life. No mourning dresses and none of Queen Charlotte's restrictions."

"If you consider a night with this lot—in borrowed clothes from the last century, no less—to be a holiday, then life at St. James's Palace must be very bleak indeed."

"Oh, I've no *life* in St. James's Palace," she commented. "At St. James's Palace, I simply exist."

He watched her drift away. She didn't complain or seek pity; she'd simply said the words. Her reality was as wretched as it was inescapable. A hot wind swept the abandoned structure of Killian's heart, rattling the boarded-up doorways.

He wanted . . .

He wanted—

He couldn't say what he wanted; he knew only that there was no easy "fix" here. Forgetting what the king had asked of him, he couldn't solve this woman's loneliness or isolation—not in a way that positioned *him* as part of the solution.

Killian understood the pain of fixes that left no room for him; Paxton Dale was such a fix. He wouldn't survive being left out again.

"Wait," he called after her. "I'll escort you."

The princess turned back with a smile that, even now, he could not believe was directed at him.

When she looped her hand beneath his bicep, the movement felt so natural and familiar—like she'd known him for years, like he belonged to her and their rightful place was linked together.

Killian hated it. He hated it because he loved it so very much.

None of it was meant to be possessive or provoking, and yet, blaggard that he was, he was provoked. The notions of fixes and futures became tiny specks on the horizon—barely discernable. Instead, he knew only the urge to touch *more* of her, to touch *all* of her.

"Lady Dunlock was kind enough to give me a tour of the manor house," she was saying. "Paxton Dale is beautifully appointed."

"Ah, yes," he managed, forcing his brain to function. Her hand on his arm was tight and possessive. Another thing he hated and loved.

"Has the interior changed so very much since you lived here as a boy?"

"It has." He sighed. "My father and brother made no updates, but in the weeks that I was earl, I mobilized all my London resources to make improvements I'd dreamed of for an age."

"You summoned the royal dukes and bade them roll up their sleeves, did you?"

"Ah, my *other* London resources. Edward told you about the buildings I own. What he failed to mention is that these properties are dilapidated when they come to me, and I work with builders and craftsmen, stonemasons and plumbers to refurbish them. *These* are my London resources. There was more to be done at Paxton when I inherited, but then Bartholomew appeared . . .

"Well, you know the rest," he sighed. "I moved out."

"Lady Dunlock seems to delight in it."

"*Lady Dunlock*," he said, "would sooner re-paper every wall in blinding colors and smother the windows in heavy drapes—and eventually, she will do. For now, there isn't money to redecorate in her preferred style. To her credit, she's mindful of the household budget I've set out, but only to a point. If a peddler comes through the village, she will deplete her pin money on trinkets and 'antiquities' with nothing left for winter essentials. Mr. and Mrs. Pile, Bartholomew's tutor and nanny, respectively, serve as friendly spies who help her think of the future."

"Oh, yes, the *Piles*," repeated Princess Elise. "I noticed that Mrs. Pile has the shrewd ability to . . . in a manner . . . *emerge* from nowhere and gently redirect Lady Dunlock. She made suggestions about my comfort that perhaps hadn't occurred to her. Mrs. Pile is a member of staff, clearly, but Lady Dunlock seems grateful for her guidance."

"Yes, the Piles are a godsend, actually. Pearl can be childlike in one instance and ruthlessly ambitious the next. Mrs. Pile has an inherent steadiness, thankfully, and she instructs with a rare balance of respect and good sense."

"Instructs the boy, or Lady Dunlock?"

"Both. When I interviewed for staff that would remain here in my absence, I searched for a husband-and-wife team who would accept a child earl—well, would accept Bartholomew, in particular . . . with all of his exuberance and unfettered sweetness—but also educate him in such a way that will prepare him for school and, eventually, society. He's made remarkable progress under the tutelage of the Piles, actually.

"It's only the beginning, I'm afraid," Killian went on.

"Bartholomew will bring friends home and press his suit with debutantes. As such, Mrs. Pile must also educate and prepare Pearl. My mother could have benefited from a gentle advisor. The Piles are meant to be allies and they've thrown themselves into the spirit of it, God love them."

"However did you find them?"

"I met with fifty couples, at least. I'd nearly given up hope when I came across their letter. One of their first signs of potential was their great honesty about how they found themselves in service. Mrs. Pile is the daughter of a baron, actually. She'd fallen in love with her brother's classics tutor and was banished from the family. Mr. Pile was that tutor, and he married her, but they had very little money. Their plan was to be hired by the same household and work as a team. Most society families shied away from the scandal surrounding her banishment, but I seized upon it. She knew manners and comportment, and he is an excellent tutor. I feel so very lucky to have stumbled upon them."

"What a perfect solution," she said.

"Yes, well. I am in the business of solutions."

"But do you provide the compensation paid to the Piles, Killian?" she asked.

"Well," he began, but then he stopped. It wasn't necessary for her to know this, of course—but what was the harm in saying it? Certainly, no one else seemed to care.

"Yes, I do pay it," he said.

"Remarkable," she whispered. "But do you support this entire estate from your private funds?"

Killian swallowed, gauging the distance to the dining room. And now they were discussing it in earnest. It hadn't been his intention to raise the topic of money. It was gauche and common and one of many things he'd asked Mrs. Pile to address with Pearl. And yet . . .

And yet all Killian's priorities felt balanced on the head of a pin, and that pin teetered on a slipping, sliding stack of money. Money motivated everything he did. So very many people relied on him.

"For the time being—yes," he finally said. "Paxton Dale had been neglected for a number of years, and we are rebuilding. My father was not an attentive steward of the estate, and my brother, less so."

"But your nephew will be," she said.

"That is the great hope," he said. "Whether he takes a personal interest or simply hires it out to a proficient steward, only time will tell. Either way, the management of the estate will go more smoothly if it's functional rather than a pit of debt."

"And what of your own property?" she asked. "You've not said where you lived after the young earl and Lady Dunlock claimed Paxton Dale."

"I returned to London," he said simply.

"To Mayfair? Near St. James's?"

He made a scoffing noise. "No. I've a house in Bishopsgate, actually. In Lamb Street. It is . . . perfectly suitable for me."

And perfectly unsuitable for a princess, he reminded himself in his head.

"But did you not think of residing here? At Paxton Dale? Everyone is so fond of you. Why not live with your family?"

"First, they are not my family—not really," he said. "Second, I do not interlope on what is not mine. This house, the lands, the title—all of these belong to the earldom, *not to me*. The only thing I inherited when my parents were both dead was the ruby wedding ring my father gave my mother."

They'd reached the dining room now, thank God, and he guided them through the doors.

"But surely they would—"

She was cut off by the enthusiastic welcome of the group assembled around the long, glittering table. Exclamations rose, greetings were gushed, deep curtsies were executed. Three dogs circled the table, barking and thwacking the legs of footmen with their tails.

Killian was loath to let her go, but this conversation had gone on too long and revealed too much. Now he would allow his nephew to do the talking, and he would try very hard not to do the thing that was second-best to touching her, which was looking at her.

CHAPTER SIXTEEN

*ℬ*UT ARE THE dinners so very lavish, Princess, at St. James's Palace?" asked Lady Dunlock, speaking between spoonfuls of fragrant soup. She sat to the right of Killian, who was seated, Elise noted, at the head of the table. He might view himself as an interloper, but the family did not.

"Well, that depends," said Elise, smiling at a footman who leaned to remove her empty bowl. She'd not realized how hungry she was until she'd taken the first bite.

"Many nights the queen and her daughters take their meals together in an annex to the main palace called the Queen's Chapel. As courtier to the princesses, I am generally included in these meals. They are quieter, less formal affairs.

"Several times per week, however," she continued, "the family will dine together, in a cavernous dining hall at the heart of St. James's, and these are much lengthier, rather elaborate productions. A veritable army of servants scurries in and out, bearing course after course of food. A taster sits beside the king and samples everything on his plate before he eats it. Depending on the night, the table may host distinguished guests from around the world. I'm not always included in these meals, but sometimes."

"How very exciting," enthused Lady Dunlock. "Imagine being seated at the table with the king and queen."

"Truth be told, these meals drag on for hours, and no one may be excused until the king declares it to be finished. Twenty courses is an uncomfortable amount of food. After about seven or eight, you begin to wonder where you will put it. And it can be rather boring, depending upon who is seated beside you or who takes it upon himself to give a lengthy toast."

"Is that how you met Uncle?" asked Bartholomew. Elise had been cheered to see that the boy was included in the meal. He sat across from his uncle. Beside him sat Mrs. Pile, and next to her sat a man introduced as her husband, Mr. Pile.

Elise opened her mouth to answer, but the boy cut her off. "Uncle is great friends with King George and the Prince of Wales and all of the royal dukes and he has been to St. James's Palace a hundred times and I know he could eat twenty courses if he had to do it."

"I was once at a horse race with King George and Queen Charlotte," commented one of the aunts, piping up from the far end of the table.

They all turned to look.

"He was as fat as a bear and rather pink in color, especially his ears," she said. "Direct sunlight is a scourge to the man, I'd wager. He was followed everywhere he went with a servant holding aloft an umbrella."

No one seemed to know quite how to reply. Someone coughed. Elise's first thought had been, *She's not wrong*.

Killian cleared his throat. "I'm doubtful the king considers me a 'great friend,' Bartholomew. I am a reliable *resource*. When he has . . . special requests, he calls upon me. I'm not included in palace dinners like the princess."

"But you are great friends with the *royal dukes*," amended Bartholomew.

"I am friendliest with His Grace, the Duke of Cumberland, although I knew him simply as Ernest when we were in school. He has introduced me to his brothers. We get on rather well, so long as I cater to their every whim."

"Oh, yes, *Eton* is the school that educates all the royals," reported Lady Dunlock, waving her spoon like a conductor. "And it is the school that educated your papa, Bartholomew, and of course your uncle Killian. In a year or two, you will also go to Eton College, just like *all* the other sons of *all* the other gentlemen in the land. But only a handful of boys will have already *inherited* at so young an age like you, Bart. You'll go in as an earl—and won't that be a fine distinction? Perhaps you will meet a member of the royal family when you are a student."

To this, the boy had no answer—his first real silence. Elise eyed him. He'd become transfixed by the path of a potato on the end of his fork as he slid it around his plate.

Elise looked at Killian. He dabbed his mouth with a napkin and replaced it in his lap. He stretched his neck right and left, as if to relieve tension. "Let us not speak of Eton as if it's a foregone conclusion," he said. His tone was indifferent, but his posture was rigid.

"Oh, but the boy must be educated at Eton, Killian," insisted Lady Dunlock, her eyes large.

He made no reply.

"He should have no less than did his papa and yourself, Killian. No less," the countess went on. She took up her spoon and scraped aggressively at her bowl. "Mr. Pile will prepare him, never you fear. He will be ready. You will be ready, won't you, Bartholomew?"

The boy lifted his fork to examine the potato, but he did not answer.

"It needn't be decided tonight, does it?" said Killian. A tight smile.

"Perhaps it's already been decided," pressed Lady Dunlock. "I said I want my boy to have the finest education, just like the son of any other gentleman, and you said, 'Yes, we shall see it done,' and I said, 'His father went to Eton College and then Oxford,' and you said, 'Yes, we shall see—'"

"What I *said*, my lady," Killian cut in, "is that the earl shall have a fine education that prepares him to manage Paxton Dale, navigate London society, and take a seat in Parliament if he so chooses. Eton is not the only route to these or any occupation. There are other schools. Mr. Pile and I—along with you—will work together to consider all of the options until we land on what is best for the boy."

"But Eton College *is* the best," insisted Lady Dunlock, her voice a little pleading, "and Bartholomew is very clever—*very clever*—everyone says it. And his father was an earl. *He* is an earl. What other boys will be clever *and* have their titles before they've yet stepped foot in the building, I ask you?"

"I know the boy is intelligent, my lady, and I begrudge him nothing," gritted out Killian. "However, I've not yet decided that Eton is the best path for him. Your late husband had a fine experience there. *I* did not. I found it rather miserable, truth be told, and what is cleverness if you are being tortured along the way? However, this is a topic for another time."

"I was courted by a graduate of Eton College," commented one of the aunts from down the table. "He had the smallest little feet I've ever seen. But do you remember, Margaret?"

"I do not remember," said the other aunt. "How can I be expected to keep tally of your great many men? What care have I for anyone's feet?"

Elise bit back a smile. Killian signaled a footman for another glass of wine and took a long, bracing drink. Lady Dunlock nibbled a hank of bread in tiny, aggressive bites, like a starving rabbit. The young earl leaned over the arm of his chair to feed potatoes to the dogs from the end of his fork.

"Lord Dunlock?" Elise asked, endeavoring to change the subject. "You asked if I met your uncle at a dinner in the palace. In fact, he was introduced to me by His Grace, Edward, Duke of Kent, at a royal ball."

"But Edward is fourth son of the king!" said the boy, popping up.

"Yes, that's right," said Elise.

Now the boy frowned. "But was there dancing at the ball?"

"In fact, we did dance," she said. "The royal duke put him up to it, I'm afraid, but your uncle is a rather fine dancer."

"Perhaps not so very fine," said Killian, "if you were led to believe that Edward *made me* do it."

Elise glanced at him, raising an eyebrow. Of course that had been precisely what'd happened.

"I know Uncle Killian better than I know anyone," declared the boy, "and I can guess that it was the dancing that was forced upon him, not you, Your Highness. He and I are not the dancing sort we are riders and shooters and men of science and letters. And also if he did not like going away to that horrid school then I won't either." He glared at his mother.

Lady Dunlock gasped. "Killian, you must fix this. He shall have the same as his father. No less. What have you said to him?"

"What I've said," Killian intoned, "is that we shall leave the topic for tonight."

Elise sipped the last of her wine. As deflections went, hers had failed miserably. The boy had draped himself over the arm of his chair to whisper to his dogs.

Lady Dunlock had begun to breathe very hard and

very fast, as if she intended to blow out every candle at the table.

The Piles, Elise noted, were vigorously engaged in cutting their lamb chops. They had the traumatized looks of innocent bystanders trapped in a shop as it was ransacked by robbers.

Meanwhile, Killian simply looked weary. What torture, she wondered, had he experienced at Eton College? She'd always thought of him as respected in St. James's Palace, but then, she'd not really known him. In hindsight, perhaps members of the royal court did not show him respect so much as regard him with *respectful caution*.

One thing was certain: the puzzle pieces of his personality had grown too numerous to count. Elise wished to have hours and hours to pore over them and find all the little corners where traits, such as Would-Be Bitter Second Son, snapped together with Protective Uncle.

But now an awkward silence had descended over the table. Lady Dunlock was shaking her head back and forth, as if she was building arguments in her head, and each point was more convincing than the next.

Elise cleared her throat, determined to make a new topic stick. "But is dancing one of the subjects you study with Mr. Pile, Lord Dunlock?"

"No there is no time for dancing I'm afraid," said the boy, not looking up from his dogs.

Mrs. Pile must've felt safe to wade into this line of questioning. She said, "But can you tell the princess what subjects you've read this summer, my lord?"

The boy ignored her, and the nanny tapped a firm finger on the table in the direction of the boy's head.

"We do mathematics," the earl recited blandly to the dogs, "writing history geography natural science Latin, French—"

"Vraiment," Elise asked, "vous étudiez le français?"
Really, but you've studied French?

And now the boy sat upright so quickly his dogs barked. He stared at her. He craned down the table to look at Mr. Pile. The man nodded his head with encouragement.

"Oui, j'étudie le français," he answered in perfect French, "et je peux vous dire que c'est préférable a d'autres choses inutiles comme la danse (par exemple)." *Yes, I have done, and I don't mind saying that I far prefer it to learning something pointless like dancing.*

"Votre prononciation est impeccable," exclaimed Elise, grinning back and forth between his mother and uncle. "Et vous parlez parfaitement. Je suis vraiment impressionnée, monsieur le conte*!" Oh, but listen to you! How perfect your accent is. And how fluent you are. I'm ever so impressed, my lord!*

The boy continued in flawless French, "But I only practice with Mr. and Mrs. Pile and *they* only speak of the most boring topics such as naming the parts of a house or the items in a wardrobe."

The boy layered a funny voice on top of the French words. "I put on my shoes. I wear boots. Where are my boots? They are in the wardrobe. Where is my umbrella? It is beside the door."

"But this is how you learn vocabulary," laughed Elise, still speaking French. "That is how everyone learns. That is how I learned English."

"But I can understand everything you are saying," the boy marveled in French. "I know exactly what you are saying can you believe it Mr. Pile it has worked everything you have taught me has worked!"

"I can indeed, my lord," said Mr. Pile, speaking also in French. "It is fortunate you have a French guest with whom you may practice."

"But have we switched to *Portuguese*?" asked one of the aunts, squinting down the table.

"It's French, madam," said Mrs. Pile, herself a little breathless, clearly proud of the work she and her husband had done with the young earl.

"*It is French*," repeated Lady Dunlock in a hushed whisper. Carefully, the boy's mother placed her knife and fork beside her plate. She brought the fingertips of one hand to her mouth, as if gently holding it closed. She stared at her son, tears filling her eyes.

"My boy is speaking beautiful French like a proper Frenchman," she said, her voice cracking. "Look at you, Bart. *Look at you.*"

"Well done, Bart," said Killian, raising his glass. "You may have just weaseled your way out of dancing lessons." He saluted Mr. Pile and gave Elise a quick wink.

Elise paused her fork halfway to her mouth. The wink hit her like a kiss.

"Your French is easily superior to mine, Bartholomew," Killian was telling the boy. "I shall have you translate when I'm next compelled to argue with the princess in a debate."

"Speaking to a French princess in her own tongue," Lady Dunlock marveled. "Ask her something else, Bartholomew. If you don't like talking about rain boots and umbrellas, ask her something different. Ask her anything."

"Of course, we would never wish to use our language skills as a parlor trick," Killian warned gently.

"Princesse?" began the earl, warming to his mother's challenge. His French really was flawless. "Depuis combien de temps habitez-vous en Angleterre au lieu de la France?" *How long have you lived in England instead of France?*

For the benefit of the table, Elise answered in English. "I came to England ten years ago, my lord. In 1793. When I was fifteen."

"But did you wait to learn English until after you arrived?" the boy wanted to know.

"Yes, I suppose you could say that," she said carefully.

"Because I'm meant to learn several languages before I ever travel outside of England so that . . . so that . . ." He frowned and looked at Mr. Pile. "Why must I learn all the languages?"

"Well, my lord," said Mr. Pile, "learning languages can make visiting travelers feel welcome in your home, as your lovely French has done tonight. But also, it allows you to read books from around the world in their original translations. And it prepares you to communicate when you travel. Perhaps you'll spend many years in a foreign land like Princess Elise and have time to study the language, but you may also visit other countries for only a fortnight and have only days to learn. How much better off you'll be if you already speak as the natives do. Travel will suit you, my lord. This has been very obvious to us."

The young earl considered this. He turned back to Elise. "When you came to England ten years ago did you intend to remain long enough to learn the language, Princess?"

Across the table, Mr. Pile gripped his goblet tightly enough to crack. Mrs. Pile leaned to whisper to the boy.

"Politeness may prevent us," Killian told the earl, "from asking after the princess's intent when she came to England. Remember there is a difference between making conversation and—"

"I do not mind discussing my move to England," Elise cut in.

This was true, but Elise took a deep breath, thinking of how to answer. Of all the dark corners of loneliness in St. James's Palace, one of the most painful was the silence surrounding her escape from France. The *whys* and *hows* of her exile felt eerily taboo, and people simply kept back.

"But will the girl *relocate* to Portugal?" asked one of the aunts. "Her language skills are quite good. She is ready, I trow."

"I'll never see that coral-colored dress again if she goes." The other aunt sighed.

"What dress?"

"The one she's wearing. She's taken it from my closet and turned up to dinner with it on. It will go directly in her trunks and then off to Portugal, mark my words."

"That's not your dress," scolded her sister. "Why would a princess be wearing a dress that belongs to you?"

"You know royals," whispered the wiry aunt loudly, "accustomed to having everything like a gift. They've come to expect it. I am happy for her to have it, honestly, but I cannot say it will be fashionable in Portugal. Not everyone is suited to coral."

Killian cleared his throat. "More bread, Aunts?" He signaled to a footman.

Elise swallowed her amusement and turned to the boy. "When I came here from Paris, I spoke very little English, my lord. Far less than your own beautiful French. My brother had been taught English, but I had not. I came to England to escape the French Revolution, and I've stayed these great many years because I am in *exile* from my home country. Do you know what that means?"

"Oh yes I know what it means but do you mean you were fleeing the guillotine?" asked the boy excitedly.

"Yes. That is what I was fleeing."

"And if you'd remained in France, would *your* head have been chop—"

Mrs. Pile made a sound of distress and clamped a hand across the boy's mouth. In the same moment, Mr. Pile shoved from his chair, a look of horror on his face.

Killian said, "Bartholomew, enough!"

"Buth sche thaid vi coulth asch—" the boy exclaimed from behind his nanny's hand.

"Pray forgive the boy, Highness," gasped Mrs. Pile, looking in horror at Elise. "He's not been exposed to gues—"

"Do as you're told, Bartholomew," recited his mother, less distressed than the others. She was occupied by the careful buttering of a piece of bread.

"Please, everyone," said Elise calmly, "the earl has committed no offense. I am not bothered by the topic of my exile or of the revolution. Truly. I . . . I believe it would do me good to speak of it. It would make it feel less . . . forgotten."

"Oh, we have not forgotten it, Princess," said the earl, pulling his mouth free. "Of course I was not yet born but I have learned about it from Mr. Pile and everyone else remembers it well except for possibly the aunts but they cannot accurately remember anything so . . ."

Mrs. Pile put a tired elbow on the table and then slowly dropped her face into her hand. She tipped her head to glance sideways at her husband. He slid defeatedly into the chair.

Elise glanced at Killian. His eyes were closed in what looked like mortification. He opened them in time to catch her gaze. Speaking softly—mouthing the words—he said, "*You wanted this.*"

She gave a small smile, hoping to reassure him, and turned back to the boy.

"Shall I tell the story of my escape from the revolt in France?" she asked. "Would you like to hear it?"

"*Oh, yes,*" enthused Lady Dunlock, answering before the boy. "We should very much like to hear it."

"Yes!" concurred the earl, waving his spoon in the air.

CHAPTER SEVENTEEN

*O*H, TO RETURN to the topic of Eton College, Killian thought. Or to watch Bartholomew feed the dogs from his plate. Perhaps the aunts could again discuss the stolen dress.

Any of it would be better, surely, than opening his mind—and subsequently his heart—to the story of how Princess Elise fled France.

Killian wasn't a coward about hearing difficult histories—he wasn't even unfeeling. What he was . . .

. . . was *unable to help*.

Because this story, which was certain to be full of heartbreak and terror and courage, was perhaps worst of all *unfinished*.

It would contain unsolved mysteries and locks with no key and a yawning need for *solutions*.

In a perfect world, Killian, being a fixer, could solve it for her. But Killian wasn't being paid to solve the problem of Princess Elise for her own good. He was being paid to solve it for someone else. And the more he learned about her, the more he knew the two solutions would not align.

If he could not fix it for her, it would be very difficult for him to hear it described.

Looking around the table at rapt expressions and meals forgotten, he appeared to be the only person to have this reticence.

"I cannot say if I would've been executed if I remained," the princess was telling Bartholomew. "My uncle was king when the revolution began—"

"King Louis XVI!" recited Bartholomew. "Mr. Pile and I spent weeks on the French Revolution didn't we Mr. Pile?"

Killian glanced at the tutor. He was staring at his plate as if he might pick it up and shatter it over the top of his head.

"That is correct," Princess Elise was telling the boy. "My uncle was King Louis XVI. You'll know from your studies that he and his queen, Marie Antoinette, were executed. I was fourteen years old when the first protests broke out. The two sons of the king, my cousins, went on to die in prison, sadly. Their sister, however, has survived. She is living on the Continent, I believe, also in exile. After the king, more and more members of the French royal family were executed, including my own father—"

"Your father!" exclaimed Bartholomew, distressed. "I'm so sorry princess but please take heart Mr. Pile has told me the way the guillotine operates and it is very qui—"

Killian shoved from his chair, but Mrs. Pile had already clamped her hand over the boy's mouth.

"Bloody hell, Bartholomew!" exclaimed Killian. "You mustn't speak of personal circumstances with such frank and vivid detail. Think of what the princess has suffered. I'm impressed with your knowledge of world events, truly, but let us remember that these are not merely 'events' to the princess; they are experiences she's actually been forced to endure."

"The boy cannot help that he is curious and insightful and remembers everything he reads," insisted Lady Dunlock.

"That is not the point," said Killian tiredly.

He looked at Bartholomew. "A large part of being a gentleman is compassion, my lord. You must be mindful of the impact of the things you say. Not every idea in your head needs to be expressed—especially to guests at dinner. Some things, you entertain *merely* as *thoughts*, and you never say them out loud. Please apologize at once."

"What's happened?" asked Aunt Millicent. "But is the boy choking?"

"No," reported Aunt Margaret, "he's refused to eat his carrots. *Leave him be*, Killian. The carrots may not suit him—they certainly did not suit me. It's the sauce."

"I'm sorry Uncle!" the boy said, turning his face away. He looked legitimately distressed.

"*Not* to *me*," ground out Killian. "Apologize to the princess."

"I meant no harm Princess!" the boy said, tears in his voice. "It's true I can be thoughtless at times my brain speeds so quickly along that I don't have time to decide what to say in words and what to think in thoughts I'm so sorry that your father had his head chopped. My father died too and so I also have no father and it is very sad even though I did not know him well and Uncle Killian is far better than any father. Sometimes it is better to have an uncle than a father but of course both your uncle *and* your father were killed so you have—"

"Bart!" snapped Killian. "This would be one of the instances where you think your statement rather than say it."

"Mr. Crewes, please," implored the princess, "do not scold the boy. There is no harm done. I invited this topic, and the earl's questions are genuine and without malice. You'll remember I said that meals at St. James's Palace were long and boring—well, no one may claim this of dinner at Paxton Dale, and good for you."

"You are beyond gracious, Highness," he mumbled.

"Perhaps," she said. "Or perhaps I'm simply grateful for the chance to talk about myself. I am largely ignored in St. James's, one of many, many princesses. When one is the only princess in the room, she should expect probing questions. The earl is clearly knowledgeable of world events—and good for you, my lord. Would you like me to tell you the rest?"

"Do not feel compelled," intoned Killian in the same moment that Bartholomew and Lady Dunlock said, "Yes!"

The princess smiled to herself. "Right. Well, where was I?"

"Everyone you knew had been beheaded or was in prison!" provided Bartholomew.

The princess nodded, taking a sip of her wine. Killian drained the last of his and signaled for another glass. When the footman leaned in, Killian took the bottle.

"My parents, brother, sister, and I had been imprisoned for many weeks before my father stood trial."

"You were a princess locked in a tower," surmised Pearl, wistfully.

"Sadly, no," said the princess. "We were held in several prisons, and all of them were dismal. Very little food, nowhere to wash, nothing to read or do but share a Bible, but no lamp by which to read it. We slept on the bare floor. We had almost no news of what had become of other members of the royal family. Meanwhile, crowds outside the prison chanted for our blood."

She took a small bite of lamb, glancing around the table. She paused at the sight of the collected expressions and replaced her fork. "Forgive me," she said slowly. "This is not suitable dinner conversation. I would not spoil the meal with talk of—"

"Do not stop on our account, please," implored Pearl spiritedly.

Killian shot her a look, and the countess added, "Unless it's too painful for you, Highness."

The princess gave Pearl a small smile. "Very well," she said. "To speed things along, I'll just say that my father was sentenced and tried in a mockery of justice, and then led away to be executed. All of this happened in one day, after weeks of waiting and uncertainty. When the execution was over, my mother and my siblings and I were hustled from the Temple Prison, in one part of Paris, to the Conciergerie, in another. As part of this transfer, monarchist sympathizers managed to slip in among the guards. They'd been lying in wait for just such a moment to . . . well, to *rescue* us. We'd been warned by our father that this might happen; we were told the opportunity for escape would come when we least expected it.

"They were, unfortunately, too late to save my father, but they came for the rest of us, employing decoys and distractions to extract us, one by one. My brother was said to have been taken by a soldier, I was taken by a nun, and my sister, then only a toddler . . ." and here the princess's voice broke, and she paused.

"*Highness*," whispered Killian. "Please. You'll make yourself—"

"No," said the princess stoically. "I would say it. My sister Danielle was but a baby, and because of this, I'm uncertain of who took her or where. My mother fled with a servant and rendezvoused with a . . . friend."

"But did you have time to say goodbye to your brother and sister?" asked Bartholomew.

The question seemed to surprise her, and she turned her head, staring directly at the boy.

He's finally done it, Killian thought. *He's finally offended her.*

"In fact, I was not given time to say goodbye to my brother and sister," she said quietly, her voice quivering again. "Thank you for asking, my lord. I don't believe anyone has asked me that before, not even the aunt and uncle who harbored me when I reached England. Not saying goodbye, standing beside them in one moment and gone the next, was . . . the most agonizing part of fleeing France."

It was a thoughtful question, Killian realized, especially as the boy himself had no brother or sister. He studied her, now staring into her empty plate. How . . . *haunted* she was.

Why does she put herself through the misery of recounting this? For what?

He'd built a robust business out of silencing, and whitewashing, and brushing wretched, regrettable things under the proverbial rug. A cornerstone of solving of problems, great and small, was to *say less*. Even better— *feel* less. *Bury* what pained you. And yet—

And yet perhaps she didn't need a solution in this moment so much as she simply needed to say the words.

"Not saying goodbye was worse than *prison*?" confirmed Bartholomew.

"Oh, yes," she said quietly. "Far worse. We were all together in person, you see. If you can think of a time, my lord, when you found yourself suddenly, utterly alone, with no clear way to return to your family, and no notion of what became of them—*that* is what it was like."

"I don't think I have ever been alone Highness because I have always had Mama even when my father died she and I were together and of course the servants and then we went to Uncle and he *rescued us* and then Mr. and Mrs. Pile came and there were more servants and of course the dogs. And the aunts." He frowned down the table.

"If you don't like the carrots," said Aunt Millicent, "do not eat them, my boy. No one ever perished for lack of a carrot."

"You are very fortunate, indeed, my lord," said the princess. "In addition to constant worry about my brother and sister, both of whom were much younger than me, I felt hopeless for my own self. My exile has felt like . . . homesickness, but more painfully acute. It has felt like grief with fear mixed in."

"I'm so sorry Princess," said Bartholomew. To his credit, he sounded and looked as if he meant it.

"Thank you, my lord."

"But after you left your family, were you forced to fight the angry mob in hand-to-hand combat to escape Paris?"

Mr. Pile choked on his wine. Killian closed his eyes. How fleeting Bart's one moment of appropriate discourse had been.

Princess Elise smothered a laugh. "In fact, I did no fighting as part of my escape. Mostly it involved dressing as a novice nun or a peasant and endeavoring to blend in. Hiding—lots of hiding. We hid in church catacombs and stable lofts and the cargo hold of a ship. There was some running, but we did not dash about so much as . . . scurry in the dark like mice. In all honestly, I don't remember much of it. I'd just witnessed my father's execution, you see . . ."

She trailed off, her voice failing her again.

"Witnessed?" asked Bartholomew. "But do you mean that when your father had his head cut off, you *saw* it?"

"I did, in fact," Princess Elise said quietly, very quietly.

"But were you standing right there, waiting in line for your own—"

"Bartholomew!" Killian said, although he wondered why he bothered.

She shook her head. "I could see a sliver of the gallows from the window of the room in which we were being held," the princess said. "My mother and governess begged me to come away, but I thought, if he could bear to *experience* it, I could bear to *watch* it. It felt like solidarity and courage, but in hindsight, it was perhaps not prudent. No child should be subjected to the sight of this. It's not something I should describe . . . here . . . in such pleasant company . . . over such a beautiful meal. Forgive me." She glanced at Killian.

"We are at your service, Highness," Killian said softly.

"You have made me feel so very safe," she said. "Part of the safety is the years gone by, and part is the very great welcome I've been shown at Paxton Dale, and this lovely meal, and your curious concern. I . . . I ceased speaking for many years after I entered exile in England."

"Ceased speaking?" asked Bartholomew.

"Impossible for you to comprehend," drawled Killian.

The princess chuckled sadly. "Yes. It was a sort of muteness. In those days, very little time had passed, and I had no feeling of safety. As I said, it feels . . . healthful to talk about it. Here and now. For better or for worse."

There was silence around the table; even Bartholomew was quietly pensive.

Killian, in contrast, was quietly outraged. Was it possible that no more care had been given to this princess than to murder her father before her eyes, rip her from her siblings, and then stash her in England to be largely ignored? And when, finally, she'd begun to emerge from the trauma of it all and search for her family, the response had been to dispatch him to "seduce her"? What of her mother, he wondered? What of any of the seemingly hundreds of advisors and equerries and diplomats in St. James's Palace who might provide useful counsel to her? Instead, they'd saddled her with Killian. Killian, who had—on more than one occasion—been asked to escort a demented royal cousin from a ballroom because he unbuttoned the fall of his trousers in front of the ladies. Killian, who crawled through parked carriages at a boxing match until he found where a royal duke had left his opium pipe.

They'd assigned her to him?

She deserved so much more. And not because she was a beautiful, royal French princess, and not because she'd been undeniably gracious to his bizarre relatives, because she was an innocent human woman who deserved more than a "fix."

And perhaps he was part of the problem. Perhaps the work he did for the royal family made unpleasant situations disappear for the palace, but compounded misery for everyone else. Certainly that would be the result if Killian followed their assignment to the letter.

He would no sooner seduce this woman than he would beat her over the head, he thought. She needed diplomats and advisors, not Killian Crewes, Royal Fixer.

"But I can see that we have put everyone off their dinners," the princess was saying. "All this talk of executions and fleeing countries and muteness. Perhaps we should accept the wise counsel given us, Lord Bartholomew, and change the subject? But do you have one, final question you'd like to ask before we speak of something more palatable?"

"Think carefully, Bart," warned Killian, "before you accept this invitation. Consider the various warnings and admonishments that have already been issued. Look at poor Mr. Pile. He has burned a hole in his plate, staring at it with such mortified dread, and I, for one, feel his pain. Let's go out on a high note, shall we?"

"Very well uncle I know just what I shall ask Her Serene Highness Princess Elise and that is what are your intentions toward my uncle?"

CHAPTER EIGHTEEN

ELISE SAT ON the foot of the bed in the guest room and stared out the window at the starless night. The rain that had threatened all day never came.

A *metaphorical* storm, however, had drenched the dining room tonight. One moment they'd been praising the young earl for his proficiency with French, and the next Elise was revealing the most painful moments of her life.

Elise couldn't remember the last time she'd talked so much—and not simply spoken words, but *described things*. True things. Terrifying things. Her own experiences and their lingering effects.

All of the talking had churned up a maelstrom of *feelings*—heartache and desperation and loneliness—and Elise had left the dinner with a torrent inside her.

Lady Dunlock and the aunts had invited her to repair to the sitting room for warm sipping chocolate, but Elise had declined. She'd drifted to her room instead, shivering and wrung out. A maid had been waiting to attend her, and she allowed the girl only to unpin her from the borrowed gown and snuff the lamps.

When the girl had gone, Elise shrugged into a borrowed night rail and sat on the end of her bed, allowing the memories to drip from her like rain.

The rear of the manor house boasted a second garden,

as beautiful as the front. Nightfall had reduced it to a dark green, shadowy void. Even darker was what lay *beyond*: a deep, dense forest. Most English stately homes were situated in the center of vast parkland, but Killian said that Paxton Dale had once been a royal hunting lodge; as such, it was nestled on the edge of an ancient wood. The forest, no doubt, teemed with deer and boar, pheasant and fox. Doubtless it contained people, too.

Perhaps her brother lived in such a wood. Perhaps he lived in *this* wood. He could, Elise knew, be anywhere in the world. He could be dead. The Road to Land's End was the only logical place to begin searching, but there were no guarantees. She must remember this as she searched for him. No guarantees.

And also no regrets. Wasn't that what Killian had told her when he ended their very strange conversation about the potential of a kiss? But what did that mean?

I should have tried harder to find Gabriel, she told herself. *I should've taken action sooner.*

If nothing else, she didn't regret tonight—not her refusal to return to Hampton, not agreeing to pass the night here, not her revelations at the dinner. Killian's family were strangers, but they were well-meaning strangers with no hidden aspirations.

And wasn't Killian's nephew a delightful surprise? Sweet and smart and without guile. Even so, most men would've resented all Killian had lost to the boy. But Killian had freely given the title and the land and the house to the nephew he'd only just met.

Lightning pulsed beneath the clouds, and Elise allowed her eyes to blur, taking in the spectacle.

How deep is the forest? she wondered, placing a hand on the cool pane.

Would she have learned that Killian was in possession of this lovely family if she'd not come here?

No regrets.

Almost as shocking as Killian's history had been the
young earl's question about her "intentions" toward his
uncle. He'd not meant to embarrass or trap her—she was
certain of this—he was protective of Killian. The boy
knew just enough about the world to understand there
might be some risk in squiring about an unattached
woman.

Killian had rescued the moment by choking on his
wine and signaling for pudding. Meanwhile, Elise's
cheeks had burned. If the young earl had discerned
some . . . attachment, it was impossible the adults hadn't
also; certainly her reaction had not gone unnoticed.

So be it, she now thought. She'd already admitted to
him that she wanted a kiss. Their attraction was clear,
even to a boy.

But is Killian attracted to me? she wondered. He
indulged her requests and considered her demands. He
would not kiss her but he'd explored her body in the carriage as if he meant to make love to her. He'd brought her
here, and since they'd arrived, the two of them had communicated through a series of looks and gestures that felt
like their own private language. Little glances that said,
Can you believe it? Or, *How funny,* or, *You predicted
this.* Elise's experience with intimacy was very stunted,
indeed, but surely this must be among the sweetest and
most exclusive forms.

Attracted or not, his reaction to her stories at dinner
could not be overlooked. While the others had regarded
her like a fascinating storyteller, Killian had seemed truly
shaken. His expression had gone from deep sympathy, to
horror, to outrage.

Without really thinking about it, Elise's fingers found the lock on the window. She tested it, pressing hard, and the tiny latch slid free.

It's unlocked, she realized. Every window at St. James's Palace was locked. Elise had encountered so many locks in the last ten years, she'd almost forgotten what to do in their absence.

She tested the hinges at the edge of the windowpane, pressing against the glass. The window slid open, exposing her to a rush of humid night air. The smell of the forest, loamy and verdant, hit her like a leafy frond.

The garden through the open window looked like a large, green chessboard of topiaries and benches. The forest beyond it, however, was a high, black wall hemming in the manicured grounds. When the wind blew, the treetops bent and swayed in a slow, undulating ripple. A heartbeat later, she was hit by the same gust; it brought the faint smell of every fresh and decaying thing it had touched as it swept through the forest. Had this same wind touched Gabriel? Had it touched Dani?

She extended her hand out the window, feeling the draft rush through her fingers. She sat on the sill and leaned, allowing the wind to catch the open V at her neckline and puff out her night rail like a sail. The fabric was starkly white against the night, and Elise watched it dance into a cottony froth. If it functioned as a sail, she wondered, would it carry her away? Where would she go, if she were to be carried away by the wind? *To Gabriel, wherever he is. To Dani.*

The wind blew again, harder his time, pulling her hair, tugging at her rail, *beckoning her.*

I could jump down from here, she thought.

I could leap to the terrace, and run down the steps, and dance about the garden. I could stomp in the soft grass and balance on the edge of the reflecting pond.

I'm not at St. James's Palace. I'm at Paxton Dale. I can talk about my family, and remember my father's death, and crawl out of windows, and feel the wind.

She was off the window sill in the next moment, her bare feet hitting the flagstones of the terrace with a slap. There was a cascade of wide steps, and she took them two at the time. The wind gusted again, and she turned into it, sprinting now, allowing the exertion to take her breath away.

She was a white streak against a dark night, legs pumping, breath heaving, night rail flapping out behind her. She darted past the reflecting pond, around the short hedge and then the tall hedge. She came to a stop only when the soft, manicured lawn of the garden met the fluffy ferns and wiry undergrowth of the forest.

Panting from exertion, pushing wild hair from her face, she looked up. Thick trees stretched skyward, their dark canopies moving in the wind.

"Gabriel?" Elise whispered harshly, peering between the trunks of the trees.

She heard only rustling underbrush and the patter of intermittent rain.

She called his name again, louder this time. "Gabriel!"

There was a gap between two trees where the shrubs and ferns had been worn low. A path, she realized. Another unlocked door.

Elise crossed to the gap and squinted into the dark tunnel of woodland. A pulse of lightning cracked open the sky with a flash of light. She could see ten yards. The path was wide and well-worn. Trees lined each side and bent above it in a leafy arc.

Carefully, Elise extended one pale, bare foot, testing the roughness of the ground. The path was cool and sandy, littered with sticks and fallen leaves. She matched the second foot to the first. And now she stood just inside the forest, and no one stopped her. And she wasn't afraid.

The wind gusted again, pressing at her back, and Elise was off, sprinting down the path.

Where she was going, she couldn't say. Why she fled, she also didn't know. She gave no thought to her bare feet on the forest path or the first heavy raindrops that dripped through the trees. She knew only that she'd been restricted for so very long, and silenced, and she wanted to run and shout and fight for the opportunity to live a real life.

"Gabriel!" she shouted, screaming her brother's name between breaths. *"Gabriel! Dani!"*

The path—already so dark—grew progressively darker; she hadn't realized there were so many layers to night. Her eyes struggled to adjust, distinguishing path from undergrowth, tree from air. Lightning popped again, turning the sky momentarily silver. The light wrecked her vision, but not before she saw an end ahead: the forest tunnel emptying into a void.

Elise sprinted toward it, chased by the wind, mindless to everything but the sound of her brother's and sister's names ringing in her ears.

KILLIAN HAD JUST shrugged from his waistcoat and tugged his cravat free when he looked out the window of the dower cottage to see a ripple of white cotton streak past the reflecting pool.

What the devil? He leaned toward the glass.

No, not a ripple—it was a billowing white garment streaming from the running body of . . .

He leaned closer to the window.

Well, it couldn't be Pearl; she was not, by nature, a runner.

A maid? This was not the attire of a maid; it was a voluminous white night rail from the last centu—

Killian's heart stopped.

He thew open the window and squinted into the wind, one hand on the sill, a leg halfway out.

"Gabriel!"

The name of Princess Elise's brother drifted to him on the wind. He paused, making certain of what he'd heard.

"Gabriel!" There it was again, anguished and tearful.

Princess Elise was running through the garden, shouting her brother's name. She was half-dressed, and the storm that had threatened all day was finally coming to a head.

But what is she doing? Killian thought, bolting after her. He cleared the steps in one jump and vaulted over the low hedge. *Why is she shouting her brother's name? Another fit of panic? Does she believe she's seen Gabriel d'Orleans?*

"Princess!" he shouted, but his voice was carried away by the wind.

He turned the corner of the large hedge and saw nothing.

But where had she . . . ?

He ran to the other side of the hedge. Nothing.

Would she run into the forest? The woodlands were dark and wild and a little daunting, even in the light of day. Surely she wouldn't—

He ran to the trail that snaked into the woods. It was a pathway he'd taken thousands of times as a boy.

"Princess!" he bellowed down the path.

Silence.

He checked behind him, making sure he'd not missed her in the garden. There was nothing; the grounds were deserted. He was sure of it.

Swearing, he bolted down the path. "Princess!" he shouted again, louder this time. He ran on memory, his vision obscured by the dark night. The path cut right, veering toward the meadow, and he almost missed it. "Elise!"

"*Gabriel*!" came the reply. "*Dani!*"

Thank God, Killian thought. He was closing in. He increased his speed, careening around another curve, swatting away low-hanging limbs.

When at last the wooded path spit him out into the wide meadow, he saw her. A flash of lightning illuminated a lone figure in the center of the meadow, on her knees, head bent. Her billowy night rail glowed ghostly white, bunched around her in the tall grass. Her shoulders shook from crying.

Oh, God, she's hurt, thought Killian. Every nerve ending, already jangling, now exploded with fear. He scrambled to her.

"Princess?" he breathed, dropping to his knees and sliding the last two feet. "What's happened? What's wrong?"

She looked at him, sucking in a breath. "Killian."

Well, she knew him, at least. She wasn't entirely out of her head. "I'm here. What's happened? Are you . . . ?"

"I'll never find him," she declared, speaking through tears. "How will I ever, *ever* find him? In the whole wide expanse of the world? He could be anywhere. My mother will not help me. The British royal family would sooner have me locked away than help me. It's hopeless. Look around," she said on a sob, extending her hands to the trees. "How can I expect to find one man—a man I've not seen since he was a boy—in all of England? And our sister? Even if I found her, she will not remember. I will be a stranger to her."

"*Princess*," he said gently. Remarkably, he felt tears in his own throat.

"If only I could know what became of them," she insisted. "Even if we are never reunited, if I could simply know that they are well, and cared for, and loved." Her voice broke on the word *loved*, and she dissolved into tears, bracing her palms flat against the wet grass.

"Highness, no," Killian said gently. "No, you mustn't give up. Tonight was . . . a trial—I'll never forgive myself for allowing it to unfold as it did—but you mustn't allow yourself to feel overwhelmed. They are memories—nothing more. They cannot—"

"I'm not," she cried, "*overwhelmed* by memories." She slapped the ground with her hands. "The memories, as wretched as they are, are all that I have. I cherish them. And you could not have stopped me from talking about my family at dinner." She sucked in a sawing, tear-choked breath. "I will never *not* talk of them. I'm finished *not* talking of them."

"Right, yes, good. Forgive me. You will talk. And—if it serves you—you'll dash about in the garden in the night. But the *rain*, Highness." He looked at the sky. "This forest is not the saf—"

"I'm overwhelmed by the thought of never seeing them again," she stated, her tears abating. "I'm furious that *no one* will help me. It's maddening, in a way. Yes, we can all acknowledge it—I've run mad. At least for tonight. I became a little undone by the tiny window of freedom afforded by a night outside the palace."

"Right," said Killian cautiously, watching her, "we're all permitted a bit of madness from time to time, aren't we? Certainly the occupants of this house have inspired me to run mad on more than one occasion."

She chuckled, as he'd hoped she would, but she also slapped both hands against the ground again—the gesture of a woman whose patience was at an end.

It was in this moment that he became aware of the rain. Intermittent drops had given way to a steady drizzle.

"Highness," he continued gently, "I absolutely support this rebellious tour of freedom; however, I'm worried for your safety. Will you let me return you?"

She didn't answer him. She didn't even look at him. She was breathing deeply in and out, in and out, staring at the grass.

He tried again. "The rain for which we waited all day is finally here. We changed our plans to avoid it, and now we'll be caught in a downpour just the same. That says nothing of the lightning."

"I don't care about the rain," she said quietly.

"Perhaps you don't, but we cannot sit in an open field during a lightning storm, Highness. It's not safe. Come. Let us make our way back before the pathway runs with mud."

Haltingly . . . bracing himself before he did it . . . he reached for her, hooking a hand around her waist. The night rail was voluminous, and his hand sank through folds of cotton before it connected with her small, taut body. He gave a little tug.

"Princess?"

"You don't understand," she declared, sitting up. She sat on her heels. Lightning flashed again, and he could see her face, splotchy and streaked with tears.

"Elise," he breathed softly, his heart breaking at the sight of her anguish. "Tell me. Tell me what I don't understand."

"It's hopeless to search for my brother and sister. I'm mad to believe I'll find them. I'll *never* find them."

"No. No. It's too soon to make this declaration. You've only visited one town—*one*. You've been at this for less than a day. I can only imagine it feels overwhelming, but please don't give up the fight."

"You cannot understand," she repeated softly. "You have a family who love you, and you don't even care. You reject them." She turned to look at him, brushing wild hair from her face.

He'd not expected her to accuse him—he wasn't the one who'd fled into the woods in a storm—and he wasn't ready with a reply.

Raindrops were coming faster now—fat, cold drops that dotted his shirt and her night rail. He edged closer to her, squinting into the clouds.

"Your nephew adores you," she pointed out. "Your sister-in-law could've been terrible, but she isn't. She adheres to you. Even the Piles seem to hold you in some affection that far exceeds that of an employer. You've a fully formed family here, and I had to force you to call upon them for *one* night. Do you know what I would give to see my brother and sister for a night? Do you know?"

Thunder boomed, suggesting the answer would be very loud and very violent indeed.

"Up you go, Highness," he said. "It's not safe to remain. You may continue telling me how ungrateful I am in the garden."

He fastened his other hand around her waist and hauled her up. She didn't fight him, thank God. When she was up, he thought to shepherd her down the path. They would dart between raindrops, side by side. He needn't touch her more than necessary. He needn't—

She clung to his arm with both hands, pinning her body to his. They shuffled two steps. She was so close, he was veritably *dragging* her. This was never going to wor—

"Ouch!" she said, hopping on one foot.

"You've no shoes?" he realized, staring at the tiny foot poking from the hem of her night rail.

"I can manage," she said, limping a little.

She'd barely said the words when the clouds opened up and dropped a day's worth of pent-up rain onto Middlesex.

Killian swore and scooped her beneath the knees, sweeping her into his arms. "Up you go," he said, darting to the path.

She made a little yelping sound, more surprise than alarm, and buried her face into his chest. Killian ducked, trying to shield her from the downpour, and she wrapped her arms around him and held on.

There was less rain under the cover of the trees, but it was more difficult to see, and Killian zigzagged down the path, trying to remember the way. Despite the prodigious yards of white fabric flapping from her body, the princess weighed almost nothing. She coiled into a tight crescent against his chest. He carried her with one arm beneath her knees, a hand splayed across her hip, the other arm at her back, that hand clutching her ribs.

"I'm sorry," she said. "I've been foolish. I . . . I hope you aren't struck by lightning. Or trip on a root and fall to your death."

"Very considerate," he grunted, running faster.

When he reached the end of the path and stumbled into the garden, it occurred to him that he had no plan for what to do with her next.

"How did you leave the house?" he shouted. Rain pelted them, and he scanned the garden, cursing himself for not installing a covered gazebo.

"I crawled out the window," she shouted back.

"Why?"

"It was unlocked."

He sighed. Was it odd that this answer actually made sense? In truth, everything she'd said and done tonight made sense.

"Right. It's safe to deposit you on a high windowsill in a storm."

He looked right and left. The window to the dower cottage stood open, exactly as he'd left it. He hadn't yet locked the door, but the lanterns on the stoop were snuffed.

Thunder boomed a warning, and the sky replied with a flash of lightning. Rain drummed harder now. He felt the princess begin to tremble.

"Devil take it," Killian said quietly, and he ran through the downpour to the dower cottage, shouldered open the door, and carried her inside.

CHAPTER NINETEEN

"WHAT IS THIS?" Elise asked, looking around.

"What do you mean?" Killian called from another room.

They weren't in the manor house. He'd changed course and carried her inside what appeared to be a cottage on the edge of the garden. She'd been deposited in front of a crackling fire in a snug little parlor.

Elise edged closer to the warmth, looking around. The room was small but formally appointed, with two matched chairs in pink upholstery, an elegant sofa with deep tufts, and a low table with ornately curved legs and little clawed feet. Oil paintings in heavy frames hung on the walls and candles gleamed from the hearth.

"This place," she called. "What is this place?"

"Dower cottage," he answered, coming back in.

She'd not looked at him until now, not really, and the sight of him in firelight, with no jacket or waistcoat, hair wet, chest exposed, felt a little like meeting a much-read storybook hero come to life. He was disordered and raw and a little dangerous.

The desire she'd felt on the roadside flickered to life. Not simply desire. The urge to go to him transcended want or even need. It felt elemental.

Meanwhile, he regarded her like a hill he wasn't certain he could climb. He stood in the doorway holding a fluffy yellow blanket, eyes narrowed, mouth set. He'd pulled the blanket taut between two hands, like a rope. He appeared . . . agitated.

Of course he's agitated, she thought. She'd been careless and thoughtless. Running through the forest calling for a lost brother did nothing to instill confidence in her sanity. Everyone at Paxton Dale had treated her with welcoming generosity, and she'd repaid them by . . . tearing through the night like a maddened thing.

"Is the blanket for me?" she asked. The sight of the thick cotton reminded her that she was wet and cold. She looked down. The night rail stuck to her thighs and belly and breasts. Her skin showed pink through the translucent cotton.

"Hold still," he rasped, striding to her. He draped the blanket over her, grabbed her arm, and began to massage the fabric into her shoulder.

"Oh," she said, caught up. His movements were not gentle. His gaze, which was fixed on her arm, was not polite. She was nearly toppled by the force of his work—firm, brisk circles applied to one specific area at the time. It was sudden and unexpected and rough, but it wasn't . . . unpleasant. On the contrary, the sensation of a strong man making solid contact with her shivering body felt a little like being rubbed back to life. Elise was plunged into a warm swirl of pleasure; sensation radiated from her arms and pooled in the swells, dips, and junctions of her body. She tingled where she hadn't known she'd been numb. Everywhere, she felt alive.

Without warning, she began to list, tipping sideways.

Killian made a noise of frustration and caught her around the waist. He held her steady with one hand while he dried her with a series of rough, circular motions with the other.

She unfurled her hand, inviting him to minister to every finger. Bit by bit, he smoothed fluffy cotton into her palm. He traced it around her thumb, her index finger. Each stroke sent a strumming pleasure across Elise's skin, like the tail of a mayfly across a calm lake. Her body seemed to vibrate with ripples.

Next, he spun her around and dropped the blanket on the top of her head and embarked on a vigorous rubbing of her hair.

"You've given me quite a fright, Princess," he told her. His voice sounded muffled through the blanket. "I understand that you value freedom, but you mustn't . . . *run away.* At night. In the rain. You shouldn't venture into the forest alone."

She lifted a corner of the fabric to speak. "Yes, yes, all of this is true. I—I can't account for what came over me. I wasn't thinking, obviously. I've not known the luxury of rash behavior for so very long. I've had no liberty to, to . . . be reckless. The price I pay for sanctuary is being forgettable. But Killian? I believe this blanket's usefulness may be exhausted on my head. My hair takes half a day to dry. My body, however . . ."

Killian paused. He tugged at the blanket away. He removed his hands and took two steps back.

"Let me stoke the fire," he said.

He reached for the poker, stepped around her, and jabbed at the crumbling logs in the grate. Swirling sparks danced upward.

I want to feel that, she thought. *That hot flurry. Inside me . . .*

"Killian?" she called softly.

"This is the dower cottage," he recited, ignoring

her—*deflecting* her. "But you needn't worry that Pearl resides here."

Elise was not worrying about Pearl. "Killian?" she repeated.

"Pearl resides in the countess's suite in the main house," he went on. "*This cottage* was my mother's residence after my father died. I lived here, too, when I was home from school."

Fine, she thought, *we will discuss the floor plan of Paxton Dale*. The flurries were postponed.

"And you reside here now," Elise guessed, "when you pass the night?"

"I rarely spend the night at Paxton. But when it can't be avoided—yes, I take my old room here."

"Very pretty," she said. "And so close to the gardens."

"It's the former groundskeeper's cottage. I refurbished the property for my mother—my first renovation. If you can call it a 'property.' I think my brother savored the idea of his father's second wife living in a glorified shed."

"This is no shed." She wrapped her arms around herself for warmth.

Killian made a growling noise and stepped to her. "Turn around," he said. He took her by the shoulders and spun her to face the fire. The blanket was still in his hands and he gave it a snap. Elise jumped and he moved in, positioning himself in her periphery.

"Hands *here*," he instructed gruffly, plopping first one hand, then the other, on the mantel. Elise had barely grasped hold when he placed a boot between her legs, his thigh nudging her bottom. She sucked in a breath and squeezed the mantel.

Like before, his touch was firm, methodical; unlike before, it wasn't brisk or rough. Now he slowly, carefully, trailed the fabric down the contour of her back, painting a wide stripe of sensation. The contact was heavenly, warm and firm and purposeful. Elise arched a little, her body forming a small slope from her shoulder to the rounded point of her hips. The position pressed her bottom against his thigh, and he faltered, just a bit, shuffling to regain his footing. She felt the jut of his erection against her lower back.

The combined sensation of his touch and his shuffle, his thigh and his hardness, took her breath away—and then he made it so much better by pressing against her, his front to her back. The contact set off a swirl of need inside of her, and she let out a little whimper.

Killian responded with a stern, "*Shhh . . .*" But he pressed again.

Something about the closeness, and the silence, and the commanding sort of power he exuded made her want to laugh. She liked it—the power—but it was so very serious. Too serious? No, but it almost begged her to challenge it. Regardless, she dared not laugh. Instead, she cleared her throat and repeated, "This is no shed."

"We turned a sow's ear into a silk purse, I think." He hovered behind her, his mouth at the crown of her head. He dipped down when he spoke.

"My brother was surprised, I think," he rumbled into her ear.

"He didn't approve?" She was breathless. She could barely speak.

"I'd been forced to go to him, hat in hand, to ask for permission to see her housed elsewhere on the estate."

"They simply could not get on?"

She closed her eyes and bent a little at the waist, leaning into his hardness. She wanted to hear this, truly she did. She was . . . so very interested in his mother and brother and the gardener's shed. But her breathing had become labored. Her body tilted and swayed and thrummed.

When he'd dried her to the waist, he knelt, sliding down her body to a crouch behind her.

"Oh," she gasped softly, unprepared for the sudden change in position. She held her breath, waiting to see where he would touch her next.

The back of her right thigh was the answer. His hand came down just beneath her bottom. Her knee gave out under the force of it, and he slid his hand to her hip to steady her.

"Careful," he said.

She made a mumbled noise of pleasure, and his hand slowed.

Don't stop, Elise thought. She swallowed and rushed to continue the conversation.

"Your mother and brother . . ." she prompted.

"Peter was terrible to her," he said. "He'd always been terrible to her, but in small ways, unseen, difficult to prove. He was a conniving, manipulative little git, and my father wouldn't have stood for the abuse if he'd known.

"My mother always hoped to win Peter over, and the carrot with which she tried to lure him was silence. She never told my father about his many small aggressions. But then, when Papa died and Peter became earl, the aggravations increased. I had no authority with him—we were bitter enemies—and anyway, I was away at school."

"Your poor mother," she said.

"He wasn't *cruel*, per se—not after he became earl, at least. I would have found some way to remove her if he was cruel. He was callous and dismissive, and she learned to keep out of his way. What choice did she have? I was too young to provide for her. In the end, he gave us this 'shed' because he was miserable, too. In a show of great magnanimity, he gave us a small budget to set the place to rights—very small, an insult, actually—but I'd saved up my own money, and I did most of the repairs myself, working alongside loyal servants. She was happy here, I think."

He reached her right ankle, and Elise raised her bare foot, hoping he would touch her there, too. He buried her foot in the blanket and rubbed deeply. The pleasure of this simple gesture was so absolute, she sighed.

Killian worked in silence, drying and massaging, circling each toe with a finger. When he was finished, he set her foot gently on the floor and pivoted to the other leg, starting beneath her left hip, drying her through the wet night rail. Elise closed her eyes, squeezing the mantel, hanging her head between her arms.

"Are you well, Princess?" he said softly.

Elise shook her head. She was so much better than *well*.

He paused in his movements.

"*More* . . ." she breathed.

The pause lengthened.

Elise made a whimpering noise. Before she could stop herself, she wiggled her bottom impatiently. "Killian," she pleaded softly.

He began again, his movements rougher, more pointed. She clung to the mantel lest her limp body fall over.

He rubbed faster now, reaching her foot in half the time, sliding his hand beneath it, drying and warming and massaging it. When he was finished, he settled it gently on the floor.

"You're ticklish. I know," he said.

"I'm perishing. I will perish if you do not kiss me."

He shoved up when she said this, took her by the shoulders, and spun her. She released the mantel and pivoted with a gasp, whipping around to face him. He loomed over her, so close she could feel his breath. She looked up into his face. His expression was something like . . . pain? Frustration? Agony? He did not look like a man in control.

"I'm not made of ice, Princess," he said gruffly. "I'm only a man."

"Please," she whispered. The lone word in her mind. She slid her hands around his neck and tugged.

He swore, and yanked her against him, and descended on her mouth.

KILLIAN HAD MANAGED to explore this woman's body two times in the length of a day. Both times, he'd done it under the guise of her well-being. And both times, the exploration had devolved into a sort of worshipful eroticism that left him shaking. He was also breathless, light-headed, and a little vacant. But not entirely. In truth, his mental state could be best described as single-minded. Or ravenous. He wanted to swallow her whole. He wanted to pound into her. He wanted all of her.

It was, in no way, *not* a seduction. It was the very definition of a seduction—for him and for her—and now, in this moment, he was so far gone, he didn't care.

He was not her Glorified Nanny.

He was not her Special Friend—unless "special," meant that he would be privy to every part of her body, and possesses her, and be possessed.

None of that seemed as important now because she was in his arms and he was finally, finally kissing her. Their kiss was one of those very rare, very fraught kisses exchanged before battle or at the end of a sea voyage; it threatened consciousness and balance. They weren't coming up for air.

She hadn't resisted; she had, in fact, met him more than halfway. He'd crushed her body to him and devoured her, and she'd leaped to him with the same voraciousness.

He couldn't account for her enthusiasm; perhaps he

knew better than to question it. He knew only his own truth: that he'd wanted this since she'd lifted that damnable veil at Tattersall's and turned up her face. One look into her eyes had been like a summons, a siren song to the deepest, most primal, most undeniable part of him.

How very good it felt to *not* be denied. He thrilled at the feel of her small body settling into place against him and the taste of her on his lips, so much more delicious and satiating in life than fantasy. They clung to each other as tightly as the wet cotton of her night rail.

That night rail, he thought, another surge of lust pulsing through him. *Bloody hell.* What man could resist the sight of pink flesh and brown nipple, round bottom and curved waist—all of it perfectly defined by the clinginess of saturated fabric and ever so thinly veiled by the fibers of cotton? *No man*, and certainly not Killian. He'd wanted her when she'd been smothered by the black shroud.

But now the lack of breath threatened to topple him, and thank God she broke the kiss, dropping back her head and gasping for air.

Killian sucked in his own breath, staring down at her. He would see her like this; he would memorize her. She was limp and yielding in his arms, weak with desire.

She knew how to kiss; this realization formed slowly. There had been no timidity, no awkward fumbling; he'd pounced on her, and she'd met his mouth and tongue with a skill that thrilled him. She'd fisted the shoulder of his shirt in one hand and the hair at the back of his head with the other. She emitted beautiful little sounds of desperation and satisfaction and desire with no trace of shyness.

"You know how to kiss," he huffed, speaking between breaths.

She swallowed. "I am French."

To this, he had no reply. So she was. He came down

on her mouth again. She received him with a moan, and Killian ate up the sound. His fingers began to seek, sliding to all the delicious places he'd discovered in the carriage and by the fire. So much useful reconnaissance. What a liar he'd been, telling himself he was controlled, and resistant, and honorable. He'd told himself he was caring for her, not . . . *memorizing* her, not storing up the shape and feel of her for fantasies that would sustain him for the rest of his life. He'd never dreamed he would later return to every well-charted inch, to touch her the way he'd *wanted* to touch her, with no pretense of gentlemanly control. Control was a distant memory now; he played her like an instrument and reveled in the pleasure he felt reverberate in moans and sighs.

The night rail was like a loose cotton net, and he was too mindless to navigate the hem or the neck. He used it to his advantage instead, taking up handfuls and rubbing the limp cotton against the curve of her lower back, down across her hip, around the perfect globe of her bottom.

The princess sighed in pleasure and pressed herself against his erection. Killian's vision went black, unprepared for the beautiful burn, the sheer goodness of it, and oh, God, how it compounded his need. One thrust was not enough; he needed another; he sought repeated pleasure; more of her, *all* of her.

"Princess," he gasped, breaking the kiss.

She followed his mouth, clawing to remain close. He blinked at her, making sure he'd read the situation correctly, that she wanted this. She was impatient and grabbed the front of his shirt with both hands, planting her bare feet on his boots. She was scrambling up his body like a bear cub climbing a tree.

Killian blinked again. Coherent thought came and

went in quick flashes. He was amazed by how much she seemed to want him. He felt sanctioned, somehow, by her desire; he felt anointed by it. Her boldness emboldened him. She seemed to welcome his desire to plunder her, to please her, to take her higher. He would not bask. He would give her what she wanted.

Killian stooped a little, catching her under the bottom. He took five steps across the room until they collided with the wall. Her back hit pink wallpaper, and he pressed against her. The framed landscape beside her clattered on its nail; an umbrella propped against the door fell to the ground. The princess seemed to barely notice. She grabbed his head and pulled him down to her.

"Killian," she breathed.

He answered with a growling noise and moved from her mouth, burying his face in her hair. He found the sensitive skin just below her ear and nuzzled, breathing in the smell of skin and soap and *her*. He kissed his way to her earlobe, dragging the stubble of his beard along her jaw and chin. He teased her, coming close to her lips but not stopping. She nipped at him, trying to capture the kiss, but he kept moving, nosing to the other ear.

"Killian," she moaned.

"Yes?" he teased.

"Come. Killian. Back. Kiss. Oh, God, don't stop."

"I am kissing you," he rasped into the whorl of her perfect ear.

She made a noise of frustration and brought her legs up, locking them around his waist. He caught her by the thigh and slid his hands upward to cup her bottom, rocking her against him. He ground forward, using the wall behind her as leverage.

She tipped up her chin and cried out. He did it again, mimicking the movement that seemed, in that moment, as natural and necessary as breathing. She dove her hands into his hair, fingers sinking to his scalp. He closed his eyes against her neck and thrust against her again.

"Killian!" she whispered.

"I have you, Highness," he growled, thrusting once more.

He was just reaching for the fall of his trousers, mindlessly making good on this promise, when the smallest, sharpest thorn of hesitation pierced his lust-muddled consciousness. It was very thin but very sharp, the stinging sort of puncture that annoyed more than hurt.

Killian ignored it and thrust again. Again the princess whimpered in pleasure.

He popped one button on the fall of his trousers, and the thorn of hesitation jabbed him again.

Killian growled and pulled his face from her neck. "Princess," he gasped.

She opened her eyes and blinked up, her hazel gaze both half-lidded and desperate. "Yes?"

But he'd forgotten what he meant to ask. She seized this indecision and fell against his mouth again. He returned the kiss—a man hit by a wave and no will left to swim. He would happily drown, he thought. This kiss felt oddly like everything he wanted but also not enough.

"Princess," he said again, huffing air in and out.

"Will you call me Elise?" she whispered, kissing his neck.

"No," he said, closing his eyes against the sweet pleasure of her small, wet lips on his throat. Why did he refuse her? He couldn't remember. Habit? His instinct to be contrary? Self-preservation?

He squeezed his eyes shut, fighting for clarity. He

should do something. He should say something. They were flinging themselves, willingly, over a cliff. Did it matter? Did anything matter but this?

Should he apologize? Should he make certain she was in her right mind? Should he—

"Are you a virgin, Highness?"

The question, useful or no, insult or accusation, was out before he'd really thought of it. Only ten percent of his brain was currently functioning. That small fraction informed him that this might be relevant. If nothing else, it was a way to *pause*.

"What?" she breathed, flicking the corner of his mouth with the delicious tip of her tongue. Her hands found their way beneath the lawn of his shirt. She explored his chest with firm, searching fingers. She touched him like she was smoothing the coverlet of a rumpled bed, feeling for a lost ring.

"Are you a virgin?" he repeated.

"Of course I'm a virgin," she mumbled. "I was brought up in France, but I wasn't . . . unobserved. I was only fifteen when I left—just newly debuted." She sucked in his bottom lip.

"*Oh, no*," he moaned, the words barely audible.

She kissed them away. "Oh, yes," she said quickly, breathlessly.

He returned her kisses—frantic, hungry—for two seconds, then he pulled away. She made a noise of extreme frustration, following his mouth.

"*Highness*," he whispered. He let fly a stream of profanity inside his head.

Slowly, staggeringly, he pushed the two of them off the wall. Her legs were locked around his waist, and he supported her with an arm beneath her bottom. With uneven, reluctant steps, he plodded to the sofa. He put a knee up, tipped forward, and released her, dumping her onto his mother's pink couch. She fell to the sofa in a boneless heap.

"Killian?" she protested, her voice part moan, part demand. She said his name as if he'd just poured expensive champagne into a flowerpot.

"Princess," he replied, trying to instill a note of warning. The word was painful to say.

"You—" she accused, but didn't finish. She scrambled to her knees and grabbed the front of his shirt in both hands, pulling him back to her. He went—no human man could resist this—but he lingered only long enough for a hard, final kiss. Then he encircled her wrists with one hand and tugged his shirt free with the other. He took a step back. Then another. Then another.

He would put distance between them—better yet, a piece of furniture. He went around the side of the sofa. He ran his hand through his hair and exhaled, willing his body to settle and his brain to work.

Behind him, Elise made a rather loud, rather unladylike noise of frustration. Killian glanced back. She'd crumpled herself into a small cottony pile, facedown on the sofa.

"I'm sorry," he said curtly.

He wasn't sorry. He was miserable. He wanted her, wanted her more than anything he could remember—and that was saying quite a lot, considering his life was largely defined by wanting things he could not have.

Withholding himself from her wasn't even the truly miserable bit; the true misery was rejecting her. He would sooner cut out his heart than make her unhappy.

"Why?" she asked into the upholstery. Her voice was not pleading, it was not bereft, it was defiant. Muffled, but defiant.

"Why did I ask about your virginity?"

She popped up and spun to face him. "No," she said. "I know why you asked that. I understand societal rules. I know there is a risk of pregnancy. We're hardly children. As an adult, I can tell you that I don't care about societal rules in this moment. And I understand there are . . . ways to avoid pregnancy. *Why did you cause us to . . . to stop?*"

Of course, she would want more than the obvious. Also, of course, he could hardly tell her more. He couldn't tell her that he was being *paid* to do exactly this thing they both wanted. He couldn't tell her that he refused to do *that thing*. And certainly he couldn't tell her that—despite this refusal—he still hoped to collect the payment.

"Killian?" the princess demanded.

His mind creaked and lurched, trying to think of some fix for this moment. He would begin, he thought, by restating the obvious.

"We cannot indulge, Highness, because one day you will be married, and you should enjoy that occasion without the complication of explaining . . . or lying about . . . *this* night."

She let out a bitter laugh. "Married? Who in God's name am I to *marry*?"

No one, he wanted to declare. *Marry no one. The very thought of you going to some other man is ripping me in two.*

Instead, he said, "Doubtless there are scores of potential husbands for a Princess of the Blood."

"Well, you're mistaken," she said, sliding from the sofa. She reached for the blanket and pulled it tightly around her. "I'm too old to be married. Also, largely forgotten. No one in the English court will make the bother, and the French court no longer exists."

He was shaking his head. "Untrue," he lectured her. "I work for the palace, remember? You think they cannot orchestrate a marriage for a French princess in a matter of days? *You're* mistaken. They multiply lands and strengthen courts and purify bloodlines as a matter of course. It takes only a handful of letters and a chest of gold."

The thought of this—nay, the *truth* of this—made Killian queasy. Had the royal duke made any indication that they would marry her off? No, he hadn't. Edward wouldn't have attached her to *him* of all people—and with the charge of seduction, no less—if the king had immediate plans to marry her off. But still. It was common enough. It *could* happen.

The princess was not so convinced. She was shaking her head, pacing aimlessly around the room.

As Killian watched her, a potential solution began to fit itself together in his mind. He reexamined his suggestion. He thought back to other female courtiers, to marriage contracts, to foreign courts. He was an engineer, rummaging through a box of loose parts, assembling a working solution. It would mean agony for him, sacrifice, and walking away with nothing—it would mean being alone—but wasn't this always his reality?

"Perhaps marriage has not been in the forefront of anyone's mind," he said, "but think about it, Princess. If you were to marry, you could leave St. James's Palace. You would be mistress of your own household. You would have some control over how you lived your life. Assuming you enjoyed some . . . accord with your husband, he could help you mount a search for your brother. A proper search."

She stared at him, illuminated on one side by the fire. Her lips had been kissed pink, her cheeks and neck marked by the scrape of his beard. Her night rail, now drier and whiter, puffed out with a thousand wrinkles. She was radiant, and he was convincing her that she should marry some other man.

"No one," she explained, "intends for me to marry." The words were emphatic, but she said them slowly. She said them as if she, herself, was examining them for truth.

"Queen Charlotte would have none of her own daughters marry," she continued. "Male callers are not welcome in the Queen's Chapel. And my advanced *age*, as I've said—"

"You are not one of Queen Charlotte's daughters," he said. "Think about it, Highness. *This plan*—marrying yourself off to some husband—would be far more welcome than your current effort. Stop asking to find a long-lost brother; ask instead for a husband to take you off their hands. A bridegroom is the natural order of things; your brother threatens the French balance of power. It's an easy fix, honestly."

For a long moment, she said nothing. She chewed on her bottom lip. The sight of this simple gesture caused a dark mist to fall inside Killian's heart.

He forged on. "You are of perfectly marriageable age. How old did you say you are?"

"Twenty-five," she said softly. "How old are you?"

He cleared his throat. Certainly this had no relevance to their conversation. "Thirty-three."

Silence fell. Killian watched her turn over this new prospect in her mind.

She was never yours, he told himself.

So very little, he reminded himself, *is yours*.

Least of all the body and virginity and love, even for one night, of this woman.

He walked to the hook by the door that held his overcoat.

She hovered close by, close enough to touch, but he snatched his hat from the next hook and held it tightly in his hands. This conversation had done much to snuff out the desire coursing through his veins, but an underlying current remained.

"Think on it," he said, trying to make his voice light. He was suddenly so very tired. He wanted to put a knee on the sofa and topple down and sleep for a thousand years.

He shoved his hat on his head. "I should walk you back to your room. You can drape yourself in my overcoat."

She looked to him, hazel eyes and tousled hair, lips the color of crushed rose petals. Killian's drowning heart did a halfway roll and gasped for air.

"I cannot say I *want* to marry," she told him.

"It's nothing that needs to happen tonight," he said. He would examine her statement for meaning later.

"Tonight," he continued, "we need only convey you to this ledge outside your window, deliver you through the sill, and lock you safely inside. If we're meant to tour Sunbury in the morning and reach St. James's Palace by early afternoon, we'll need an early start."

She hovered a moment more, considering this. After a beat, she said, "Do you regret it, Killian?"

"Regret what?" He prayed she would not press this.

"Kissing me? What happened here tonight?"

"No regrets," he said. The truth.

He held his overcoat up, draped it across her, and ushered her out into the rain, repeating it softly. "No. Regrets."

CHAPTER TWENTY

"GOOD MORNING TO YOU, Highness!"

Elise was scarcely out of her bedroom when she encountered the breathy, excitable voice of Lady Dunlock. The countess wilted into an exaggerated curtsy, her scarlet morning dress puffing around her like an ottoman.

"Oh, good morning, my lady," Elise said carefully. She'd risen early and dressed quickly, despite her sleepless night. She wasn't certain her reserves of energy were prepared for Lady Dunlock.

"We are to take breakfast together," proclaimed the countess excitedly, spouting upward and thrusting a note at Elise.

Elise startled at the sudden motion—what an acrobatic dancer Lady Dunlock must have been—and accepted the folded parchment. Lady Dunlock chuckled a little, not unlike a schoolgirl passing a note, and hovered beside her. Elise was given no choice but to read it while her hostess waited.

Highness,

I bid you forgive my absence this morning and carry on with breakfast in the company of Lady Dunlock. I've pressing matters to discuss with my nephew and must meet with the boy alone. The countess is an eager breakfast companion. I hope the meal will be unremarkable in the best sort of way.

After you've taken breakfast, I've arranged for the earl's carriage to convey you to Sunbury. You'll be accompanied by an experienced driver and three grooms. Assuming the vehicle manages to stay upright, you should be perfectly safe in their care for the short distance. I'll meet you beside Sunbury Green by ten o'clock. We'll see to your inquiries and set out for London no later than noon.

Regards,
Killian Crewes

Elise read the note two times and tucked it into her pocket. Beside her, Lady Dunlock was staring at her expectantly. Elise pasted on her most serene smile and looked up.

"I'm to be treated to breakfast in your company, my lady," Elise said.

"So you are!" trilled Lady Dunlock, clapping her hands together. "Right this way, Highness. I've had Cook do up something special. If it pleases Your Highness, we'll take it in the dining room."

Elise inclined her head and trailed behind her. The countess chattered on about her extreme preference for breakfast over every other meal of the day, the best temperature for milk in coffee, and butter molds. Elise heard but wasn't really listening.

Of course Killian would carry on, Elise thought, as if nothing had happened in the cottage. As if she'd not made a wild flight into the forest, as if he'd not introduced his strange plan to marry her off to someone else, as if they'd not almost made love.

Of course.

He would not reference it. God forbid he acknowledge this great shift in their relationship; God forbid he use it to build a new intimacy.

In the puzzle that was Killian Crewes, this was a corner that she'd actually worked out. This . . . avoidance. The more profound the experience, the less he would regard it. It had happened after the corridor in the palace, and again after the carriage toppled. It had happened after she declared they should kiss on the horseback ride to Paxton Dale.

Why? She couldn't say. Perhaps that would be the next section of the puzzle to solve. Or perhaps she would never know.

No, she thought, *I heretofore banish the notion of "never" from my life.* She *would* discover it. Just like she would discover the location of her brother, and discover some path to her own freedom.

She would fit together all the mismatched pieces of Killian Crewes and discover why in God's name she enjoyed him so very much.

Because honestly, he was a lot of work.

But now she would follow Lady Dunlock, still talking, into the dining room laden with a breakfast feast for twenty people.

So be it, Elise thought, watching as the footman poured a steaming cup of coffee. Let him send her notes and tuck her into carriages alone and meet her in village squares. He would manage the memory of last night in his own fashion, and she would manage it in hers. But first, she would eat.

Or, she would endeavor to eat. Any encounter with Lady Dunlock was a chatty, spirited affair, and breakfast was no different. They'd not eaten so much as volleyed question and answers back and forth, speaking around the leaning bodies of footmen who stooped to ladle eggs and porridge and cups of raspberries.

Lady Dunlock wanted to know about London fabrics, and necklines, and colors, and hats. At one point, the countess departed the table and returned with three maids holding aloft three gowns from her wardrobe. She bade Elise make some judgment on which of the three was the most consistent with current London stylings.

When, finally, they'd made some small dent in the feast and discussed shoes for every season, Lady Dunlock conveyed Elise to an upstairs sitting room, where Killian's elderly aunts were taking a private breakfast. Rallying the old women to rise, the countess compelled all of them to embrace and clasp wrists and say repeated farewells.

Here, Elise fielded questions about her journey to Portugal and was informed of the best way to remove stains from the coral-colored gown.

But then the clock struck a quarter after nine o'clock and, with almost reverent precision, Lady Dunlock's questions and demonstrations stopped. She snatched up Elise's hand and marched her to the front door. With an unerring sense of duty, the countess bustled her into a waiting carriage, positioned herself outside the open door, and dropped into another of her reverse-bloom curtsies. The boy earl appeared then, bounding around the corner of the house, three dogs on his heels. He danced about his mother, waving and imploring Elise to return as soon as possible.

Killian was, as promised, nowhere to be seen.

Elise thanked the boy and his mother from the window and promised to return. With no command from her, the carriage pulled away—and that . . . was that.

Elise dropped back on the carriage seat, a little stunned. As much as she loved Paxton Dale—and truly, she'd loved everything about it—and as annoyed as she was that Killian was, for all practical purposes, *hiding from her*, the silence and stillness inside the carriage was a welcome respite. She was tired. Her head swam from the company of Lady Dunlock, and she longed to engage in her new favorite pastime, which was remembering last night.

She'd spent sleepless hours examining their encounter from every angle. She'd not lied when she'd told him she'd been kissed before. Her debut season in Paris had been littered with dark corners of crowded ballrooms, strolls behind high garden hedges, and rides into park thickets. But kissing those boys had been as different from Killian Crewes as washing hands was from swimming in the sea.

He'd kissed her, yes—but he'd also engaged every part of her body, every sense. She'd tasted him. She'd heard the hungry sound he made when he was aroused. She'd felt his eyelashes on her cheek. He'd traced his index finger around her smallest toe. He'd slammed her against walls and palmed her bottom. He'd touched her with feather lightness and firm possession.

And he was so very good at all of it. It was as if he'd expertly untied the ribbons of her heart, slid them over her body, bound her up, released her, and then retied all of it with a new knot, known only to him.

And then there was the bit about the dower cottage, more of the history with his brother and his mother, the revelation that Killian had rebuilt the cottage when he was still in school.

Finally, randomly, there'd been the strange suggestion that Elise ask the British royal family to . . . marry her off. Or, at least that's what she took him to mean. Honestly, it had been very difficult to grasp the topic of another man so soon after her body had been worshiped by *him*. It had been like going from lemon ice to calculus.

In the end, logic and equations—her virginity plus her future—had won out, and he'd led her down the garden path to her room. The aftermath hadn't been ideal, perhaps, and the future was uncertain, but she had no regrets. This had been his suggestion, hadn't it? No regrets. Whether he really believed this, she had no idea. Because, naturally, he was absent.

He is a coward, she thought, dosing against the carriage seat. *Coward, coward, coward.*

The journey to Sunbury was not long—less than an hour. But by the time the vehicle bounced to a stop, she was lost in a swirl of cottages and pink wallpaper and lightning strikes above a dark forest. A groom, leaning through the door, awakened her with the gentle call of her name.

Sunbury sparkled in the morning light—a village washed clean by a night of storms. The River Thames coursed through the town center, narrower here than in London, hardly placid but not deadly. She squinted against sunlight on the water and crinkled her nose at the smell.

Looking around, she conjured up the memory of that moment she'd spotted Gabriel from the carriage window and transposed it over the roadside before her. Sunbury had a short row of shop fronts, bisected every building or so by an alley. There was a village green arranged around a small fountain, a church, a—

Killian Crewes leaned against the nearest building, arms crossed, shoulder to the cornerstone, watching her examine the layout of the town.

Elise's breath caught at the sight of him; her heartbeat leaped. He didn't stand out—not really, the town was crowded with men milling about in long overcoats and hats—but the moment of recognition was no less jarring. It was a little like being lost and then turning the corner and realizing you knew where you were. Familiar and, in a way, *found*.

When he saw her recognize him, he reached a hand

to his hat and tipped it, a slow sort of salute. It was the smallest movement, barely an acknowledgement, but it caused the ribbons on Elise's heart to cinch tighter.

She took a deep breath and lifted her hand, giving him a small wave. He pushed off the building and walked to her. Elise waited, watching his unhurried grace and self-assured stride. He had very long legs. She remembered the feel of them pressing her to the wall. She remembered—

"Morning, Highness," he said.

"How do you do, Mr. Crewes."

"You've made it, I see."

"I did, in fact. How comfortable your nephew's carriage is."

"I owe you my thanks for managing on your own. This morning's conversation with Bartholomew will grant me several weeks in London before I'm pressed to return."

Elise thought of this, thought of the strange balance of obligation and care he felt for the boy.

"Also," he went on, "I wanted to reach Sunbury in advance of you—to make some inquiries on your behalf that might *concentrate* your search. That is, if you would be so amenable to a concentrated search."

"I'm sure I would be," she said. He extended a hand, gesturing to the street, and she set out.

She'd known they would speak only of logistical matters, her search, his nephew. And how very correct she'd been. There would be no reference to last night. At least, the brusque terseness was absent. He spoke to her like a friend. Is that what they were? Friends?

She did not feel like his friend. She wanted to touch him. Her need to touch him had become like a puppeteer's string, pulling, always pulling, the most proximate part of her body to him. Her shoulder to his bicep. Her fingers to the back of his hand.

"When I hired the carriage that will convey us back to London," he was saying, "I took the stable master aside and asked how locals typically conduct horse trades in this town. He was very forthcoming and is happy to discuss what he knows with you. If you are amenable."

"Truly?" she said, laughing a little. If he was her friend, he was a very good one, indeed. "Thank you, Killian. Absolutely. Lead the way."

The next hour was spent discussing horses, horse trainers, horse breeders, surgeons who treated cows and horses and sheep, jockeys, and wealthy racehorse owners who lived nearby. From the stable master to the youngest groom, everyone gave some suggestion, and Elise listened to each in turn. She was shown animals, bills of health on new foals, and lists of reliable men who might have horses available to sell. It was impossible to make sense of all the information, but she took down everything in her notebook to pore over later.

When, finally, they left—Killian with a new riding crop for which she was certain he'd paid too much, Elise with a book about the horse market at Newmarket—they nosed in and out of shops for a half hour more. Killian bought a loaf of bread and hunk of cheese, four apples, and a length of dried beef at the mercantile.

"Luncheon," he told her.

"Lovely," she said with a smile. "Shall we find a bench with a view of the water?" The morning had been so productive, she'd learned so much, and Killian, although quiet and detached, had felt almost like a collaborator. It warranted a small celebration.

"Unfortunately, no," he said. "A movable feast is the

order of the day. Inside the carriage. We cannot keep you from London any longer."

"But will you join me?" she asked. "Surely this food is not all for me."

"I will ride with you until Hampton," he said. "Remember, my horse is stabled there."

She bit her lip to hide a smile. Her stomach gave a small flip. She'd not expected him to consent.

Heartbeat speeding, skin flushed, she made her way to the carriage. "So you will," she said.

CHAPTER TWENTY-ONE

*K*ILLIAN TOLD HIMSELF that he'd succeeded.

Success.

He'd managed it—nay, he had managed *himself.* He'd squired her about for more than a day, just as the palace requested.

He'd taken seriously her search for the missing brother.

He'd rallied locals to explain country horse trading.

Through it all, he had *not* seduced her. Or, he had not seduced her *much.*

This was success.

If also he'd touched nearly every part of her and kissed her against the wall—he'd put a stop to it in time. She was an innocent, still. She would recover from . . .

Well, he'd forbidden himself from dwelling on all the things from which they both might not recover. He would focus instead on the fact that, because he'd removed her from St. James's for a time—and not just a few hours; she'd been detained overnight—he'd succeeded. It was more than the palace had in mind for their first outing. He would *get paid.*

And after he was paid, he would be offered the warehouses in Limehouse, and he would combine what he'd earned with what he'd saved for this very purpose. He would buy the warehouses, and refurbish them, and offer them up for lease. Sea captains and import companies would pay him to house cargo shipped to London from around the world. The money from those leases would pay for a myriad of things, including sheep for Paxton Dale, salaries for staff, and repairs to other of Killian's properties.

One success was inextricably linked to the next work in progress. And *that* work was connected to another new enterprise. All of it was very carefully balanced, and none of it left any time to worry about what would happen to Princess Elise because of last night—or what would happen to himself without her ever again.

It was enough of a success to earn him the privilege of being alone with her one last time. A brief carriage ride. Where was the harm? The distance between Sunbury and Hampton was short, and her attention was on her brother, and blinding daylight streamed through the carriage windows from a public road. They were alone, but not really. It was private but not personal.

"How went the conversation with your nephew?" she asked him now. She was seated opposite him in the springy carriage, one gloved hand braced against the seat.

"Productive, I think," he answered. He would deflect any suggestion that they were . . . *familiar.* He could sit across from her, they would share a meal, but he would not intimate any life revelations. There could not be a repeat of last night at dinner. Success relied upon the cessation of mutual knowledge.

"How went," he inquired, "breakfast with the countess?"

She regarded him but did not answer. Killian shifted in his seat. He'd not realized the very smallness of this hired carriage. It felt cocoon-like. It felt like a private, rolling booth for two.

Finally, the princess said, "You were correct when you said the countess is impossible not to like."

"*Impossible* may be a strong word, but I appreciate your graciousness about her. About all of them."

"No grace is required, Killian. I enjoyed every resident of Paxton Dale. Very much. Even the aunts."

He nodded. Fine. Topic closed. Now he would offer her luncheon, and they would eat in companionable silence. Success endured.

"What did you discuss," she asked, watching him unwrap the bundle of food, "with your nephew?"

Killian paused, the bread in his hand.

"Not more scolding about last night's dinner, I hope," she continued. "The boy did nothing wrong, in my view."

"He is too familiar," Killian told her. "He presumes too much."

"Perhaps, but he was not trying to embarrass or unsettle me. It was curiosity. He's trying to make sense of the world. Looking back on my life, I can see I've asked far *too few* bold questions."

Killian tore the loaf in two. He removed the knife from his belt and sliced the cheese. She leaned toward him and plucked an apple from the bundle.

"In hindsight, curiosity is a difficult trait to introduce midstream," she mused. "It alarms and unsettles people when they are not accustomed to you speaking out. Best not to suppress it. Let the boy go as he intends to finish."

"Alarming people will be the least of his worries if he enters school without some modicum of reserve," Killian said. "He is too earnest. Too . . . open."

"Enters school at Eton, you mean?"

"He will not go to Eton."

She regarded him. "His mother seems rather determined to have him there."

"His mother will not pay the fees, so she will not decide. In the end."

"Eton is too expensive," the princess guessed.

"On the contrary. I've money set aside for whatever the boy may require, including advanced degrees at Oxford. The reason I'll not send him to Eton is that the other students would eat him alive. He is too trusting, too"—he exhaled tiredly—"sweet I'd no sooner send him to a workhouse than Eton College. The damage would be no greater. There are other ways for Bartholomew to prepare for university."

He was shaking his head, sawing at the cheese with his knife. How had the conversation found its way to *this*?

"What happened to you at Eton, Killian?" the princess asked in a soft voice.

"Nothing that bears repeating." He glanced at her and then away. She was so lovely, it almost distracted from the impossibility of her question. Almost. The last thing they needed was to explore what happened to him at Eton.

He handed her a bundle of bread and cheese on a crumpled sheet of newsprint.

Princess Elise accepted it, eyeing him, but did not press—thank God, for once, she did not press. Instead she took up the apple again.

Killian held up his knife, offering to slice it, and she handed it to him. He cut a slim crescent. She smiled and accepted it, nibbling the corner. Her notebook lay beside her on the seat, and she turned to it, flipping open to the notes from Sunbury.

"I'm astounded at the amount of information I've gleaned from one visit to Sunbury," she ventured. "It begs the question of what I missed in Hampton yesterday. Did I call to public stables in Hampton? I was at a stable, but I don't suppose I understood if it was a public enterprise or operated by the inn."

"It was the stable yard of the inn," he told her. "Forgive me for not lending more of a hand yesterday. I was . . . I was being unhelpful for no good reason."

She thought about this and nodded, turning back to her notes.

She was wearing her hat, he'd noticed. She'd managed to revive it from yesterday's carriage accident. She'd tucked away most of her hair beneath it. Only the halo of curly tendrils escaped, framing her face and the base of her neck.

She looked up from her notes and gave him a smile that shone sunlight into the foggy windows of his heart. It felt happy and bright but also hopeless. Light gave off warmth and was illuminating, but it exposed neglect.

He began to see himself less in terms of success or failure, and more like a man who would spend a lifetime toiling for one thing, when what he *really* wanted was something else entirely. A farmer who wanted to practice law; a soldier who longed for the stage.

He cleared his throat.

"In future," he said, "when you visit these villages, call first to stables and ask for the man in charge. For all practical purposes, you were already making these inquiries in London. You were on a good path."

She lowered the piece of apple from her lips. "Will you not travel with me? In future?"

The muscles in Killian's chest went slack. He'd not anticipated this question.

"*In future*," she repeated, "I will go alone to the villages?"

"I . . . I cannot say." The truth. He *didn't* know if she would be alone in future. He couldn't even say for certain if her future would provide for repeat trips outside of London. He knew almost nothing about what the palace intended for her.

Gently she closed her notebook and balanced her slice of apple on top. Killian watched the fruit rock with the motion of the carriage. He was unable to look at her.

"Perhaps I'm asking the wrong questions," she said, her voice suddenly sharp. He actually loved it when she used this tone. There was an entitlement there; *she* was a princess, and *he* was just a man, and now he would do her bidding.

Except, he wouldn't. The prevailing activity of this carriage ride was not eating luncheon or chatting. It was evasion—evading her. He could see that now.

"Perhaps," she said, "we should postpone the topic of whether you will escort me in future. Perhaps we should explore why you escort me *now*."

Killian didn't answer.

"Tell me again," she said. "No—tell me, perhaps for the very first time, why the royal duke dispatched *you* . . . with *me* . . . to tour the countryside. Explain to me why I was allowed to leave London. Why I was *encouraged* to leave London. With you. You've made references to 'favors' you do for the king. Other times, you refer to these favors as a 'job.' So, am I a favor or a job—or something else entirely?"

"Highness." He ate a piece of cheese from the tip of his knife.

"Surely I'm entitled to know this. Perhaps *this* will inform whether you will escort me again. Since you are so very unclear on the topic."

How foolish he'd been to ride alone with her. The journey now offered him two choices: *lie* to her about her future or to *explain* to her about his life.

Wait, no, there was a third choice. It popped and sparkled between them like hot ashes rising up a chimney. His other choice was to reach for her. To kiss the questions from her lips. It would put an end to the lying and the truth telling.

He sighed and slid his knife back into the scabbard. *Fine*, he thought, the *truth*.

"Just to be clear, I work for my living," he began. "There is no inherited wealth. Any potential wealth at Paxton Dale goes to Bartholomew, and good riddance. There are no favors for the king. I am a paid employee."

"You've said as much." She sounded impatient and bored.

"Right. So, the royal duke dispatched me with you," he said, "because I serve as the Royal Fixer. In this work, I am paid by the royal dukes, or the king, or the queen sometimes—anyone in the royal family, really—to 'fix' problems in court that cannot be easily solved by a diplomat, or a governmental official, or someone who enforces the law, like a soldier or a guard. I fix things that no one else has the capability, or ingenuity, or anonymity to fix. And you, Highness, were viewed as a problem for which the palace had no other fix, and so they hired me to . . . in a way . . . manage you."

"Manage me?"

"*Distract* you."

"*Why?*" She sounded genuinely confused. She did not, he realized, sound appalled at the nature of his work—or, for that matter, that he worked at all.

"I am not a 'problem,'" she insisted. "I'm all but invisible. Why me?"

"The specifics are unclear to me, honestly. Part of my job is to ask very few questions. I know only that the royal family wanted to have you, in a manner, 'contained.' They want you making less of a fuss about your brother, fewer inquiries; they don't want you to prowl outside the palace unaccompanied. They want you *oc-*

cupied. In particular, this week they seemed to want it very bad indeed."

"And yet they allowed you to squire me about Middlesex, searching for Gabriel?"

"I didn't ask them what was allowed. The glaring lack of *whys* and *hows* is reciprocal. The royal family do not ask my methodologies. I chose the Road to Land's End because you wanted me to take you there. You asked me in the corridor, after the ball, remember? You implored me. I couldn't—"

He stopped himself and took a deep breath. He began again. "I wanted to give you what you wanted."

"Just to be perfectly clear," she informed him, taking up the apple slice, "you have *not* given me what I wanted."

Killian closed his eyes. *Me neither, Princess. Me neither.*

"What are examples of other jobs you've been hired to do on behalf of the palace?" she asked. "Other fixes?"

"Princess." He sighed.

"Tell me. I want to know."

Fine, he thought. Perhaps it was for the best that she understood all the dirty, illegal, petty things he did for money.

"Well," he said, "most commonly, I'm charged with following or watching people—family members, visiting dignitaries, government officials. I report the things I observe."

"Their wrongdoing," she guessed.

"Sometimes. Other times I substantiate their innocence; I prove that they are who they claim to be. Or not—if they are lying. Sometimes I simply gather secrets they wouldn't want revealed—evidence the king may later use to compel them to vote a certain way or make some financial decision. In essence, I learn secrets."

"What else?"

"Really?" he breathed.

"Really."

"Ah, I've been hired to dissuade or, if you will, 'threaten' acquaintances of the royal family who overstep, or inconvenience, or embarrass the palace. I've set up lodging and livings for mistresses who are deemed too distracting to the royal dukes. I stand guard over favorite nephews who frequent late-night boxing matches, I pay gambling debts, I procure liquor and antiquities and exotic birds that are otherwise unavailable in London shops. But look, Highness, I've made no effort to hide my occupation from you. I didn't overstate it, perhaps, but it's not something I generally discuss. I alluded to the fact that I've been, in a manner, *'assigned to you'* by Edward. You seemed not to care. You seemed only to want to find your brother. I'm not a man prone to long conversations, this current exchange notwithstanding."

"You're correct—I didn't care. The reason Edward introduced us felt inconsequential compared to the opportunity to leave St. James's and search in earnest for Gabriel. It is my primary goal."

"Right," he said. "A bit of advice. I'd downplay your ambitions on that score. That, in particular, seems to make everyone . . . uneasy."

"I don't care about their unease. What about you? Can you defy them? Can you escort me outside of London even if scouting for my brother makes them 'uneasy'?"

"I don't know."

"Why?"

"Why?" he repeated, a pathetic attempt to stall.

"Yes, *why?*"

"Fine. If they offer me the job of squiring you about in future, I'm doubtful I would accept it." *There*, he thought, he'd said it.

"Again: Why?" Her voice was as hard as a slap.

This, he would not say. He wouldn't tell her that he could barely sit across the seat from her without touching her. He wouldn't tell her that he had a very damaging habit of wanting things he could not have, and he wanted her very badly indeed. He wouldn't tell her that he only survived this habit by removing himself from the object of his desire.

"I find myself at a loss for words, Highness," he said.

A long, heavy pause. They stared at each other, air crackling.

"Convenient, *that*," she replied.

The carriage rolled on, and Killian wondered if the driver had chosen the longest possible route to Hampton. Had they detoured through Yorkshire?

"If you will not tell me why you'll refuse future jobs that involve me," she said now, "tell me something about yourself. Tell me how you came to serve in this role in the palace."

"What? Why would I delve into that?"

"Because I regard you as a puzzle. You might as well know this. You're a puzzle that I want to assemble, and I'm missing too many pieces. How does one become a 'Royal Fixer'?"

"No," he tried. He wanted to tell her he was no puzzle, he was a temporary distraction. If she knew what was good for her, she would look away.

"*Yes*," she countered.

She cocked her head and raised an eyebrow. A wordless challenge. Naturally, he was thrilled by this. He wanted to reach out and trace that perfectly arched brow with the tip of his finger, to follow the line of her face beside her ear, around her jaw, and to nestle it in the center of her lips.

"Killian," she said. "If we cannot speak of my future

because neither of us seems to know it, then let us speak of you. We must pass the time somehow."

"I knew the king's son Ernest in school," he said. "The job sprang from there."

"How does the son of an earl become the hired fixer of a royal duke because of a friendship in school? Pray do not forget that I've spent many years in the palace, and I know the friends of the royal dukes, and I know the hired staff, and you seem like neither."

How do I seem? He wanted to ask her.

Instead, he said, "From my earliest year at Eton, I was forced to counteract the bullying of my older brother."

"You were that close in age? To be in school together?"

"My first two years overlapped with his last two. And during that time, he worked very hard to cast me as unfit."

"Unfit . . . how?"

"Too common, too mannerless, too beneath the lot of them. He worked very hard to have me banished, and I was determined to rise above it. These early schoolyard reputations have a way of baking themselves into the great pie of society, and the stench of being an outcast can follow one throughout life."

"How could he banish you?" she asked. "What did he do?"

Killian shook his head. *No.*

"Alright, tell me this: How could he sully your name and not his own?" she asked. "You were brothers."

"*Half* brothers. His mother was a gentlewoman and mine was a dancer, and he never allowed anyone to forget it. *He* was the heir, not me—another constantly repeated fact. I was young and terrified. He was about to graduate and advance to Oxford. I . . . could not outpace his resentment or his bullying. I was, however, an enterprising little rotter. I had a knack for anticipating difficult-to-meet needs and providing for them. And I had the very great fortune of living across the hall from King George's fifth son. Combining all of these, I forgot about my brother and made myself invaluable to my royal hallmate."

"And by invaluable, you mean . . ."

"I *mean*, I fulfilled the twelve-year-old-boy version of the same role I fill now. I became a trusted and reliable source for tobacco, whiskey, illustrations of beautiful women in diaphanous scarves, answers to questions on assignments. Whatever Ernest wanted, I procured. I arranged pig races and wrestling matches and fiddle players. I created diversions and hid the evidence of pranks. *And*," he said, "I was droll and haughty about it. From the beginning, it was a business. I always charged for my services. There are two ways you can play at 'royal lackey': doormat or resource. I am a resource, and I demand a very high price."

"'Created *diversions*,'" she repeated. "That's what you've done for me. You've become a diversion. That has been the 'fix.'"

"I meant only to suggest the fancies of a twelve-year-old bo—"

"*How much* are you being paid to divert me?" she demanded.

Killian stared at her. What a fool he'd been to allow this shared ride to Hampton.

"How much?" she repeated.

"We've not worked out a price," he said. "Procurement of *goods* comes with a known fee. *Services*, however, are generally at the discretion of the royal dukes. I learned quickly that I get paid more if I allow them to decide. Money means almost nothing to them. They've no notion of how much anything costs.

"And also, I receive a side benefit for my work. It's an

informal arrangement involving property the palace is looking to sell. They offer the buildings to me, and me alone, in advance of any other potential buyers—and at a good price."

"The properties you refurbish," she realized.

"Yes. Those." He wasn't sure why he'd told her this. She hadn't asked. It was certainly no boast to remind her that he worked for his living. She had a way of making him reveal things.

"So now you know," he concluded. Puzzle piece revealed. Thank God.

"Well, I know more *about* you," she countered, "but not *my* future. I know virtually nothing of what the palace intends."

"What of marriage?" he tossed out. "We discussed this last night. You could ask the queen and king to pursue a suitable match for you. Surely—"

"You would raise this?" she challenged, her voice loud and hard. "Again? You were so . . . *unaffected* by last night that you persist with this plan to marry me off to a stranger?"

Killian couldn't look at her. *Unaffected by last night?* He was forever changed by last night. He would never recover.

"Surely you would not kiss me twelve hours ago, say nothing more about it, and then suggest that I mount up a search for a husband?"

"I'm trying," he gritted out, "to help you. Do you think I'm so heartless as to hear your situation and not determine some way out?"

"You mistake me for a client, Killian. I've not hired you to fix my problems. I'm simply trying to . . . have a discussion. We're alone together in this carriage—a circumstance we may never again enjoy—and I'm simply talking. Is there *nothing* you'll say to me?"

"What? I've never spoken so many words in my life." Now *he* was angry. "I do not *know*, Highness, what the palace intends for you. My experience at Eton is a private misery that I share with no one. And I won't help you because I cannot seem to be in your company without kissing you. And I've *no excuse* for kissing you, except that you are the most beautiful, clever, alluring woman I have ever encountered, and I cannot resist you. Not last night, and not now."

He reached for her then, his hands at her shoulders and neck. She met him more than halfway, launching from her seat and slamming against him. Arms closed, mouths met. He fell back, taking her with him, kissing and kissing and kissing. They sank together, descending into the mindless swirl of their inevitable embrace. He gathered her up, armfuls of skirts and legs and knees, breaking the kiss only to suck in air.

"Elise." He whispered her name into the skin of her neck like an oath.

The choreography of the kiss felt as practiced as a duet they'd danced their entire lives. He knew her taste and her tongue and exactly where his hands fit. She knew where to hold on—or rather, she knew that he would hold her and allow her fingers to roam his body. She knew he would gasp when she breathed into his ear.

"Killian," she murmured.

"Stop. Talking. Please," he implored her, speaking around kisses. "Five minutes. Let us . . ."

"Yes," she whispered, "let us . . ." She pounced on his lips.

And this was the volatile alchemy of the carriage. He'd gone from what felt like success, through the wringer of fifty topics he had no wish to discuss, and landed, finally, on what he'd really wanted all along. Any other motive was a lie. He would never have coerced her, but he'd hoped. The miles they spent on opposite seats had felt like a very rickety bridge onto which he walked, farther and farther, until finally he realized that it did not connect to the other side but dropped off into the abyss. When Killian came to the drop, he did not turn around. He dove.

"Hat—*gone*," he said, tugging the lavender millinery from her head and digging his fingers into her hair.

"Coat—remove," she countered, pulling his overcoat from his shoulders. Next she grabbed the folds of his cravat and pulled. This afforded only a little slack—the tie was looped around his neck—and she whimpered in frustration. Killian found an end and worked it loose with his fingers, unspooling it. The princess pulled away to observe this, fingers idly popping open the buttons on his waistcoat. Her expression drove him mad—eyes half-lidded with desire but also dark and wild with excitement. He paused to kiss her again. She made a noise of frustration and pushed him away.

"Take it off," she breathed, pulling open his waistcoat.

Killian slid the cravat free with a yank, and her hand went to his neck, delving beneath his collar, searching for bare skin.

For a long moment, Killian allowed his hands to drop, to simply rest on the sides of her hips as she balanced on his lap, kissing him, exploring his chest. The swaying of the carriage rocked her, ever so gently, against him, and they rode out the motion, kissing a little harder on the bumps and a little softer on the bounces. She pulsed against him like a heartbeat.

When her hands had fanned across his clavicle and chest, his belly and ribs, she bumped possessively against the waist of his trousers. The fluttering probe of fingertips felt like the splash of a wave. He wanted to dive in.

He wanted to be awash in her touch. He wanted more of everything. He wanted the carriage ride to never end.

Without thinking, he tipped to the left and turned, spilling her from his lap to the carriage seat. Elise hit the seat with a sigh, reaching for his shoulders, pulling him down. Balancing above her on a knee and a hand, he hovered, pausing only to consider what part of her he would kiss next.

He gathered up her left leg and hitched it over his hip. Her skirts were a constricting, obstructing menace, and she released him long enough to hike them up to her waist. He wanted to see this, to gaze upon her beautiful body, but she was pulling him down again, and his want became her want; he thought only of eliciting more sounds of pleasure from her, of pressing the most demanding part of himself against her arching body.

He left her mouth to nuzzle her neck, the irresistible hollow in the center of her collarbone, and then to nudge lower still, to the creamy expanse of skin above the neckline of her gown. He followed with his hand, his fingers trilling over her bodice, eliciting a sigh, and tickled them up again, turning the sigh into a little moan. He palmed her breast, a perfect fit for the hollow of his hand. She called his name in a soft, lazy plea.

He was just about to slide his pointer finger beneath the neckline of the gown when the carriage lurched heavily, crushing them against the seat back, and then— *whoosh*—rolling them the opposite direction. Killian dug his boot into the carriage floor, resisting the force, and caught the princess at the waist.

She cried out, clinging to him, and Killian dropped his head over her shoulder. He swore, knowing what was happening—*hating* what was happening—and he squeezed her to him, endeavoring to imprint her body on his memory, trying to absorb her.

"We've arrived, I'm afraid," he grumbled into her ear.

"What?" Her voice was weak, breathless.

"Hampton," he said. "The driver has reined in. He's navigating other vehicles. Traffic. A midday crush. We are . . . no longer alone. Back to civilization."

Now the vehicle was stationary, and Killian rose up. He ran a finger through his hair and yanked his shirt squarely on his shoulders. Keeping a hand securely on her waist, he peered out the window.

"Yes," he confirmed grimly. "We've arrived."

He glanced down at her. She was rumpled and disheveled and tinted pink from his kisses.

"Up you go," he said, and extended a hand.

She accepted it and came up on one elbow. "Killian—"

"There is no time to discuss it, Highness. There is no time to ask why, or how, or what's next, or what happened in 1781 when I was at Eton. Let me help you with your hat."

"How convenient," she said, finding the hat but refusing his help.

"Take a deep breath," he said. "That's it. The driver will navigate us to the mews where I stabled my horse. I'll be riding out for the journey to London. For obvious reasons."

"Obvious to whom?" she asked tiredly. She closed her eyes and dropped her head back, allowing it to hang. She struggled to catch her breath.

The sight of her neck, of her upturned profile, hair falling back, was more than Killian could bear. He swept her to him once more, kissing her hard. Kissing her as if it was the last time. It *was* the last time.

She kissed him back, but when he pulled away, she did not pursue him. It was one of his favorite things, that pursuit, and this felt like a small slap. Foolish, he knew. They'd clattered into town by the skin of their teeth.

He'd not succeeded, perhaps, but he'd not fully seduced her—not yet.

"No regrets," he said, giving her a little shake.

"I think you and I have a different understanding of regret," she said.

He stared down at her, hoping to look his fill, to remember her like this—languid in his arms, hair loose, eyes flashing. He said, "I've bungled this. Everything is my fault."

"Would that that were true." She sighed, wiggling to break free. "Things are easier to endure when there is someone to blame."

CHAPTER TWENTY-TWO

KILLIAN LACKED THE authority to summon a royal duke, but he could make the request. It was his only thought as he cantered into the courtyard of St. James's Palace. If he couldn't resist the princess—which, clearly, he could not—at the very least he would have some answers about what they intended for her.

He parted ways with Elise from his saddle; he didn't want to give the appearance that he would linger. She was handed down from the carriage, he gave a small salute from horseback, and then her maid was there. She paused for a moment, presumably waiting for him to speak. When he said nothing, she shook her head and followed her maid inside. She did not look back.

As it should be, Killian told himself.

The best result.

What we both require.

Then he asked for parchment and pen to scrawl out his request for an audience with the royal duke.

Ten minutes later, he was shown into a small, out-of-the-way library. His Grace, Edward, Duke of Kent, awaited him, sprawled in a chair. Killian wasn't surprised. Of course they'd receive him. The more Killian thought about the introduction at the ball, the more he believed that Princess Elise was less of a nuisance and more of a priority to the royal family.

But *why*? *To what end?*

Learning all he could was his only usefulness to her now. And the alternative was untenable. He would not ruin her opportunity to live the life to which she'd been born. He would not lose his primary source of income and the warehouses, only to *not* have the princess in the end. Instead, he must find a way to do the least amount of damage while also making the largest amount of money.

"Killian, there you are," said Edward, looking up. He'd been pretending to read.

"Highness," said Killian, bowing. "Thank you for seeing me on such short notice."

"The French girl has been returned, I presume?"

"Yes. Just. I apologize for the unplanned detour to Paxton Dale. And also for the damage to your carriage. The accident we suffered on the Road to Land's End proved quite an ordeal. I was forced to leave the vehicle in Hampton. I'm not certain it can be repaired, but the—"

"It was the most perfect diversion," cut in the royal duke. "A harrowing carriage accident? Even the queen could not quibble. Naturally the princess would require an overnight stay to recover. Honestly, I couldn't have planned it better. You do the best work, Killian."

"The accident was purely that—an accident, Highness."

"Oh, yes," drawled the royal duke, "these things often are."

"I would never endanger the—" Killian stopped, took a breath, and started again. "I would never endanger an innocent woman. It's a miracle that no one was harmed."

"You are nothing short of a miracle worker. That is why we do love you so," said Edward. "Sampson is waiting with your first payment. Worth every pound."

"Thank you, Highness."

His chest constricted with a heavy clamp of guilt, the pressure tight enough to crack a rib. Killian ignored it. He'd been assigned a job. He'd done the job. The princess had been restored with minimal damage to body and spirit. Now he would get paid. He'd done this a hundred times before.

"And the warehouses, Highness?" Killian prompted. "In Limehouse. Does His Majesty still intend to offer those for sale?"

"Perhaps he does and perhaps he doesn't," Edward said, making his way to a drinks cart. "Let us think of the buildings as incentive, shall we?"

"Incentive . . . ?"

"To complete the job, naturally."

"Naturally," repeated Killian. "If it pleases you, I should like to know a bit more about the completed job."

"More of the same, really. Dazzle the girl, Killian. Enchant her, take her to bed. Make her forget. This messy preoccupation of her missing brother must stop. Above all."

"Right," Killian said, but in his mind, he was thinking, *Why me? Was it not enough to want her but have no future with her? Must I also be asked to quash her life's purpose as well?*

"For what reason," Killian asked, "can Princess Elise not search for her missing brother?"

The royal duke paused in the act of taking a drink and considered him. He swirled the amber liquid in his glass.

Killian saw his mistake and tried again. "I can better distract her if I understand why the search is forbidden."

"Could you do?" challenged Edward.

"For example," Killian said, "if the brother is actually *dead*, the princess might be told as much. That would be the end of it. Or, if he's in another country, she might realize the futility of a search. If the brother is somehow a danger to her . . ."

"A danger to her?" asked Edward. "No, no, it's not that. And—I might as well tell you—the brother is not dead. Well, so far as anyone knows, he's not dead. Honestly, I've no idea where he is, and I don't care. But the two of them have an uncle who aspires to be king of France. Assuming the French can pull themselves together and restore a king, *any* king. A rather large assumption, if you ask me. All things considered."

Killian hadn't known about the uncle.

"We hosted a French delegation yesterday," explained Edward. "The uncle, Louis-Stanislas and his sad, little exiled court. He is the only surviving brother to poor headless King Louis—may God rest him. When you spirted the girl away from St. James's, Father could finally grant an audience to this uncle."

"The princess's uncle was in London? At St. James's?" asked Killian, all pretense of casualness lost. His heart began to pound. Access to an uncle—someone who could explain her situation to her, who could give her details about her future and her family—would have been endlessly helpful to Princess Elise.

"*Was he here*?" asked Edward. "I thought the man would never leave. He's passed his exile in Austria, but he's been in England for a time, awaiting an audience with Father. With the girl finally absent from the palace—and reliably so, thank you very much, Mr. Killian Crewes—we were able to receive him."

"I see," drawled Killian, recovering his careless tone. But he didn't see. Not at all.

Stalling for time to think, Killian pointed to the crystal decanter in the corner. "May I?"

"Help yourself," said Edward.

Killian sloshed brandy into a glass and took a slow drink. "I see now why the overnight stay in Paxton Dale was fortuitous. If the princess had been in St. James's when her uncle called . . ."

He let the statement dangle, hoping Edward would fill in the gaps.

"*If* the princess had been *here*," Edward said, "she would've plagued the man with her excessive questions, especially about her brother. And in doing so, she might have—no, she would have—ruined everything. *This* is why I sent the carriage. *This* is why I introduced you at the ball. It's very delicate, these dealings with Louis-Stanislas. We could not risk complications caused by Princess Elise."

Delicate, why? Killian wanted to shout. *Dealings about what?*

He couldn't guess, and the royal duke was being purposefully evasive. Killian knew only one thing for sure: when Princess Elise learned that Killian had caused her to miss an opportunity to meet with her uncle, she would be furious, and rightly so.

If he ever saw her again. *If* she did not strangle him before he could croak out the excuse. *If* there was some excuse beyond the unbelievable *I didn't know*. Which, in hindsight, sounded careless and lazy in addition to being unbelievable. But it was the truth. He hadn't known. The circumstances of the fixes had never mattered to him before her.

Nothing had seemed to matter before Princess Elise.

ELISE HAD HAD a bath and a meal, and now Kirby was plaiting her hair. She winced as the maid worked a comb through the tangles.

"Your head was bruised in the accident?" Kirby guessed, horrified.

"Oh, no, it's not that, Kirby," said Elise. "My hair is tangled, nothing more. Carry on. Ignore me."

"I'll not add insult to injury. Whoever heard of someone walking away from a carriage accident without a scratch?" Kirby picked gently at her hair. "And then to be forced to climb on a horse and ride through the fields? Chased by a storm?"

Elise thought back to the horseback ride to Paxton Dale, balanced on Killian's lap. Riding through the fields and hearing about his history had been one of her happiest memories in years.

"It was only a mile or so," Elise said. "Not so very bad."

"Look who's returned!" said an excitable voice from the doorway. Her cousin Juliette. Elise took a breath, bracing herself. She caught Kirby's gaze in the mirror.

"How worried we were," trilled Juliette, sweeping into the room. "Well, some of us more than others, perhaps? Because *first* we were told you were quite well, and *then* we were told you were in the care of Mr. Killian Crewes . . ."

Juliette came behind Elise, shouldered Kirby out of the way, and stooped to embrace her. She squeezed her to the back of her seat like she was strapping her to the chair.

"When I heard the royal dukes had sent you off with Mr. Crewes, I thought, 'Lucky little thing,'" proclaimed Juliette. "I assured everyone their fear was misplaced. I always had a good feeling about him, you'll recall."

"Yes, how insightful you are," said Elise.

"And *then* came the news that you'd pass the night at Mr. Crewes's country house, and I was green with envy. But whatever was he like, Elise? Just as I always thought, surely. Charming and dashing and the perfect gentleman? What of the estate? Was it grand?"

"Not everyone aspires to have their carriage tip over,"

said Kirby, speaking through a mouthful of pins. "The princess has been through quite an ordeal, I assure you. She may not wish to describe it until she's recovered."

"Oh, look at her," Juliette cajoled. "She looks rather rosy-cheeked and fresh-faced if you ask me. In fact, I can't remember our princess ever looking quite so pretty. But *was* Mr. Crewes so gallant and resourceful when the carriage collided with the tree?"

"It didn't collide with a tree," Elise said. "The wheel hit a rock in the road, and the carriage tipped over."

"Was he gallant and resourceful when the carriage tipped?"

"He was," confirmed Elise, willing herself not to respond. "He worked with villagers, I believe, to hoist the thing upright. I cannot say for certain. I was speaking to local women who stopped to observe. It was quite a spectacle."

"'Hoist the thing upright,'" repeated Juliette reverently. She stared into the distance as if imagining Killian, shirtless, lifting a carriage from the road with his bare hands.

Elise frowned. "I'm sorry to have slipped away yesterday. All of you have been so loyal to accompany me in my search for Gabriel. But then the royal duke suggested an outing beyond London, and it was meant to be a very quick, uncomplicated jaunt. Mr. Crewes could ride out for a handful of hours, and we'd return by luncheon. I never meant to stay the night with his family. I never meant to worry anyone." She glanced at Kirby.

"Funny," said Juliette, wandering to the bed and dropping down with flourish. "This is not what I was led to believe." She began to carefully arrange her skirts.

Elise turned to her cousin. "Whatever do you mean by that?"

"Hmm?" asked Juliette innocently.

"What have you been led to believe?"

Before Juliette could answer, Elise's third lady-in-waiting, Marie, appeared in the doorway.

"She returns," said Marie. She smiled at Elise but shot a warning look at Juliette.

"Don't scowl at me," Juliette snapped at Marie. "No one could *find* you. You're always *praying.*"

Marie ignored her and ducked into the room.

"*Marie,*" breathed Elise, an unexpected lump in her throat. Marie had only returned to Elise's life these last four weeks, and she wasn't accustomed to the relief of seeing her friend pop into her bedroom.

"I'm here, Marie, and I'm perfectly sound," Elise told her friend. "I'm so sorry to have worried you."

Marie crossed herself, bobbed a curtsy (Marie and Kirby never failed to curtsy) and sank to her haunches beside the vanity. She studied Elise like she wasn't certain if she was the real princess or an imposter.

"I've had a new brush with death to add to my collection," Elise reported. "Toppled carriage."

"May this be the last one," Marie said.

Elise wanted to fall against her friend and tell her everything, but of course they were not alone. Juliette's behavior was more pointed and annoying than usual. She could feel her cousin's eyes, tracking her every move.

"But have you heard, Highness," Marie asked quietly, "what happened here in the palace while you were away?"

"What do you mean?" Elise shook her head. "I've heard no news from the palace."

"I was just about to tell her," called Juliette from the bed.

"Juliette?" asked the nun. "May I have a moment alone with the Princess?"

This surprised Elise. They trod very lightly around Juliette; a direct dismissal would mean days of pouting.

"I should prefer to stay," declared Juliette. "And I'm affronted you would ask, Marie. You're in no position to—"

"Juliette, will you leave us?" Elise said sharply.

"*Elise,*" complained her cousin.

"I will tell you everything I know of Mr. Crewes shortly," Elise lied. "Pray, allow me speak to Marie alone."

"Fine," said Juliette, swanning from the room. "I feel quite certain I already know all of her many *secret revelations.*"

Elise turned to her lady's maid and shot her an imploring look. "Kirby?"

"Of course, Highness," said the maid, bobbing a curtsy. She collected her comb and pins and closed the door as she left.

Elise spun back to Marie. "What is it?" She couldn't imagine. Virtually *nothing* happened in the palace that called for private discussions. For years, boredom had reigned.

"While you were out of the palace with Mr. Crewes," said Marie softly, "your uncle and his entourage called on King George and the Prince of Wales."

Elise shot to her feet. "*My uncle?* Which uncle?"

It was a stupid question. She had only two paternal uncles—her father's two brothers. One had been the King of France, Louis XVI, and he'd been killed by the guillotine. The other . . .

"Louis-Stanislas," Marie said solemnly. "Contender for the French throne."

THE ROYAL DUKE poured himself another drink and held out the decanter to Killian.

Killian raised his half-full glass. He worked to maintain a neutral expression and keep his tone light.

"What of your meeting with the princess's uncle? Is Britain not at war with France?" he asked.

"Well, Britain is at war with Napoleon, aren't we? And Napoleon has seized control of France. The French royals are another story. As such, Louis-Stanislas wants something from us. But in order to *get it* . . . we'll require something from him. It's always a negotiation, these things."

And what are we negotiating? Killian want to shout. He ambled to a bookshelf and stared up. After a long moment, he mused, "Nothing gets you nothing, I suppose. Question is, who has the most to gain?"

"Indeed," agreed the royal duke.

Killian swore in his head. He tried again. "Anything you require from me in your dealings with the princess's uncle?"

"More than keeping the girl out of sight and *away* from her brother?"

"Aye," said Killian. "Easy enough to keep her from the brother if no one knows his location."

"Well, keep the girl away from the *idea* of him," Edward amended. "It's the *threat* of her brother, isn't it? Louis-Stanislas is determined to reclaim the French throne. No small task, mind you. He'll have to contend with the tyrant Napoleon, not to mention millions of French citizens who, just ten years ago, were shouting for his head. It's an uphill battle, and I don't envy the man. The last thing he wants is a *family* squabble on top of everything else."

"A fight with the princess?" guessed Killian.

"No, no—*her brother*. But don't you see, Killian? This is the point. The uncle wants to be king. But Princess Elise's brother could, theoretically, be king. This is why she must leave off looking for Prince Gabriel; he is a threat to her uncle."

"And King George wants the *uncle* for France? *Not* the brother?"

"Father is less concerned about which of them endeavors to rule France," dismissed Edward. "He wants what the uncle *will give us* if we help to keep the brother . . . *lost.* For lack of a better word."

"We?" asked Killian.

Edward exhaled, exasperated with having to explain. "Princess Elise's brother is in England somewhere. Well, *probably*, it should be said, he's somewhere in England. Can you see: because the *brother* is in England, and *Princess Elise* is in England, their uncle wants *our family* to keep both of them suppressed and out of the way."

"The uncle believes they will challenge him?"

"Well, not the princess. In France, only a male heir can rule. But the princess's brother could challenge Louis-Stanislas, certainly. Regardless, the uncle wants both of them to be largely forgotten. In the instance of the brother, this means 'lost'; in the case of Princess Elise, it means 'quiet.' Do you see?"

"And what does King George stand to gain if you—" Killian paused to rephrase. "What does the king gain if *we* manage to subdue the princess and *not find* her brother?"

"Oh, it's no small thing, I assure you. Louis-Stanislas doesn't have much with which to barter—exile is not the Palais-Royal is it?—but he's finally come to us with something that would benefit England very much . . ."

"LOUIS-STANISLAS WAS HERE?" exclaimed Elise. "Yesterday? Exactly yesterday?"

Marie nodded.

"For how long was he here? In St. James's Palace?

The castle in which *I* reside? The place I've been, effectively, *trapped* for five years with almost no contact with family?"

"He was here all day, Highness," Marie said solemnly. "And he dined with the royal family in the evening. I was told he left near midnight."

"What?" cried Elise. It was a useless exclamation but quite literally the only word in her brain.

"But how could he call on the *precise day* that I am away?" Elise demanded.

Elise thought of the number of letters she'd written her uncle—twenty at least—imploring him to tell her news of the French court, of what was intended for her, of the location of her brother and sister. She'd begged for any direction on how she could safely leave the protection of the British royal family.

He'd written back one letter to her every five. In these letters, like those of her mother, he'd said almost nothing of consequence, he'd bemoaned the very great challenges faced by their family, the importance of steadfastness and faith and patience—*blah, blah, blah.*

Elise spun away and began to pace.

"But what did Louis-Stanislas discuss with King George?" she wondered out loud. "Was the queen also in attendance? What of the king's sons or the girls? What of other courtiers?"

She stopped and stared at Marie. "Was everyone present but me?"

"I cannot say who met with your uncle," said Marie. "I do believe all members of the royal family *dined* with him in the evening, Her Majesty Queen Charlotte included. This comes from a footman, and he suggested that nothing of consequence was discussed at the meal. But he did not serve during the closed-door meetings with the king and Louis-Stanislas. He cannot say what they discussed."

Elise heard this statement in snatches . . . *The queen . . . nothing of consequence . . . he cannot say . . . closed-door meeting . . .*

She resumed pacing.

"This makes no sense," Elise insisted to Marie. "He called on the palace the exact day I was away?"

"It was remarkable to me," said Marie.

Elise stared at her, and Marie stared back, and a terrible intuition passed between them. Not a formed thought, no accusation—a suspicion. It crept into the room like a serpent, squeezing beneath the door. Elise refused to see it for what it was. It wasn't a snake, it was a length of rope. It was a vine. It wasn't a villain, it was . . . Killian.

"It's more of this new regard I've endured," Elise said. "The way I've been treated since seeing my brother. They view me as some sort of a threat. They don't trust me."

She stopped, considered this, then began to pace again.

"My uncle would want to hear about the sighting of Gabriel," Elise said. "Louis-Stanislas and my brother were great friends. Gabriel was only a boy before we fled France, but Louis-Stanislas had been a loving uncle to him. He doted on Gabriel—he loved Gabriel, I'm certain of it. *Louis-Stanislas would want to hear that he's alive.*"

"We can speculate for days," said Marie, "but there are important bits of the story we do not know. I am trying to learn what Louis-Stanislas discussed with the king. Your uncle traveled with an entourage, but his servants were rude and dismissive of St. James's staff. My only hope is to learn something from a footman or guard who served the king during that private meeting. I need more time."

God love Marie, thought Elise. She'd always been more warrior than nun. It was no wonder that she'd been chosen to steal Elise out of France.

"In the meantime," Marie went on, "it's necessary to take special care with your safety. Tread carefully on your alliances. Even Juliette, perhaps, should not be taken into confidence."

Elise turned to her. "You believe me to be in danger?"

Marie raised her hands in question. "I know only that you were conveyed away from the palace within hours of the arrival of your uncle. And while you were away, you were in a life-threatening accident."

"You believe they tried to have me *killed*?" And now the serpent/rope/vine began to wrap around her throat.

"I cannot say," assured Marie. "'Tis only speculation. Before we left France, I vowed to protect you with my life. Your safety is my priority."

For this, Elise had no reply. Marie was fierce and loyal, but Elise always thought of her more as her friend than an avowed protector. She exhaled heavily and sat on the foot of the bed. She dropped her head into her hands and stared at the floor. She tried to remember the last two days—not the breathless, intimate bits, but how she came to leave St. James's. She climbed over every moment like a woman picking her way over steep rocks. To what could she hold fast? What was slippery or might crumble? Was any footing safe?

Putting aside their first suspicion—that she was removed from the palace on purpose—she thought of the carriage accident. Was there any way it had been *intentional*? Had they meant to kill her? She thought of Killian riding out and then riding in. She thought of the moment the wheel cracked, of his worry over broken bones. She thought of the distress of the driver, a career servant.

She looked up, shaking her head. "The carriage accident was entirely happenstance. It was not planned. I am certain of this."

"Very well," said Marie. "Good. I struggle to find any motive for killing you. But there *is* motive for killing your brother, Highness—there is no getting around the truth of this."

"I *can* get around it," insisted Elise. "The revolution has been over for ten years. Who would want Gabriel dead? Clearly, no one cares if he is alive except for me—but who would want him *dead*?"

"If Louis-Stanislas wants the French throne restored—if he wants himself on it—Gabriel is better left *undiscovered*. Does your uncle want him dead? I cannot say, but certainly Prince Gabriel is better unaccounted for. If I had to guess, *this* was on the agenda when Louis-Stanislas met with King George."

"But why would they send me away to discuss this? Why not simply tell me to . . . shut it?"

Marie chuckled. "You've not demonstrated a spirit of cooperation these last weeks, Highness. You have failed at shutting it."

"But does King George believe he's *protecting me* by keeping me from the ambitions of Louis-Stanislas?"

"This I do not know. I can't even say if you were sent away by design or if it was coincidence."

Elise began shaking her head. *She* knew. This was no coincidence. The timing was too perfect; the stakes—previously unconsidered, and how naive she had been—were too high. She'd been sleepwalking for years.

She charged to the door.

"Highness," called Marie. "Highness—wait."

"No," said Elise. "He's still here. Killian—Mr. Crewes. He would have me believe he's gone, but he's not. He'll want to be paid. And he's a natural lurker and shadow dweller and a spy. He's here and he *will* give me answers."

She thrust open the door.

"WHAT PAYMENT, HIGHNESS?" Killian asked the royal duke. "What will Louis-Stanislas offer King George if we can keep Princess Elise and her brother out of his way?"

He'd never worked so hard to appear careless in his life.

"Troop movements," Edward declared. "If you can believe our very great fortune. Troop *movements*, troop *size*, the potential for reinforcements in key battle-grounds. Munitions storage. The chain of supplies that feeds, clothes, and provides weapons to French soldiers."

"Louis-Stanislas would sell out his own army?"

"Remember what I said? *Napoleon* is fighting the English. Likely, Louis-Stanislas will fight Napoleon. His desire for the throne is strong enough to trade his inside knowledge of the French military to keep his niece and nephew out of view."

"But can Louis-Stanislas speak reliably about Napoleon's army?"

Edward shrugged. "It's only been ten years since his brother was king. Napoleon may have reordered things, but forts and battlements remain the same. Docks and garrisons have not moved. Men and provisions are ferried around the country by the same routes. Our spies can only learn so much and dispatch it to us so quickly. My father is asking to get Louis-Stanislas in a room with our generals, a table of maps before them. If he'll consent, Louis-Stanislas is a valuable resource, I assure you. He is determined to defeat Napoleon and will seize any advantage. And, our end of the bargain is simple. As simple as hiring you."

"Right," said Killian. Finally he understood. "Sub-due the princess. End discussion of her brother. England learns military secrets about France."

He longed to take the heaviest book from the shelf

and hurl it through the window. He wanted to shout, *It's cruel to make this girl and her brother into pawns.*

He wanted to quit this room and tear through the palace, searching for Princess Elise—to tell her everything and haul her away from here. But what would that achieve? And would she even speak to him? The princess was no idiot. She would have learned her uncle had been to the palace by now. It was obvious that Killian had conveniently removed her just in time to *not see the man.*

She would be furious. She would not be seduced by him. She would throttle him.

"Just to be clear, Killian," said Edward, "the cost of the warehouses is seeing this through to the end. If you want the properties and the balance of your fee, you must keep the girl complacent and contained. The king will have these state secrets from her uncle. In exchange, she will be kept quiet, and the brother will remain missing. There *is* a simple fix for making all of this happen. So, Royal Fixer? Do your job. *Fix this.*"

PRINCESS ELISE STRODE from her chambers. Marie called to her from behind, but Elise waved her off. Killian would answer for this. He would tell her the truth—all of it—no deflections. He would—

"I'd wager I know a piece of the story that the nun did not . . ."

Elise stopped at the sound of her cousin's voice. She whirled around.

Juliette loitered in the darkness of the corridor.

"What do you mean, Juliette?" Elise asked. "Come out of the darkness. Stand in the light."

Juliette moved just enough to position half of her face in the lantern's glow.

Elise willed herself to keep calm. "*What* is this missing piece?"

"Well, only *you* could confirm this, of course," said Juliette coyly, "but I was told that the palace *paid* Mr. Crewes to take you away—"

"I'm aware that Mr. Crewes was paid to escort me."

"But is that all he was paid to do?" her cousin wondered. "*I* heard the precise assignment was to *seduce* you. *I* heard that if he compelled you to fall in love with him, you would cease all your . . . rambling about town and searching for Gabriel. *That* is what I heard."

"What?" Elise's illusion of carelessness vanished. Her face grew hot. Her heart had stopped doing its job and hung, suspended, in her chest.

"What, indeed?" mocked Juliette. "And just look at that blush. Come now, Elise, you claimed Mr. Crewes was beneath your notice. Not handsome. Not dashing. You called him a stalker, remember?"

"You've no idea what you're talking about," Elise said, but she could hear the lack of conviction in her voice. Tears burned behind her eyes.

"Don't I?" Juliette asked in a soothing tone.

"Please," Elise said flatly, "do not speak of this again. Do not gossip about it—not to Marie or Kirby or anyone. You've no notion of what you're talking about."

"Then tell me the truth," Juliette demanded, popping off the wall. "Did Mr. Crewes . . . *touch* you? Do you fancy yourself in love with him? This is the way court works, Elise. Knowledge is power. I'm trying to help you. It is my job, as your lady-in-waiting, to navigate court intrigue. Finally, we'll claim some notoriety in the palace—you'll be known for more than being boring, and sad, and pathetic."

"No, Juliette," Elise breathed, beating back panic. She would not have Juliette cast her as a philandering courtier. She wouldn't be discussed at all. She didn't want notoriety. She didn't want to play games. She wanted *out* of this place. "You are mistaken. What you've heard are lies. If you repeat them, you perpetuate *lies.*"

But who's lying now? Elise thought. *Juliette's accusation makes perfect sense.*

Killian Crewes had willfully, purposefully kept Elise from her uncle. He had touched her, and she did believe herself to be falling in love with him.

A fresh surge of anger hit her like a wave against a rock. Juliette snickered, but Elise barely heard over the crashing sound in her head. Fury drowned out the threat of tears. Fury drowned out reason. She backed away from Juliette.

"Keep out of it, Juliette," she warned her cousin. "You will make a fool of us all with baseless gossip."

"If it's baseless," lectured Juliette, "then I should be permitted to say so. I would *defend* you, Elise."

"You will not. You are no ally to me if you repeat a single word. If you defy me on this, hear me now: I'll have your trunks packed and send you back to your parents without a backward glance."

She gave her cousin a hard look and turned away, hurrying to the mews.

CHAPTER TWENTY-THREE

KILLIAN RACED THROUGH back passages and servants' stairwells to the stables. He would see no one. He would speak to no one. He would slip away from here and never return.

"Killian!"

The sound of his name rang through the courtyard like a rifle. He felt it like a shot to the gut.

He spun around.

"Stop," she called.

Killian followed the sound to a columned passageway. Princess Elise moved quickly to him, skirts clutched in both hands. The sight of her—merely the shape of her, as he could not yet see her face—caused every cell in his body to lean in. How unnecessary it was to tell him to stop. Of course he would stop. She immobilized him.

"What have you done?" she demanded.

"I beg your pardon?"

If he thought she would keep her distance, he was wrong.

If he thought she would give him the benefit of any doubt, he was wrong.

She strode from the shadows into the fading afternoon light, skirts swishing, braid swinging, mouth set.

Killian had the errant thought that he wouldn't move. That he would allow her to simply collide with him. She would hit him at speed and he would absorb the force, and then he would gather her up and carry her away from here.

But they did not collide; she rounded on him, eyes flashing. She raised her hands, like she held the evidence of his every crime.

She wore a gown he'd never seen before, a simple blue-gray silk. Her hair had been plaited into a thick braid. She looked clean, and beautiful, and furious.

"My uncle was here," she told him. "Here. In this palace. After ten years of living with strangers—no contact with blood relations, except my hateful cousin Juliette and her enterprising parents. My uncle was here, and *I* was *not*. And why? Because you took me away. You bundled me into a carriage and conveyed me miles and miles away. *On purpose*."

"Princess," he tried.

"You allowed me to tell you of my loneliness, and my confinement, and my desperation—and all the while, you conveyed me in the opposite direction. You moved me out of reach from someone who might help me."

"Highness," he gritted out, "I did *not* know."

"That is a lie," she declared. "I don't believe you. The timing was too perfect. The carriage was too ready. I *cannot* believe you—and do you know why?"

Killian had been prepared to hear her out. He would offer one (and only one) excuse and then simply accept whatever view of him she held. Having her accuse him, and blame him, and hate him would actually make it easier for her to lose him.

But now he could neither make excuses nor listen to her, because he saw movement out of the corner of his eye. It was a servant or an aide hurrying from one door to the next on the opposite end of the courtyard. He had to get her out of sight.

"Careful, Highness," he told her quietly. "Come away—come inside. We'll talk. We mustn't have this exchange out—"

"Oh, lure me inside, will you?" she tossed out. "Is this so you can continue your seductio—"

Killian lunged, fastening one hand over her mouth and another around her waist. Looking right and left, he swept her from the courtyard into a passageway that led to the cellars. Ducking through an arched doorway, he deposited her against the wall of a dark, empty corridor and leaned in.

"Shh, Highness," he breathed into her ear. "Please. I beg of you. Hate me, banish me away, send me to the devil—but we must be mindful of what you say in earshot of others. Can you stop shouting?"

She turned her face to the side, sliding her mouth from beneath his hand. She sucked in air.

"Don't touch me," she said.

Killian released her and stepped away. "I'm sorry, Highness, but it's not safe for you to openly discuss what's happened these last two days. You cannot rail about your uncle. Or me. Or our time away. No one else should hear, do you understand?"

She was leaning against the wall, breathing hard. She nodded. She looked down at her hands. They were balled into fists.

"I know you're angry," he said.

"You know everything, don't you? How very angry I am. The great danger that I invite if I shout. Who will visit the castle. Who will be absent when they come." She looked at him with hard pain in her eyes. *"You knew."*

"Princess," he vowed, "I did not know your uncle was due to call on the king; I promise you, I did not. I've only just learned myself."

"Why would you spirit me away on the same morning?"

"Because you asked me to take you to the Road to Land's End to find your brother. Remember—in the corridor, during the ball? It was a request that fit perfectly with my assignment from the royal family. Completing assignments on behalf of the royal family is my job, and I do whatever they ask—largely without knowing why. I've told you this."

"Is it also your job to kiss me? To . . . carry me across the room and hold me against the wall? To almost make love to me? What about to climb on top of me in a carriage? Was that also your job? Because this is what people are saying. My cousin Juliette has just *ever so casually* informed me that you'd been hired to *seduce me.* You should have seen her delight in relaying this morsel of information. She's poised to tell everyone in court the delicious news that the exiled princess has fallen into the arms of the Royal Fixer."

Killian was, for a long moment, devoid of words. He'd suspected she would learn of her uncle's visit. He had *not* thought she would learn about the seduction.

He squeezed his eyes shut and dropped his head, a man who'd just taken an unexpected punch. He swore under his breath.

"Who told her that?" he asked, speaking to the floor.

"I didn't ask. I don't want to know. I want it to be a lie."

Killian pivoted and leaned, shoulders first, against the wall beside her. He bounced his head against the bricks like a man testing the hardness.

She turned her face, watching him. "Tell me it is a lie, Killian."

"I can explain."

"Oh, God," she cried, and she dropped her face into her hands.

"You can believe your cousin, or you can believe me," he rasped. His voice sounded desperate—he *was* desperate. Why had he fought so hard to resist her, only to have her believe the worst?

"I trusted you," she whispered. "Outside of Marie, you were, in a way, my very first"—she looked up, searching the shadows for the word—"friend. In the palace. The first person in whom I'd confided *for years*."

"You misunderstand."

"Yes, I think I have misunderstood," she said bitterly. "When you listened to me, when you were appalled on my behalf, when you looked after me—*when you kissed me*. I thought you had formed some . . . affection for me. That I mattered. And you're so very handsome. And capable. How could I not want you? You *knew* I would want you. All women want you."

"I tried so very hard, Princess. It was like dying a little each time, *not* touching you."

"Why?" she demanded, lifting her head. "Why resist, if that was your job?"

"Because," he said, pushing off the wall, "I thought it was cruel and needless to feign romantic interest in a lonely young woman who'd been dealt a very bad hand. The last thing you needed was me, panting all over you. *And*, despite the very real fact that my romantic interest was *not* feigned, I thought I could do what the palace asked—"

"Withholding me from my uncle."

"—*distracting you*," he corrected her. "I thought I could distract you without putting my hands on you. My plan was to take you to Hampton and Sunbury and Lyne and follow along behind you as you interviewed blacksmiths. And herdsmen. I failed at this, obviously. You're too beautiful and clever and I wanted you and—God help me—I took what you offered. I tried so very hard to keep us from doing any lasting damage. I tried to keep it from going too far."

"I don't believe you," she said again, but the words sounded like a burden. It sounded like she'd tossed them out, just to be rid of them.

In the end, it didn't matter what was said. She wasn't listening. And he wasn't staying.

"Listen, Highness," he said, "I'm going. You'll never have to see me again. But please, please take care. Your cousin is correct about palace gossip. It will hound you now. Trust no one—do you hear me?"

"Well, you've given me a painful preview of how to do that."

"Right. So be it. You're welcome." He cleared his throat. "Trust no one. If possible, postpone your search for Gabriel until this business with your uncle is over. Louis-Stanislas may come again—he may come several times."

"What? He'll come again?"

"I don't know his travel plans. I do believe he's been in London for some time, just waiting for King George to grant him an audience. I believe the palace waited for the two of us to get distracted by the countryside before they ushered him in. But when he finally arrived, *this*"—and now Killian edged closer and looked right and left—"is what your uncle offered. Are you listening?"

"Of course I'm listening."

"Louis-Stanislas will trade information about French troops to King George in exchange for your suppression."

"My what?"

"The British royal family have promised to keep you quiet and out of everyone's way in exchange for military secrets. Make no mistake, King George *will* force your silence and compliance."

"*You* will force it," she corrected him. "He will hire you to do it."

He shook his head. "I mean to resign. I'm walking away."

She stared at him, hazel eyes huge. Killian wanted so very badly to kiss her in that moment. He took a step back.

"Why?" she asked.

He shook his head.

"*Why?*" she demanded, and he thought of how, despite the heartbreak of this conversation, he loved the sound of her voice when she wanted something.

"What could it matter, Highness? You don't believe me."

"Then why these warnings?"

"*For your safety*," he intoned. "I assure you, there's nothing in it for me, Princess. I only hope you'll take it to heart."

"You're being paid to lie to me. You want your warehouses."

He raised his hands in surrender. "I'm walking away, Highness. *You're* furious and hurt and betrayed. *The palace* asks too much. I'm *out*. I cannot. My closing salvo is to warn you. *Watch yourself.* Leave off your search for Gabriel for the time being. Try again in six months. A year. Allow things to settle."

"A year!" she shouted, and he rushed forward and clamped his hand on her mouth again.

She bit him, and he yelped and pulled back.

"I can't abide another day among these people," she said, breathing hard. "And what if my uncle does return? I'll be foisted on some other fixer?"

"Go back to your chamber, Princess," he told her quietly. "Put on your black and your veils. Stay close to your ladies. Be wary of your cousin. And bide your time. The British royal family are not exactly your friends, but they are also not your enemies. If you cease rambling, if you pause in searching for your brother, they will let you be."

"How very familiar this all sounds," she said, her voice breaking. "I've come full circle. Back to where I started. Silent and invisible. Meanwhile, you simply walk away?"

Killian closed his eyes.

She pushed off the wall. "You would leave me?"

In his chest, Killian's heart started beating again—he could feel it thudding away, like an actual working organ. Some small part of her wanted him still. She didn't want him to go. It was . . . something.

"Of course you would leave me," she was saying. "I was only a job to you."

"*Not true*," he sang, shoving his hat on his head.

"I was money, and property, and you did whatever it took," she said. "It's no different with your nephew. He is duty and obligation, and you do for him only what is necessary. There is no sentiment. You feel nothing."

"You are hurt," he said, his voice ringing with warning. "Because of that, you are trying to hurt me, too. Well, congratulations. I hurt."

"Yes, you are hurt. But you're well enough to walk away. A double rejection. You cannot cope with emotions that are large and uncomfortable and fiery. You conceal your motives, make your 'fix,' earn your payment, get paid, and run away."

He took a step back, shaking his head.

She continued, on a roll now. "You manage Paxton, buy old properties, transform them, sell them. It's all a cycle to you, and now the cycle has veered off course, and you don't like it, and you're walkin—"

Something inside Killian snapped in two pieces, and a terrible puff of loathing escaped. He loathed the royal family, he loathed her uncle, he loathed his constant need for money and the very thin thread that kept all of it aloft. He loathed everything *but her*.

He reached for her before he realized he had moved. One minute he was standing beside her, listening to her accuse him, the next, his hands were at her waist, and he was hustling her back.

She bumped into the wall with an "*Oof,*" and he fell against her, pressing his body to hers, dropping his face to the soft, warm curve of her neck. His hat fell to the ground. He breathed heavily in and out, in and out, awash in the smell of her.

"*Killian,*" she pleaded, tears in her voice. Her hands slid beneath his coat, and she caught the lapels of his waistcoat and held on. "Killian," she repeated.

"I am not dead inside, I assure you," he whispered. "I experience emotion like any other man. But my life is a balance of survival and obligation, and neither leaves excess time to manage how I *feel*. Because of this, I am better off not becoming mired in situations or with people who may distract me or upset the balance of my life. The lives of the people for whom I am responsible depend on it."

"That's not it," she accused him. "You're *still* lying. There is always room for love, Killian. Even the most cynical man will make room in his overburdened, complicated life for love."

Fool that he was, it thrilled him to hear her call him out. She was correct, of course. He made a growling noise against her neck. He pressed his body to hers. She whimpered in pleasure.

"Fine," he said. "You want the truth? The truth is, I've lost too many times in my life, and I cannot cope with losing again. And I *would* lose you, Elise. Because of *this*, I cannot love you." He made a noise of frustration and slapped the wall. "Hell, I've lost you already. You don't trust me. I was set up to fail. But no more. I'm going. I've left it. I'm gone."

"Killian, wait—" she cried, but he stumbled back, breaking free of her hold. He picked up his hat and shoved it on his head.

"Watch yourself, Princess," he said. And he turned and staggered from the passage.

When he reached the courtyard, he ran.

$\mathcal{N}$INE HOURS LATER, Elise slipped belowstairs and tapped softly on the door to Marie's small corner room.

The door opened a crack, revealing a sliver of her friend's face. When the nun realized it was Elise, Marie bobbed a reverent curtsy and poked out her head to scan the corridor.

Elise stepped to the side, proving they were alone. She'd waited ten minutes in the stairwell to make certain. Marie looked at Elise's gray hooded cloak and the heavy cross hanging from a pendant around her neck.

"We're running," Marie stated. "Forever or for a night?"

Elise's eyes filled with tears. If she had nothing else, she had a very loyal friend. "Only tonight," she said.

Marie nodded. "Can you make your way to Marlborough House Gardens? Meet me at the far corner?"

"Yes," Elise whispered. "Thank you."

"Go," her friend told her and disappeared inside, closing the door soundlessly behind her.

Elise shrank into her hood and made her way down the corridor, careful not to appear rushed. Her face was obscured and most servants were abed, but the sight of an unfamiliar nun in the servants' quarters would not go unnoticed. The corridor was unlit, and she felt her way with a hand on the wall. Kirby had drawn a diagram of the warren of passageways belowstairs at St. James's Palace.

The consequences of leaving the Queen's Chapel at night . . . without permission . . . were incalculable. Elise didn't care. For five years, she'd done everything exactly as they'd asked. And what had been the result?

Now she fled the palace like she was being chased—not by the royal family, but by regret. It was a tangled net around her body. She'd been so very wrong, and she was determined to set things to right.

When she emerged on the ground floor, she cut left through the empty ballroom. Squeezing around potted palms and stowed tables, she skirted the wide acreage of the vacant dance floor to the wall of glass doors. These doors were polished twice weekly by a cadre of maids. The chore amounted to hundreds of panes, inside and out, and the maids could be careless with the locks; this was a hint she'd learned from the queen's daughters.

Too late, she thought of sharing this hint with Marie, but Marie already knew most shortcuts and evasions. She'd prowled every foot of the palace—her first order of business when she'd arrived—and learned all its secrets. She'd made friends with staff members who were Roman Catholic, setting up a network of spies. Why, in God's name, had Elise waited so very long to send for her?

The second-to-last door was the winner—not only unlocked, but slightly ajar—and Elise opened it just enough to slip onto the veranda. Then it was down the steps to the garden, up the winding path, and finally over the wall. She landed on the other side in a flutter of wool. Freedom.

Heart pounding, eyes adjusting to the absence of lamplight, she ran down The Mall to Marlborough House. Ten minutes later, Marie met her there, bobbing a curtsy.

"Where are we going?" her friend asked. She'd dressed in her own gray cloak and cross. These had been their traveling clothes when they fled France.

"Bishopsgate," said Elise.

"Without or Within?"

"Within. But do not ask me where, because I don't really know more than the name of the street."

"Which is?"

"Lamb Street. Do you know it?"

Marie shook her head. "In Bishopsgate, I know only St. Anne's, the church."

"Can we get a hackney cab at this hour?"

"If not, we will walk," said Marie, poking her head around a juniper. "We walked across France, did we not?"

"Your loyalty astounds me, Marie," Elise said quietly. "Thank you."

Marie chuckled. "There is only one part of being a nun that I actually enjoy. That is serving as guardian and escort to you, Highness. It is a job required of almost no holy sister, and desired by even fewer. I was fortunate enough to both want it and have it land in my lap."

"I'm sorry I waited so many years to send for you," said Elise. "It wasn't clear to me that I was at liberty to make this request."

"You were not at liberty. I'm only here now because they wish to placate you."

Elise sighed. "*You* were sent to placate me. *Killian* was sent to distract me. I wonder if anyone thought to simply sit down and talk to me?"

"Doubtful."

Marie looked around and then nodded toward the road. The Mall was lined with lanterns, and they kept out of the flickering light. Carriages rolled by, a few men on horseback, but no hackneys.

"Would Lamb Street," Marie asked, "be the location of the King's Problem Solver?"

"Actually, the correct term is 'Royal Fixer,'" Elise said. "And yes. He lives on Lamb Street."

If Elise expected Marie to say more, she did not. If she expected her to ask why, she did not. They reached the imposing height of Admiralty House and trudged around it to Whitehall. Coaches, horses, and tired-looking oxen pulling a cart clattered by.

"There's a hack," said Elise, pointing half a block away, "there."

Two gentlemen spilled from a hackney cab, punching each other on the arms and barking with laughter.

"Hurry," said Marie. "Someone will poach it if we're not quick."

A minute later, they were squished inside the hackney, lurching their way to Lamb Street. The driver sat on the bench outside, singing to himself.

Elise lowered the hood of her cloak and took a deep breath. "He didn't know, Marie. Killian—Mr. Crewes—he didn't know."

"I trust you," her friend said.

"He didn't," Elise insisted.

"I trust you," Marie repeated.

The reality of Killian's innocence had come to Elise like a dip in the lake. First she'd waded into the possibility; then she'd paddled out to her chest, finally, the bottom dropped away and she swam about in the truth of it. *Of course* he'd not known about her uncle.

"You've spoken to him?" asked Marie. "Mr. Crewes?"

Elise nodded. "I confronted him immediately after I left you in my bedchamber."

"No one saw you or heard, I hope?"

"No. He dragged me to an empty corridor."

"He dragged you?"

"Well . . . I was not behaving, in that moment, like a rational person," Elise said. "Nor was I open to being marched about."

"Meaning . . . ?"

Elise cleared her throat. "I've exhibited one or two irrational . . . tendencies since making the acquaintance of Mr. Crewes, I'm afraid."

"Proximity to any man would certainly incite irrationality in me."

"He is not the source," Elise said. "It's not his fault."

"Oh, yes. The very great innocence of Mr. Crewes. I detect a trend."

Elise chuckled. "What I mean is, he did not cause me to behave irrationally. I am, in a manner, emerging from a sort of *hibernation*. It comes in fits and starts. Until I saw my brother, I was sleepwalking. Now I've awakened. The result is, there are moments when I'm overwhelmed by panic . . . or heartbreak . . . or—"

"Obscured judgement?" suggested Marie.

"*Goodwill*," Elise finished. "At times I am overwhelmed by goodwill. For Killian."

"'Killian,' is it?"

"Yes."

"Would that we were all so overcome," said Marie.

Elise added, "He makes me feel safe enough to . . . sort of . . . fall apart? For ten minutes or so."

"Gives you all of ten minutes, does he?"

"Well, I'm coming back to life—not running mad. Sometimes ten minutes is enough."

Marie looked out the window. "You would be well within your rights to run mad, Highness. I'm gratified to see you come into your own. If it takes finding your brother and . . . 'goodwill' toward the Palace Forager, then so be it. A lesser woman might not have survived the execution of her father and the loss of her home and family. It's remarkable, really. You are very resilient."

"Have I survived, do you think?" Elise wondered out loud.

"Yes, you have survived. Are you not stealing out of palaces in the dead of night? Seeking out shifty men in shifty parts of town? Hibernation over, I'd say."

Elise fingered the large cross hanging from her neck. "This visit to Mr. Crewes comes with no guarantee that he'll receive me. Just to be clear. I was very angry when we spoke earlier today."

"Perhaps he'd be more likely to receive you if the palace *paid* him?" suggested Marie.

Elise snorted. "He was honest about being paid to distract me. And he didn't know my uncle would call to St. James's while I was in his company. It can't be said enough. Unfortunately, this was not what I *said to him*. When last I saw him. Hence, this outing."

They rode for half a block in silence.

Finally, Elise said, "I do wonder why King George did not send me off with the queen and their girls if he wished to be rid of me. God knows they drag me to Weymouth often enough; what is another journey before autumn begins in earnest? I could hardly unsettle my uncle if I'm in *Dorset*."

"Perhaps they believe holidays to Weymouth might invite another 'sighting' of your brother."

Elise stared at her. "They think I'm mad, don't they? The royal family think Gabriel exists only in my head? An illusion?"

"On the contrary," said Marie. "They've invoked the Royal Finisher, haven't they? I've researched the man, and he does not work for cheap. They know Prince Gabriel is out there somewhere, but they want him kept a secret."

"Royal *Fixer*, Marie," corrected Elise. "Killian is the Royal Fixer."

"He is a paid lackey," said Marie, "but that does not mean he can't be an ally."

Marie had been watching outside the window, reading street signs and checking the location of the moon. "We're getting close, I think. Can you smell the river?"

Elise inhaled, choking on what was surely the combined scent of every passenger to ever inhabit the cab, especially the last sodden two.

"When we *reach* this unknown house of Mr. Crewes," confirmed Marie, "you plan to . . . reassure him that you do not blame him?"

"Oh no," said Elise. "I plan to apologize. For blaming him entirely."

"Now I see the urgency."

"My irrationality, you'll remember," reminded Elise. "I accused him of knowingly keeping me from my uncle. I called him a liar. I accused him of taking advantage. He offered excuses, and I wouldn't hear them. I was terrible, actually."

"Well, you returned from Middlesex to quite a shock. He will accept your apology."

"He may not. He may send us away. Also, I accused him of seducing me. Juliette suggested this—she stopped me in the corridor, veritably bursting at the seams to tell me. She'd heard he'd been paid to take me to bed to distract me from Gabriel."

Marie looked away from the window. "Juliette is a child and a menace. The value she brings to your entourage isn't worth the headache."

"I mean to return her to her parents," said Elise. "It will be complicated, but you are correct. She must go. *You* have come, and *she* will go, and also . . ." Now Elise paused. She swallowed. She took a deep breath. "And I will marry Mr. Crewes. That is the final reason I'm seeking him out. To suggest that he and I marry."

Marie paused in the act of reading street signs. She turned. She stared. Very levelly, calmly, she said, "Highness."

Marie never raised her voice—it was one of Elise's favorite things about her. When she was very, very alarmed, she would repeat Elise's title. Which she did now. "Highness."

"It was his idea," Elise told her. "Well, marriage in general was his idea—he thought I would have more freedom if the palace pawned me off as someone's wife. But I spent hours this afternoon sifting through what he'd done . . . and what he'd *not* done . . . and my own future in light of Louis-Stanislas's visit. In the end, a very clear solution revealed itself. It was like . . . a missing key that had been hanging on a string around my neck all along. I was searching through drawers and under furniture, too frantic to see it."

The hackney cab lurched suddenly, pitching them forward. The driver leaned down and called, "Lamb Street, sisters."

The two women ignored him. Elise held Marie's gaze.

"Do you think it's rash and imprudent and ill-advised?" Elise finally asked.

"Honestly, Highness," said Marie, "it's not my place to say. I'm sworn only to protect you and, if possible, restore you to reign in France."

Elise made a horrified face. "I hope to never be restored to reign in France."

"Fine. Then only to protect you."

"When you are acquainted with Mr. Crewes," Elise assured her, "you will see."

"This is almost never my experience when I meet men, but mine is not the place to judge. I'm here to serve."

"You will see," Elise repeated, singing the words, and they slid from the hack. Cool air rushed to meet them, sinking through their cloaks and gloves. The pungent smell of East London was more pronounced than the stench of the cab: soot fires, uncollected rubbish, latrines, and, in the distance, the Thames.

There was little fog tonight, remarkable for this time of year, and the lamps pushed back the dark. Up and down the street, houses slumped together, their roofs sagging, paint chipped away, windows cracked or boarded. It was a drunken hodgepodge, but Elise tried to see it as Killian would—full of potential, waiting to be shored up and restored.

"Luck is on our side, perhaps," Marie whispered, beginning to walk. "It's not a long street. Do you mean to . . . knock on doors? It is five o'clock in the morning—just a reminder."

Elise shook her head. "We look for the house that has been cared for, the one that looks refurbished and new."

"And if several look this way?"

"*Then* we knock on doors, I suppose. At the very least, we peer into windows? He told me he's bought up almost every property on the street, but he's only renovated one. That is where he lives."

"The one renovated house," repeated Marie, gazing up at the first building. It was missing a front wall on the upper floor, revealing the hollowed-out shell of two rooms.

"Thank you for including me in this venture, Highness," Marie said. "It would have been unwise to set out alone."

"Thank you for making no judgment," said Elise.

"Oh, I'm judging you," said Marie, "but silent, like."

Elise laughed and glanced back.

Marie cocked an eyebrow. There was a broken glass on the sidewalk, and she pointed. "Careful, Highness."

Crunching through the debris, Elise went on her toes to see around a slight bend in the road. There was a narrow alleyway and then, illuminated by two flickering sconces, was the broadest, tallest house on the block.

"This is it," breathed Elise, coming to a stop. "I know it."

In the line of sad, defeated houses, this property jutted proudly out, a hero with a chest of medals. It had fresh white plaster and green half timbers. The front door was shiny black with a brass knob. Heavy stone planters flanked the door, geraniums frothing upward and ivy spilling over the sides.

While Elise gazed at it, Marie peered down the thin alley between the house and its crumbling neighbor.

"How pretty it is," Elise marveled. "I count three stories, but perhaps there are four floors? A cellar, perhaps?"

"It's on fire," said Marie, coming back around.

Elise didn't hear her. She wondered if Killian would accept compliments about the house. He'd acknowledged her praise about Paxton Dale.

"Could he know how lovely it is?" she wondered.

"This house is on fire," Marie repeated.

"So pristine, despite the condition of the street. Imagine the maintenance—"

"Highness," Marie said, louder now, "do you hear what I'm saying? *This house is on fire.* Look. Look at the smoke from the window in the alley."

"What?" asked Elise, finally hearing.

"*Fire*," said Marie.

CHAPTER TWENTY-FIVE

𝒦ILLIAN WAS ROUSED from a drunken sleep by a very small, very frantic demon in a gray hood, shaking him by the shoulders.

"Get up, get up, get up!" the demon shouted.

True to so many demons, it had taken on a female voice—familiar to him and . . . hysterical? It almost, he thought, sounded like Princess Elise. Bloody hell, how drunk had he gotten? Clearly, the whiskey had done nothing to help him forget her, if her memory had arrived in demon form.

He squinted up, his eyes struggling to focus, but the gray hood obscured the demon's face. Also, the room was filled with black smoke—no doubt, the demon appeared in a great, suffocating puff of it—and his eyes burned.

Take me, he thought. *Take me to hell.*

"Killian, get up!" And now the demon had him by the boots and was dragging him across the floor of the library, knocking over empty bottles of whiskey with a terrible clatter.

"Ouch!" the demon cried, and its distress was so loud and sharp, Killian tried to sit up. His head was plunged into thicker, blacker smoke, and he was beset with a fit of coughing. The combination of sitting upright and uncontrolled coughing shot lightning pain through his skull, and he thudded back to the floor in agony.

His head felt like a detonated cannonball. His throat was a lit fuse. And he couldn't breathe. Hell was not a slow burn. It was a frying pan.

"Put this around your mouth and nose," said another female voice, and he had the errant realization that *all* demons were women.

Before he could open his eyes, someone jerked up his head and secured a gag over his nose and mouth, tying it securely with a yank. Now it occurred to him that he wasn't descending into hell. He was being robbed.

He forced his eyes open and tried again to sit up. Suddenly Hodges was there, stooping over him, obscured at the edges by black smoke.

"Killian!" Hodges shouted, reaching for him. He saw his manservant in small, fuzzy gaps where the smoke thinned. Hodges's white hair, usually oiled back to cover his bald spot, hung limp down the side of his head.

"Move. Away. From. Him," commanded the voice of the second demon-robber. "Stop. You'll topple over, and you're too heavy to lift. Go to the door. Go. We've got him. Highness, take him by the arm, and let us try again to drag him."

Highness?

Finally Killian achieved something close to sitting—a position that sent Hodges windmilling backward into the black smoke.

Killian ripped at the gag on his mouth, coughed, and then pressed the cloth back to his face. Sense returned to him all at once. This was not a robbery or hell. He was on the floor of his library in Lamb Street. The room was on fire. And, remarkably, horrifyingly, *Princess Elise* was here.

She appeared by his face, feeling her way down his arm until she could take hold. When she found his right elbow, she began to pull. In the same moment, someone pulled his right boot. The motion flipped him on his side—and then they were dragging him.

"Wait, wait, wait," he gasped, tugging his limbs free. "I'm awake. I can manage. You shouldn't be upright. Get down! The low air is better."

He scrambled to his hands and knees, trying frantically to make sense of the flashes of gray wool pawing beside him. He spun, searching for flames. He saw only black smoke.

"Elise!" he called again—he'd lost sight of her—and he struggled to one knee. "Elise?"

Suddenly she was there, coming down hard beside him, a whoosh of arms and knees and gray wool. He fell toward her, coughing.

"Who is with you?" he shouted. He'd seen movement through the smoke and heard another voice.

"Marie!" she shouted back.

"You must get out," he shouted. "How did you get in?"

"The window! We saw the smoke and broke a window and climbed inside."

"What?" he yelled. Surely he'd misheard. This made so little sense. *How did she find my house? Why did she come? What princess and nun crawled inside a burning house instead of running away from it?*

"It doesn't matter," she shouted back. "We must get out. Is there staff elsewhere in the house?"

"No!" he said. "No one lives in save Hodges." *Bloody hell—Hodges!* "I have to find Hodges!"

"I have him!" called the nun, wading through the thick smoke. At her side, Hodges leaned limply with an arm around her shoulders. The nun was taller than Hodges, but the older man outweighed her by three stone. Even so, she was taking long, sideways steps, dragging the two of them toward the door.

"Marie, I'm coming!" he shouted. "Let him fall and get yourself down low!" To the princess, he said, "Crawl to the door, Highness! Go! Hands and knees!"

Killian swam through the smoke to Marie and rolled the manservant from her shoulder to his.

"I have him," he shouted. "Get as low as possible."

Killian took a step to follow but was overcome with a fit of coughing. He staggered through it, bending at the waist to find better air. Hodges hung from his right shoulder like a bag of rocks. Killian's eyes refused to open against the burn of the smoke. His lungs were useless. Securing Hodges with one hand, he reached out with the other. He knew the layout of his library, but he'd become disoriented in the smoke. He couldn't find the wall or the door. He thudded on, coughing, tangling his feet with Hodges's boots. All the while, he thought, *Elise. Elise. Please let her survive this. Elise.*

When at last his searching hand hit the smooth wall and—a few feet over—the door, he collapsed against it. He thrashed around with his free hand, feeling for the doorknob. *Why had they closed the door? Did they mean to lock us in?*

Killian nearly dropped Hodges, trying to kick the door, but then it gave way, and he fell through, Hodges on top of him.

The women were there, dragging him out and shoving his legs out of the threshold so they could slam the door shut again.

"The smoke is contained in the library," said the nun. "If we keep the door closed, we'll enjoy the fresh air here in the corridor and trap the smoke in the library. Breathe, Mr. Crewes. Breathe."

"The fire." Killian coughed. "I have to go back in. Get out—all of you. It will devour the house."

"The fire is extinguished, Killian," said Elise. She was suddenly there, hovering over him, alive, smiling. She wiped at his face with a cloth.

He inhaled and was consumed with another coughing fit. She rolled him onto his side and rubbed firm circles on his back.

"How can you know the fire is out?" he gasped, trying to get on his hands and knees.

"Marie and I beat it out," Elise said, "with cushions from the sofa. Then we smothered it with soil from your potted plants. It had only just sparked when we came upon you. There was prodigious smoke—how you'll ever clean the soot and smell from your library, I've no idea—but the greater house is sound. Your philodendrons are not likely to survive."

"My what?" he asked, flopping over. He sat up, still coughing, and felt the wood of the closed library door. It was cool.

Beside him, Hodges made a choking noise, then sputtered, then rolled onto his side and began to cough. Marie slapped him on the back.

"That's right," Marie said, "get it out."

Hodges honked like a goose—but he was alive. All of them were, miraculously, alive. If what Elise said could be believed, his house had been spared. Another miracle.

Now she was crouching beside him, her small hand on his shoulder. "If you've caught your breath, go in. See for yourself. Take a lantern, cover your face and mouth. We opened the windows, but you've seen the smoke. It appeared that someone set an open candle too close to the window and the drapes caught fire. We ripped them from the wall and heaped them in the center of the floor. You'll find them covered in soil."

Killian struggled between coughs to comprehend what she was saying. She offered him a cloth, and he took it and held it to his face. He went up on his knees and opened the door a crack. The first rays of dawn glowed through the window, dulled by hanging smoke. The air was thick with it, but the billowing had subsided.

He closed the door, staggered to his feet, and took a sconce from the wall. Holding his breath, he opened the door again and went in.

Ten minutes later he stumbled out, coughing, rubbing his eyes with his wrist. The women scattered, allowing him to drop to his hands and knees. Hodges was sitting up against the wall, his shirt open to the waist, his hair a one-sided waterfall.

"It's my fault, Kill," Hodges wheezed. "I was the one who took up residence under the window. I didn't think about the candle."

"We were both stupid," said Killian between coughs. "We could have burned the entire block—we could have burned all of London. Drunken carelessness is exactly how it starts. Do we deserve to have been spared? I'm not so sure."

He glanced up. Elise and Marie looked down at him like they'd come across a dead body on a stretch of deserted beach.

"Thank you," he said to them. "I am mortified that you put your lives at risk. You're correct about the fire. The drapes are a smoldering heap. We would have likely burned without your heroism. But . . . Highness? Sister? Why were you here?"

For a long moment neither of the women spoke. Finally, the princess cleared her throat and said, "I would speak to you, Killian. When you have found your breath. On a matter of—well, several matters of—importance."

Killian blinked. She sounded like a clerk in the solicitor's office. "Alright," he began, climbing to his feet. He was overcome by another fit of coughing. "But *how* did you get here?"

"We hailed a hack near Admiralty House." This was from Marie. She did not sound like a member of the clergy. She sounded like someone who'd missed a night of sleep to hail hackney cabs and fight fires.

"How did you get in my house?"

"We broke a window," said Elise, "in the next room."

They broke a window in the next room. He squinted down the corridor. His head pounded, his throat stung, and his eyes burned. His brain struggled to process that a French princess and a nun had saved his life and his home by breaking windows and throwing plants at flaming drapes.

"What window?" It was all he could manage to ask. The more he understood of the situation, the more horrified he became. He was a careless, reckless, sodden miscreant.

"Just . . . there?" the princess said, pointing one room to the left. The parlor. For no good reason, he trudged to the room in question, stepping over Hodges in the process. The first pinks and oranges of sunrise shone through the parlor window, now open to the morning. There was a pile of broken glass on the floor.

He turned back. "I'm sorry. Clearly I've inhaled too much smoke. Are you saying that you crawled through broken glass into a burning house?" This question came out at a near shout. He'd been a lot of things in his life: spare heir, dancer's son, Royal Fixer, aspiring landlord. But surely drunken victim who endangered the lives of innocent women was the very, very worst.

"Please take into consideration," the princess said, her own voice rising, "we thought you were in danger."

"*I* was in danger?" he repeated. "You thought *I* was in danger? What about you? I would never, ever expect you to put *your* life in danger for me, Highness. Never. Why didn't you call for help? Why didn't you—"

"If you don't mind," the nun cut in, "I would just as soon leave the two of you to sort out whose life was in more danger and who should've been left to burn alive. The palace cannot awaken to both of us gone; I'm no help to the princess if I've been sent back to Ireland. Can I trouble you to borrow a mount, Mr. Crewes? Now that we've all been reunited, I should take my leave."

"You're going?" Killian rasped. "You would go and leave her?"

"The princess is very motivated to see you," said Marie.

"Well, to *speak* to you," the princess cut in.

"To speak to you," amended Marie. "Fully conscious. And not on fire. Perhaps the best way to characterize it is, her work here is not yet done. Mine, on the other hand . . ."

She looked at the princess. Elise nodded her head.

"I leave her in your capable hands. I should add that she is perfectly capable herself—the window was her handywork, and she was the first one through the jagged teeth of the broken glass—but two is generally better than one."

Killian couldn't think. "But how will we restore her to the palace? Without gossip? Her reputation—"

"She has some idea about this. But if you please: A horse?"

Killian tried to comprehend what they were asking— the princess wanted to see him. She had some plan. *She'd crawled through a broken window.*

"I can always set out on foot," Marie was telling Elise.

Killian stepped to Hodges and nudged him with his boot. "Can you manage to escort the sister to St. James's, Hodge?" He turned to Marie. "You and the princess saved two lives tonight, Sister Marie—not to mention thousands of pounds in property. I am forever, forever, in your debt."

"You're welcome," the nun replied. "My advice to you is, never drink yourself into a stupor around open candles and heavy drapes."

Hodges rolled to one knee and sucked in a few deep breaths.

"There's a good man," Killian encouraged, hauling him upright. "Off you go. You heard the nun. We are better off as two."

He turned to the princess.

"*You*," he said.

She smiled at him. She actually smiled.

"We've several pressing matters to discuss," she said.

CHAPTER TWENTY-SIX

$\mathcal{K}$ILLIAN, SILENT AND enigmatic, led Elise to the basement kitchens. He did not take her by the hand. He did not tell her why. She trailed behind him, passing beautiful rooms and interesting art, saying nothing.

If he'd seemed *open* to talking, she would have complimented the beauty of his home. She would've asked him questions about the paintings. Each room told her a little story, and she would've held up her interpretation to his vision.

The parlor said, *Snowy morning with the broadsheets.*

The drawing room said, *Drinks with friends before the opera.*

Meanwhile, Killian said . . . nothing. And Elise was too wrung out from the sleepless night and the fire to cajole him. She would need all her energy for the apologies. After that, the proposal. If he wished to wind her through the empty house in silence, so be it.

They passed a large mirror in a bronze frame, and Elise caught her reflection. Her hair was limp and lifeless, her dress streaked with soot. Before Marie had gone, Killian had shown them to a basin where they could splash water on their faces. They'd removed their gray cloaks and hung them outside. The smell of smoke still clung to her, but she wasn't quite so grimy. Without the nun's cloak, her green dress looked . . . if not "smart," then less like a nun.

"Sit here," Killian said when they reached the kitchens. His first words.

The belowstairs kitchens told Elise yet another story. She could imagine an exacting cook and her staff busily preparing a feast for Christmas. The rooms were illuminated by high windows that lined the ceiling and looked out on the walkway above. There were wide stone counters, devoid of a single crumb or stray spoon, a wooden table that could double as a barge. Shelves were laden with pots and pans in neatly ordered stacks.

"Coffee, Highness?" Killian asked. He was kneeling before a large stone hearth, laying a fire.

"Alright," she said.

He inhabited the kitchen with precise movements, setting the kettle to boil, scooping coffee from a barrel. Elise had never actually seen anyone make coffee—coffee had always appeared before her—and the process fascinated her. She was also fascinated by Killian's takeover of this kitchen, efficiently moving from fire to cabinet, from basin to stove, in his shirtsleeves and trousers. He'd changed shirts since the fire, and scrubbed his face enough to push soot to his hairline. His coffee-making routine was efficient but also graceful, quiet except for the *clink* of a dish on the stone counter, the slide of his boots on the floor.

"Mind the temperature," he said, presenting Elise with two things: steaming coffee in pretty blue china, and a pile of new pieces to the puzzle that was Killian Crewes. One piece was his proficiency in a kitchen. Another was her strong preference that he never again wear a waistcoat or a jacket.

After the coffee came a fragrant loaf of bread, dotted with currents and glazed on top with sugar. He placed this on a wooden board and set it beside two small plates.

Next, a floppy bunch of purple grapes and a triangle

of cheese. He piled these on a second board before her, along with a knife.

Elise hadn't felt hunger, but now her mouth watered. She flashed him a shy, grateful smile.

"Eat," he said.

"Will you take some?"

"My cook and housekeeper will arrive soon," he said. "They'll not expect me to be in the kitchens. I'll keep watch." He pointed to the windows that looked up to the street.

Elise nodded and tore off a corner of the bread. It occurred to her that she'd not really scripted how she might raise her apology. Was it possible that she'd come all this way with no real plan? It made her laugh, thinking of all she'd hoped to say to him yet with no strategy for introducing it.

"What?" he asked.

She shook her head and took up the coffee. "I called to your house, so I suppose the burden of introducing conversation is on me . . ."

"You saved my life, Highness. Surely that is enough of a burden for today."

"Meaning?"

"Meaning . . . it will take some time for me to reckon with everything you've done for me. Crawling through broken glass? Fighting a fire to—"

"Stop." She held up a hand. "Your very great shock at being rescued has been made clear. But the more you belabor it, the more you demonstrate a lack of confidence in me. I am perfectly capable of navigating a crisis, thank you very much. I'm not helpless, nor am I unwilling to come to the aid of someone in a burning house."

He blinked. "No, I—"

"It's an insult, really, when it comes down to it. I know we've become acquainted with each other at a very odd time. I'm sheltered and, in a way, muzzled by my . . . my benevolent overlords. But please remember, I fled my home and family with only the clothes on my back. I am not helpless, nor am I without courage. Your speech-lessness and shock are misplaced. Of course I broke a window and put out the fire. Let us go forward from it—honestly. We've more important things to discuss."

"Alright," he said, crossing his arms over his chest. "Your point is well-taken. And . . ." Now he looked away. The next bit came out as a low chuckle. "Did you know I love it when you put me in my place?"

Elise paused, the cup halfway to her mouth. "I beg your pardon?"

"You"—a tired sigh—"delight me."

"Thank you." She'd not expected praise. Was he flirt-ing with her?

She cleared her throat. "This is delicious."

"You are delicious."

So he *was* flirting. She stared at him with narrowed eyes. He gazed back. Invisible sparks popped and spun be-tween them, hotter and wilder than the fire in his library.

First things first, she thought. She moved her coffee to the side and placed her hands flat on the table. She looked to him. "I should like to make an apology for what I said yesterday in the courtyard."

He raised one eyebrow.

Elise swallowed and continued, "I behaved abomina-bly. I was callous. I dismissed your reasoning. I accused you of seduction. I called you a liar. After you'd gone, I had time to think on the events of the last few days. In hindsight, I was very wrong about all of it. I have reasons for leaping to conclusions, but I'll not muddy my apol-ogy with excuses. I know you to be an honorable man; I believe your intentions were well-placed. You have been truthful with me, despite this job you do for the king and your obligations to your nephew, which I know hinge on the money you earn. I'm so sorry, Killian. If you cannot see past it, I understand. But if you would consider absolving—"

"Do you feel seduced, Princess?" he cut in.

Elise blinked. This was a question she had not anticipated. "What?"

"Do you feel seduced? By me?"

"I . . . I don't know." What she felt was a jump in her heart rate. She felt a low hum in parts of her body previously dormant and exhausted. She was suddenly wide awake. All of her.

"I meant to apologize for all of my accusations," she told him. "Not just the, er, suggestion that you seduced me."

"I hear your apology, but I would like you to hear my defense. If I set out to seduce you, Highness, you would know it. Just to be perfectly clear. Overturned carriages and uncomfortable horseback rides in the company of my nephew are not seductions."

"Oh," she said.

"Yes," he confirmed. "*Oh.* That's more like it; the sound of someone being seduced. *Properly* seduced."

And then suddenly, he was coming for her. One moment he was standing on the other side of the table, arms folded, the next he was sliding chairs out of the way, leaning to her, shoving dishes aside.

He lowered his face a whisper away and breathed, "May I, Highness?"

Elise didn't answer; she turned her face up and met him, locking her mouth to his.

Killian cupped her cheeks in his hands and went deep. Their tongues met; the hum in Elise's body turned into the shimmer of a cymbal.

Without breaking the kiss, Killian crawled onto the tabletop and balanced before her on his knees. Elise rose up to meet him, settling each of her hands on his thighs, fingers spread, digging into the muscle. His legs were like iron; his mouth was like heaven. He tasted like smoke and coffee and *him*.

And then he was lifting her, not breaking the kiss. Elise went, grasping for his ribs, his shoulders, his head.

In one swift movement—an arm beneath the hips, another across the shoulders—he swept her from the chair and laid her out on the table. Elise settled in with a sigh, releasing his neck and dropping her hands over her head. At the foot of the table, cutting boards and china hit the floor with a clatter.

Killian sat up and stared. "Oh, Princess," he rasped, "just look at you."

Lifting a knee, he straddled her, positioning his body to answer so many unspoken requests. His heaviness pinned down the bits that were floating away. Elise's eyes dropped closed at the sheer pleasure of it, the weight, the security.

But now he was tracing the line of her throat, splaying a hand on her chest and teasing the neckline of her gown with a finger.

"May I?" he rasped.

She nodded, moving to help him. The bodice was tight, and her fingers fumbled in frustration, trying to peel back the fabric.

"*Shh*," he soothed, and he lowered over her, dropping to one hand. With the other, he worked at the bodice.

"What about now? Do you feel seduced *now*?" he whispered, pressing a lingering kiss to her lips. He rolled his thighs, pressing against her center.

She made a little gasping sound. "*Killian.*"

"Is that a yes?" He rolled again and dipped in for another kiss.

She whimpered.

"Right. Unclear about the seduction. We'll return to it. But what about *absolved*? Do you feel absolved? Of the guilt that drove you to my home in the middle of the night?" he asked.

"I feel . . . I feel surprised. I thought you would hate me—that you wouldn't want me. I thought I would have to beg."

"Begging? Now there's an interesting notion." His fingertips had finally wiggled into the neckline of her gown. He peeled back the silk and nestled his palm against the stays that barely covered her breasts.

Elise sighed and arched her back. "Killian," she pleaded.

He lowered his lips to her breast and kissed her nipple through the mesh fabric between the boning of her stays. She called his name again.

He smiled and peeled the bodice from her other breast, roving over it with his palm until his fingers found the burning tip. He returned to the other breast, repeated the torture; he went back and forth. The sensation was part pleasure, part *not enough*. Desire sluiced to her center. She wanted him to never stop, but she also needed him to do more.

She began to, ever so slightly, press up against him, to writhe and sigh. He dropped his mouth to her ear, breathing hard. "What do you want, Elise?" he whispered.

"Yes," she huffed.

He chuckled, a low vibrating rumble that raised goose bumps on her sensitized skin.

"Tell me what you want," he repeated in her ear.

"All of it. Everything. I want you."

"I want you, too," he said, nuzzling his way back to her mouth. "I want you so bloody much." He kissed her hard, and Elise surrendered to it. All reason and purpose left her. She dug her hands into his hair and squeezed.

"Good morning to you, too, Mrs. Danvers. Can you believe this sun, so late into September?"

Unfamiliar voices pierced the haze of their desire.

Killian jerked his head up. He swore.

Elise craned around, following the voices.

"I said the same thing to my husband this morning, Mrs. Feeney," came the cheerful reply. "But, do you smell smoke in this alley?" A cough. "Breathe in, Ruth. Do you smell it?"

Through the narrow windows at the ceiling, she saw the hems of two skirts and the soles of two pairs of sturdy work shoes.

"My housekeeper," Killian said. "And the cook. *Bollocks!*"

He sat up, looked around, and then said, "Up you go."

Taking her by the hands, he rolled her to a sitting position. Elise made a small cry of alarm, clutching her wilting bodice. He was in her lap—they were nose to chin now—and he dipped to kiss her one time, quick and hard. Then backed off her body and hopped to the floor. Next he reached for her, scooping her to the edge of the table and tugging her to stand.

"Hurry, hurry, hurry," he whispered. "If they see me, I'll need a half hour to explain about the fire. If we escape, Hodges will return and sort them out."

A moment later, they were at the stairs, scrambling up. Elise tripped on her skirts and laughed. He put a finger to his lips, and she clapped a hand over her mouth.

When they reached the ground floor, he pulled her through the center hall to a U-shaped staircase.

"Shh," he warned again, pulling her up. Elise followed, holding her skirts in one hand and her bodice in the other.

When they reached the top of the stairwell, Killian looked right and left, almost as if he didn't know the way.

"I don't know where to take you," he admitted.

"*Emmenez-moi dans votre lit*," she whispered, falling against him. *Take me to bed.*

"God save me," he said, pulling her to the right.

They came to the first door, and he pushed it open. It appeared to be a small office. Two large desks faced opposite walls, the surfaces littered with architectural drawings.

"Not here," he said, and kept walking.

"Killian, I am not particular—"

"Don't want to presume too much," he mumbled, stalking past three doors.

"What do you mean?"

"I mean, there are bedrooms on this floor, obviously, but I'm not a complete blaggard. Yet."

They came to the last door in the hallway. He hesitated a moment and then pushed through. The room inside was mostly vacant; sunlight shone on a stray chair. There was a plush rug in the center of the floor.

"Let's try this," he said, pulling her in and slamming the door behind him. She was barely inside before he gathered her up and crowded her against the closed door.

"Highness," he said, coming down on her mouth again.

"Call me Elise, please."

"*Princess*," he whispered.

She made a whimpering sound and nipped his lower lip. He laughed against her mouth and moved closer. He hooked his hand under her knee and hitched her leg up.

"Elise," he said, "we should pause for ten seconds." Another kiss. "It would be wildly irresponsible if we didn't pause and indulge in your favorite thing."

"Swimming?" she asked after his next kiss.

"*Talking.*"

"Talking is not my favorite thing."

He kissed her again.

She pulled away, breathing hard. "About my apology?"

"I accepted your apology. It's finished," he said, kissing her. "We need to talk about how I'll restore you to the palace. We need to talk about what more I can do to keep you safe. I was a fool to think I could just walk away."

Elise nodded, kissing him back. In her head, she thought: *this is it*. This was her opportunity. There would be no better chance to raise it.

She dropped her head against the door. She put her hands on his face. "Yes. I agree. Let's talk. I have something to tell you—something to *ask* you."

She lost heart then, closed her eyes, and kissed him.

"Right—good," he breathed, pulling back. "Will you begin? Princesses first."

Elise nodded, swallowed, and said, "I want you to marry me."

CHAPTER TWENTY-SEVEN

KILLIAN WAS FALLING.

He was falling through a hole in the floor, followed by a hole into the next floor, and through the cellar and into hell. The burning drapery had been only a preview. Now he would take up actual residence, because hell was the ultimate destination for careless, avaricious men who wanted too much and tempted fate. Now fate was fed up. He was being proposed marriage by the woman with whom he'd fallen so madly in love. The one he could not have. The royal princess who lived in a palace and whose brother or uncle might become king of France. *Him*. Killian Alexander Crewes.

He had wanted too much.

"Killian?" she asked, looking at him with those large, expressive hazel eyes. She cupped his face in her hands, preventing him from looking away. He could only blink at her or kiss her.

He kissed her.

"Killian," she repeated, laughing a little, evading the kiss. "Did you hear?"

"Yes."

"*Yes*, we should marry," she asked, "or *yes*, you heard me?"

He gaped at her, and she laughed again. "How very

nerveracking this is. I've no idea how men routinely make proposals."

"Stop, Highness." He wrapped his hands around her wrists. Gently he pulled from her grasp and moved away.

"Oh my God," she realized. "You're going to refuse me."

He glanced up. Her expression was so mortified, he stepped back to her and took her in his arms. "I'm not refusing you."

She wiggled free. "You are. You're refusing me."

Now she sounded angry. She rolled from the door and began to amble about the room.

"And I thought the apology would be the difficult bit," she was saying. "*The apology* was the thing to reject. *There* was the wrongdoing. *Not* the proposal. The proposal is the most sensible, logical thing. *You* raised it. It was *your* idea."

"What?" He tried to go to her, but she moved away.

"*You said* the solution for my freedom was to be married. *You said* my future husband might indulge my search for Gabriel. *You said*—"

"*I* would never presume to be that husband, Highness. Princesses do not marry members of the palace staff. It's unthinkable. No one would allow it."

"Stop. You're hardly a footman. And I wouldn't care if you were."

"I'm not certain you have the freedom to care. There is an order to things in this world, Highness. Your family . . . other royal families of Europe . . . ? They'll have someone in mind for you—a prince or a count who leverages your lineage and his lineage and future alliances and borders and international trade, for God's sake. The only thing leveraged if you marry me is . . . is—this house, which sits in the middle of a slum, and is currently absent a library."

"I like this house," she said.

"Perhaps, but you cannot make your life here. It's not safe; there are footpads and prostitutes up and down the block. You'll be robbed or worse. No friends would call to bloody Bishopsgate. *No one* comes here unless they have the very bad luck to live here."

"Better to be unsafe in Bishopsgate with you than locked in St. James's Palace with indifferent strangers. And spare me your international altruism, please. The future treaty of Hanoverian-Prussia or Franco-Bulgaria? I've given enough to *France*, thank you very much—and the British royal family is currently very low on my list of priorities. The rest of Europe? I could not care less. I want *you*, Killian. I am a flesh-and-blood woman whom you seem to regard rather . . . warmly"—she yanked at the slanting bodice of her gown—"and our two individual lives are my only concern. I . . . I've fallen in love with *you*, Killian. What care have I for any of the rest?"

They were circling each other in the empty room. When Killian cycled past a chair, he grabbed it, lifted it, and put it down hard. If he could, he would crumble it to kindling. How had it come to this?

"Careful with the furniture," she warned. "Wherever will the royal princess sit if you damage your lone chair?"

"You mock," he said, "but you've passed most of your life inside one palace or the next. You are accustomed to a certain life; meanwhile, I have very little to give you. I have dreams, I have plans, I have run-down properties that I hope to restore—but they are years from being suitable for a wife. Paxton Dale belongs to Bartholomew. I could put you there, I suppose, but think on it, Highness: Is a country house filled with dogs, a dancer, two old maids, and a child better than St. James's Palace?"

"I am unseen to the inhabitants of St. James's Palace," she told him. "Except when an *actual* member of my *real* family comes to call—then they hire you to send me away. I'll not be used as a pawn—not for France, not for Britain, not for anyone. I'll marry for my own future happiness, and I *want* to *marry you*."

"How dare you," he asked quietly, closing his eyes, "come here . . . save my thankless life . . . and then offer me what I want most in the world? How dare you?"

"I dare because I refuse to live like a rare bird in a golden cage for another minute. And I want to find my brother. And I've fallen in love with you, Killian."

He made a growling noise and spun away. Why must she repeatedly ply him with every single thing he wanted?

"You know what your problem is?" she asked him. "Your problem is that you always say, 'Absolutely not.' Your first answer. Every time. And I'm so very weary of it. If I thought you didn't like me, I could understand. But you aren't saying no to me. You're saying no to your-self. You won't allow yourself. If you want me—here I am—stop refusing the both of us."

She took a deep breath and held up her arms. She looked like a dancer at the end of a performance.

And oh, the irony of that metaphor. Killian wondered idly why he was not partial to dancers. Why not carry on the family tradition? Why must he fall in love with princesses instead?

"Not to belabor the point," he asked, "but how am I to provide for you, Highness? If we marry? I'll be sacked for marrying the woman I'm meant to be keeping out of trouble. Fine—I am unbothered by their dismissal. I was going to walk away, but that was when I only supported Bartholomew, Pearl, the two aunts, and myself. Oh, and Hodges—who, I might as well tell you, is my mother's brother. That's right, my manservant is also my uncle. Meanwhile, your uncle is the future king of France—if your brother doesn't beat him to the punch. But do you see my point, Elise?"

"Hodges is your uncle?"

"My mother wanted to provide for him," he said dismissively. "He insisted upon working for his living, so she attached him to me. We get on very well. It's a story for another time, surely, but the relevancy here is, he is the opposite of royal and yet very much a part of my life."

Elise was shaking her head. "We will find a way, Killian. I'd rather have a humble existence than be without you."

"You say that, Highness, but let us explore the notion of that humble existence. What if you're forced to find *work*? Are we to become like Bartholomew's tutor and his wife, Mr. and Mrs. . . . bloody *Pile*? Remember Mrs. Pile? Amelia Pile was born to live a life of privilege and marry a gentleman. She married her brother's tutor instead, and now she is destined to chase Bartholomew and his dogs around Paxton Dale. And she's *lucky* to have the job."

"Mrs. Pile did not seem unhappy to me," the princess shot back. "Given the choice between my current life and serving *any* function at Paxton Dale, I should choose Paxton without hesitation. Even if you'll not have me, perhaps you would offer me employment instead."

"I would never 'not have you,' Highness." He sighed, running a hand through his hair. "I want only you. From the moment you lifted your veil at Tattersall's, I wanted only you. But I learned years ago that the things I want most are, in the end, *not* destined to be. Decades of heartbreak have shown me this."

"Ah, this again. The crux of the matter, at last. Tell me," she said. "Tell me of these years of heartbreak."

He shook his head. He would not burden her with

what he'd gone through as the hated half brother to Peter Crewes.

"Fine," she said, "don't tell me. However, *I* can tell *you* that a pattern is not the law. What happened in the past is not absolutely preordained to happen in the future. You'll have to do better than that."

He laughed at her then. He couldn't help himself. She was so very confident, and she was not afraid of him—not to tell him their future and not to love him. Apparently. Remarkably. He wanted her with every thud of his heart.

"May I ask you," she ventured, "what was your plan here, exactly?" She'd begun another circuit of the room. Killian saw her coming in his direction and moved to the wall.

"What plan?" he asked. "There was no plan. I planned to get drunk and have one night's respite from this damnable situation. Even that was stolen from me by the great drapery fire of 1803."

"Not last night—*today.* You laid me out on the kitchen table, Killian. You led me, half-dressed, upstairs. I can only assume that you intended to make love to me, and then what? If you will *not* marry me? This is not an accusation, mind you—I've made no secret of my desire for you, and I would have followed you half-dressed anywhere. But I know you to be a man of honor, and I'm curious. What did you intend to do with me next?"

"Well . . ." he began, and he felt his face redden. He was blushing. Against all odds. Mortifyingly. Perhaps for the first time ever.

". . . I thought to," he continued, "give *you* pleasure . . ."

"Come now, Killian," she sang, "do not tell me you intended to make me your mistress or have a torrid affair, because I won't believe you. You could have done that and gotten paid by the palace for your trouble."

He frowned. "Right, *Highness*, if you would have it so

spelled out, here you go: there is a way to give you pleasure that does not risk pregnancy or your innocence . . ."

She had the decency to look confused. "There is?"

"Yes. There is. However, please be advised. My intention was to leave you innocent in a physical sense but not
in practice."

And now who was blushing?

"*Oh,*" she said, her eyes going wide.

Killian watched her turn over his threat in her mind.
She was radiant—almost too beautiful to look upon—
clutching a handful of her skirts, biting her lip, gazing at
him through lowered lashes.

"*After that,*" he continued, "I thought I would smuggle
you into the palace, and we would . . ." Here he trailed
off. He couldn't finish. It was a lie to say that he could've
walked away. Not from his princess. He could see that
now. It was always a shite plan.

"*And we would . . . ?*" she prompted. "*What?*"

He sighed. "I never imagined a world where we would
marry, Highness. I couldn't allow myself."

She stopped her circuit of the room. She turned to
him. "*Imagine it,*" she said.

Killian half laughed, half swore. "I need a moment."

He walked to the window and looked down at Lamb
Street. Neighbors—working-class people in drab clothes
trailed by skinny children—greeted each other in the
street. She would have him bring her *here*? A royal princess, making her home in Bishopsgate?

It was unthinkable—and yet . . .

"What is this room?" she asked, advancing on him.

He watched her come. Something about the look in
her eye made his mouth water and his body harden.

"The room has no purpose at the moment."

"The light is nice," she said. "It is warm, even with
no fire."

"I thought . . ." he said softly ". . . I thought eventually, it could be a nursery."

"What?"

"I said"—he turned to face her—"I thought it might one day be a nursery."

"A nursery? So you intended to marry someone. You just hadn't intended to marry me."

"How could I ever dream of marrying you, Elise?" he asked softly.

She closed the distance between them. "*We* are getting married as soon as possible." She bumped up to him. "But first, what was that you said about ridding me of my innocence?"

And with that, he lost all grip on self-control. He gathered her up and lowered them to the floor.

CHAPTER TWENTY-EIGHT

ELISE WAS BEING a bully, and she didn't care.

If she must be a princess, and she must be exiled in a palace of apathetic opportunists, and she must be a pawn of several nations—then she would also order people about.

Well, she would order Killian. At least while he was being so very obtuse. And for what? Reasons that probably felt very personal and important but that otherwise blocked the fortuitous road to happiness that stretched before them.

The bullying stopped, however, when he pulled her to the floor.

How lovely—the floor. Also, the tabletop, the wall in his mother's cottage. He knew all of these inventive places to kiss her. In this, she was grateful to cede control. She wanted him to take her up and sweep her away.

There was a rug in the center of the room, and they rolled to it—legs entwined, arms clutching, his hand protecting the back of her head—kissing all the way.

When she was flat on her back, Killian on top of her, he broke the kiss and smoothed the hair from her face.

"Fine?" he asked.

She nodded, tracing a finger down each of his biceps.

He winked and descended again, kissing his way southward. He'd not shaved since Paxton Dale, and his jaw was stubbled with delicious little whiskers that scraped and tingled as they brushed her skin. He began with her neck, licking, nuzzling, breathing into the little hollows and notches of her throat and collarbone.

She had the errant thought that this area of her body had misled her all these years. She'd always considered it to be so very boring and practical—a means to hold up her head—but now it sang and shimmered with the most tantalizing sensations.

After he'd kissed and tasted and teased until she was gasping his name, he dipped lower, using both hands to peel back the bodice of her gown.

Cool air teased her breasts through the thin fabric of her stays. She raised her head just in time to see him slowly, reverently, *plucking* the ties at her shoulders, releasing the stays until her breasts peeked free. Her skin tingled, alive with anticipation, but he didn't touch her. He craned up to gaze at her, to drink in the sight of her bared before him, to worship her with his eyes.

Witnessing this was almost as delicious as his hands (almost), and some previously unknown instinct caused Elise to arch, bowing up, tipping her breasts completely free.

He swore beneath his breath and dropped drunkenly to his elbows, a man shoved to the ground.

"*Elise,*" he breathed, finally touching the bare skin of her breasts. "Elise, you are so beautiful—so much more beautiful than I imagined, and I imagined quite a lot."

It was very poetic and terribly sweet—Elise enjoyed praise and admiration—but she'd stopped listening. His hands on her breasts elicited a newer, higher, more intense feeling of pleasure. She arched again—not for his perusal, but to position her body closer to him. She called his name. She raised her hips, seeking, seeking,

seeking something hard enough to satisfy the burn inside of her.

"Do you feel innocent, Highness?" he huffed against her breast.

She made a muffled sound of pleasure.

"Yes?" He sucked on her breast.

Elise made a small cry of pleasure, and he slid back to her mouth, kissing away the sound.

"The servants have come," he whispered against her ear. "We may divest you of your innocence, but we must be quiet about it. They will be unsettled when they discover the fire."

"But will you do that last bit again?" she panted.

He chuckled and re-kissed the path to her breast. He homed in on the burning tip, and the explosive pleasure shot through her body again. Again she screamed, her blissful reaction too surprised and too urgent; her control was lost. How dizzyingly, burningly *good* it felt; how it radiated such a lovely little burn to so many other parts of her body.

Her thoughts came and went in hot, fevered flashes.

Yes.

Love you.

Marry.

Yeeessss.

But then he was leaving her breasts and dragging his face lower. Elise whimpered, not wanting him to stop. She was suddenly so curious about his next destination. As good as his attention felt at her breasts, the sensation in her body spiraled downward. Pleasure had pooled between her legs, a bright, shimmery throb, and the more she'd pressed against him, the brighter it burned.

Maybe if he meant to . . .

Perhaps if he could . . .

"Killian," she panted, placing her hands on his shoulders as he descended.

"You're killing me, Highness," he grunted. "In case I forget to tell you. I'm deceased. Fortunately, everything about this encounter has made my life worth living."

She half chuckled, half cried and called his name, the only word she could manage.

When his head was level with the crux of her thighs, Killian dipped against her, pressing his face into her skirts, breathing in.

It was a heavy, muffled pressure, and the thrill of this, was so all-consuming, Elise could no longer cry out. She let out a breathy little moan.

"Ready, Highness?" he said, peeking up.

"What?" she whispered.

"Innocence *almost* lost? As I promised. Ready?"

Elise pushed up on her elbows. "Wait."

He was in the process of raking up her skirts, but he let them fall. He gaped at her with an expression of horrified panic.

"No, no," she amended, "not, *wait, I'm not ready*. I mean, *wait, I want it all*."

"What does that—" His voice broke. He cleared his throat. "What are you saying?"

"I want all of it. All of you joined with all of me. I want this resolved and finished, and I don't want some fraction of the experience. I want all of you."

"Highness . . ." He rolled back on his haunches.

"Do not tell me no again, Killian, I swear to God."

He laughed at this, as she'd hoped he would, and looked at the ceiling.

Channeling her newfound instinct to entice, Elise rose from her elbows to her palms, arms straight behind her. She was naked to the waist, and her skin glowed pink where he'd touched and licked and scraped her. She shook her head, swinging her hair. Slowly, she raised one inviting eyebrow.

Killian drank in the sight of all she offered. He looked away, swore under his breath, and then vaulted up, taking her by the hand.

Elise let out a little yelp—one moment she'd been posing before him, and the next she was on her feet, being led from the room. She yanked up her stays with her free hand and clutched her gown to her chest.

"Where are we going?" she asked. "Are you aware, this marks the second time today you've dragged me, half-dressed, through the corridors of your house? Am I being seduced or taking a tour of the property?"

"*Shh*," he warned, cracking the door. He looked right and left down the corridor.

"Where are we going?"

"To a proper bed."

He slipped out, tugging her behind him. They dashed three rooms down, to a room she'd not seen him consider when they'd first canvassed the corridor. Killian cracked the door and pulled her inside.

Elise blinked, her eyes adjusting to the darkness. Velvet drapes blocked the windows, but a varied landscape of heavy furniture took shape in the dark.

"Where is this?" she asked. She shimmied and bounced to smooth her stays back in place.

"My bedchamber," he told her. He left her near the door and stalked to a piece of furniture in the corner.

"May I let in the sun?" she asked.

"If you like," he called, still rummaging. "The servants know to keep out until I descend for breakfast."

Elise found a thick braided cord and tugged the drapes away from the window. Daylight cut into the room. She squinted, trying to determine the story of this room. It said, *Bachelor* (the paneling was stained wood, the paint was masculine blue); it said, *Styled just so* (the furniture was not a matched set, but each piece existed in harmony with the room); and . . . *Architect*? There was another desk littered with schematics for buildings and gardens.

"Here it is," Killian said, turning from the bureau.

"What?"

He walked to her, holding out a small gold ring. The center stone was a ruby, large enough to be seen from across the room, surrounded by what appeared to be diamonds. Killian presented it to her with a cautious smile. Elise, fool that she was, was more captivated by the smile than the ring. As a general rule, Killian Crewes did not smile.

But he was smiling now, and she smiled back, and they stood in this beautiful bedchamber, beaming at each other over this ruby ring.

"What is this?" she whispered.

"My mother's wedding ring. It is, quite literally, the only thing I inherited when both my parents were gone. She was a beautiful soul, and my father loved her very much. He had this ring made for her. It is . . . only an object, obviously, but it has a great deal of value to me. I would be honored if you would have it. As a symbol of our . . . betrothal."

Light shone into Elise's chest like the window. A sunbeam of hope. Perhaps she'd bullied him, but he wanted her. He wanted her enough to give her his mother's gorgeous ruby ring. He wanted her enough to stop their lovemaking to prove his commitment.

"Yes," she said, "yes, I should be honored to accept it."

She held out her hand, and he tried several fingers before it slid securely on the pointer finger of her left hand.

Elise gazed down at it, shifting her hand this way and

that to admire the twinkle. It really was beautiful, and look how it—

"*Now* . . ." he ventured.

Elise glanced up.

His smile was gone. He looked at her the way a starving man looked at a feast.

Elise was suddenly, inexplicably shy. "*Now* . . ." she repeated, dropping her hand.

"But perhaps the moment has passed?" He raised his eyebrows and studied her.

She shook her head. She wanted him. She wanted what he'd been doing to her and more of it. But she was unsure of how to get from here to there. She glanced over his shoulder at the giant bed.

"I don't know what to do," she whispered. She looked again at the ring.

"Will you give me a kiss, Highness? Here?" He pointed to his left cheek.

Elise glanced up. Well, yes of course. She went on tiptoe and placed a soft, slow kiss just below his eye. His skin was warm. He smelled like smoke. She lingered half a beat and then pulled away.

"Thank you," he said.

"You're welcome."

"And what about another kiss—here?" He pointed to the other cheek.

She chuckled and went up again, kissing him—a little slower this time—beneath his other eye. She lingered longer here, reveling in the closeness. He blinked, and she felt his eyelashes on her nose.

It occurred to her that she wanted to kiss his mouth—it was just *there*, so close—but he'd pointed to his cheek, not his mouth. After a long moment, she pulled away.

"Very nice. But what about one more kiss . . . right

here?" And now he pointed to his lips. He tapped his finger two times in the center of his mouth.

Elise didn't hesitate. She wrapped her arms around his neck and kissed him, full on the mouth. Just a peck at first, like the others. And then one peck became two, and two pecks became three—each of them longer. And then she wasn't pecking, she was kissing, really kissing—eyes closed, fingers sliding into his hair.

He waited for what seemed like an eternity to reach for her. When he finally fastened his hand around her waist, she'd long since stopped pecking and slanted her head, invoked her tongue.

"Is this alright?" he breathed into her ear.

"Yes."

His hands left her waist and followed the curve of her body downward. He palmed her bottom and gently scuttled her against him. "What about this?"

Elise nodded, allowing her brain to float away on the heady sensation of building a kiss with Killian. She hoped he would stop asking her for permission. She hoped he would carry her to his large bed. She hoped—

He stooped a little and lifted her, poker straight, above him. It was a slow lift, and she broke the kiss only when he'd slid her so high, she could no longer reach his mouth.

"Bed?" he asked her.

She nodded, and he carried her to the bed and toppled her back.

"Elise?" he asked, crawling on top of her.

"Killian?"

"This can happen so many different ways, as you may know." He paused. He looked into her eyes. "Did you know this?"

She chuckled and gave a shrug. "I cannot make sense of what I know."

"Right," he said. Another long kiss.

She wanted to kiss him, truly she did, but she was also keenly interested in what he was about to tell her. "Continue," she prompted.

"Right. So, one of the ways is more of what we were doing in the empty room—which is exciting and breathless but difficult to recapture outside of the moment from which it . . . erupted. It can be done but—" He shook his head. "I'm sorry. I shattered the mood because you said you wanted more, and it seemed very important that you have the ring. It was, perhaps, unsporting of me."

"Go on," she said, smiling a little. She was so very happy.

He cleared his throat. "Right. Another way is very slow and reverent, with a sort of ritualistic removing of clothes, and a lot of eye-gazing and breathing each other's names. I've never actually experienced this, but I can envision it."

"Oh, similar to when you were examining my legs for breaks?" she asked.

It felt so very good to have him on top of her—large, and hard, and stabilizing. She hooked one leg over his boot.

"The examination of your legs was done in the spirit of deep concern and in a manner wholly clinical in nature. Strictly scientific."

Now she laughed harder, and he laughed, too, peering down at her. "I love you," he whispered. "God help me, I tried not to, but I love you."

"I love you, too," she whispered back, sobering a little.

And then she asked, "But what is the way that *we* will carry on with, er, it?"

"Well, I wondered, in the interest of being steeped in smoke, streaked in soot, exhausted from the night, and also plunged into the blinding brightness of this room, if we might endeavor some combination of several ways? A bit reverent, but perhaps without peeling off every stitch of clothing. A bit breathless, but without threatening to expire. And a bit of something that is singular to this moment?"

Elise nodded. "Yes. I like it. That sounds very nice."

He made a face. "'Nice' is not necessarily what a man aims to achieve the first time he makes love to his wife, but I promise we will never stop exploring the great many ways to embark upon . . . this."

She nodded.

"You're certain?" he asked.

"I'm very certain."

And so he made love to her . . . on top of his coverlet . . . with the morning sun pouring into the room. They gathered her skirts to her waist and unbuttoned the fall of his trousers but didn't make time to remove their shoes.

He kissed her senseless instead, worshiping her mouth while she roved over his shoulders and back and chest with her hands.

By the time the burning, shimmering desire pooled again between her legs, Killian was draped on top of her. Her body responded by pressing up, again and again, that glorious rocking she'd done on the kitchen table, and he adjusted them so they could rock together, their bodies touching but not yet joined.

"Killian, please?" she said—the words out of her mouth before she even realized she was going to say them.

"Yes?" he confirmed.

"Yes, yes, yes."

He reached to tuck each of her knees over his hips,

and Elise thought how lovely it was to embrace him with not only her arms but her legs as well. Lovelier still was how very essential this position felt.

"Careful," Killian gritted out, reaching between them, and Elise wasn't certain if he spoke to her, or himself, or the universe. But then she felt his erection against her, and he cupped her bottom, and she felt a sting, and then a fullness. So *very* full. Too full? She wasn't prepared to judge this right away. He was kissing her again and the kisses felt somehow deeper, more intimate than before. She struggled to keep up.

She opened her eyes and looked into his face, so close to hers. His eyes were closed, but he felt her gaze and blinked.

"Are you alright?" he asked.

She nodded. "Are you?"

He laughed at this, an awkward, pained sort of breathy sound, and she realized she'd said something foolish. She frowned, a little abashed, but he kissed her again, and she realized the fullness had dissolved into something more like . . . completeness. Elise rocked a little, repeating the delicious motion they'd enjoyed before he'd entered her, and that felt rather nice. The fullness had a purpose. Something to sort of . . . press around. Press against? She couldn't work through it because her ability to think kept getting hung on little tickles of pleasure. And then the very demanding instinct to press upward overtook her, and her ability to think was not hung, it dissolved. *Poof.* No thinking, only feeling.

Above her, Killian began to, ever so slightly, move up when she moved down, to move in when she pressed out. This had the effect of making everything *more* interesting, and she could only press . . . and kiss . . . and feel the fullness and the completeness and the pleasure. It was like a beautiful dance that she'd never been taught. And yet, somehow, she knew the most important steps.

"Killian," she heard herself call.

"I have you, Princess," he answered.

"Killian," she called again. They worked toward something; she could sense that now—the rocking and the kissing and the touching culminated into—

"Killian!" she shouted. Her insides were suddenly tossed, gloriously, into the air like coins at a wedding. They spun and twinkled. Her metaphorical self hovered there, resplendent with pleasure. And then she fell, settling back inside herself. Almost all the parts dropped back into their original positions except for possibly a few jagged edges of her heart.

Above her, Killian seemed to experience his own toss and spin. He, too, hovered, and then she felt his body empty within her. She understood.

When it was over, they lay, panting, in a tangled heap. Finally, Killian lifted his head.

"Are you . . . well?"

She opened one eye. His face looked gravely concerned.

"I am well," she told him. She raised a hand and laid it on his cheek.

"No regrets?" he asked her, rising on his elbow.

"No regrets."

He kissed her.

"May I sleep?" she asked. "Here? For just . . . perhaps ten minutes . . . before we sort out what to do about the palace?"

"That sounds glorious," he said, lowering his head to the crook of her shoulder. He rolled off of her, an uninvited retreat that felt a little like an act of aggression. It had felt so very good to have him lying on top of her. She was cold and weightless without him.

But then he was gathering her against him—and that felt good, too. He caught the edge of the coverlet and folded it over them. That felt even better.

"Just a half hour," she mumbled, snuggling into him.

"No more," he agreed.

And they fell asleep.

CHAPTER TWENTY-NINE

HEY AWAKENED WHEN Hodges came, whistling, into the room, carrying a bundle of firewood.

Killian's first awareness was that he was not alone in the bed. He opened his eye and saw brown hair and pale skin.

The princess.

His whole world had changed, and there was so much more change to come. Good change—glorious change—but also planning, and unraveling, and sorting. It would be the biggest "fix" of his life.

He sat up, tugging the coverlet over her body. "What time is it, Hodges?"

"Kill," the man said. "I thought you was out dealing with Her Serene Highness. Sorry, should I come back—"

"A fire would be welcome, but can you tell me the time?"

"Three o'clock in the afternoon, Kill. Have you eaten? I can have something sent up."

"What became of the nun? Marie?"

"She asked to be let out in The Green Park, which is what I did. Where is Princess Elise?"

Killian felt Elise go tense beside him, and he laid a steadying hand on her hip.

"She is here, actually. But I would take something to eat, I think. Can you have Cook send up a full breakfast?"

"Breakfast? But it's—"

"Yes, yes, it's afternoon—but just the same. A full breakfast. For two. Have Barlow leave it outside the door."

And now Hodges, eyes wide, firewood forgotten, slowly raised his chin and craned his head, trying to make out the unfamiliar contours beneath the coverlet. Killian gave him a stern look and a warning shake of his head.

"Right, Kill," said Hodges, a smile on his face. "Breakfast for two. I'll see to it presently." He deposited the timber in the fireplace. "Anything else?"

"What of the library?" Killian asked on a sigh.

"It's bad. The damage from the smoke. Could have been worse, though. They saved us, to be sure."

"Aye. Keep the maids out of there, will you—it's not safe. I'll write to one of my builders, have him send a few men."

"Right. I'll tell the staff. What else?"

"Merely . . . I'll require all of your good discretion and undying loyalty, Hodges? In the coming days?"

"As ever, Kill," Hodges said. He winked at him and left the room.

When the princess heard the door shut, she sat up.

"Good morning," he said, his heart thudding to life at the sight of her. Her hair was rumpled, and her bodice sagged, revealing the most tantalizing view of one perfect breast. Her creamy skin had been abraded by his beard to the most gorgeous raspberry pink.

"It's not three o'clock in the afternoon," she said.

"It is, I'm afraid. Not cause for panic, but we need to think carefully about what to do."

"I've been gone all day. Marie can only lie on my behalf for so long." She dropped her head in her hands. His mother's ruby ring caught the light and flashed. The sight of it on her finger made Killian feel gratitude, and pride, and something like triumph all at once.

"Oh, Marie," she breathed. "I've taken terrible advantage. I must send a note to her. When we determine what happens next, I'll send her some cryptic version of events. Let me think . . . Where will she be at this hour? How could we have slept for so long?"

"Lovemaking can have that effect. Also, firefighting, drunken benders, hackney rides in the middle of the night. You needed the sleep, and for this reason alone, I don't regret it. But we cannot"—he watched hungrily as she took up her stays and smoothed the undergarment against her glorious body—"tarry."

Determined to put some distance between them, he slid from the bed. If she was within arm's reach, he would touch her. If he touched her, he would have her.

"Tell me about the patterns of a normal—What day is today?" He knelt before the fireplace.

"Tuesday?"

"Right. What happens on Tuesdays in the Queen's Chapel?"

"Well, every day is very much the same. They will take tea at four thirty. If we could manage to get me back by teatime . . ." She slid from the bed.

"What will Marie have told them?"

"I cannot say. She'll have to be located. She is allowed to attend me, but she is not necessarily welcome to meals or teatime. She devotes much of her time to marshaling spies among members of staff who happen to be Catholic."

"I don't like this," he said, speaking to the grate. "I don't like sneaking about and the risk of you being reprimanded because you've left court alone. I cannot say how long it will take to procure a special license—and to a royal princess, no less." He swore to himself. "It will not happen quickly. I will do what I can, but let us not pretend it will be easy. I am not Catholic. You are not Anglican. At this point, I don't have the permission of a guardian. I have to find a way to reveal to the palace what we intend . . ."

"Wait," she said. She'd been smoothing her skirts, but now she stopped.

"Killian," she said excitedly, "why not carry on as you've been? Complete your assignment from the royal duke to seduce me?"

"What? Elise—no. It was always a crass and cruel way to solve their perceived 'problem,' which is why I refused to do it in the first place. I wouldn't do it when I barely knew you, and I'll certainly not do it now." He arranged the wood in the grate with swift, frustrated movements.

"It was crass and cruel when I was an unwitting *pawn*," she explained. "But now that I *know* you're meant to seduce me, and now that I am *so very fond* of being seduced, and now that you've already taken me to bed? Let us see it through. Then you can claim to be plying me with your wiles, and the royal duke can make excuses to Queen Charlotte, and we'll be left alone for a time. You can use it to sort out the marriage license."

He was shaking his head. "You'll be the talk of court. I'll not have you be the source of ugly gossip."

"What care have I for gossip in court? When we marry, and I can quit the palace forever."

"It could take weeks for me to find a way for us to be legally wed."

"I can tolerate palace gossip for weeks, I assure you," she said. "Especially if I'm freely allowed to engage in a torrid affair with the Royal Fixer. Let's see . . . I can play it one of two ways. I could return to my black dresses and veils and deny everything, or I could accept it and say I've finally emerged from my malaise and I'm ready to be the French courtier everyone expected me to be. It doesn't really matter; they care for only one thing—not finding Gabriel. As long as I don't speak of him, I can comport myself however I like. Although . . . the most believable thing may be to return to the way I was. Quiet. Biddable. Forgotten. If I can manage that, it will appear that you're doing a crack job."

"But what is the end result? If I claim to be seducing you, how do we walk away? Do I go to them and claim, 'Oh, and by the way, as a result of seducing Her Serene Highness, I also fell in love with her, and now we intend to marry'?"

"Why not?" she said. "Oh, but buy your warehouses first. Think of it!"

"This will not happen," he said.

"It could. How vehemently did you bemoan the fact that you cannot provide for me? If you have your warehouses, we'll be that much further along. I may not be able to find employment like Mrs. Pile, but I can make money indirectly as a pawn in King George's court."

"Absolutely not."

"*Absolutely yes.* And the best part is, we'll not need an elaborate web of lies to sneak in and out of the palace. Our 'affair' will be an accepted thing. We needn't be brazen about it, but if Edward approves it, the queen will turn a blind eye."

Killian shoved up from the fire and strode to the window, looking out. He shook his head. First he would remove her from everything she knew to marry him—and then use her to earn money along the way?

"This will not end well, Highness," he said.

"You're not thinking like the fixer, Killian. We have a problem—yes. But here is the fix."

"This is different. There is so very much at stake. I've seen what can happen if you endeavor to outsmart people in a position of power. Eventually they discover the ruse. Or they realize you're taking advantage. Or they feel you've presumed too much. And do you know what they do next? They arrange for the natural order of things to be restored. It's one thing to lose the protection of the palace, it's another to have the palace come after you with a grudge."

There was a knock at the door, and Killian poked his head out, spoke to a footman, and then wheeled in a trolley laden with eggs and toast, coffee and tea, beans and bacon.

"Will you eat?" he asked, maneuvering the cart before the fire.

"Killian?"

"I kept you from eating when we were in the kitchens before—brute that I am. You've not eaten all day. Come, take something. Did you taste the bread when we were belowstairs? My cook is rather good, for all that."

"Killian," she repeated.

He eyed her and took up a plate, heaping it with eggs and bacon.

"What do you mean by 'the natural order of things being restored'?"

He made a scoffing noise. "I mean that I've been paid to do their dirty work for years. I cannot also make off with a spare princess. It's not the natural order."

"But you are a gentleman—the son of an earl. You move seamlessly through court. You claim to require money, but you've restored two beautiful homes. There is some gap here."

"If nothing else, drink something. I can ring for cider if you don't want coffee."

She sighed. "Remember how I said I regard you like a puzzle? There are so many bits of your nature that do not align and even now, something is still missing. Tell me."

"I'm not a puzzle, I am a man, same as any other."

"If you were the same as any man, I would not be joining my life with yours. I find you remarkable, in case I've failed to convey it. But part of you remains a mystery."

He looked at her and then away. He'd told her his mother was a dancer. He'd told her the earldom had slipped from his grasp into the lap of a child. That was enough.

"Please understand," she continued, "when *I* think of people in power, I think of hapless, helpless *victims*. In France, the powerful elite were rounded up and murdered. I, myself, have been miserable in exile and powerless to do anything about it. You behave as if we're beholden to outsiders who would steer the very course of our lives. That has been my plight, perhaps, but I am a woman. You are a man. You buy and sell entire buildings. You are personally acquainted with the king. I don't understand."

He poured coffee and drained the cup.

"Tell me what happened," she said.

He sighed. "When?"

"Whenever!"

He held out a plate. "Come, sit, eat."

"I will if you explain to me why you're so uncertain of your authority to marry whomever you desire."

"It's no small thing to take an exiled Catholic princess as my wife."

"Perhaps it isn't, but is it *impossible*? You are not a common laborer, Killian."

"Fine," he said. "But what if I say there is no story here? What if I tell you I've endured a thousand small demotions over the course of my life? That my mother had been a dancer and my half brother never let anyone forget it?"

She took the plate and filled it with fluffy eggs. "Fine. Say the worst thing. Remember dinner at Paxton Dale? My conversation with the earl? That's what I did; I said the worst thing."

He laughed. She was beautiful and demanding, and he couldn't believe he would reveal this to her—of all people. That was the magic of Elise: he was dazzled by her royalty, but she wanted them both to be human, above all.

"It's a boring story," he warned her, wiping his mouth. "Painful to me—but nothing like what you've endured."

"Do not return to the topic of shock and awe over my survival. I'm sturdier than I look; we've already covered this."

"Right," he said, "fine. When I was in my first year at Eton . . ."

"Oh, it's the Eton story," she exclaimed, munching toast, "finally."

He shook his head. She was trying to make this easier for him, and—honestly—it was working. She made him more human, but she also made humanity seem less . . . wretched.

He cleared his throat and started again. "When I was in my first year at Eton, my brother, Peter, lured my mother—my beautiful mother, who wanted nothing more than to be a good stepmother to him—from Paxton Dale to Eton College under the guise of visiting me. He told her there was an event—a mother-son dinner—and that she should come as my guest.

"She kept her distance from my school," he explained, "because of how coldly she was regarded by other society families. But when Peter insisted that I would be the only boy without his mother present, she rallied her courage and came."

Killian took a deep breath. "And of course there was

no dinner. Peter, who was in his last year, had arranged an unofficial 'salon' for his classmates, complete with prostitutes and dancers brought in from London. When my mother arrived, nervous and hopeful, Peter met her and, under the guise of not having a mother himself, escorted her with unusual solicitude to this entirely fictional mother-son dinner.

"You can guess the rest," Killian said. "My mother was led into a room of randy, pubescent boys who'd been promised a tawdry, ribald show. She was introduced *not* as Countess Dunlock, but by the name she'd used to perform on stage. The girls brought in from London were hustled in beside her and instructed to preen and dance about. My mother was stunned, and mortified, and— although a proficient performer—caught entirely off guard.

"Myself and some other boys—the most influential and popular boys in my year—had been dragged to a back door to witness the spectacle. Because this was an unsanctioned event, it was held in an empty barn. It was cold and muddy, and the boys waiting for the 'show' devolved into a cacophonous scrum of hoots and shouts. They threw things—*threw food*—at my mother.

"The irony was, I had been excited to be included. I was about six months shy of understanding the older boys' ravenous slavering over London prostitutes, but I knew they considered it a very special night. And I knew that only the most esteemed boys from my class had been tapped to see it. Imagine my horror when I realized that the entire show had been designed for the sole purpose of humiliating my mother and me, and sealing my reputation for . . . baseness in the minds of every future peer and gentleman's son at Eton."

"Except for the royal duke—your mate from across the hall?"

"In the early days at Eton, he was never without his personal attendants and royal guards, and they minded him with a very heavy hand. He hadn't yet learned how to attend underground student gatherings. He did hear about it—everyone heard about it—but by that time, I'd already made myself invaluable to him."

"But what happened, Killian?" Her voice was gentle now. She spun the ruby ring on her finger.

"Peter had his mates release me—I was fighting to free myself from their grasp—and I raced to their make-shift stage. I covered my mother with my own small coat—she never dressed as provocatively as Pearl, but she was no shrinking violet, and Peter had told her the theme of the dinner was *A Midsummer Night's Dream*—and I pulled her to the door. Peter and his friends had, naturally, blocked it, so we were forced to wind our way through leering, jeering boys to the back door, which, by that time, was also locked. My mother was hysterical when I finally found a way to get her out—and honestly, so was I."

"Oh, Killian," Elise said, and she rose to crouch beside his chair. "I'm sorry I was so cavalier about it. That is a horrifying story. My God. No wonder you mother suffered attacks of panic."

"She loved my father so very much, but she never enjoyed being a countess. They would not accept her, and she felt like an imposter. *And* she had this bitter, hateful stepson, who worked, tirelessly, to reinforce that feeling. This has been my worry for you, Princess. I do believe you love me, but can you live a different life?"

"It's not the same, Killian," she said. "It's not remotely the same. It's simply not."

"Perhaps not. However, when you ask me about approaching the royal family to offer for you? This . . . this is the source of my trepidation. For years, they've paid me to redirect, curtail, contain, and punish anyone who crossed them. I have been always on the outside, and now I presume to take one of their own as my wife? I am loath to cross Edward, no matter how highly he regards me. I've always kept the royal family at arm's length. They pay me well, but I ultimately have very little protection from them. I've no title, no alliances with titled gentlemen, and no family—save those who rely upon me—and a very tenuous bank account." He took a deep breath. "I am vulnerable, in a way, and we must be . . . very careful how we handle this. Do you see?"

"I do," she said, laying her cheek against his hand. "And I'm sorry for baiting you. After years of exile, I am overeager; I am ready for any risk. You, in contrast, could benefit from risking *less*. We will find some middle ground, Killian. When we are married, we will find it."

Killian pulled her into his lap and buried his face in her neck. "I love you," he said. Not a promise, not a wish, simply the truth. It was all he needed for now.

"What of this?" she suggested, toying with his hair. "Let us make the tentative plan to carry on with the seduction. You were asked to seduce me, and I will be so very seduced. I will search for Gabriel only in private—studying maps and reading books about horse traders—but be otherwise subdued. When you sort out our path to marriage, we will reveal ourselves to the royal duke; we'll admit that we've fallen in love. After that, we'll ask them if we may simply walk away. Complete honesty should mean lower risk. No deceit or betrayals; a man fell in love with a woman—nothing more. You'll ask for no payment; no money need change hands. You'll miss out on the warehouses, I'm afraid. I'm so very sorry."

"It's nothing," he said. "Nothing I could buy or sell has value compared to you."

It must have been the correct thing to say, because

she made a little whimper, and turned in his lap, and straddled him.

"Is this," she murmured into his ear, "one of the ways?"

Killian dropped his head back and let her come to him; to kiss his mouth and splay her shirt open with his hands and touch the skin of his chest above his heart; to move her hands lower and touch more of him, to touch all of him. She allowed him to escape the burden of being human while engaging in marginally animal behavior. In the love that, surely, transcended both.

$\mathcal{U}$LTIMATELY, KILLIAN CONSENTED to Elise's plan, if for no other reason than it allowed them to restore her to St. James's Palace that afternoon with little more than a note to the royal duke.

Killian told Edward that he'd taken her to one of his properties, they'd lost track of time, one thing had led to the other, and they'd spent the night. He told him the seduction was well underway and that Her Serene Highness needed a bath and a meal on a tray and otherwise to be allowed to sleep off their night of passion.

"She'll not be bothering you with talk of her brother anytime soon," he'd written—a final flourish of Elise's design.

The princess had sent her own note to Marie, and the nun, along with her maid Kirby, had met her in the courtyard and ushered her to her chambers.

Sure enough, the royal duke sent back his thanks and assurances that he would smooth over comings and goings with the queen.

If it bothered Killian that he and Elise wouldn't enjoy a proper courtship, with chaperones and tea and turns around the garden, Elise said she didn't care. The less-than-proper experiences of their "affair"—carriage lovemaking and kissing against trees in a thicket of Hyde Park—were far more satisfying.

When they were away from the palace, they made love—or, made some approximation of love; he was careful after their first time not to risk pregnancy. He did not return with her to the house in Bishopsgate. God willing, she would be mistress of that house one day, and he would tolerate nothing less than respect from his staff.

When they were not together, Killian worked tirelessly to sort out how he might marry her. He could take her to Gretna Green in Scotland, where virtually anyone could marry. He could take her to France and search for a sympathetic priest. In London, the options were far more limited. Her Catholic faith and his Anglicanism were a huge complication. Also, their lack of permission from a guardian. Meanwhile, her friend Marie was making discreet inquiries with priests, and the princess had written her mother in Spain. With every letter and interview, they risked someone learning that the exiled princess was endeavoring to run away with the Royal Fixer.

Despite the absolute delight and restorative qualities of their faux "affair," the stress of managing the wedding was slowly ripping him in two. He spoke to solicitors and clergymen until his head swam with contingencies and caveats, then he would see her, and she would stitch him back together. He'd been severed and sewn so many times he felt like an old sail, and he prayed he would eventually manage to catch a strong wind and carry them where they needed to go.

And then, after two weeks of loving her in the day and lying awake at night, trying to sort out some way to love her always—to *legally* love her—he received a summons from the palace.

The note was so unexpected and the summons so urgent, there was no time to safely send word to Elise. He would have to speak to her afterward. And in case he was forced to steal Elise away and flee the country, he scrawled out a note for Pearl along with the solicitor he'd arranged to manage Paxton Dale should something befall him. *What is the punishment for what we are doing?* he wondered. Was there recourse? Perhaps he was sailing—but into an abyss.

He rode to the palace with breath held. He felt like a very full cup of boiling water; if he jostled, even a little, scalding anxiety would spill out.

"Killian!" Edward, the Duke of Kent, boomed, when he presented himself to the private library reserved for their meetings. "Come in, come in. I've very good news for you."

Some rare impulse nudged Killian to say, "I've news as well, Highness."

If, on the off chance that Edward seemed amenable, perhaps he would simply reveal the truth to the man. He'd fallen in love. He'd proposed marriage. He would remove Elise from the palace's list of concerns. No charge, naturally.

"More questions about property, no doubt," guessed Edward. "How savvy you are with the buying and the rebuilding, Killian. It has occurred to us that we should cease selling our cast-off buildings to you and hire you to make them new and profitable again instead."

"It's not about property," Killian said.

"No? Well, next time, perhaps. I hope your news is not a bad report on Princess Elise. *My* good news hinges on her very good, very *manageable* behavior. How well you've done, Killian, taking her in hand. I can only hope the Prussian court has someone as effective as you on staff."

A long, cold needle of dread entered Killian's body in the back of his neck.

"I beg your pardon?" he said.

"Oh, the Prussians," Edward went on. "Do you reckon

they have a fixer? Surely they do—I've never heard of a palace without one. Typically there are several, but you are so very effective, we manage with only one."

"What about the Prussian court?" Killian gritted out. The dread continued to descend, slicing him open.

"Oh, do forgive me. I've leaped ahead. The *reason* we summoned you here is to tell you that the French royal family are taking Princess Elise off of our hands. They've found a Prussian count . . . Count Wilhelm or some such, third son of Prince Ferdinand VI . . . who will marry the girl. When it's done, he will relocate her to his castle in the Alps.

"But do you know what this means?" continued Edward. "You may cease your minding her, Killian. She'll be the problem of the Prussians now, and good riddance, honestly. We were able to get our military secrets from her uncle before she went. Now that Louis-Stanislas is out of bartering chips, he's arranged this marriage for her. The man has little confidence in our ability to keep her subdued. Ha! He does not know your handywork, Killian. But sending her to the mountains will also get the job done. It will be difficult for the girl to find her brother if she's living in an Alpine castle."

"Marry?" It was the only word Killian could manage. The needle of dread had pierced his heart. He couldn't breathe. He couldn't stand.

"Well, don't look so sullen, Killian," said Edward. "This is good news. Now you shall have your wash-houses."

"Warehouses," Killian corrected him—for no other reason than it prevented him from shouting, *She. Will. Be. My. Wife.*

"Oh, yes, the *warehouses.*"

"But do you believe the princess wishes to marry the Prussian?"

"I cannot see why she wouldn't," said Edward. "The girl has always struck me as sort of, oh . . . restless? And unhappy—here, in our court. The French are difficult to entertain, actually. Easily bored. Not big on reading or instruments, are they? The women especially. Oh, and just look what the count has sent as an engagement gift."

Killian saw the box before Edward reached for it. It was sitting alone on his desk like an explosive, waiting to go off. Killian watched the duke take it up; he saw him flip the box into the air and catch it; he saw him pop the lid.

The ring inside was grotesquely large. A white diamond protruded like a navel from two loops of smaller stones. Killian was made sick by the sight of it.

He closed his eyes.

He saw his mother's ruby ring—now Elise's—in his mind's eye. They'd felt it was imprudent for her to wear it in public, so she concealed it until they were alone together.

"What girl would refuse *this*?" Edward was asking. "And there's more than jewelry. He sent a trunk full of leathers and furs. He means to woo the chit, I suppose. I didn't have the heart to tell them that she refuses to wear anything but gray and black."

"When will you ask her?" Killian forced out.

"Well, that's why I've summoned you, Killian. At this point, you know her better than any of us. What do you think is best? Should Mama tell her about the proposal? Should I? Perhaps the whole family and all of her ladies-in-waiting? Should we have the Prussian consulate here and make a party of it?"

"The count will not come here?"

"Well, he'll come to collect her, I presume. I hope the French don't expect us to finance the girl's sojourn to Prussia. But he'll not make the journey to propose—that's why he's sent the ring and the gifts. And a letter, of course. But perhaps we should show her the letter first?"

"I think," managed Killian, "you should broach the subject with her in a way that allows her to decide what she wants. And give her time to search her mind. She has been an interloper in this court for many years. Allow her some agency over her life."

"Well, and isn't that a progressive notion? Is that what she's told you? She believes herself to be an interloper? Thankless chit—it's been a trial to harbor her, honestly. My mother and brother were kind to take her in, but I'm glad to be rid of her. 'Search her mind,'" mimicked Edward. "Really, Killian. My own sisters would marry a Prussian count in a heartbeat, but my mother won't let them out of her sight. If Elise must complain about the very dismal time she's had in England, living on the goodwill of our family, let her do so to the Prussians."

For this, Killian had no reply. There was a great roar echoing somewhere deep inside his chest, and he could not say when it would well up and escape his mouth. He knew only that he shouldn't be in the presence of the royal duke when the roaring began.

He bowed suddenly—not certain if he'd been dismissed, not caring—and backed from the room. He wound his way through the palace to the courtyard. He walked in the direction or the stables . . . or The Green Park . . . or Bishopsgate . . . he'd stopped paying attention.

He looked up to the bright blue of an unfeeling sky. He'd known he wasn't fit to have her. He'd known she could never be his wife.

He gave himself up to the roar, and it came out as six painful words: *I. Knew. She. Couldn't. Be. Mine.*

CHAPTER THIRTY-ONE

FOR THREE DAYS, Killian did not call on Elise. On the first day, she thought perhaps he was busy with some progress on the wedding. On the second, she began to worry—it was not like him not to write. She told herself that he had traveled, perhaps, to Scotland or to France. Perhaps something was amiss at Paxton Dale.

When the fourth day came and went with no sign from him, she asked Marie to slip from the palace and make some inquiries. He'd been so very steadfast and devoted to her; since the beginning, he had never wavered in this. But there was an alarming sort of . . . hollowness to the four days without a single word. It was like an eerie whistle that stalked her as she went about her day. She was sitting down to write him a note when her cousin Juliette burst into the room.

"Elise, Elise," Juliette sang, "come quickly. Queen Charlotte and the girls—plus several of the royal dukes—are in the grand salon, and they would see you."

"What? What do you mean, they would see me?" The whistling in Elsie's head came to an abrupt stop. She heard nothing but the patter of Juliette's feet scurrying about the room.

Elise had not been in the direct presence of Queen Charlotte for more than a month, and Elise herself had never been summoned before the royal dukes. Fear skittered up her body like a spider. There was a very specific sort of anxiety born of maneuverings inside a palace. It could be jealousy, or ambition, or vanity; it could be maddened peasants rattling the palace gates to haul your father away.

And hadn't Killian predicted this? Hadn't he said that they risked too much with their very loose, evolving plan? Hadn't he—

But Killian was not here. She'd not seen him for four days.

Breathing deeply, carefully, Elise forced herself to smile at her cousin.

"But I am not dressed," she tried.

"What?" Juliette frowned. "You always look the same. What difference is there between one gray dress and the next? Kirby is not here, and the queen is waiting now. Come, *come*, Elise. There are . . . presents! In a shiny trunk! And a painting beneath a velvet cloth. Something is happening . . ."

"Presents?" repeated Elise, forcing her brain to examine every detail. "What presents? A painting?"

But perhaps, Elise thought, it was someone's birthday. But wait—was it *her* birthday? No, she'd been born—

"You look like you're being led to the gallows." Juliette laughed, insensitive as ever. "It's not a bad sort of summons, I assure you. Everyone is happy. They are drinking champagne!"

Champagne? thought Elise, confused, only barely keeping panic at bay.

Saying nothing, seeing nothing, she allowed her cousin to take her by the arm and pull her down the corridor.

"I know," said Juliette, "you would like Mr. Crewes to be here. But remember what I've told you? All the useful little tidbits I've learned about Mr. Crewes and his women?"

Oh God—no, thought Elise. And now she was to endure this? Juliette's salacious review of every affair in which Killian had embarked with court ladies? It was one of her cousin's favorite topics—especially now that Elise had added herself to their number.

"The gossip in court is," prattled Juliette, "on the rare occasion Mr. Crewes takes a lover—and aren't you a lucky little thing to be one of the rare, chosen few—he won't acknowledge the lady openly in court. Queen Charlotte would never allow it. What he'll do, as we've seen—"

"Quiet, Juliette," snapped Elise. "Tell me more about this gathering. How many of the royal dukes are in the room? What of the Prince of Wales?"

By some miracle, Juliette seized this question and gave a preview of the scene inside the grand salon. She detailed everyone's gowns and hats and shoes and where they'd all been seated. Elise barely heard. What did it matter, they were nearly to the door.

Happy voices from inside drowned out her cousin's chatter. She could smell the perfumes and pomades of an assembled crowd. Servants came and went with trays of cakes and—yes—champagne. Elise saw swishing silks and bobbing feathers and fluttering fans. Besides the rare appearance of the queen and so many of the royal dukes, the gathering was not unlike any of a hundred afternoon diversions she'd endured in the palace. She had no reason to believe anything was amiss, no reason to feel threatened or in danger—except . . .

Killian had been gone for four days.

Now the spidery fear felt more like the precipice of an icy black lake. This wasn't an infestation, it was a drowning. She was about to be plunged into something from which she could not escape. She was certain of it.

Elise wore the ruby ring on a chain concealed beneath her dress. She felt for it against her collarbone; it was like a tiny little handle that she might grab and hold. She thought of it attached to a hidden door, and if she pulled hard enough, the door would open and she could crawl inside, and move down a passage, and out of this place.

"In we go," said Juliette, bustling Elise inside.

The room contained the queen, four of her daughters, and all of their collected ladies-in-waiting. The grand salon was generally used to host drinks before small dinner parties, or afterward, when someone would play the pianoforte or groups would gather for cards. Now it looked like a little theatre, set up with a stage and spectators.

On the makeshift stage stood four of the royal dukes. Beside them was an open trunk of items that sparkled and billowed and a piece of artwork on an easel beneath a velvet drape. In the corner sat the queen and her daughters.

The courtiers sat in what would be the audience, studying Elise with cold expectation. She was stricken, suddenly, by the lack of feeling in that look, the open search for how Elise could advance their own causes, whatever they might be.

No wonder I kept myself hidden and forgotten for so long, she thought. *I have been friendless here.*

She pressed her palm to her chest, feeling the outline of the ring.

"Ah, there she is," said Edward, the Duke of Kent. "We've been waiting for you, Princess Elise. Please, Highness, will you come before the queen and my brothers? I've something very exciting to reveal to you."

Elise and Juliette dropped, immediately, into reverent curtsies before the queen and her children, and then Juliette gave Elise a little shove. For the hundredth time, she asked herself why she'd not sent her cousin home to her parents.

But now she was given no choice but to slowly traverse

the crowded room and stand before the royal duke. When she reached him, she curtsied again.

"There's a good girl," said Edward. "But the reason we've arranged this little gathering"—now he raised a flute of bubbling champagne and saluted the room—"is to tell you that *your family* . . . in France . . . may God preserve them . . . have arranged for you, Highness . . . to be *married*."

He could have told Elise she would now march to the guillotine and she would have been no more shocked or horrified.

"Marriage . . . to whom?" she asked—because she had two choices in this moment: she could allow fear to prod her into silent acquiescence, or she could begin to advocate.

"To . . . His Excellency, Count Wilhelm Phillipe Celestine, son of Prince Ferdinand of Prussia."

Behind Elise, the room burst into gasps and then reluctant applause. There was a loud *pop!* of a newly opened bottle of champagne.

Elise began to shake her head. The word *no* began to march up her throat at a steady clip. But did she have the liberty to tell the royal duke no? Regardless, she mustn't lose her composure in front of the queen and her court. She must think, she must strategize, she must comply until exactly the most sensible moment to bolt. She would allow the celebratory noise and increasing applause to distract from the fact that she was not saying yes.

She looked around. The illustrious trunk now resembled an open mouth, spitting up shiny furs and golden trinkets. The painting beneath the velvet drape would be, she now realized, none other than a portrait of the Prussian count.

Elise knew this because open trunks and draped paintings were precisely how these things were done.

She'd been present at the engagement of a young, beloved aunt before the revolution. The groom-to-be had been an Italian duke, and he'd also *not* been present for the happy occasion. Her aunt had been forced to admire his portrait, and paw through a shiny box of gloves and reticules made of Italian leather—all gifts of the duke. There had also been a small keening monkey in a wire cage—a pet to entertain her aunt until her future husband could be bothered to make the journey to France.

Elise had been only a child when she'd witnessed this, but even she had thought it was odd to bind oneself to a strange Italian who'd sent a monkey instead of himself.

In this instance, however, Elise was lucky the Prussian count was absent. It was one thing to flee from a trunk of gifts and a portrait—not ideal, but she would do it—but another to evade a flesh-and-blood man.

"It may come as a bit of a shock, my dear," Edward was now saying. "But when you've had a moment to peruse the great many treasures he has sent to honor your engagement and to"—and now he paused in his speech, held out his hand to an aide, and snapped his fingers—"see the *betrothal ring* . . ."

The aide dropped a small leather box in Edward's hands, and he popped it open, shoving it at her.

". . . and what do you say to that, Your Serene Highness?"

Juliette was suddenly beside her, gasping in delight at the garish, bulbous projectile of a diamond ring. Elise gaped at it, her eyes stinging with tears. Inside her gown, Killian's ruby ring burned against her chest. She clamped a hand over it, searing the shape to her throat.

"Oh, Highness," said Juliette, invoking the title that she otherwise never used, "but how stunning it is! Why, imagine the weight of it!" She began to slightly hop up and down. "Put it on, put it on, put it on!"

"Will you take it from him, Juliette?" Elise stammered. It appeared the royal duke would not retract his hand unless someone unburdened him of the jutting, blinding thing.

Her cousin bowed again to Edward and then reverently lifted the box from his gloved hand.

"His Excellency has also sent a letter, introducing himself to you and expressing his pleasure over the betrothal." Edward snapped his fingers again, and a piece of parchment, drooping at the top with a royal seal, appeared in his hand. He thrust it at Elise, and she was given no choice but to take it.

She looked down at the paper through tears. She looked up. "This is written in German," she said. "I cannot read it."

"But can we get a German translator here?" Edward asked his aide.

Elise looked again at the paper. The small, tight handwriting, so unfamiliar to her, and the wild, strident signature were more abhorrent than a proposal she couldn't read. It was like this person—this count—was already here, claiming her, telling her she must adhere to him, and that she must learn yet another foreign tongue, and leave with him. It was like he was hauling her away from Killian, and her brother, and Marie, and the life she had only just begun to build.

The royal duke was saying something, making some pronouncement about gifts and the very great esteem of two noble families and the joining of peaceable nations for a stronger, more prosperous Europe, but Elise had stopped listening. Her brain was scrambling for ways to oppose this, or run from it, or—

But where is Killian?

Why did she face this alone? Had he—

And then it occurred to her. The four-day absence. The silence.

He'd learned this would happen. He *knew*.

They'd told him she was being betrothed to a Prussian count, and he'd . . .

She looked around the room. Through tears, she saw laughing, gossiping, champagne-swilling courtiers; she saw the royal dukes, who watched her with annoyed confusion. She saw Queen Charlotte, sad and tired, as always, clutching the hand of one of her sad, bored daughters. She looked to Juliette, who was prying the ring from the box, asking her to hold out her finger.

Inside the bodice of her gown, the ruby ring burned hotter, and Elise began to fumble with the chain. Frantically, with fingers that shook, she pulled at it, trying to get to the ring. The chain bit into her neck, and she pulled harder. It snagged on her stays and she yanked again.

And then, there it was, the cheerful ruby winking at her, the gold band warm from her skin.

She wanted to ask Juliette to unclasp the chain, to remove the ring, to help her put it on. It didn't fit her ring finger, but she would force it. She would lodge it in place so that no other ring could take its place.

Juliette, of course, would not help her. She was coming at her with the big diamond, instructing her to hold still, to hold out her hand.

Behind her, the royal duke was beckoning her to the portrait, his hands hovering over the velvet drape. He would show her, he crooned, a likeness of Count Wilhelm, so she could see how dashing and handsome he was.

Another duke held out a fur coat, the lapel swinging with the pelts of four dead rabbits, and Elise realized that she could not, in this moment, fight the spider or the icy lake. There were too many eyes on her. She'd been caught off guard. She'd lost her ability to speak. She was entirely alone.

Killian had been correct.

She was not at liberty to marry whom she wanted. She had no liberties.

He'd proclaimed this, and then he'd abandoned her to . . . to—

"Highnesses, Your Majesty, Princess Elise, I beg your pardon . . ." said a loud voice from the doorway.

Elise turned to the familiar sound.

Killian.

He had come.

KILLIAN WAS SWEATING, his breathing was quick and labored, and the hair on the back of his hands stood on end. Even so, he strode into the grand salon with measured steps.

He leveled a quick knowing look on Elise—his first look.

She gaped at him, confused and near panicking. It took every ounce of self-control not to go to her.

The room, previously loud with chatter and laughter, fell silent. These people knew him, they knew his reputation in court—and they also knew he'd engaged in some familiarity with the French princess. And now here he was, striding into the announcement of her betrothal.

This would be the best seat in town; court would not see better entertainment all year.

The royal dukes paused in their milling about the trunk and the portrait to watch him. He bowed respectfully to the queen and her daughters. He bowed to the royal dukes. Finally, he bowed to Princess Elise, locking eyes and trying wordlessly to convey his steadfastness and love.

She took a step to him, then paused, uncertain. If he'd needed motivation to make this stand, the sight of that small, uncertain step, the *doubt* she endured, propelled him. Oh, but he needed no motivation.

For the last ten minutes, he'd lurked in the doorway, restraining himself until he could bear it no longer. He'd been waiting for Elise to make a clear choice. He'd wanted her to hear what the Prussian offered her, to see the gifts, to be reminded that *this* was the natural course for a royal princess. He'd wanted her to see it all and remember it all—and to choose *him* instead.

When he'd seen her scramble for his ring, her choice had been made clear. He let fly his self-control and burst into the room. Sweating. Breathing hard. Prepared to toss her over his shoulder and run from this place if it came to that.

But first, he would endeavor to talk their way out of this.

Edward met him halfway across the room.

"What is it, Killian?" the royal duke asked quietly, speaking between the two of them. Courtiers craned to listen.

Killian bowed again. "I've something to say, Highness. If her majesty and the royal dukes would hear it."

Edward was shaking his head. "You're not needed in this. You wouldn't listen when I explained the offer for the girl, and we moved on without you. You're *off* the assignment. Obviously. I'll deal with your insubordination later. For now, the princess should enjoy her happy moment without you to distract her."

"I don't believe the princess is happy," Killian said.

Edward gaped at him. "She's being showered with gifts and promised the moon. Of course she's happy."

There was a murmur among the courtiers. Chairs slid. Someone stood up.

Killian said nothing, staring levelly at the royal duke.

"I beg your pardon?" demanded Edward, louder now.

"Oh my God. Have you—Has your time with her led you to believe that she somehow . . . fancies you? *You?* The man we pay to remove dissidents from the palace gates?"

"If you'll not permit me to address the queen or your brothers," said Killian, "I would speak to the princess, Highness."

"Speak to us? No. Speak to her? Also, no. I knew there was something odd in your manner these last two weeks, and now I see why. You've gone and gotten yourself attached to the girl. A princess, Killian? Really? Now, that *is* ambitious. She may be in exile, but she's hardly a run-down building that can be bought up on the cheap."

Killian's vision was blurred by a fine red mist. Anger was like a living thing inside him. Only his hope for some future with Elise kept him from putting his hands on the man.

"Oh, and now you're angry, are you? Well, I'm not so happy myself, to be honest. We've somehow managed to be rid of the girl, and I'll not have you mucking it up with an overblown sense of romance or some white knight rescue fantasy. This may come as a shock to you, Killian, but good looks and brute strength only go so far. In the end, most women are sensible. They will choose a royal count and an Alpine castle every time."

He'd just said this—the words *Alpine castle* still hung in the air—when Elise barreled around him and collided with Killian's side, clutching him.

The assembled courtiers gasped. Elise's cousin made a yelping noise and clapped her hand over her mouth. She closed the ring box with a snap. In the corner, Queen Charlotte and her daughters straightened from their slouches.

"Oh, for Christ's sake," said Edward, spinning away.

Killian wrapped an arm around Elise, banding her

to him. It was clear to him that he would have no better moment. He took a deep breath.

"Your majesty," he began. "Highnesses. Princess Elise. I beg your pardons for my interruption of this lovely gathering; however, the circumstances of the festivities compel me. Two weeks ago, I proposed marriage to Her Serene Highness, Princess Elise, and she has accepted me. We plan to marry as soon as it can be arranged. She cannot, I regret to inform you, marry the Prussian. She will marry me."

"This," said Edward, glaring back and forth between Killian and Elise, "is impossible. And likely against the law. Seditious. She cannot marry you. She is a Princess of the Blood. And you are the son of a—"

"I will marry him," declared Princess Elise, stepping up.

After she said it, she repeated the words in French.

After that, she said another thing in French, and another, and another, and Killian thought he would absolutely become fluent in French so that he could speak to her in her native tongue. The more she spoke, the louder she became. She rattled off French accusations and declarations in the spitfire voice that Killian knew and loved but that was entirely new to the royal court.

As she spoke, Killian glanced around. He'd not planned what would happen next because he hadn't known how the presentation of the betrothal would happen. He'd been lurking about the palace for four days, waiting for them to tell Elise, waiting for her to decide without his interference.

His plan to wait her out—to sit idle as she made an unbiased decision about her future—had been agony. Not only could he not see her, but he was not entirely convinced that she would, in the end, choose him. He thought she would . . . but he wasn't certain.

He'd not planned to be inside the palace when they

made the offer to her, but he'd not ventured far in the last four days. It was her friend Marie who came to him at his rally point in the stables and told him Elise had been summoned before the court. The nun didn't know the purpose of the gathering—she'd only just learned of it from a footman. But Marie had been made uneasy by the surprise nature of it and the size of the crowd. She could not watch over the princess because she'd been summoned by a priest with an urgent note, posted through the Catholic church.

Killian had thanked her and run. In his opinion, Edward had fully expected Elise to reject the proposal. She'd hardly demonstrated a spirit of cooperation since the sighting of her brother. The champagne and the guests and the presence of the queen were meant to stun her into acquiescing.

But Killian had gotten there just in time, thank God. He'd witnessed Elise's choice and strode into the room to take on the sons of the king. He deplored packed rooms, brimming with esteemed people; ever since the day his mother had been shamed at Eton, he'd hated them. Now he cast off the anxiety like a wet coat that no longer kept him warm. He shoved every bad memory aside and thought only to extricate Elise.

It had been a pleasant surprise that no one had shouted insults or threw food. Instead, the courtiers watched with expressions of titillated excitement. Edward looked to be on the verge of heart failure. His brothers had stepped up to calm the princess—who, for more than a minute now, had continued her diatribe in angry French.

But this could not go on forever. Eventually Elise ran out of things to say. Edward had already made a ruling on what came next; he'd rejected Killian and proclaimed she *would* marry the count.

Ernest, the king's fifth son, was among the royal

dukes circling Elise. Ernest had been Killian's first client within the royal family—his old hallmate from Eton— and Killian looked to him. If he had any ally in this room, it would be him.

To Ernie's credit, he did not look away. He blinked once, slowly, an acknowledgment, and then he deftly, slyly, pointed his eyes at his mother.

Killian felt a tiny spark of hope. He gave Ernest a slight nod and looked to Queen Charlotte.

Remarkably, the queen seemed to be waiting for Killian's eyes.

He nodded to her, a subtle bow. She acknowledged his attention and then tipped her head ever so gently in the direction of the door.

Killian's heart stopped. He widened his eyes.

Go? he asked with his expression.

The queen nodded. *Go.*

Killian bowed again. He took Elise by the hand, and they went.

Behind him, he heard Edward bluster and call for them. Then he heard Queen Charlotte's voice: "Leave them."

When they escaped through the door, Marie was waiting for them in the corridor.

"Highness," she said, extending a mud-splotched envelope, "this has just come for you at St. Christopher's. From Spain. Your mother, Highness. She has answered your letters."

CHAPTER THIRTY-TWO

THEY WERE MARRIED not in Scotland, nor in France but, remarkably, in Spain. In a small, ancient church high in the Pyrenees. It was an autumn wedding, and the wall outside the church was frilled with the fat leaves of a muscadine vine in every shade of yellow, gold, and orange. Elise wore a pale green gown and, upon her mother's insistence, an emerald-studded crown.

Elise was pregnant at the time of the wedding—a fact known only to Elise, Marie, and the priest they compelled to marry them quickly and without a lot of fuss about paperwork.

They were allowed to marry by permission of Elise's mother, Louisa, and her maternal grandfather, a Spanish prince.

The lack of concern that Louisa had shown Elise during her ten-year exile seemed to vanish when her daughter's needs pivoted to that of someone who could grant her permission to marry.

Louisa and Elise's grandfather dispatched letters from the Spanish court to King George, rejecting the proposal of the Prussian count. Elise's late father, may God rest him, would've never agreed to any bridegroom chosen by his brother. And if Elise had fallen in love with the dashing second son of an earl, why shouldn't she have him?

Killian and Elise departed London for the Spanish village of Torla-Ordesa with due haste—within a fortnight of the Prussian count's remote proposal—but Elise asked Killian to include Bartholomew and Lady Dunlock in the festivities.

Alas, Killian could not manage the logistics or the expense of transporting so many people to Spain—"An early taste of life on a budget, Highness," he'd told her—but he promised they would have a small party at Paxton Dale when they returned.

And so Elise's only real guest at her wedding had been the mother she'd not seen in ten years. Their reunion, for all that, was rather stilted and impersonal. Her mother's lover never left her side, and it was immediately clear that Louisa would make no excuses for not answering Elise's many cries for help during exile. Also not part of the reunion: basic sympathy or some inquiry about Elise's well-being. Her mother wished only to speak of plans for the wedding, to discuss the details of the gown she'd brought from Seville, and to flirt with Killian.

Elise allowed her mother's lack of compassion—or was it more a lack of attention? Lack of maternal regard? There was a deep gap there, whatever it was, and it was painful, but Elise let it go unexplored. What choice did she have?

And honestly, when Elise had really, truly needed her mother, she had not failed her. She'd moved swiftly and demonstratively on the matter of Killian. She'd granted permission and invited them to Spain to celebrate a proper wedding. She had made the Prussian count disappear.

Elise accepted this as enough, but every time she thought of it (and it haunted her more than she would've liked) she patted her belly and vowed never to impose the same neglect on her own child.

The night after the wedding, as Killian and Elise lay tangled in the crisp white sheets of the sturdy bed of Torla-Ordesa's only inn, Elisa found the words to tell him that he would be a father before next summer.

"Killian?" she asked softly, tracing the splendid contour of his bare back with her index finger. He lay facedown in the sheets, snoozing after their first very enthusiastic coupling—real coupling—now that they were married.

"Yes, love?" he asked.

"I've something to tell you."

He lifted his head from the pillow.

"In English, I hope?"

He'd spent the day navigating Spanish relatives, Latin church services, and Elise's and Marie's rapid-fire French.

"Yes, of course."

"Remember when we made love after the morning of the fire?"

"Let me see," he teased, "can I remember the first time we made love? Oh, yes, it's coming back to me. Ever so faintly. Did you wear your shoes?"

She hit him with a pillow. "Well, despite how very careful we were every other time, I'm afraid . . ." She cleared her throat. "It seems that . . ."

She squeezed her eyes shut.

"What is it, Highness?" he whispered, his face tightening with concern. He sat up.

"Nothing bad—well, nothing that, hopefully, we cannot manage. It's just that I know you are so very worried about providing a nice living for me . . . and you have so many obligations to Paxton Dale. And now you've lost a substantial source of income from St. James's Palace . . ."

"They'll come crawling back," he said carefully, watching her, "as soon as one of them owes money or covets an unavailable Arabian stallion. But what is this hesitation, Highness? You know you can tell me anything. Have you begun to worry about surviving a cruel, harsh winter?"

"No, no—it's not that. It's . . . I'm going to have a baby, Killian. That is, we are. I'm pregnant. From . . . that night. When I was . . . wearing my shoes."

Killian's eyes went wide. He took a long moment to study her face, and then he scooped her up, cradling her in his lap.

"*Elise*," he whispered, breathing into her hair. "Highness. I am thrilled—I am beyond thrilled. What is more than thrilled? Ecstatic. Are you happy? But how long have you known?"

"About a week, actually. Not long. It's very early. But . . . of course you should know. It was so expensive to travel to Spain that I was loath to burden you with the news of . . . well, of another child to feed, and clothe, and educate, and . . ."

"Please put it out of your mind," he said, holding her tighter still. "In the first place, we are not destitute, regardless of how I may have portrayed myself when I was trying to convince us both that I did not deserve a royal princess as my wife."

She chuckled into his chest. "I've seen your art collection. I had some idea."

"And second, I've something to tell you, too."

"In English?" she asked.

He laughed. "God, yes. Although you raise a good point. What I'm about to tell you was communicated to me in Spanish, and I had only Marie to translate."

"Oh, Marie speaks excellent Spanish."

"So she does. Luckily, your grandfather allowed her to do the honors, despite his strong preference for a male translator."

Elise made a disgusted noise. "But what did he tell you?"

"He told me, Highness, that you happen to be . . . heavily dowered."

Elise pulled away.

"What?"

"Indeed. You've a substantial dowry, actually. Pesos and pesos of it. Even now, I'm endeavoring to reckon with the fact that the man simply . . . gave it to me."

"To *you*?" She raised her brows.

"Well—to us, that is. I suppose it's yours, isn't it?"

"Is it enough to buy the estate you wanted?" she whispered. "One to call your own, like Paxton Dale belongs to Bartholomew?"

"I could not use your money to buy myself an estate, Highness."

"Would you buy it for us? For our baby? If there is enough?"

He dropped his head. When he looked up, his eyes were bright. "I did not marry you for a fortune, Elise. I'll admit that I was dazzled by your . . . haughtiness, your regality, your very . . . *my-serene-highness-ness*. God help me, that does thrill me. But I married you because of my very great love for you. I had no aspirations to a Spanish fortune. It came as quite a shock. I was going to tell you, but I wanted to make love to you first . . ."

"To seal the union?" she guessed.

He laughed. "For the obvious reason that—while you experienced the pleasure of *almost* making love again and again in the weeks of our 'affair'—my almost-lovemaking remained wearily . . . less experiential—"

"That's not entirely true!" She laughed.

"It was also not entirely satisfying. Lovely, to be sure, but not equal to what we've just . . . er, enjoyed. And *that* is why I waited to tell you. Imagine my bitterness now that I've learned we put a baby in you the very first time, and we could have been doing this all along."

"Are you so very bitter?" she teased, and he reached for her, toppling them back on the pillows.

"Seriously, Killian," she said, looking up at him through her hair. "How much is the dowry? Can we manage an estate in the country? Not that I do not adore the Bishopsgate house, but you—"

"The Bishopsgate house will never *not* smell like smoke. And yes, it is enough for a country estate."

"*No* . . ." she marveled.

"Yes. Do the French not tell their princesses the value of their dowries? In France?"

"I was barely out of the schoolroom when I left. I had not been told. But . . . how much is it?"

And now Killian dipped his head and whispered the very large sum into her ear. Enough for an estate, and to buy the warehouses, and to refinish the properties he already owned and sell them or lease them. Enough to realize the very careful dream he'd been building all these years.

Later, Elise would mull over the unfairness of living in near penury at St. James's Palace. The little room and the meager wardrobe. One maid in dear Kirby, for whom she struggled to buy even a small token of thanks at Christmas. And all the while, there had been a literal chest of gold just waiting to go to . . . her husband.

In the years to come, Elise would appreciate that Killian considered all financial decisions in conjunction with her. She had little interest in money, and she was happy to have him manage it, but he always asked. *And* he took the dowry and multiplied it many times over. He brought Paxton up to speed and then paid back the money to Elise's estate. They provided for Hodges, Kirby, and Marie (despite Marie's vow of poverty, she was partial to fine boots, expensive wine, and fast horses); for the Piles and Bartholomew; for the maiden aunts and Lady Dunlock.

But dearest to Elise's heart was perhaps the money spent to hire an investigator to begin a real search for her brother, Gabriel.

Because they left Spain not only with a pile of money; they left with a thin file of careful notes . . .

"I've one more thing to tell you, Highness," Killian said that night.

"Well, this is a night of revelations," she said, coming to her elbows on his broad chest.

"I hope you'll not be cross that I didn't raise this first."

"Cross? My God, what is it?"

"Well, after Marie and I met with your grandfather, I encountered your mother in the gardens. We exchanged pleasantries—I can speak a little Spanish—and then she handed me a packet of papers and . . . and let fly a long paragraph of rapid Spanish. Before I'd even translated the first sentence, she hurried away. Luckily, Marie was there."

"But what was it?"

"It was notes, Elise, about your brother."

Elise scrambled to her knees, her eyes wide. She clutched the bedsheet in both hands. "What notes? What did they say?"

"After your mother had gone, Marie translated what she'd said. Basically she knew you wanted to find your brother, but for years she did not think it was safe for Gabriel to be . . . I guess the word is *found*. But now she thinks that perhaps he is old enough to defend against the likes of your uncle . . . or anyone else who might vie for the French throne."

"I cannot believe you're telling me this," said Elise. "Mama *knew*. She knew all along. And she withheld the information. Does she know about Dani? Our sister? My God, how can this woman just . . . lull about Spain with her paramour and not seek out her own children?" Elise cradled her belly and broke into sobs.

"Shh," Killian soothed, pulling her to him. "We'll sort it out, Highness. Together we will find them. Marie has looked at the notes. She says it is a very good start."

"So there are clues about Dani?"

"Just a few," he said. "Fewer than about Gabriel. Honestly, the wedding was about to begin, and we couldn't study it overlong. But what I did learn is . . . you were correct about the market towns along the Road to Land's End. There is a very good chance that you *did* see him. Your brother was—according to the notes—taken to a horse trainer in south-central England, and the Road to Land's End bisects this area of the country. He served as an apprentice to this man. I have his name and his general location. It's a start, Highness. It is a start."

And now Elise was crying again. Killian held her, pressing his lips to the top of her head and promising they would not stop until they found him.

When, at last, she had run out of tears, she asked, "Why did my mother give the notes to you, I wonder? Why not give them to me? I'd written her countless times, begging for any clue."

"Honestly?" he asked. "I think she was a little afraid of you. Likely, she feels some remorse for the way your family was split apart and exiled after your father's execution. But she is a different sort of parent than, perhaps, you or I will be. It's cold consolation in a way, but she delivered us when we needed her. I was prepared to leave Britain for America with you, Highness—to start over in a strange land from nothing. That had been my best option when I strode into the grand salon during the announcement of your 'betrothal' to the Prussian. Her intervention was, however, a far easier path to security. It will be less burden on the child, simpler for all of us."

"Yes," Elise said, sniffling. "Yes. I suppose she did. And now we will have this baby. And we will be together. And we will find my brother and sister."

"Yes, Princess," he said. "Now it will be done."

AUTHOR'S NOTE

*M*UCH OF THE history here has been massaged in an effort to keep this book light on its feet and the love story in the spotlight. I implore readers to indulge these distortions, but I can share a little of what is real and what has been manipulated.

First, the idea for this series came from my neighbor Michelle, who introduced me to a podcast called *Noble Blood*. I was immediately sucked in by the history of royal intrigue, royal executions, fleeing royals, dethroned royals, royals separated at birth, etc. Michelle and I brainstormed, and the Hidden Royals trilogy was born. My original thought was to invent a small European country in turmoil and create lead characters fleeing from this imaginary land. My agent, however, urged me to research actual countries that sent actual exiled royals to England at the turn of the nineteenth century. Thank you, Patricia Nelson, because this advice made the book so much richer. The precise historical facts, however, required a bit of shoehorning.

Here is what's real in *Say Yes to the Princess*:

The French monarchy boasted several "cadet" branches—these were cousins and nephews to the king—who lived the royal life in palaces throughout France. They enjoyed lavish wealth and extreme privilege and were married off to other royal offspring around

Europe. When the people of France, starving and oppressed, revolted and heads began to roll, these "lesser royals" became targets, just like King Louis XVI and Queen Marie Antoinette. All told, 17,000 people were beheaded in the French Revolution, including the king and queen and so many of their extended family members. Relatives who weren't killed fled France and lived as exiles.

Royal families from Spain to Russia watched in horror as their French counterparts were imprisoned and beheaded, and many helped to arrange sanctuary. French aristocrats managed to settle throughout Europe, including Britain, and a few traveled as far as America.

Depending on their proximity to the throne, some French aristocrats carried on with their presumed royal lives, waiting for the turmoil in France to end. Their existence was radically scaled down, and resources were few. They lived in borrowed chalets, often bouncing from country to country, biding their time. Court intrigue endured, however, as some ambitious members of the family viewed the line of succession to be up for debate. I touch on this in the book.

My research showed that Queen Charlotte was very possessive of her daughters, and she refused to allow most of them to enter into courtships or marry. She preferred instead to keep them cloistered for her own security and companionship.

Finally, there *is* a branch of the French royal family known as the Orleans. The father, Philippe d'Orleans, *was* beheaded, the mother *was* an incredibly wealthy Spanish princess who returned to Spain with her lover, and their children *did* flee France after their father's execution. However, those facts are mostly where the truth ends.

Here is what is *not* true (or less true):

Instead of three children, there were *five* Orleans siblings. Four of these siblings were, unhelpfully, named either Louis or Louise. For this reason, and also because I'm particular about the names of my protagonists, I invoked the Orleans surname but *renamed* the siblings Elise, Gabriel, and Danielle—and reduced their number to three to make a tidy trilogy. The real-life Orleans brothers and sisters bear no resemblance to my fictional Elise, Gabriel, and Dani—not their lives in exile and not their personalities. Although Queen Charlotte was particularly sympathetic to lesser French royals who fled their country, and the Prince of Wales was a close friend to the Prince d'Orleans, there is no evidence of an Orleans daughter being granted sanctuary within St. James's Palace. I used the Orleans family as a jumping off point, and then I flapped my arms and flew.

The biggest leap is that I upgraded the Orleans branch in the order of succession to the French throne. In essence, I amalgamized the cousinly Orleans with King Louis's *brothers*. I did this for timeline reasons and because a beheaded father and a rich Spanish mother better matched the real-life circumstances of the Orleanses while the nature of exile (houseguests instead of vagabonds) and the proximity to the throne worked better with children of one of King Louis's brothers.

I also invoked the title of "Princess" for Elise with a very heavy hand. In my research, the Orleans children were often referenced as "Princes of the Blood," or "Princesses of the Blood." Their form of address was, "Your Serene Highness." However, the patriarch of this branch was most commonly known as the *Duc* d'Orleans rather than *Prince* d'Orleans—not always, but mostly. For dramatic effect, I leaned in to the "Princess of the Blood" distinction and referenced our heroine as "Princess Elise" throughout the book.

READ MORE BY CHARIS MICHAELS

AWAKENED BY A KISS SERIES

A DUCHESS BY MIDNIGHT

WHEN YOU WISH UPON A DUKE

A DUCHESS A DAY

THE BRIDES OF BELGRAVIA SERIES

YOU MAY KISS THE DUKE

ALL DRESSED IN WHITE

ANY GROOM WILL DO

THE BACHELOR LORDS OF LONDON SERIES

ONE FOR THE ROGUE

THE VIRGIN AND THE VISCOUNT

THE EARL NEXT DOOR